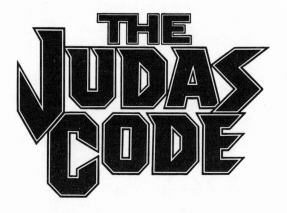

By the same author

Novels

The Red Dove
Angels in the Snow
The Kites of War
For Infamous Conduct
The Red House
The Yermakov Transfer
Touch the Lion's Paw (filmed as Rough Cut)
Grand Slam
The Great Land
The St. Peter's Plot
The Memory Man
I, Said the Spy
Trance

Autobiographies

The Sheltered Days
Don't Quote Me But
And I Quote
Unquote

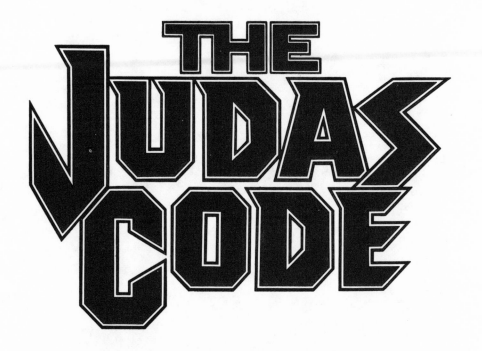

DEREK LAMBERT

STEIN AND DAY/*Publishers*/New York

For Len and Dorothy Wellfare

First published in 1984
Copyright © 1984 by Derek Lambert
All rights reserved, Stein and Day, Incorporated
Designed by Louis A. Ditizio
Printed in the United States of America
STEIN AND DAY/*Publishers*
Scarborough House
Briarcliff Manor, NY 10510

Library of Congress Cataloging in Publication Data

Lambert, Derek, 1929-
   The Judas code.

   1. World War, 1939-1945—Fiction.   I. Title.
PR6062.A47J8   1984   823'.914   83-40371
ISBN 0-8128-2948-4

AUTHOR'S NOTE

It should not be forgotten that this is a novel. But neither should it be forgotten that it concerns an established and bewildering fact: despite all the evidence, Josef Stalin refused to believe that Hitler intended to invade the Soviet Union in June 1941. If he had heeded the warnings—and there were many—two tyrannies might have remained relatively unscathed, and the world today would have been a very different place. When such a momentous fact is the pivot of a novel, one wonders if the accompanying material is also true. Who knows, perhaps it is.

And what of Stalin? How was he reacting to the fact that almost the entire German army was on his doorstep? Incredibly, he appeared to ignore it. Was he the victim of some kind of hysteria that deprived him of the ability to act? Or were there other powerful reasons for not acting—reasons known only to him?

—*Russia Besieged* by Nicholas Bethell
and the editors of Time-Life Books

Despite all the indications that war with Germany was approaching, neither the Soviet people nor the Red Army were expecting the German attack when it came.

—*History of World War II,* editor-in-chief, A. J. P. Taylor

Never had a state been better informed than Russia about the aggressive intent of another.... But never had an army been so ill-prepared to meet the initial onslaught of its enemy than the Red Army on June 22, 1941.

—*The History of World War II* by Lt. Col. E. Bauer

It is almost inconceivable but nevertheless true that the men in the Kremlin, for all the reputation they had of being suspicious, crafty and hard-headed, and despite all the evidence and all the warnings that stared them in the face, did not realize right up to the last moment that they were to be hit, and with a force which would almost destroy their nation.

—*The Rise and Fall of the Third Reich* by William L. Shirer

PROLOGUE

My advertisement in the personal columns of *The Times* read, "Would anyone with the key to the Judas Code please contact me." The response was prompt. At 9 A.M. on the day of publication a man called at my London home and threatened to kill me.

The threat wasn't immediate, but as soon as I saw him on the doorstep, smiling and tapping a copy of the newspaper with one finger, I sensed menace.

He was in his sixties, with wings of silver hair just touching his ears and what looked like the scar from a bullet wound on his right cheek. He wore a light, navy blue topcoat with a velvet collar and carried a furled umbrella. The elegance and the legacy of violence combined to give the impression of a commando who had retired to the City.

"Your request interested me," he said. "May I come in?"

Wishing that I hadn't unlocked the ground-floor door by remote control and allowed him to reach my apartment on the top floor of the old block near Broadcasting House, I said, "It is rather early. Perhaps—"

"Nine o'clock? You look wide awake, Mr. Lambert, and I won't take up much of your time." He took a step forward.

"Before we go any further, Mr. . . ."

"Chambers."

"Do you mind telling me how you found out where I live? I only gave a telephone number."

"It's not so difficult to obtain an address from a telephone number. If you know how to go about it, that is."

"And my name?"

"The same source. Now if you would be good enough—"

"To step aside? I don't think I would, Mr. Chambers. Perhaps you would be good enough to telephone me to make an appointment."

"Aren't you being a little formal for someone as obviously enterprising as yourself?" He tucked *The Times* beneath his arm on his umbrella side.

"I've always been a stickler for protocol."

"Really? You surprise me. I had heard quite the opposite." His voice frosted. "Let me in, Mr. Lambert."

"Get stuffed," I said, terminating my brief relationship with protocol.

He, too, abandoned niceties. He leveled a Browning 9-mm automatic at my chest and said, "Don't try slamming the door. It's only in Hollywood that wood panels stop bullets. Now turn around and go inside." The door clicked snugly behind me. "That's better," he said as we entered the living room. "Now sit down in that easy chair beside the fireplace."

I sat down, feeling slightly absurd in a red silk dressing gown, rumpled blue pajamas, and leather slippers savaged by a friend's dog, and waited. Chambers sat opposite me and appraised the room—books scattered across the worn carpet; a bottle of Black Label and its partner, an empty glass; punished leather sofa; windows looking across the rooftops to the pale green treetops of Regent's Park. In short, fading elegance; in fact, the workshop of an author who commuted to a house in Surrey where his wife and children lived.

Having completed his inventory, Chambers waved the gun and said, "Do I really have to go on pointing this at you? I know I'm much older than you. Forty-five aren't you?"—I was forty-four—"But I think I'd get the better of you in physical combat, and I'm not just being conceited."

He could well have been right. Anyway, I told him to put down his gun and tell me what he wanted. There was always the possibility that I might be able to surprise him later.

He stood up and slipped off the topcoat. Underneath he wore a charcoal-gray pinstripe with a waistcoat and a gold watch chain with a seal fob looped across it. He slipped the Browning inside the jacket without spoiling its shape and sat down again. "And now," he said pleasantly, "tell me why you want to know about the Judas Code," one finger straying to his cheek. (The bullet must have taken bone with it because the scar was almost a furrow.)

"You must have guessed that. I'm writing a book."

"*The Judas Code* . . . a good title. Why did you choose it?"

"I didn't, it was unavoidable. Kept cropping up while I was research-ing a book about the last war. I wanted to know why Stalin ignored all the warnings that Germany intended to invade Russia in 1941."

"That's simple. The warnings came from Churchill and Roosevelt and other interested parties, and he interpreted them as mischief-making. Most accounts of World War II have made that quite clear."

"But it doesn't wash, does it? He also ignored warnings from his own spies. Richard Sorge in Tokyo, for instance. And the evidence before his own generals' eyes: the buildup of the German army on his borders."

"And why are you, a novelist, so anxious to put the record straight?"

"Three reasons. One, because I abhor flawed logic. Any history student who suggested in an exam that Uncle Joe misread Hitler's intentions just because he thought the Allies were deceiving him would deserve to get a C minus.

"Two, because if Stalin had got it right, then you'd have to redraw today's maps of the world. If, for instance, Germany and Russia had persevered with their unholy alliance, if their armies hadn't bled each other for more than three years, then Britain might be a Nazi or a Soviet satellite."

Chambers took a silver cigarette case from the inside pocket of his jacket, on the other side from the Browning. He didn't offer it to me—perhaps he even knew I'd given up smoking—and selected a cigarette. He lit it with a gold Dunhill lighter and inhaled with pleasure. A true smoker, not a chain-smoker. "And the third?"

"Because it's my guess that the real reasons behind Stalin's apparent stupidity will make a better story than any novel I've written."

"I see." He blew a jet of smoke into a shaft of dusty sunlight. "Yes, I can see that." His voice had assumed an introspective quality and I wondered if I could jump him. I had never been an athlete, let alone a fighter, but I was big enough and fairly fit. He said crisply, "Don't try it," followed by, "But you haven't explained about the Judas Code."

"Why don't you explain it? It seems to have worried the bejaysus out of you."

"Because I have the gun," slipping his hand inside his jacket.
I told him.

To try to plug the gap in appraisals of World War II caused by Stalin's apparent aberration, I had traveled all over Europe winkling out people who might once have had access to secret information that could explain it. Spies, in other words—among them former members of Britain's XX

Committee, various branches of America's OSS, Germany's RSHA VI (foreign intelligence) and Abwehr, and the Soviet Union's two European espionage organizations known as the Red Orchestra and the Lucy Ring.

Predictably, most of the agents denied that they had ever been spies. Who wants to admit to a furtive past if he is currently a burgomaster or the chairman of a bank? But a few, mostly the very old, whose cloaks of secrecy were now in tatters, did agree that the history books should be rewritten. Watching their reactions to my questions was like peering into coffins and seeing corpses momentarily resuscitated. From a number of coffins came a dusty whisper: "The Judas Code." No more. Aging reflexes belatedly recognized indiscretion, coffin lids snapped back into place.

Chambers seemed to relax; relieved, I guessed, that I appeared to know nothing more. "If I were you," he said, "I should forget all about it." He crossed his legs, revealing black silk socks.

"Why? It was important enough to bring you around here like a dog after a bitch in heat."

"There are some secrets that are best left undisturbed. For everyone's sake."

"You would have to be more explicit than that to convince me."

He was about to reply when the phone on the coffee table between us rang, as intrusive as a fire alarm. I reached for the receiver but Chambers beat me to it.

He gave the telephone number, paused, and said, "Yes, I inserted the announcement. Can you help me?"

As I tried to snatch the receiver, Chambers backed away and, with a pickpocket's agility, plucked the Browning from his pocket and aimed the barrel between my eyes.

"Yes, my name is Lambert. Can we meet somewhere? . . . Very well, midday . . . Yes, I'll explain then . . . Thank you for calling."

"So where are *we* meeting?" I asked as he sat down again.

"You are not meeting anyone."

"Are you in the habit of impersonating people?"

"Not recently. In the past, well yes, it has been known." He handled the gun with love, then asked, "Do you have a price?"

"They say everyone does."

"What's yours?"

"A niche at the top of the best-seller list."

12

"Alas, the one bribe I can't offer you, because if *The Judas Code* achieved that distinction it would negate everything I have set out to achieve."

"Which is?"

"To persuade you to abandon your inquiries."

"And why would you want to do that?"

"I can't tell you that. Would ten thousand pounds persuade you that I had good reasons?"

I shook my head.

"Twenty thousand?"

"I'm going to write the book."

He stubbed out his cigarette fastidiously, making sure he didn't soil his fingers with tar, and stared at me without speaking. In the hall, the grandfather clock chimed 9:30; a pigeon on the windowsill pecked at the glass; I became aware of the hum of the traffic far below.

Finally he said, "If you continue to follow this up I shall kill you."

He took a gold hunter from his waistcoat pocket and consulted it as though he had another pressing appointment to threaten someone with death.

"I'm going to call the police," I said.

"Please do so," he said. "But have the courtesy to wait till I've gone." He stood up, walked to the window, and gazed at the dignified streets below. "You have a wife and three children, I believe?"

"You keep them out of this!"

"Don't worry, I won't touch them. But they're very fond of you, aren't they? Would it be fair to deprive your wife of a husband, your children of a father? Because, please believe me, Mr. Lambert, I mean what I say. Try and crack the Judas Code and you're a dead man."

Throat pulsing, the pigeon backed away along the windowsill.

Perhaps I should have said, "I don't scare that easily," but it wouldn't have been the truth. Instead I said, "All right, you've had your say, now get out."

He shrugged, buttoned his overcoat, walked to the door, said, "Please be sensible," and was gone.

I considered calling the police, but even if they traced my visitor—I doubted whether his name was Chambers, but he couldn't escape the scar—he would merely deny everything.

As I was making a cup of instant coffee in the kitchen, the phone rang again.

A man's voice: "If you want to meet Judas, go to the lion house at the zoo at eleven this morning. Be carrying a copy of —"

"*The Times?*"

"The *Telegraph*. And appear to be making some notes." Click, as he cut the connection.

So I had more than an hour. I shaved and dressed in a blue lightweight suit and took the antiquated elevator to the ground floor where the porter, Mr. Atkins—I had never known his first name—had stood guard ever since I had come to the musty old block ten years ago. He was as permanent as the stone horsemen on the portals and just as worn.

"Good morning, Mr. Atkins."

"Good morning, Mr. Lambert. Fair to middling this morning."

I don't think he ever left the hallway, because the weather was "fair to middling" even if a blizzard was raging outside.

I walked down Portland Place toward Regent's Park. An April shower had washed the street, the sun was warm, pretty girls had blossomed overnight. A chic woman in gray waited patiently while her poodle watered a lamppost; a man in a bowler hat, carrying a briefcase, danced down a flight of steps; a nun smiled shyly from beneath her halo; an airliner chalked a white line across the blue sky.

Faced by all this, Chambers's lingering menace dissolved. The gun probably hadn't been loaded anyway.

I crossed Marylebone Road and the Outer Circle, Nash terraces behind me benign in the sunlight, and walked down the Broad Walk between the chestnut trees.

Nursemaids were abroad with prams, and for a moment I imagined them steering them toward clandestine meetings with red-coated soldiers.

And that scar—he had probably fallen onto the railings at school.

Inside the lion house my mood changed. The big cats hopelessly padding up and down their cages, their prison smelling like sour beer. I displayed the *Telegraph*, took out a notebook, and began to make notes: *Lions watching the spectators brought there for their delectation . . .*

The young man in the fawn raincoat said, "I'm afraid you won't meet Judas here." His voice and dress were irrefutably English, but there was a Slavonic cast to his features. He had gray, questing eyes and was, I guessed, in his late twenties. "You see, you've been followed."

My earlier optimism was routed. A lion bared yellow teeth behind its bars; captivity tightened around me.

14

"Who are you?"

"That doesn't matter. Just an intermediary. We had to do it this way, otherwise," he shrugged, "you would never have got your story."

"How did you know I wanted a story?"

Without answering, he took my arm. "Let's get out of here, I can't stand jails. But, before you go, take a look at the man in the tan jacket with the patched elbows looking at the tigers."

Casually I glanced toward the tiger cage. The man in question seemed absorbed with the occupants. He was squat, balding, powerfully built, about the same age as Chambers.

We left the cats dreaming about wide-open spaces and returned to the sunlight.

"And now," he said as we walked past a polar bear sunning itself beside its pool, "I have another assignation for you. But first you'll have to shake off your tail and make sure that he hasn't got a backup."

I stopped and gazed at the bear, glancing at the same time to my right. The man in the tan jacket was standing about seventy-five yards away consulting a handbook.

We walked on. "One more word of advice," he said. "Don't use your telephone on Judas business—it's bound to be bugged. That wasn't you who answered the phone the first time, was it?"

"It was a man who says his name is Chambers."

"We thought as much. It was he who hired the private detective who's following us."

"Do you mind telling me what this is all about?"

"I can't; Judas can."

"And when am I going to meet Judas?"

"Soon. But first of all, do you mind telling me just how you intend to use any information you might get hold of?"

"Write a book. You seemed to know that."

"We've known about you for a long time, Mr. Lambert. Ever since you started making inquiries. We've checked you out and you seem to be an author of integrity."

"Don't forget I write novels. In my particular field it pays to be sensational."

"At least you're being honest. That's what I want to establish—before you meet Judas—that your book will be honest."

"I can give you this assurance: I want to write a book that puts the record straight about the Second World War. Our civilization is shaky enough without being saddled with false premises. There was, for instance, no way Britain could have stood alone in 1940-41 unless something occurred behind the scenes that we know nothing about. The Battle of Britain was a famous victory, but it wasn't sufficient to deter Hitler from calling off the invasion. There was something more behind that decision, just as there was something more behind Stalin's refusal to believe that Germany was going to attack Russia. Stalin, after all, was a very wily Georgian."

"And you'll stick to the truth? If, that is, you believe what you're told?"

"As I said, I'm a novelist. I may use the fictional form to mold the facts into a digestible composition. But, yes, I'll stick to what I learn. If and when I learn it."

A flock of schoolchildren shepherded by a harassed woman in brogues passed by, watched from aloft by a giraffe. I turned, ostensibly to watch the children, and spotted the man in the tan jacket.

The young man seemed to accept my assurance. He glanced at his wristwatch. "I wonder," he said, slowing down as though he were about to break away, "if you realize just what you're getting into."

"When you're forced into your own flat at gunpoint you get the general idea."

"He wasn't playacting, you know."

"The gun didn't look like a prop."

"Well, so long as you understand—"

I said impatiently, "Where can I meet Judas, for God's sake?"

"It's eleven-thirty now. At Madame Tussaud's in one hour."

"Where at Madame Tussaud's?"

"Beside the figure of Winston Churchill." Where else? his tone seemed to say. "Good luck, I'll take care of our friend. But it will only be a temporary measure, so take care."

He turned abruptly and hurried away—straight into the man in the tan jacket. The man fell. I raced past a line of cages and, while they untangled themselves, took refuge in Lord Snowdon's aviary, watched incuriously by a blue-and-red parrot. There was no sign of my tail.

I emerged cautiously from the aviary and, leaving the jungle squawks behind, made my way to the zoo's exit. At Camden Town I took an underground train to King's Cross on the Northern Line and changed onto the Bakerloo Line, alighting at Baker Street.

At 12:25 I entered Madame Tussaud's waxwork exhibition and made my way into the Grand Hall on the ground floor. Churchill, hands clasping the lapels of his suit, chin thrust out belligerently above his bow tie, seemed about to speak. To offer, perhaps, nothing but "blood, toil, tears, and sweat."

It was exactly 12:30. The voice behind me said, "He could tell the story much better than I. But I'm afraid you'll have to put up with me."

I turned and came face-to-face with Judas.

THE JUDAS CODE

PART ONE

1

July 11, 1938. A wondrous Sunday in Moscow with memories of winter past and prospects of winter to come melted by the sun. The golden cupolas of the Kremlin floated in a cloudless sky, crowds queued up for *kvass* and ice cream, and in Gorky Park the air smelled of carnations.

In a forest behind a river beach, thirty miles outside the city, a blond young man who would one day take part in the most awesome conspiracy of modern times was courting a black-haired beauty named Anna Petrovna.

If anyone had hinted at his future role to Viktor Golovin, he would have dismissed that person as a madman. And abruptly, too, because it was his nineteenth birthday and he hoped to celebrate it by making love for the first time in his life.

It was a daunting prospect. In the first place, he feared his inexperience might be ridiculed; in the second, being a serious young man, he believed that the act of love should involve more than casual pleasure. It should, he reasoned, be a seal of permanency. But did he truly desire permanency with Anna Petrovna?

Standing under a silver birch, where coins of light shifted restlessly on the thin grass, he bent and kissed her on the lips and gazed into her eyes, seeking answers. She stared boldly back and gave none. He slipped his arm around her waist and they walked deeper into the forest.

The trouble was that although he loved her there were aspects of her character that angered him. Not only was she supremely self-confident, as any girl desired by half the male students at Moscow University was entitled to be, but she was politically assertive. She believed that Josef Stalin had made a travesty of Marxism-Leninism and she wasn't afraid to say so. Could love transcend such considerations?

He glanced down at her. She was small but voluptuously shaped, with full breasts that he had caressed for the first time two nights ago. There was a trace of the gypsy in her, an impression heightened today by her red skirt and white blouse. She was three months older than he and unquestionably far more experienced.

She smiled at him and said, "You're looking very serious, Viktor Golovin. Let's sit down for awhile and I'll see if I can make you smile."

She tickled his lips with a blade of grass as he lay back, hands behind his head, and tried not to smile. He could feel the warmth of her body and see the swell of her breasts.

Finally he grinned.

"That smile," she said, "is your key."

"To what?"

"To anything you want."

She unbuttoned his white, open-neck shirt "to let the fresh air get to you." He wondered if her previous words were an invitation and whether he should accept in view of his misgivings about her character. But when she kissed him—such a knowing kiss—and when he felt the pressure of her thighs on his and heard her sigh, his principles fled.

He lost his virginity with surprising ease. With none of the fumbling and misdirected endeavor that he had feared. His need was such that it didn't occur to him that his accomplishment owed not a little to her expertise.

She helped him with his clothes. She lay back, skirt hitched to her hips, legs spread, breasts free. She touched him, stroked him, guided him. And when he was inside her, marveling that at last it had happened, wondering at the oiled ease of it all, she regulated their movements. "Gently . . . stop a moment . . . harder, faster . . . now, now . . ."

For awhile they didn't speak. Then, when he had taken a bottle of Narzan mineral water from his knapsack and they were sipping it from cardboard cups, she said, "It was the first time for you, wasn't it?"

"Yes," he said, "it was. Are you surprised?"

"Why should I be? You're young."

So was she, and for a moment the obvious question about her experience hovered between them; but he knew the answer and then, in

her way, she answered it. "At our age a girl is much older than a boy."
She stroked his hair. "You're very attractive, Viktor, but what I really
like about you is that you always seem to be searching for the truth. I
think you're going to have trouble with your conscience some day."

He grinned at her. "I wasn't just now."

She was serious, however, and, not smiling, said, "It's a pity you don't
search for the truth in politics."

"The truth was the Revolution."

"That was more than twenty years ago, and we need another one."

"That tongue of yours will lead you to Siberia, Anna."

"Oh," she exclaimed triumphantly, "and what sort of a country is it
when one can end up in a labor camp for saying what one thinks?"

"A better country than Germany!"

"As if Germany were the only other country in the world." She stood
up and smoothed her skirt. "You must have heard about the purges."

Of course he'd heard, but some of the rumors were too outrageous to
be believed, and the others told of things that might well be justified.
After all *there were* traitors to the Revolution. Even now, somewhere in
Mexico, Leon Trotsky, like a malignant spider, was spinning his web.
Oh, no, Viktor only wondered how she could be so foolish. Lenin and
Stalin had given self-respect back to Mother Russia. He knew older
people who, before the Revolution, had lived on potato skins, black
bread, and tea.

"He's quite mad, you know." She began to walk back toward the
beach.

"Who?" picking up his knapsack and following her.

"Stalin, of course."

"They say genius is close to madness."

Through the birch trees, he could see a glint of water. Faintly, he could
hear the babble from the beach and the sound of Ping-Pong balls on the
tables beside the sand.

"I wonder," Anna said, "what it would take to convince you." She
kicked a heap of old brown leaves and her red skirt swirled.

"We have a good life," he said.

"*You* certainly do, Viktor Golovin."

He knew what she meant. For an orphan he had enjoyed a protected
upbringing; and his foster parents seemed to have had rather more than
their share of communal benefits. An apartment near the university on

the crest of the Lenin Hills, a small dacha in the village of Peredelkino, where the writers lived. Not bad for a librarian and his wife.

"It must be difficult," she said, "to hold forth about equality when you've had such luck."

"Everyone has a slice of luck. The trick is knowing what to do with it."

"Rubbish. Not everyone has luck. It isn't lucky to be an army officer these days."

"Ah, the purges again."

They emerged from the green depths of the forest into bright light. Beyond the table tennis players and the fretted-wood restaurant where you could buy beer, *kvass* and fizzy cherryade, pies, and cold meats, the beach was packed with Muscovites unfolding in the sun. Flesh burned bright pink but no one seemed to care. Rounding a curve in the river came a white steamboat nosing aside the calm water.

The doubts that had reached Viktor in the forest dissolved. Ordinary people wouldn't have been able to enjoy themselves like this before 1917. . . or so he imagined. Possessively, Viktor, lover and philosopher, took Anna's arm.

"But do you?"

"What?"

"You haven't been listening, have you?" she said.

"I don't want to hear anything more about purges."

She pulled her arm away. "Of course you don't. You don't want anything to interfere with your precious life. Least of all truth."

"I don't believe it is the truth. Let's go and have a beer."

They sat at a scrubbed wooden table and drank beer from fluted brown bottles. Around them families ate picnic lunches and guzzled beer; in one corner a plump mother was feeding a baby at the breast.

"I was asking," she said, "whether you would like to see some proof of what I've been saying."

"If it will please you."

"Please me!" She leaned fiercely across the table. "It won't please me. But I shall look forward to seeing that smug expression wiped off your face."

"Not so long ago I was always searching for the truth—"

"In everything except politics."

Some of the men and women sharing the long table were looking curiously at them. "Keep your voice down," Viktor whispered, covering her hand with his to soften the words, knowing that at any moment now she would accuse him of cowardice.

"I will for your sake," which was the same thing. "We can't have you thrown into Lubyanka, can we?"

A man with a walrus mustache, who was peeling an orange, pointed his knife at them and said, "Cell 28. I spent three years there. Give my love to the rats."

Viktor said, "You see, everyone can hear you, even when you lower your voice." He felt ashamed of his caution, but really there was no need to be, if she had been speaking the truth then, yes, he would have sided with her.

"Am I to speak in whispers all my life?"

He thought, Yes, if I'm to share my life with you. But the possibility was becoming less attractive by the minute.

The man with the walrus mustache bit into his orange and, with juice dribbling down his chin, sat listening. The woman in the corner transferred the baby to her other breast.

Viktor said, "There are a lot of informers about. Even I admit that."

"I suppose you think they're a necessary evil."

He thought about it and said, "Yes I do," waiting for her voice to rise another octave.

Instead she spoke softly. "I meant what I said, Viktor. I will show you the proof. Or I'll arrange for you to see it."

The man with the walrus mustache frowned and edged closer.

Viktor tilted the bottle, drained it, and wiped the froth from his lips. "Make the arrangements," he said.

"What arrangements?" asked the man with the walrus mustache. He spat out an orange pip. "I remember there was one rat who got quite tame. I called him Boris."

"Let's get out of here," she said.

Without speaking, they made their way along the dusty path beside the river. The bushes to their right were the changing quarters and from behind them came shrieks and giggles, the smack of a hand on bare flesh.

As they neared the bus station, she said, "You know Nikolai Vasilyev?"

"Your private tutor? I know of him."

"He's a good man," Anna said, and from the tone of her voice Viktor guessed that he was, or had been, her lover. "Sometimes when our sociology lesson is finished, he talks about what he believes in. The dreams that peasants dreamed, before Stalin made nightmares out of them."

Exasperated, Viktor punched the palm of one hand with his fist and said, "This proof. Tell me about it."

"Nikolai's best friend is an army officer, a captain. He will show you the proof."

"Proof of what?"

"You must see for yourself. If you have the stomach for it."

Then he couldn't refuse.

In the red-and-white coach packed with Muscovites radiating heat from their sunburn, Viktor considered Anna's jibes about his privileged upbringing. In fact it had bothered him long before she mentioned it.

He had been born in 1919, when the Red Army was still fighting its enemies in the civil war that followed the Revolution. There were many orphans in those days but not many who had the good fortune to be farmed out almost immediately to a respectable but childless young couple.

From what he had subsequently gathered, the Golovins had become remarkably self-sufficient in the dangerous, disordered streets of Moscow. They had found a small house in a relatively tranquil suburb; his father had been given a job at the library, where he helped Bolshevik authors rewrite history. His mother had devoted herself to the upbringing of Viktor.

In photographs he looked an uncommonly smug child—scrubbed, combed, smiling complacently at the cameraman.

It wasn't until he was sixteen that his father had told him that he was adopted. And it was only then that he began to question the uneventful security of his life.

To the inevitable question, "Who were my parents?" his father, bearded and patient, replied, "We don't know. There were thousands of children without parents in those days. You see, it wasn't just the men who were killed in the Revolution and the fighting after it, women fought side by side with them."

"But how did you find me?" Viktor asked.

"We didn't *find* you. You were allocated to us. We knew by this time that my wife, your mother . . . foster mother? . . . no, let's always call her your mother. We knew that she couldn't have a child, so we went to an orphanage. You had been taken there by an old woman who left without giving any details about your background. Perhaps she didn't know them; perhaps she was your *babushka*; we shall never know." His father put his hand on Viktor's shoulder. "But we do know that we were very lucky." A pause. "And I think you were lucky, too."

But it wasn't the mystery of his birth that bothered Viktor, because it was true that a baby could easily have lost its identity in those chaotic days when a new creed was being spawned. What bothered him was the cloistered life that he and his *parents* lived. Questioned on this subject, his father had no real answers.

"We're decent, upright citizens," he said in his calm voice. "Your mother keeps a good home." Which was true; she was a fair-haired, handsome woman in her early forties, who cooked well and was obsessively house-proud. "And I work hard," continued his father. Viktor later discovered this wasn't quite so true, because his father had taken to nipping vodka behind the bookshelves in the library off Pushkin Square. "So why shouldn't we have our security? We've earned it."

When he was seventeen Viktor pointed out that the apartment on the Lenin Hills, to which they had just moved, *and* the dacha were hardly commensurate with a librarian's income. And it was then that he first heard about his father's biography of Tolstoy. "I was given a considerable advance by my publishers," he confided. "They have high hopes for my project."

Viktor's doubts were assuaged until he discovered that the great work consisted of an exercise book half-filled with jumbled notes and a letter from the state-controlled publishers saying that they would consider the manuscript on its merits when it was delivered. Which, judging by the scope of Tolstoy's life and the paucity of his father's notes, wouldn't be for another century.

The bus swung around a corner and the standing passengers swayed together laughing, still drunk with the sun. Viktor loved them all, but he wasn't one of them—his parents had seen to that.

At school he had subtly been kept apart from other children. Even now at the university, where he was studying languages—English, German, and Czech (he could have taken a couple more because foreign tongues gave up their secrets to him without a struggle)—his privileged circumstances created suspicion.

Through the grimy windows of the coach he could see blue and pink wooden cottages tucked away among birch and pine; then the first scattered outposts of Moscow, new apartment blocks climbing on the shoulders of old houses.

Pride expanded inside him. So much achieved during his lifetime. What scared him was the gathering threat to the achievement. War. Fermented in the East by Japan and in the West by Germany. Viktor, orphan of war, was a preacher of peace. Russia had most certainly had her fill of war, but would the belligerents of the world let her rest?

By the time he and Anna alighted from the bus and made their way toward her lodgings in the Arbat, her mood had changed. She seemed to regret what she had proposed.

"Of course you don't have to go," she said. When he protested, she insisted, "No, I mean it. You're entitled to your opinions. I was being possessive."

"No, I must go."

It was early evening and heat, trapped in the narrow streets of leaning houses, engulfed them. In the distance they could hear the rumbling of a summer storm.

She slipped on the cobblestones and he held her and she leaned against him.

She said, "There's no one in the house. Come in and I'll make some tea."

She slid the key into the door of the tenement, owned by a baker and his wife. The stairs creaked beneath their feet, splintering the silence.

Her room was a revelation. He had expected garish touches, photographs of film stars, vivid posters from Georgia, beads, and powder scattered on the dressing table. But it was a shy, chaste place, and he wondered if he had misjudged her. On the mantelpiece above the iron fireplace stood a photograph of her parents, and the only beads on the dressing table were those strung on a rosary.

She lit a gas ring in the corner of the room, put a blackened kettle on it, and sliced a lemon. "What are we doing this evening?" she asked.

"Whatever you like." He was fascinated by the change in her.

"You know something? You're the first man who's ever been up here."

He believed her.

"I always kept it reserved for . . . for someone special."

"I'm honored," he said inadequately.

"How do you like your tea?"

"Hot and strong."

"I wish I had a samovar. Perhaps one day. But I have a little caviar."

She poured the tea into two porcelain cups and spread caviar on fingers of black bread.

As he sipped his tea, sharp with lemon, he said softly, "You know, you really should take care. The way you talk in public will get you into trouble."

"So, who would care?" She was estranged from her parents; he didn't know why.

"I would."

"But we must be free to say what we think." She popped a finger of bread loaded with glistening black roe into her mouth. Then, temporarily abandoning her cause, said, "How about going to the Tchaikovsky?"

Her suggestion was hardly inventive. They went there most evenings since they had paired off together. It was a student café, strident with debate and none too clean; but the beer was cheap and the company stimulating.

"Why not?"

"Look the other way while I change."

He stared through the window, thinking it was strange that a girl who only that afternoon had lain half-naked beneath him in the forest should suddenly be overcome by modesty.

Thunder cracked overhead. Blobs of rain hit the window and slid down in rivulets. Behind him he heard the rustle of clothing.

Another crack of thunder and he turned; she was naked and he reached for her.

The summons came ten days later.

His father took the call in the living room.

"It's that girl," he said, exuding displeasure, and handed the receiver to Viktor.

"Do you still want to go through with it?" Anna asked.

"Of course. Where shall I meet you?" He wanted to stop her from committing any indiscretion on the phone.

"Nikolai says—"

"Forget about Nikolai. Just tell me where to meet you."

"At the Tchaikovsky in half an hour. But Viktor—"

"I'll be there." He hung up.

He glanced at his watch. 6 P.M.

"That girl," his father said, stroking his gray-streaked beard. "Anna, isn't it?"

"How did you know her name?"

"I've heard you talk about her."

Viktor, who didn't remember ever discussing her, said, "Well, what about her?"

"I've heard," his father said, "that she's a bit of a firebrand." His voice didn't carry authority, but it was a voice that wasn't used to being contradicted.

"Really? Who told you that?"

"We get a lot of people from the university in the library."

"And they discussed your son's friends with you?"

"Just one of your friends. They seemed to think she wasn't desirable company."

"What were they implying? That she was a whore?"

"Viktor!" exclaimed his mother, entering the room, which was clean and bright from a good dusting that morning.

"I'm sorry, Mama, I didn't hear you come in."

"What kind of excuse is that? I won't have that sort of language in my house." With one finger she dabbed at a trace of pollen that had fallen from a vase of roses on the table.

Viktor turned to his father. "Why did they think she was undesirable, whoever *they* are?"

"Apparently she has an *ungovernable* tongue." He emphasized long words as though he had just invented them.

"She's got spirit, if that's what you mean."

"Misdirected, by all accounts. I really think, Viktor, that you should give her up."

"There must be some nice girls in your class," his mother said.

What would they say, Viktor wondered, if they knew that he had celebrated his release from celibacy by making love to her twice in one day? Twice! He almost felt like telling them.

His father said, "Wasn't there some gossip about her and her private tutor?"

"Was there?"

"Your father's only telling you for your own good," his mother said.

Viktor wondered if his father had been fortified by a few nips of vodka. "And I'm grateful," he said stiffly, "but I'm nineteen years old and capable of making my own judgments."

His father drummed his fingers on a bookcase crammed with esoteric volumes discarded by the library. "You're going to see her now?"

"You were listening to my conversation; you know perfectly well I am." He consulted his watch again. "And I'm late."

His father's fingers returned to his beard but the combing movements were quicker. "You realize you are distressing your mother and me? Do you think we deserve that?"

"I'm sure you don't, but I'm a man now. And I have the right to choose my friends."

His father turned away, saying, "I've warned you."

Viktor kissed his mother on the cheek. "I'm sorry, but there it is: your little boy has grown up. And now I must rush."

He took a tramcar to the center of the city. It was another fine day, cumulus clouds piled high on the horizon. Two more months and the jaws of winter would begin to close. But Viktor didn't mind the long, bitter months. Perhaps his parents had been Siberians. That would account for his blue eyes.

He walked briskly through the Arbat, past sleeping dogs, a group of children wearing scarlet scarves and red stars on their shirts, and old people in black becalmed in the past.

She was waiting for him at a table by an open window. A breeze breathed through the window, stirring her black hair. She wore a yellow dress with jade beads at her neck. She was smoking a cardboard-tipped cigarette with nervous little puffs.

"I'm sorry I'm late," he said. "Coffee?"

"We haven't time. Come, we can't talk here." Outside, she said, "You've got to promise me, Viktor, that whatever you see you won't tell a soul. You won't say where you've been or whom you've been with. Do you promise?"

"Of course. Where am I going?"

She was silent for a moment. Then she said, "You'll find out soon enough."

Apprehension began to grow inside him; she seemed so confident.

She took his arm and led him along the sidewalks to Theatre Square. There they caught a No. 18 tram to the Kaluzhskaya Zastava and then a No. 7 to the Sparrow Hills.

"And now?" He looked at her apprehensively. An old gray limousine answered his question. Anna pulled open the rear door and he climbed in. The car moved off, leaving her behind.

The driver had cropped brown hair and his accent was Ukrainian.

He handed Viktor a flask over his shoulder. "A little firewater, perhaps, to prepare you for what lies ahead?"

Viktor took the flask. He had only drunk vodka once and had considered himself quite sober until he had walked into the fresh air, whereupon he had collapsed. He took a sip and handed the flask back to the crop-haired enigma in front of him.

The vodka felt like molten metal in his stomach.

From the crown of the Sparrow Hills he could see the valley of the Moskva River, fields of vegetables, the Church of the Redeemer, the towers of the Kremlin. To his left stood the Novo-Dyevitchi Convent, to the right, on the wooded slopes of the river, the Merchants' Poor House. It all looked very peaceful in the evening haze.

The Ukrainian took a rambling route, as though trying to confuse anyone following. In the outlying suburbs, where the Tartars had once lived, men were coming home from work to wives and children standing at the doors of houses surrounded by wooden fences threaded with dog roses. The homecomings had an ordered rhythm to them that soothed Viktor's doubts. And yet . . . why had Anna gone to such elaborate lengths to prove something to him?

"Another nip?" The Ukrainian handed back the flask, silver with a family crest engraved on it. Viktor took another sip; if the Ukrainian was trying to get him drunk he had another think coming. But the liquor did embolden him to ask, "What sort of farce is this we're acting?"

The Ukrainian laughed, massaging the bristles on his scalp. There were a couple of incipient creases on his neck; he wasn't so young. "A tragedy," he said, "not a farce."

"You don't seem to be taking it too tragically."

"That way lies madness."

"I suppose you believe all the purge stories?"

"Of course I do. You see I deal with them—I have become a desk-bound soldier, a military clerk, after being wounded in a skirmish with the Japanese. But a clerk with a difference. I was considered bright enough to be enrolled in Military Intelligence, better known as the GRU. Do you know how the GRU came into existence?"

"It seems irrelevant."

"But then you wouldn't know, would you, because it was born of defeat, and defeats don't have any place in our history books." He swung the old car around a bend in a dirt road, sending up a cloud of dust. "In 1920, the Poles invaded the Soviet Union and stormed through my country. The Ukraine, that is," he explained. "They were thrown out eventually; then Lenin made a mistake." He turned his head and grinned. "Heresy, Viktor Golovin? But a mistake it certainly was. His intelligence, the Cheka Registry Department, got it all wrong and told him the Poles were ripe for revolution. As ripe as green apples as it turned out. The Red Army attacked Poland and got torn to ribbons for their pains. As a result, the GRU was formed and Yan Karlovich Berzin was put in charge."

Viktor said, "What's all this got to do with purges?"

"The GRU is in charge of military purges, even though we're only a branch of the secret police, the NKVD. The NKVD itself didn't do too badly in the purging business under a man named Genrikh Grigorevich Yagoda. But apparently he didn't purge quite diligently enough, and he was shot in Lubyanka Prison. Now they have a fellow named Nikolai Yezhov in charge. He's doing a good job, but it's only a question of time before they cart him off to Lubyanka, too."

"I don't believe any of this," Viktor said.

"Where have you been, comrade? In solitary confinement?"

"Why are you doing this for me today?" Viktor demanded.

"Because I'm in love with Anna Petrovna. So is my friend Nikolai Vasilyev. So, I believe, are you. Wouldn't you do anything she asked?"

Viktor thought about it, then said firmly, "No."

"Ah, but you are young. Perhaps you are the sort of young man she needs. Someone who will stand up to her."

The Ukrainian's words surprised Viktor. He seemed to be the sort of man who would stand up to anyone.

The Ukrainian went on, "But I assure you that what I'm doing is not entirely selfless. I've heard all about you from Nikolai. You're something of a hothouse plant, and in my book, naiveté, feigned or otherwise, is as much to blame for tyranny as anything else. It will give me pleasure to disillusion you."

Viktor felt a sudden, uncontrollable shiver run up the length of his spine, but he still attacked. "You admit you play a part in these purges. Are you proud of that, comrade?"

"I have saved as many as I can."

"So you select the victims?"

"Don't interrogate me."

"Not much of an achievement, to save a few of the people you've made a career condemning."

"Then you believe me?"

Viktor was almost afraid he did, but something within him still resisted. "What if I tell the authorities about our trip today?" he said.

"Then you, too, will be executed. Comrade Stalin doesn't like to have people in the know around too long. Yan Berzin's days are numbered. So are my own. I don't really care what you do or say."

He pulled into a track leading to a farmyard and parked the car in a stable. "And now, my patriotic young friend, we walk."

The Ukrainian was shorter than Viktor had imagined. He wore a brown tweed jacket and gray trousers and an open-neck gray shirt. He walked with an unnatural stiffness, and when he saw Viktor staring, he said, "The bullet hit me in the spine, so I wear a steel corset. I'd like to think it might stop another bullet one day except that in Lubyanka they pump them into the back of your head." They turned into the dirt road and headed east. "You're not a very inquisitive young man, are you? You haven't even asked me my name. It's Gogol, like the author. Mikhail Gogol."

Bats fluttered in the calm air, swallows skimmed the road ahead of them. In the fields peasants were scything lush, green grass. A bearded *muzhik* wearing brown carpet slippers wandered past, eyes vacant.

"We're on the outskirts of a village that was once called Tzaritzuino-Datchnoye," Gogol told Viktor. "Does that mean anything to you?"

"Not a thing," replied Viktor, with the terrible certainty growing upon him that it soon would.

"Well, the village was given by Peter the Great to Prince Kantemir of Moldavia. In 1774, Catherine the Second—Catherine the Great—bought it back for Russia. She started to build a huge dacha here but abandoned it. There's a theater—also unfinished—next to it, and there are lakes, lawns, gazebos . . . but all overgrown. In fact the grounds are a jungle," Gogol said.

"Why the history lesson?"

"You must know your background. One day, perhaps, you'll write about it."

"I might," Viktor said. "But it will be fiction."

"Touché."

Gogol stopped for a moment, holding his back as though it pained him. He thumped the base of his spine with his fist. "I can't walk very far these days."

"Why are we going to a decayed dacha?" Viktor asked.

"I forgot to tell you why Catherine abandoned the place. It was because it reminded her of a coffin. Think about it."

From behind his cover, Viktor could just see the dacha over the top of the ivy-covered wall surrounding it. And it did resemble a coffin. A long, low building surmounted with spires that looked like funeral candles.

He was crouching behind a clump of dusty-leaved laurel bushes. Facing him, across a stony path, was a massive wooden door, studded with iron spikes, that opened into the wall. Set into it was a smaller door. Both were guarded by a gray-uniformed sentry, who every ten minutes marched along the length of the wall, first to the right and then, repassing the door, to the left. According to Gogol, who had brought Viktor through the undergrowth to the rear entrance, the smaller door was unlocked and only needed a push to open it. Clearly the sentry, a shabby-looking fellow with pock-marked features, didn't expect intruders, because he marched dispiritedly, staring at the ground; nor official visitors either, because he had taken off his cap and was smoking a cigarette. Locals, said Gogol, had been warned not to come anywhere near the mansion.

"Make your move when he's halfway to the right-hand extremity of the wall," Gogol had instructed Viktor, before making his way to the front entrance of the mansion, where, apparently, he was expected. "Then make your way through the shrubbery to the theater. At the back you'll find a potting shed, wait for me there. If you get caught, then I've never heard of you. I still have a faint instinct for survival."

The sentry took a deep drag on his yellow cigarette, pinched out the tip, and slipped the remainder into the pocket of his jacket. Then, carrying his rifle as though it were a cannon, he started out to the right of the door.

Viktor tensed himself. Twigs cracked beneath his feet. Dust from the laurel leaves made him want to sneeze.

Halfway across the path he slipped, righted himself, and made it to the door. The sentry, one hundred yards away, didn't look around. Viktor reached out one hand and pushed the smaller door. But it didn't move.

Perhaps Gogol had locked it from inside. Perhaps he wants me dead with a bullet in my back.

The sentry was turning. Viktor pushed again. The door swung open with a creak. He was inside, closing the door, peering around, sprinting for a privet hedge enclosing a shrubbery. He crouched behind a rhododendron. In front of him, a spider on a web suspended between dead blooms was devouring a fly; through the web he saw a man wearing a brown smock pushing a handcart. A gardener—that seemed reassuring.

Turning, Viktor ran through knee-high grass strung with brambles until he came to a lichen-covered wall surrounding a stagnant pool. Through a crack in the wall he could see a stone cherub with a ruined face smiling crookedly at him. A fish with a white, speckled body surfaced briefly in the pool before returning to the moss green depths with a flick of its tail. Viktor crawled to the end of the wall; keeping low, he raced to a thicket of holly bushes. Above him loomed the walls of the coffin.

On one side lay the half-finished theater where Catherine the Great had planned to watch the cream of Russian thespians. It looked like a dull place from the outside, dead-eyed and brooding, but then theaters often did. Beside it stood the potting shed, ferns growing from its windows.

Inside the shed, Viktor waited. Outside, the shadows were lengthening. The swallows and bats had vanished, but somewhere in the tangled undergrowth a bird sang.

Gogol said, "Follow me," his voice reaching Viktor through the ferns. Viktor joined him outside.

"Right through that gap," Gogol whispered, pointing at a space in the wall of the theater intended for a door. Gogol got there first. Inside the doorway he paused, grinding his fist into the base of his spine. "Now you've got to be careful," he said. "Just around the corner you'll see a passage, just like the corridors behind the auditorium at the Bolshoi. Take the first door on the right. You'll find yourself in a box. If you stand in the shadows at the back, you can't be seen from below; but you'll have one of the best seats for the show." He grinned fiercely. "Wait for me there afterward," and was gone.

If there had once been a stage it was no longer there. Nor were there any seats, just a rubble-strewn arena cleared at one end in front of a wall that would have been the back of the stage. Half a dozen civilians strolled restlessly about, smoking. Leaning against another wall opposite Viktor's box stood a collection of old M 1891 rifles and two green boxes of ammunition.

The men below were selecting rifles. More civilians, all in shirt-sleeves, entered the arena and picked up the rest of the guns. Crisply they loaded them. Outside he heard a vehicle, a big truck by the sound of it, draw up.

Viktor bit deep into the flesh inside his lower lip and tasted blood.

From behind the wall he heard shouts. Hands clenched, body taut, he awaited the entrance from the wings. Shouldn't there have been an orchestra? A conductor in white tie and tails?

In came the players. Middle-aged mostly. All men. All wearing military trousers, all in shirt-sleeves. They walked erect but there was a strange docility about them. They were obviously officers. Did those trained to command accept commands just as readily?

Desperately Viktor wanted to leave his vantage point and return to the sanctuary of his adolescence.

The officers were blindfolded and lined up against the wall, hands behind their heads, elbows touching. Thirty of them. Nikolai Yezhov's daily ration? I don't believe it. Viktor's legs bent and he had to steady himself with one hand against the wall of the box.

The firing squad lined up opposite the blindfolded men and raised their rifles. Some of the condemned men crossed themselves.

They slumped. Blood appeared at their breasts. It seemed to Viktor that he heard the explosions from the rifles after the impact of the bullets.

The abruptness of the transition from life to death astonished him; he could barely comprehend it. A second volley of shots made the bodies jump as they slid to the ground.

Two of the executioners propped their rifles against the wall, drew pistols, and walked along the lines of bodies shooting out any vestiges of life.

Then the *gardener* made his entrance pushing his handcart. But Viktor, unconscious on the floor of the box, didn't see them load the bodies into it.

He waited the following evening at the Café Tchaikovsky for three hours. From seven in the evening, the hour at which they usually met, until ten.

But she didn't come and some inexplicable perversity—nothing had rational explanations anymore—stopped him from calling at her lodgings. Perhaps the whole episode had been an act of cruelty on her part, and like Gogol, she had merely wanted to knock him off his smug perch. Perhaps even now she was naked in the arms of Nikolai Vasilyev. Or Gogol.

She hadn't attended her class that day, but she had sent a note explaining that she had to visit a sick relative at Kuntsevo. Well, she had a grandmother in Kuntsevo (Stalin also had a house there) but that was only seven miles away, so she could have been back by seven, eight at the latest, especially when she knew what he had been through.

Later, he decided that he had done so little about finding her because he was still in a state of shock. He believed nothing anymore, least of all the earnest babble of the students in the Tchaikovsky.

When she didn't appear in class the following day, he telephoned Nikolai Vasilyev; and then, when he didn't get any reply, went around to Anna's lodgings on the lunchtime break. Her landlady, an old crone with features as sharp as a claw, told him that Anna had packed her belongings two nights before—the night of the massacre—paid a week's rent, and disappeared.

Viktor didn't believe her. He threatened her and offered money, but fear (the new Viktor Golovin suddenly knew fear when he saw it) had efficiently silenced her.

He called at Nikolai Vasilyev's house in the north of the city, but he, too, had disappeared. The woman who answered the door was in her thirties, blonde, pretty, and distraught, possibly Vasilyev's mistress. She didn't know what had happened; he had been missing for two days. But she had an address for Gogol.

Gogol lived in an apartment near the Alexander Brest railway station. Viktor rang the bell but its chime had a lost quality to it. Neighbors told him that they had seen Gogol leave with four men in civilian clothes. Leave? "Well, 'escorted' would be a better description," said one old man. "But don't say I said so," he added, pocketing Viktor's ruble.

When Viktor continued to pursue his inquiries, his father took him aside and said, "Best leave it alone, Viktor. What's done is done. You can't bring them back . . ."

Them? Again Viktor wondered about his father's source of information.

What astonished him most, as with suicidal recklessness he asked his questions, was the lack of reprisals. He was suggesting treason to those he cross-examined, and yet he remained untouched and privileged.

When he had finally ascertained beyond all reasonable doubt that Anna, Vasilyev, and Gogol had been purged, Viktor took the only step left to him.

He, too, disappeared.

2

It is difficult enough to determine when a conspiracy is born. Is it at the moment when all doubts are cast aside and plans are carefully prepared, or is it when two schemers meet on the same train of thought?

It is well nigh impossible to decide when a conspiracy is *conceived.* A chance remark, an afterthought, a memory . . . any such stimuli can do the trick without the potential conspirator realizing until much later what has happened.

So it would be foolhardy to suggest that, when he sat up in bed to eat his breakfast on September 28, 1938, the man in the crumpled blue pajamas had conceived the plan that was to reach out for the soul of Viktor Golovin.

What was certain was that he was enjoying a hearty meal: partridge, bacon, hot buttered toast, and marmalade in the bedroom of his English mansion.

He ate rapidly but fastidiously—his hands were remarkably small for such a bulky body—and as he put away the food, he read the newspapers. His features were a mixture of petulance and pugnacity, unrelieved by the boyish smile that so often disarmed his critics.

The previous evening, the Prime Minister, Neville Chamberlain, had broadcast to the nation: "How horrible, fantastic, incredible it is that we should be digging trenches and trying on gas masks here because of a quarrel in a faraway country"—bracketing Czechoslovakia with the moon!—"between people of whom we know nothing . . ."

Dear God, the glib insularity of the man!

"I would not hesitate to pay even a third visit to Germany if I thought it would do any good. . . . I am a man of peace to the depths of my soul."

43

After making the broadcast, Chamberlain had received a letter from Hitler, and there was no doubt that it was an invitation to appeasement.

With a sigh, Winston Churchill pushed aside his tray, climbed out of bed, put on a dressing gown, and sauntered onto the lawns of Chartwell, his country manor, near the village of Westerham in Kent. He had come here from London so that he might have a brief respite from the crisis.

War clouds were gathering over London, Berlin, Paris, and Prague; but here in rural Kent they were not visible. Bonfire smoke wreathed the seventy-nine acres of grounds; the trees were autumn red and gold; chrysanthemums still insisted it was summer despite the first frost on the grass.

He lit a cigar. War would undoubtedly come. But Churchill did not think it would come about because of a breakdown in the present negotiations over Czechoslovakia. No, he was confident Chamberlain would return to Germany and sacrifice the Czechs on the altar of compromise. It was ironic that those who had failed to heed his own warnings about the Nazi threat now expected war immediately, whereas he still gave it twelve months or so.

But if Chamberlain does return with peace in his pocket, then watch out, Winston, because there'll be no place in Britain for a warmonger.

He made his way to the foundations of the cottage and with a mason's trowel scraped a few crusts of cement from the first row of bricks. Warmonger! He had borne that cross ever since. . . . He supposed it went back to those dashing days in Cuba, India, the Sudan, and South Africa when, as soldier and journalist, he had always breathed gunsmoke.

Then it hadn't mattered so much, but after the Gallipoli campaign in the First World War, which, as first lord of the admiralty, he had devised and promoted . . . after that catastrophe (205,000 dead) . . . it had hurt, and it had stuck, and it had been damaging both politically and personally, if the two could ever be separated. And yet his instincts had been right. The war might have been shortened by his plan, if it had received full and intelligent support.

It was Churchill's personal opinion that he only reveled in battle when his sights were set on peace. Let them call him a warmonger now. When the war began they would need a man who was not the flinching sort. Then they would turn to him . . . that was his comfort and his conviction.

For several years, Chartwell had been a Foreign Office in exile.

There Churchill had conferred with his closest associates, Robert Boothby, Duncan Sandys, and Brendan Bracken.

There, energetically but impotently, he had drawn up the policies he would have pursued had Stanley Baldwin or his successor, Neville Chamberlain, given him office in the Government.

There he had furiously denounced Hitler's occupation of the Rhineland, Austria, and now the Sudentenland territory of Czechoslovakia.

Today with the Munich Crisis over—solved in the groveling fashion he had been anticipating when he took that morning stroll a few days earlier in the garden of Chartwell—he recalled Chamberlain's playacting after his betrayal of Czechoslovakia. Waving his meaningless agreement to the crowds outside 10 Downing Street and telling them, "I believe it is peace in our time."

And his own words in the Commons after the debacle: "All is over. Silent, mournful, abandoned, Czechoslovakia recedes into darkness. . . . Do not suppose this is the end. This is only the beginning of the reckoning."

No one had wished to heed those words in the euphoria that followed Chamberlain's homecoming.

As he paced the reception room at Chartwell, he pointed a finger at Bracken, the Irish-born newspaper proprietor and Member of Parliament, and said, "I wouldn't mind so much if Neville believed any of this eyewash himself. But he doesn't. Even when he was waving at the crowds on his way back from Heston, he told Halifax, 'All this will be over in three months.'"

"He believed it once," Bracken remarked. "You must give him credit for that."

Churchill nodded. "In the past, I've always respected his idealism— whatever follies it led him to." Pouring himself a whisky and soda, he continued to patrol the book-lined room littered with newspapers. Finally he said decisively, "It seems to me the sincerity's been dissipated, Brendan."

"I assume he's only buying time," Bracken answered, running his hand through his crinkly, ginger hair.

"He's buying it rather late."

"Yes, but he *must* buy it. And he cannot very well admit in public that he is appeasing the Führer just to give Britain the chance to rearm. Hitler would march into the rest of Czechoslovakia tomorrow. No doubt he has expressed his real views to his confidants; I don't have to remind you, Winston, that you aren't one of them."

Churchill grunted and lit a cigar from a fresh consignment from John Rushbrook in New York.

Bracken regarded Churchill fondly from the depths of a sighing leather armchair. He had known the man for more than twenty-five years, from the time Churchill had moved to the admiralty after his tempestuous reign at the Home Office. Like Churchill, Bracken enjoyed talking and his favorite topic was Churchill; youthful adoration was behind him, mature understanding in its place.

He understood the melancholia, veiled from the public; he understood the flamboyance summoned to smother doubt, the bravado employed to mask fear. "You can't be a hero without being a coward," Churchill had once told him.

Churchill, thumbs in the waistcoat of his crumpled gray pinstripe, stared at a portrait of his grandfather, the seventh duke. "What about Joe?" he said.

"Joe who?"

"Stalin. I wonder what he thinks of this groveling policy of ours—if he's got time to think in between his purges."

"He's furious, of course. He'd prefer to see the capitalist powers fight each other to a standstill."

Silence.

Somewhere a clock chimed. Bracken could hear the crackle of Churchill's cigar as he rolled it between his fingers.

The silence persisted. Nervously, Bracken cleared his throat.

Finally Churchill said, "That's a very interesting remark, Brendan."

But hardly an original one, Bracken thought.

"Let's put it to one side for a moment," Churchill said. "But we may return to it," as though they were in for a long session that, Bracken knew to his cost, could last until 4 A.M. "Don't think for one second that Stalin is hoodwinked by Neville's scrap of paper. He knows there'll be war and he'll have to decide who's going to win, Germany or us. Whom do you think he'll put his money on, Brendan?"

"Well," Bracken said, giving his spectacles a polish, "he's been chasing an anti-Hitler coalition for three years."

"As indeed he might," Churchill said. "Two years ago Hitler was bellowing that the Ukraine and even Siberia should be part of the *lebensraum,* Germany's living space."

"But he also thinks we've allowed Germany to rearm so that she can fight Russia. Munich will convince him he's right. On the one side he's got the aggressor, on the other the betrayer. An unenviable choice."

Churchill wheeled around, waving his cigar so vigorously that Bracken feared his faulty shoulder would pop out. "I'll tell you what I would do if I were he." Churchill sat down opposite Bracken and took a swig of his whisky and soda. "I would wait until the Fascists have thrashed the Reds in Spain, then I'd throw in my lot with Hitler. You see, Brendan, it's really his only option. He knows that one day Hitler will turn on him and he's got to delay that inevitable moment until Mother Russia is prepared."

"That will take a few years," Bracken remarked. "Stalin has purged more than thirty thousand Red Army officers and disposed of nearly all the Supreme Military Council."

They were interrupted by Clementine, who came into the room to say goodnight. She looked very well, lovely for her years, and at peace with herself, but Bracken did not wonder that there were occasional wry edges to her smile.

"Goodnight, Brendan," she said, "please don't get up." And to her husband, "It's nearly midnight, dear, will you be much later?" The question, Bracken suspected, was purely academic.

"Not much longer," Churchill said, kissing her lightly. "You run along, now." And when she had gone, "What a lucky devil I was, eh, Brendan?" Churchill regarded the glowing tip of his cigar. "She's never liked these things, you know," and ground out the long stub in a gesture of penitence. "And now, where were we?"

"Stalin. You prophesied he would go in with Hitler."

"That's my guess." Churchill gave himself another whisky and siphoned soda water into it. "Now let's get that phrase of yours back off the shelf."

"What phrase was that?"

"'He,' Stalin that is, 'would like to see the capitalist powers fight each other to a standstill.' It made my hair curl, Brendan, what little there is left of it. Of course you're absolutely right, that's just what he would like."

Patiently, Bracken waited for enlightenment.

Holding his glass of whisky in one hand, pausing to tap some of the books in the cases with one small, plump finger as though they contained the answers to the problems facing him, Churchill began to pace the room again. There was his own novel, *Savrola,* written in his youth; there was *The Aftermath,* in which he had poured out his postwar hatred of the Bolsheviks. "It's strange," he said, "but my fear of the Reds has always been greater than my fear of the Nazis. We shouldn't have squeezed the Germans so hard, we should have left them a little pith."

Still Bracken waited.

"Supposing," Churchill said, turning to study Bracken's reactions, "we reversed Stalin's equation. Supposing we made sure that Russia and Germany fought each other to a standstill?"

"But what about the pact you believe they're going to sign?"

"I'm sure they will sign, but it won't fool either of them. Hitler intends to march through the steppes, and Stalin knows it."

The distant clock chimed again. A single note. It was 12:30 A.M.

Now Churchill was an exultant prophet, his glass of whisky his crystal ball. "What we must do," he said, "is cut into the time Stalin thinks he's buying."

"You're talking in riddles, Winston, and I'm afraid I don't understand."

Churchill's words lost their ring. "No more you should, Brendan. I'm not even sure that *I* do at this moment. But it will come, it will come."

He sat down abruptly and, suddenly somber-voiced, said, "I tell you this. Unless some terrible measures are devised, this island of ours will be pillaged by the barbaric hordes of either the Nazis or the Bolsheviks." Without warning, he stood up, drained his crystal ball, and said, "Come on, Brendan, there's a good chap, you're keeping me from my bed."

PART TWO

PART TWO

3

By the second week of June 1940, much of Europe lay in ruins, the people dazed and beaten by Hitler's blitzkreig. Poland, Denmark, Norway, Holland, and Belgium had fallen, and France was poised to throw in the tricolor.

But in Lisbon you could have been forgiven for forgetting there was a war on at all.

The sun shone; the boulevard cafés on the cobbled squares and wide avenues were crowded with customers, British and German among them. The broad, flat waters of the Tagus estuary were scattered with ships of many nations; the little yellow tramcars butting along their shining rails and climbing the steep hills were stuffed with cheerful, sweating passengers.

In the grand arenas of the Baixa, business in the banks was brisk, hotels were full, shops were relatively well stocked. In the precipitous maze of the Alfama, women garlanded their leaning cottages with laundry, dogs slept in the alleyways, and the hot air was greased with the smell of grilling sardines.

It was only on closer inspection that you realized that the Portuguese capital had not entirely escaped the war. There was a restlessness abroad in those sidewalk cafés; conversations were muted, money changed hands surreptitiously. And in the grand hotels, the Avenida Palace and the Aviz, the atmosphere was majestically clandestine.

The perpetrators of this atmosphere were mostly refugees, but quite a few were spies. The refugees had flocked to neutral Portugal from countries overrun by the Nazis, following in the footsteps of the Jews who had fled from Germany itself.

At first they all had but one aim: to get out of Europe through Lisbon, the gateway to freedom. The rich usually managed it, liberally tipping the custodians of the city's portals. Their poorer brethren, accustomed to using the tradesman's entrance, didn't escape so easily.

And it was they who were the most furtive. Selling jewelry, worthless bonds, secrets, and their bodies if they were well nourished enough. Lying, cheating, cajoling, bribing. Doing anything to get a berth on a ship or, more ambitiously, on a New York-bound Clipper seaplane. A passage to the United States had preference. Britain, being at war, was less hospitable to aliens, and South America was a long way off and had suspect political allegiances.

They wore incongruous clothes, these fugitives. Long coats and cloaks, slouch hats and peaked caps, moth-eaten stoles, and peasant blouses. They looked like extras from a dozen period movies; and the longer they stayed, the more threadbare became their costumes, the more humble their homes.

The really tough persevered, in particular the Jews, who were used to such privations. Others, dogged by ill luck, double-crossed by swindlers, took to the hills or one of the shanty settlements on the outskirts of Lisbon, where they could share their poverty without humiliation.

Their empty seats in the cafés were immediately filled, their rooms soon occupied by newcomers feverish with optimism. Some were luckier than others, in particular the British—many of them in transit, via Spain, from the South of France—who were accommodated outside the city. After all, Portugal was Britain's oldest ally, even if she had to placate the Germans. You didn't upset Hitler, not if you were as small and unprepared as Portugal you didn't.

On June 13, the eve of the German occupation of Paris and a fine, dreamy day in Lisbon, the plight of the refugees was starker than usual.

Or so it seemed to the tall young man in gray flannel trousers and white shirt striding loose-limbed along the Avenida da Liberdade, the Champs-Elysées of Lisbon, on his way to meet a girl in the Alfama.

It was *feira,* the festival of St. Anthony of Padua, Lisbon's own saint, and the groups of dark-clad aliens seemed so remote from it; particularly the children with their hollowed eyes, pale skin, and sharp bones. They should have been part of it—the processions, the feasts, the fireworks—because *feira* is a time for children as well as for lovers and drunks.

Today Josef Hoffman was determined not to be affected by the refugees. He had earned a day off from their suffering. He was 22 and had been in Lisbon for a year now, working with the Red Cross. At first his work had been coldly selective, weeding out the frauds—German agents mostly—and the rich from the deserving. With his Czech passport and his way with languages—he was already fluent in Portuguese—he was a natural *agent provocateur*.

But he had soon sickened of this. He wanted no more contact with spies or men who would offer him five thousand escudos to help them jump the line in the American Export Line offices. He wanted to help the helpless, that was why he had joined the Red Cross.

As he made his way across the Praça Rossio, the city's main square, he could hear firecrackers exploding like gunfire. He stopped and bought a red carnation, its stem wrapped in silver paper, from the flower seller beside the fountains—to give to the girl whose name was Candida. She was slumberous and warm-limbed, and she would cut the stem off the carnation and wear the flower in her hair that shone blue-black in the sunlight. Hoffman wasn't in love with her, which, he thought, was a pity.

He left the square by the Rua da Betesga and turned up the Rua da Madalena, intending to climb toward the ramparts of the Castelo de São Jorge, St. George's Castle, which stands astride one of Lisbon's seven hills. Or was it eleven, or even thirteen? The travel guides begged to differ.

Josef Hoffman was unaware that he was being followed by a man carrying a Russian-made automatic pistol in the pocket of his raincoat. The man had puffy features, and he walked as though the pointed brown-and-white shoes he was wearing hurt his feet. In normal times the heavy gabardine raincoat and wide-brimmed hat would, together with the shoes, have been conspicuous on a hot evening, but not these days, when it was common enough to see a Bohemian or a Slovakian in outlandish clothes hurrying to some secret rendezvous.

Hoffman turned left and began to climb, the walls of the castle ahead of him. He was early for his appointment and intended to spend ten minutes or so wandering around the battlements of the castle, with their sensational views of the city and the Tagus.

The man with the pointed shoes followed.

Absorbed in the thought of the pleasures to come that evening, Hoffman almost collided with a woman carrying a basket of fruit on her head. She cursed him but kept her balance with dignity. A procession of children in national dress scattered, as a firecracker thrown by urchins fell hissing in their midst; when it exploded everyone screamed delightedly.

The man in the pointed shoes felt the gun in his pocket, crooked his

53

forefinger around the trigger. The gun felt heavy, like himself. Why couldn't they have given him an older quarry instead of a mountain goat? Hoffman didn't have the build of a natural athlete, but he was slim and supple.

Hoffman strode along a short street lined with linden trees and entered the castle grounds. The castle was Phoenician and Moorish and Christian; apart from the walls there wasn't much of it left.

In a dusty clearing just past the gates, teenage girls were performing an impromptu folk dance. They wore long skirts striped in green and gold and red, white blouses, and green-and-red head scarves. A woman spectator, bursting with knowledge, told Hoffman that they were from the north and were affronted that *feira* in Lisbon was such a discreet affair.

Not in the Alfama, he thought, nothing was ever discreet down there. He walked over to the stone parapet and gazed down at the labyrinth below, rooftops like a discarded pack of mildewed playing cards. So closely were the hillside terraces packed, so sturdily were they planted, that they had resisted the earthquake that devastated the rest of Lisbon on All Saints' Day, 1755, and the tidal wave that had followed it. Down there every day was *feira*.

The man with the pointed shoes moved nearer, then paused. He hadn't expected Hoffman to come to this public place. He turned and looked at the dancers tripping about self-consciously in front of a statue. Putting his free hand into the other pocket of his raincoat, he fingered the purchase he had made that morning: a dozen firecrackers.

Hoffman gazed across the city and at the Tagus, called the Straw Sea because it was often gold at sunset. It was gold now. So broad was the estuary that visitors often thought that the open sea lay to the left of the city, whereas, of course, the Atlantic lay to the right through a narrower channel.

Hoffman walked on toward the remains of the fortifications. Apart from the girls dancing, the festival had not come up here. You could feel space. A few Americans carrying cameras strolled the ramparts. He thought that there would be Americans taking pictures on Judgment Day.

He knew one of them, a rangy young man from the American consulate, who did his best for the endless queue seeking visas to the United States. It was a hopeless task, but at least he was polite and he treated all the old ladies as he would treat his mother.

He pointed at the ships becalmed in the golden waters and said, "Kind of hard to believe that Europe's in flames, isn't it?"

Hoffman asked, "Has Paris fallen?" The American, whose name was Kenyon, knew about such things.

"Not quite, but it's there for the taking. Tomorrow, I guess. Then France will quit. The only neutral countries in Europe will be Switzerland, Sweden, Spain, Turkey, Ireland, and, of course, Portugal. And Britain will stand alone. But not for long unless some sort of miracle occurs."

"Churchill deals in miracles," Hoffman said. "Dunkirk was a miracle."

"A miracle? Perhaps. It was a retreat just the same, a defeat. That's the kind of miracle they can do without."

"I suppose," Hoffman said, choosing his words, "the sort of miracle they need is American intervention."

"Fat chance," Kenyon said. "Last year Roosevelt promised that there would be no 'blackout of peace' in the States. If he does decide to stand for a third term he can hardly go back on his word."

"But if and when he does become president again?"

Kenyon shrugged. "Perhaps, who knows? But it may be too late. No, Churchill will have to pull that miracle first and not just with words. If he doesn't, then one day the whole world will be full of refugees."

A firework fizzed and exploded. A small boy watched from behind a pillar. Behind him Hoffman caught sight of a man wearing a raincoat and a broad-brimmed hat. He had a lost air about him; a refugee probably. He turned to look at the decorative birds pecking the dust, and Hoffman forgot all about him.

The birds were either black or white, the colors of Lisbon's mosaic pavements. There was even a white peacock.

Hoffman glanced at his watch. In five minutes time he was due to meet Candida Pereira. He bade farewell to the American and retraced his footsteps. They would have some *bacalhau,* cod, served with baked potatoes, onions, and olives, and one of the honey-sweet desserts washed down with a bottle of *vinho verde* and then . . .

Hoffman walked faster.

So did the man in the pointed shoes, wincing with each footstep. But at least they seemed to be heading for the teeming streets of the Alfama, which was where he wanted Hoffman.

Hoffman plunged into the maze of streets. Above him the rooftops reached for each other. From the walls hung pots of pink and red geraniums and birdcages, from which only the song of the captives escaped. From the dark mouths of bars came shouting and laughter and music; sometimes Tommy Dorsey or Bing Crosby on scratched phonograph records, sometimes the *fado,* the lament of Portugal.

He stopped at the foot of a flight of steps named Beco do Carneiro. Old hands still got lost in the Alfama. He turned and, over the heads of the crowds, noticed a broad-brimmed hat glide into a doorway. It didn't register; he was imagining the invitation in the slumberous eyes of Candida Pereira and was by now alarmed that he might be late. However slumberous their eyes, the Candida Pereiras of this world didn't wait around.

He hurried on, emerging eventually in the Largo de Santo Estevão. He had come the long way around, but it wasn't far now.

Near the café where they had arranged to meet, the scene was particularly boisterous. A group of men who looked like American gangsters' barbers were singing lustily, children were wrestling, and from the windows above women were shouting across the street.

The man in the pointed shoes took the firecrackers from his pocket. He gave three to children and told them to light them and throw them.

He moved up closer to Hoffman and, reluctantly, let go of the butt of the automatic. He lit three more firecrackers—Whizz Bangs they were called—and threw them just ahead of Hoffman. As they landed, the children's firecrackers exploded, cracks as loud as pistol shots in the cramped space.

He returned his hand to his pistol and through the gabardine aimed the barrel at Hoffman's back. He waited for his own Whizz Bangs to detonate, finger caressing the trigger.

The three explosions were almost simultaneous. In fact everything happened at once. The man who ran full tilt into Hoffman, knocking him sprawling; the explosion behind him; the screaming.

When he got to his feet, Hoffman was surprised to see the man he had noticed wearing the broad-brimmed hat in the grounds of the castle lying on his back, pointed brown-and-white shoes pointing toward the sky.

"What I don't understand," Hoffman said, "is how you just happened to be there at the right time."

The suntanned man in the navy blue lightweight suit said, "We didn't just happen to be there. We had been keeping tabs on the man who tried to shoot you."

"Shoot me? Why should he want to shoot me? Why should anyone want to shoot me?"

The man, who had told him his name was Cross—"Double-cross," with the mechanical laugh of one who had made the joke many times before—said, "We rather hoped *you* would be able to tell *us* that, Mr. Hoffman."

Us? Only Cross was present; although in the Alfama there had been two of them.

As he had picked himself up after the gunshot, one of the men—Cross he thought—had thrust him through the throng and said, "Let's get out of here before all hell breaks loose." Hoffman had thought, "They must know about me."

If not, he reasoned as they hustled him down steps and alleys to a waiting car, they wouldn't have been so sure that he would be willing to be bundled away from trouble.

Beside the car, a black Wolseley, he had made a token resistance: "Before I get into that thing I want to know just who the hell you are."

"We're from the British embassy. We want to help you."

And he had believed them. In the society in which he moved, "British" or "American" had a reassuring ring.

"Is the man who tried to shoot me dead?"

"We think so."

The car, with the second man, obviously junior to Cross, at the wheel, had taken them along the waterfront to an old, comfortable-looking block of flats in the Belém district, close to Jerónimos Monastery.

The apartment itself, presumably Cross's, was splendid. The living room was spacious and filled with light; the curtains were gold brocade, the furniture Regency-striped. Through the windows, before Cross drew the curtains, Hoffman could see the first lights of evening.

Cross, who had identified himself as a second secretary at the British embassy, was interrogating him in the nicest possible way. He held up a cut-glass decanter and said, "Scotch?"

Hoffman shook his head. Cross made him feel immature, and yet Cross couldn't have been all that much older. Twenty-five perhaps, but contained and assured—some might have said condescending—in the way of some Englishmen; those, Hoffman divined, who were not quite of the noble birth to which they aspired, but formidable just the same. And well-heeled, because few diplomatic services, least of all the British, would provide a twenty-five-year-old with a flat as luxurious as this.

"Well, I'm going to have one. Are you sure you won't have a wee dram?"

"No, thank you," sitting back to study Cross as he poured himself a drink.

Hoffman had met quite a few Englishmen since he came to Lisbon, but somehow this one didn't quite fit. He was elegant enough, suit not too keenly pressed, striped tie deliberately askew, and his manner was languid. His smooth hair was a warm shade of brown, and his features were handsome in a military sort of way. (Odd, then, that he wasn't in the army.) But Hoffman could sense contradictions about him and they bothered him.

The suntan, for instance—diplomats were never bronzed. And his hands were too big, strangler's hands, making an absurdity of the white silk handkerchief tucked in the sleeve of his jacket. Hoffman couldn't imagine Cross playing the English game of cricket; blood sports would be more his line. His voice was modulated but controlled. When Cross appeared to be wasting words, he was wasting them for a purpose. No, Hoffman thought, your appearance is camouflage; beneath those casual graces lurks a hunter.

Glass in hand, Cross walked to a coffee table standing in front of a coldly empty marble fireplace and picked up a pistol. "Taft, the man who drove us here, took it out of the pocket of your assassin's raincoat pocket. Would-be assassin," he corrected himself. He held the automatic by the barrel. "Crude but effective, as they say." He pointed at the letters CCCP on the barrel. "No doubt where it came from." He sat on the sofa opposite Hoffman, still holding the gun.

"Was he Russian?" Hoffman asked.

Cross laid the gun on the striped cushion beside him and drank some whisky. "I think perhaps I should ask the questions," he said. "A rescuer's privilege." He gave a cocktail-party smile. "How long have you been in Lisbon, Mr. Hoffman?"

"About a year."

"Czech passport, I believe. And you work for the Red Cross."

Hoffman nodded.

Cross said, "When did you leave Czechoslovakia, Mr. Hoffman?"

"In 1938, when the Germans marched into the Sudetenland."

"You were from the Sudetenland?"

Hoffman shook his head. "From Prague."

"Weren't you a little premature in leaving?"

"On the contrary, that was the time to get out, before the whole of Czechoslovakia was occupied."

"What language do you speak?"

"English," Hoffman said.

Cross didn't smile. "Your native language?"

"Both Czech and Slovak and a little Hungarian."

"I wish I had your talent for languages," Cross said. "It's not our strong point—we think everyone should speak English."

Is he dead?

We think so.

So casual. The reply had barely registered. A man who tried to shoot me is lying dead in a Lisbon street, and here we discuss languages.

"Did you leave anyone behind?"

"Sorry, I don't quite . . . I will have that drink," Hoffman said, "if you don't mind."

"Not at all," in a tone that did mind just a little.

Cross poured him a whisky. "Soda?"

"Please."

He sipped his drink. "Did I leave . . ."

"When you left Czechoslovakia, did you leave any relatives behind?"

"Only my mother. My father died five years ago."

"Wasn't that a little callous?"

"She had married again. To a man who had all the makings of being a good Nazi when the Germans finally took Prague."

"And where did you go to?"

Hoffman, who felt that Cross knew the answer to this and most of the other questions, replied, "To Switzerland."

"How? Across Germany?"

"Austria."

"Same thing by then."

We think so. Hoffman took a gulp of whisky. "It wasn't too difficult. I had forged papers, and foreign languages didn't surprise people in that part of Europe in those days. The Balkan tongues had spilled over—"

"Why the Red Cross?" Cross asked abruptly.

"Should I be ashamed of it?"

"It's a vocation, not a job. You were very young to choose it."

"I knew what was happening in Europe and to the Jews in Germany. I knew what was coming and I wanted to help."

"But not to fight?"

"Apparently you didn't wish to fight either, Mr. Cross."

Cross didn't look as angry as he should have, but the interrogation lapsed for a few moments. A ship's siren sounded its melancholy note.

Cross poured himself another whisky. Then he said, "For a pacifist that was a very belligerent remark, Mr. Hoffman."

"Pacifist? I suppose I am. I think I can do more good working for the Red Cross than becoming another freedom fighter."

"Quite a cushy number," Cross remarked. Hoffman hadn't come across the word "cushy" but guessed its implication and sensed that Cross was trying to needle him. "Like mine," Cross added. "Did you go to Bern?"

"Geneva. I spent a year there. I learned English there. Second secretary of what, Mr. Cross?"

"Chancery," Cross said without elaborating.

The phone rang.

Cross spoke into the receiver. "Yes . . . He is, is he? . . . Yes, he's here . . . No, we won't . . . I won't forget . . . I'll ring you back."

He replaced the receiver, saying to Hoffman, "Yes, he's dead all right."

"Do you mind if I ask a few questions?"

"Fire away, but don't expect too many intelligent answers."

"I presume you're with British Intelligence."

"You may presume what you wish, Mr. Hoffman."

"Who was he?"

"Your would-be assassin? A man named Novikov."

"Russian like his gun?"

"As far as we can gather. As you know Portugal doesn't recognize the Soviet Union. But quite a few Russians managed to infiltrate during the Spanish civil war when they were backing the Communists. They settled here with false identities and kept their heads down."

"And why were you following him?"

"He worked as an interpreter—like you, he was quite a linguist—and did a lot of work for us. But, of course, he was a Soviet agent. He was also a hit man." A breeze breathed through the open window, ruffled the curtains, and, with a tinkle, spent itself on the chandelier. "We had penetrated his set-up and knew that today he had a contract. We didn't know who, but it became obvious that it was you. Why, we didn't know; still don't," raising an eyebrow at Hoffman. "At one stage Taft and I thought he was going to clobber you in the castle grounds."

"Then why didn't you stop him?"

"We wanted to know where you were leading him, and then, perhaps, why he was after your blood."

"Mistaken identity?"

Cross grimaced at such a preposterous suggestion.

Hoffman put down his glass; he wasn't used to hard liquor and the whisky was affecting his reasoning. There was a catalog of questions to ask, but he had to search for them.

"Until today I was a stranger to you?"

"Not quite. We make a point of checking out Red Cross personnel. I admire your dedication, Mr. Hoffman, but it's not unknown for a few devils to flit among the angels of mercy."

"Why did you kill him? It was you, wasn't it?"

"As a matter of fact it wasn't. Taft took care of it."

"And you think you'll get away with it?"

"I'm quite sure we will. There are a lot of unsolved murders in Lisbon these days, as I'm sure you know. The PIDE can't follow up the death of every stateless middle-European. Perhaps he had stolen someone's family jewels, their papers, their seat on the Clipper . . ." Cross spread wide his hands. "My turn again?"

"What more questions can there be? I don't know why he tried to kill me, nor do you."

Cross leaned forward, gray eyes looking intently at Hoffman. "Novikov worked for the NKVD. Have you really no idea why the Russian secret police should be so anxious to remove you from the face of this earth?"

"No idea at all," lied Viktor Golovin.

4

"So," Churchill said to the tweed-suited man sitting opposite him on the lawns of Chartwell, "contact has been made in Lisbon?"

The man, who had fair hair needled with gray and a withdrawn expression that looked as though it had been recently but permanently acquired, nodded. "Some weeks ago."

"You didn't inform me," Churchill said reprovingly.

"With respect, Prime Minister," said Colonel Robert Sinclair, head of the Secret Intelligence Service, "you told me not to worry you with details."

"You're right, of course." Churchill smiled at him brilliantly through the smoke from his cigar and the spymaster's pipe. "I've had a few things on my mind recently."

In the distance they heard the wail of air-raid sirens; then the alarm at Westerham groaned into life.

A few things on my mind, Churchill thought, and all disasters.

Since he became first lord of the admiralty, when war was declared on September 3, 1939, and then prime minister on May 10, 1940, after Chamberlain's policies had finally collapsed, the Nazi jackboot had crushed most of Western Europe. Now its toe was aimed across the English Channel.

Hitler had, on July 16, issued a directive for an invasion. And, judging by the armadas of Messerschmitts, Dorniers, Heinkels, and Junkers swarming across the skies, had every intention of carrying it out.

Or had he? Wasn't it more likely that the attacks were aimed at softening up Britain so she would make the sort of deal Hitler had always dreamed about?

Indeed only three days after issuing the directive, Hitler had told the Reichstag, "In this hour, I feel it to be my duty before my own conscience to appeal once more to reason and common sense in Great Britain as much as elsewhere."

Hitler was perfectly willing to leave the British Empire, or most of it, unscathed. His ambition lay elsewhere—to the east.

It was this belief of Churchill's that formed the cornerstone of the plan that had been gestating within him ever since he first suggested to Brendan Bracken, two years earlier, that they should make Germany and Russia fight each other to a standstill.

From the south there came the drone of approaching aircraft.

Clementine called from the house, "You'd better come in, Winston."

Churchill, who was wearing a painter's smock and gray trousers, pretended not to hear and shaded his eyes to look at the enemy squadrons. They were flying high in the summer sky, in parade-ground order.

Churchill said, "I wish I had my field glasses, but if I go in to get them, Clemmie will collar me."

"So she should," Sinclair told him. "We can't afford to have our prime minister strafed by a Messerschmitt."

His tone was almost flippant and it surprised Churchill. Sinclair, who looked like a Scottish laird, was canny but dour. In the past he had never shown animation except when talking about his only son, Robin: Robin had died on the beaches of Dunkirk.

Perhaps imminent danger brought out the flippancy in him; it was a drug that affected men in many different ways.

Suddenly, from the direction of the afternoon sun, Spitfires attacked. Machine guns chattered; the neatly arranged squadrons of German aircraft broke up and Churchill was on his feet shouting, "Bravo!"

Clementine came running out and handed them both steel helmets. "If you won't take shelter," she said, "you'd better wear these."

The sky above the serene countryside was now daubed with skeins and whorls of white smoke. From the midst of the high-battling planes, one fell spinning toward the ground, trailing black smoke.

"One of theirs or one of ours?" Sinclair asked.

"God knows, poor devil." Churchill sat down again on the garden seat beside Sinclair. "But I do know this, we can't afford to lose many more. Beaverbrook is doing a superb job, but even he can't replace aircraft at the rate we're losing them. You see, people only count the planes we lose in battle. They forget the ones destroyed on the ground when the Huns bomb our airfields."

"At least we know where they're going to hit," Sinclair said.

"Ah, ULTRA, my most secret source. But we'll have to do better than that. If they continue to hit the airfields, we're done for. I wonder," said Churchill thoughtfully, "if a bombing raid on Berlin would taunt Hitler and Göring into bombing our cities instead of our defenses . . ."

Two aircraft detached themselves from the battle. A Dornier chased by a Spitfire. They roared so low over Chartwell that Churchill and Sinclair could see the pilots. The Spitfire's guns were blazing, shell cases clattering on the roof and terrace.

Black smoke burst from the Dornier. It turned over slowly with funereal majesty and disappeared as the Spitfire climbed exultantly. The battle was almost over. The battered armada was returning home, discharging its bombs onto the countryside as it went.

Churchill brought the conversation back to Lisbon. "This contact, this man Hoffman, or Golovin as he used to be called, is he sympathetic?"

"He's being cultivated," Sinclair said.,

"In what way?"

"As you know, he works for the Red Cross, and he's a pacifist. We are at present putting him in touch with some of the leading peacemakers in Lisbon, and that's how we'll keep him happy and occupied until the next stage of the operation begins."

"So he has no idea he is being manipulated?"

"No, he wouldn't stand for it. Hoffman—we both know that his real name is neither Hoffman nor Golovin—is no doubt somewhat naive, but I believe he has a strong character."

"An inheritance from his father, perhaps?"

Sinclair shrugged his shoulders and gave one of his dour smiles.

At that moment, Clementine appeared from the house, carrying a tray with a bottle of Pol Roger and two glasses on it. Churchill's face lit up. She put the tray on the wooden table in front of them and said, "I'm going back for a cup of tea, but I thought you'd like a victory celebration."

"As if I needed an excuse," Churchill said, easing the cork out of the bottle and, as it sprang out, pouring foaming champagne into the glasses. When Clementine had left, he turned toward Sinclair and said, "Let's run through Phase One again."

The plan they had devised was simple in its main intent but more complicated in the execution. The Western democracies, in Churchill's view, had to regard Germany and the Soviet Union as two equally threatening and repulsive tyrannies. Britain's purpose must be to lure the two states into war with each other—preferably a prolonged engagement in which they would bleed each other dry. To a superficial mind there would seem to be dim prospects for this, because on August 23, 1939, Stalin and Hitler had signed a nonaggression pact, with Poland as the shared spoils. But it was a flimsy agreement between thieves, and the Führer's ultimate designs on the Soviet Union were no secret.

Great Britain, however, could not allow events to proceed according to the Führer's schedule. If Britain were to be saved—and militarily she was in no position to save herself—then she must *turn* Hitler's mind toward the east.

It was that change of direction on Hitler's part that constituted Phase One. The first step in it was to blast the Luftwaffe out of the skies and sink as much as possible of the invasion fleet being assembled across the Channel. It was essential to emphasize to Hitler that the invasion of Britain—Operation Sea Lion—would never be easy and might even be a mistake.

"Hitler's heart isn't in it, anyway," Churchill said, lighting a fresh cigar. "And now we come to the crux of Phase One. Hitler must believe we are preparing to make peace with him. If he believes that, then we can encourage his natural desire to crush the Russians; indeed we can make it an essential condition of the peace maneuvers."

"Of course, our success at this stage hinges on Hitler's willingness to believe we've been forced to the edge of the negotiating table," Sinclair said.

"Yes, and if he's to believe that, he must think any peace feelers come from me. Hitler will understand that we can't move through the normal diplomatic channels. If word got out I was contemplating a deal with Adolf, the outcry would shatter every window in the House of Commons." Churchill paused and puffed on his cigar. "Therefore, my dear Sinclair, what have you devised?"

"The intelligence will come from a source Hitler trusts—as much as he trusts anyone," Sinclair said firmly.

Churchill waited.

Sinclair contemplated the grass, silently and stubbornly, and pretended to pull at his unlit pipe.

"Very well," Churchill said after a few uncomfortable seconds had passed, "let us consider Phase Two. All our efforts will be for naught if Stalin realizes the Nazis intend to attack. He will mass his troops, purged or otherwise, on the borders, and there will be two possible outcomes."

Churchill paused as he caught sight of Clementine at one of the windows of the house. She was pointing at her wristwatch. The message was clear: time for your nap. He waved at her.

"There might be one hell of a battle," Sinclair said.

"Yes, although, personally, I doubt it, and if there were, it might not lead to the sort of long war I desire. One side or the other might be clearly victorious in the first month. The more likely outcome is that the two dictators would patch it up. They'd slap each other on the back, blather about military maneuvers, withdraw their armies, and prolong their alliance. How would you rate those two results, Sinclair?"

"The first would be a catastrophe, and the second might be worse."

"Exactly. On the other hand, if we succeed, two questions will always torment historians chronicling this war."

Sinclair tilted his head politely. "And they are?"

"One, why Hitler exposed himself on two fronts by invading Russia before Britain was beaten."

"And two?"

"Why Stalin ignored warnings that Hitler intended to attack."

"Warnings from whom?"

"Myself among others," said Churchill enigmatically.

Sinclair knocked out his pipe on the heel of one of his brogues. "It is a very narrow rope we're walking to cause the sort of war you require."

"Inevitably, yet it can be done. Let us imagine Stalin caught unawares and Hitler fooled by his lack of preparation. Then the Nazis will attack, but unless they can time their assault in early spring, they'll come face-to-face with the Russian winter before they ever reach Moscow. Then the two sides will grind each other down, out there on the steppes. God willing, they'll be so palsied, it'll be a decade at least before either one can trouble us. And by then we'll be prepared."

Sinclair said levelly, "What you are suggesting could involve millions of deaths."

"Millions?" Churchill said quietly. "You're probably right. What you have to remember is the alternative, and that is the end of civilization as we know it. The end," pointing at the green tranquillity in front of them, "of all this."

"Winston." Clementine's voice reached him from the house, but

Churchill ignored it. His deafness, not as bad as some people believed, was a great asset.

Sinclair said, "Odd to think that the key to the whole thing is a young man named Hoffman who hasn't the slightest inkling of what's afoot."

"The key to Phase Two certainly, but first we must convince Hitler that he will have our good intentions when he does attack Russia. You were about to explain to me how you intend to accomplish that, weren't you, Sinclair?"

"Excuse me, Prime Minister?"

"Who it is you will send to convince Hitler of my eagerness to negotiate."

"Ah, yes."

"Please be a little more explicit, Colonel."

Sinclair scraped the charred bowl of his pipe with the blade of a silver penknife. "The fewer people who know the better."

"Is there anyone in England besides the two of us who knows about this plan?"

"No."

"Good. Now who is your agent?"

Clementine was walking across the lawn, determination in her stride. Sinclair glanced toward her and then, looking back toward Churchill, said, "You told me you weren't concerned about details."

"I no longer regard this as a detail."

"Are you quite certain you wish to know, sir?"

"Yes."

Sinclair paused, searching for another evasion. Clementine was fifty yards away, rounding a bed of red, white, and blue petunias. Churchill gave him a peremptory, bulldog glare, and he submitted.

"Admiral Wilhelm Canaris, head of German military intelligence."

"Thank you, Colonel," and to Clementine, who was now standing beside them, "There you are, my dear."

"Here I am," she said, "and there *you* are, which is not where you're supposed to be. It's long past time for your nap."

Churchill gave her a peck on the cheek and Sinclair a wink. "Very well, my dear, just off."

"And so am I," said Sinclair, bowing to Clementine.

As Churchill walked thoughtfully across the lawns, the siren at Westerham began to moan another warning.

5

The softest touch for a creator of disinformation is someone who wants to believe his lies.

So I am lucky in this respect, Sinclair thought as he walked his dog, a red setter, in the woods near his home in Berkshire: Hitler wants to believe Britain is ready to acknowledge his genius and make a deal.

I'm also lucky that Hitler still trusts the purveyor of the lies, Admiral Canaris, head of the Abwehr, the intelligence section of the German High Command.

But I am unlucky in my own state of mind. The head of an intelligence agency should be impersonal, clinical in his judgment. That is no longer true of me. Since the death of Robin, I'm fueled by hatred and hatred distorts judgment.

He picked up a stick and threw it for the dog, who disappeared among the rotting silver birch trees. A gun emplacement had blocked the natural drainage, and the trees were dying like overwatered house plants. But it was a quiet place, becalmed among green fields, especially on evenings such as this, with shafts of fading sunlight reaching its bed of moss. A place to contemplate. A place to plan. A place to hate.

The dog came bounding back and placed the stick at his feet, and he threw it again, thinking, "Admiral Canaris and I have a lot in common. We are both confused by hatred. I loved my son, and so now I hate Germany; he loves Germany but hates Hitler."

Once more he threw the stick for his tireless, slavering pet. Enticing Canaris to Lisbon shouldn't be too difficult; he was already involved with Franco in neighboring Spain, and Lisbon was the European capital of espionage.

To anticipate the reactions of Canaris he would have to study him more deeply. As he walked down a flinty lane toward his home in Finchampstead, he poked a particularly bright flint with his walking stick and found that it was a jagged sliver of shrapnel.

When he reached the big rambling house, he called to the setter, "Robin, come here." But the dog's name was Rufus.

In his study, he consulted the file on Canaris.

He lit his pipe, and as the day died, the admiral emerged from the dossier and took a bow.

He was fifty-three years old but looked older. His silken hair was prematurely gray, and he was known as Old Whitehead.

He had served with distinction in the navy in the last war. On one occasion, his cruiser had been scuttled off the South American coast by the superior guns of a British warship. He had been interned on an island close to Chile but had escaped to the mainland in a rowboat, disguised as a Chilean. He had crossed the Andes on horseback, taken a train to Argentina, sailed to Amsterdam on a forged passport, calling at the *British* port of Falmouth!

A man to be reckoned with.

His escapades had continued in spectacular fashion, his star in the ascendancy until he had fallen foul of Admiral Erich Raeder, who had blocked his promotion in the conventional navy, thereby setting him on course for espionage.

Ironic, mused Sinclair, that Raeder had advocated defeating Britain before attacking the Soviet Union.

On January 1, 1935, his forty-eighth birthday, Canaris had become head of the Abwehr.

He was five feet three inches tall. He had pale blue eyes. His manner was mild. He had difficulty in sleeping. He was a hypochondriac, although his only known complaint was bad circulation, which accounted for the coldness of which he continually complained.

He was a pessimist. He detested Hitler because of his persecution of the Jews, and he feared for his country because he believed its leader was a madman.

He was subject to fits of melancholia.

In Lisbon the approach would have to be circumspect. Canaris was cooperating with British Intelligence, but he certainly wouldn't cooperate to the extent of bringing about Germany's downfall.

So he would have to be persuaded that Churchill genuinely wanted to settle for peace; that, with the specter of war on two fronts removed, Hitler would be able to concentrate on crushing Russia.

What if Canaris still had lingering doubts about *Albion perfide*? Well, there was one way in which the admiral could be *persuaded* that it was in everyone's interests to tell Hitler about Britain's change in policy. Blackmail.

From the kitchen came his wife's voice. "Dinner's ready, dear. Spam fritters and scrambled eggs—dried eggs, I'm afraid."

Old Whitehead winced at the first scream.

He abhorred cruelty. But then he reminded himself that the man being beaten up in the adjoining room was a draft dodger and felt a little better because he also abhorred that particular brand of cowardice.

Admiral Canaris's hands trembled as he turned the pages of *Signal,* the services' propaganda magazine. What a mess he had become since the death-and-glory days when he had been a U-boat commander and subsequently captain of the cruiser *Schlesiens*—since he had been diverted into espionage.

But perhaps that is your true vocation, intrigue, because you even intrigue with yourself. Furthermore you are a pessimist, Canaris. The admiral turned a page of the magazine and stared at a photograph of a sailor with his arm around the waist of a girl with her hair in braids. The sailor's face was bold—like mine once was, in those far-off days of youth and optimism.

He turned another page and Adolf Hitler stared at him.

From the room next door another scream and a voice shouting in English, "I don't know! I . . . tell you . . . I . . . don't . . . know."

A thud followed by the sound of a body falling.

Canaris glanced at his wristwatch. Another couple of minutes and he would call it off, because in all probability the Englishman was telling the truth.

He was one of the many informants who, during the past couple of weeks in Portugal, Switzerland, Sweden, and indeed, in London itself, had reported a dramatic change in Britain's policy.

According to the reports, Churchill, despite his swashbuckling oratory, wanted to make a deal with Hitler because he realized that the position of his bombarded and besieged islands was hopeless.

In his offices in Tirpitzufer in Berlin, Canaris had studied the reports with skepticism. There were too many of them at once.

Then two highly plausible sources had come up with the same information in Lisbon, and he had flown to the Portuguese capital.

But before confronting them he had decided to put a lesser informant to the test. A dispensible informant such as the draft-dodging Englishman—of whom there were quite a few in Lisbon—who was at this moment having his teeth knocked down his throat in the basement of the German minister's residence.

Canaris shivered despite the heavy leather overcoat he wore. He felt cold. From a silver pillbox he took a white tablet to aid his circulation and swallowed it.

He opened the door to the adjoining room and told the two shirt-sleeved inquisitors to put down their rubber hoses.

The Englishman, who had been propped against a wall of the bare room, slid to the floor. Just like they did in the movies, Canaris thought. Although, unlike movie interrogators, the two sweating Gestapo bully-boys did not appear to have been enjoying themselves. Presumably they preferred more refined and less exhausting methods of extracting information, which he didn't permit—that was the domain of Reinhard the "Hangman" Heydrich, Himmler's deputy and head of all SS security, which included the Gestapo.

Perhaps one day, men such as this will interrogate me, Canaris thought, and felt even colder.

He said to the Englishman, "Get up."

The body on the floor moved. The bloodied head turned. Eyes slit between swollen flesh regarded Canaris. Did he see hatred or gratitude there? With a face in that condition you couldn't necessarily tell.

To one of the interrogators Canaris said, "Bring him a chair." When the Englishman was sitting on the kitchen chair beneath a naked electric light bulb, Canaris gave him a cigarette and lit it for him.

The Englishman, whose name was Spearman, inhaled and coughed and inhaled again as if the smoke was a medicant. He was young, about twenty-three, with fair wavy hair and a face that, before the beating, had been half-saint and half-delinquent. According to Abwehr records in Lisbon, he was a homosexual.

To one of the interrogators, both beefy men running to fat, Canaris said, "What was it he didn't know? What was the question?"

"He didn't know whether it was true or not."

"Whether what was true?"

"The information he brought, whatever that was," the man said sullenly.

So the Gestapo, who unfortunately handled all interrogations in Lisbon, was learning at last: don't tell your inquisitors too much, thereby keeping risks to a minimum.

To the Englishman he said, "Why aren't you fighting for your country?"

Spearman spat out blood. "This is a neutral country, and I shall report you to the authorities."

"Really? What authorities, I wonder? The Portuguese? We Germans really are calling the tune here, you know, and their police won't risk upsetting us. The British? I don't think so, do you? They would lock you up or, worse, make you fight. But you didn't answer my question. Why aren't you helping to defend your country? You see, I am a patriot and the reasoning of a traitor interests me."

"I'm not a traitor," the voice was slurred.

"What are you then?"

"A pacifist."

"Then you should have registered as a conscientious objector in England."

"I prefer the sunshine," Spearman said.

"Where did you get this information?"

"At the casino at Estoril, where else?"

"A hundred and one places," Canaris said. "The Aviz or the Avenida Palace, in Lisbon, the Palácio or the Hotel do Parque in Estoril . . ."

"I like to gamble."

"Who gave you the information?"

"I gleaned it."

He spoke beautiful English. Perhaps he had been to Cambridge University, where the Russians were so assiduously recruiting agents.

"Who from?"

Spearman put two fingers inside his mouth. They came out holding a tooth. Then the spirit seemed to go out of Spearman, often the case when a homosexual realized his looks had been damaged.

Sensing that the moment had come to change the approach, Canaris dismissed the two Gestapo thugs. They hesitated, unsure of Canaris's authority.

Without raising his voice, Canaris said, "Get out."

They went.

Canaris sat down opposite Spearman, gave him another cigarette, and said in a friendly, almost paternal, tone, "Come now, stop being so obstinate. An admirable quality, I agree, and very British, but entirely misplaced at the moment."

Tears gathered in Spearman's eyes. "I just don't understand," he said. "I pass on information, that's all. I don't pretend it's true, I never have. And what happens?" His voice trembled, and he brushed at his eyes with blood-stained fingers. Canaris felt almost, but not quite, sorry for him. "This is what happens . . . It isn't fair."

"If you cooperate, it won't happen again. Believe me, I don't want to see you hurt. And if you do help us, we might even increase your reward."

Spearman stared at Canaris beseechingly. "But I have cooperated."

"Your informant, who was he?" Canaris hardened his tone a little.

"I told you it was only hearsay."

"A homosexual?"

"Does that make it more suspect?" he asked, a little spirit returning to him.

Canaris shook his head. "It makes no difference. Gossip is gossip." He handed Spearman a handkerchief. "Who was he?"

Spearman pressed the white silk handkerchief to his eyes. "Yes, he's queer all right."

"Your . . . *friend?*"

Spearman nodded.

"British?"

"Swiss."

"You move in exalted circles, Mr. Spearman," because there was no such mortal as a poor Swiss here or anywhere else for that matter.

"And your *friend* . . . what is his profession?"

"Does it matter?"

"Oh yes," Canaris said, "it matters very much."

"Very well then, he's a businessman."

"You're not giving very much away, Mr. Spearman. I understood you were going to cooperate."

"I thought it was an unwritten law," Spearman said, puffing away at his cigarette, "that informants weren't obliged to give away their source of information."

"I just rewrote that law."

"Very well, his business is cork."

"Along with every other businessman in Lisbon. But hardly a profitable enterprise for a Swiss. After all, they don't produce that much wine, and none of it particularly memorable. Are you sure it's cork, Mr. Spearman?"

"I understand he's a middleman."

"Ah, but he wouldn't be anything else, would he?" Canaris touched his gray eyebrows, a habit of his. His wife had clipped them for him at their home on Lake Ammersee in Bavaria just before he left for Portugal. He wished profoundly that he was back there now. He unbuttoned his overcoat, leaned forward, and snapped, "His name, please."

"I can't give it to you. You'll have him beaten just as you've beaten me."

"A Swiss businessman? I doubt that. I doubt that very much," Canaris said. "British draft dodgers, yes, we beat the hell out of them. But not Swiss businessmen. In any case, we might need his cork, if cork it is, for some of our Rhine wines. He is German Swiss?"

"No, French . . . Shit!" Spearman stamped on his cigarette butt. "That was bloody clever."

"At least it narrows the field. You might as well tell me his name, I'll find out soon enough. If you die during further interrogation," his voice still pleasant, man-to-man, "then it will merely be a process of elimination."

Spearman began to shiver. "If I do, you won't—"

"Reveal the source of *my* information? Certainly not. I am an officer and a gentleman, although that may have escaped you."

Spearman gave him a name. Cottier. Canaris stood up and began to pace the floor. Cottier? It meant nothing to him.

"In any case," Spearman was saying, "he only heard it indirectly at a party. You know those Estoril parties . . ."

"No, I don't," said Canaris, thinking of France, Belgium, Holland bleeding from the wounds of war. "And who was *his* informant, for God's sake?"

The transfer of responsibility seemed to cheer Spearman a little. He uttered a name that stopped Canaris in his tracks. It was the name of one of the two sources that had brought him to Lisbon.

Half an hour later Canaris lunched with Fritz von Claus, head of the Abwehr operation in Portugal, in his small terrace house overlooking the flea market.

He usually enjoyed himself there. It was so cramped, so full of books, so bachelor, and the schnapps was so smoky on the tongue that it reminded him of his youth.

To Canaris, von Claus always seemed like a professor, although he was the younger of the two (the deformity on his back, not quite a hunch, had added years to his fragile frame) and, of course, junior in rank.

By the time they were halfway through a bottle of schnapps, washed down with pale beer imported from Munich, the present was an unwelcome stranger to their conversation. But an intrusive one.

"So, what do you think?" Canaris asked, dousing the schnapps in his throat with beer.

"About the rumors? As you say, they're a little too thick. I wouldn't have suggested that you come to Lisbon if they hadn't been backed up by two of our prime contacts."

"I'm glad you did," Canaris said. "I like it here. It's a forgotten outpost of the Germany we once knew. Before—"

"Careful," von Claus whispered.

"What's this? Are the British so alert?" But his voice was hushed.

"The Gestapo are, you must know that."

His words sobered them both. Von Claus switched on the radio.

Canaris swirled the schnapps around in his glass and finally said, "What's for lunch, Fritz?"

"Frankfurters," said von Claus. "Frankfurters that spit their juice at you when you sink your teeth into them. Sauerkraut and potato salad."

Canaris licked his lips. "If you eat like that every day, why don't you put on any weight?"

"I have enough trouble as it is getting suits tailored to fit me," said von Claus, who was as dapper as he was deformed. "But tell me, Wilhelm, if this is an elaborate disinformation operation, how could it possibly benefit the British?" He turned up the volume of the radio.

Canaris shrugged. "God knows. But I wouldn't put anything past that *bloeder hund* Churchill. On the face of it, his strategy is logical enough:

persuade us to smash Russia so that Britain and Germany can coexist without the Bolshevik menace. I'd like to think it's as simple as that."

"Except that in our world things never are? Have another drink, Wilhelm. Blast the suspicions out of that old gray head of yours."

"Not so old," Canaris said, accepting a tot of schnapps and a glass of beer. "You see what Churchill is saying to Hitler is this: 'We will cause no trouble in the West, leaving you free to pursue your dream of expansion in the East.' Or 'We, the British, will allow you to go to war on only one front.'"

"So?"

"You don't fool me, professor. You just want me to express your own doubts."

"And they are?" smiling his pinched smile.

"Timing, my dear Fritz, timing. Just suppose Hitler was delayed? Drawn into the Russian winter. And then just suppose Churchill didn't keep his side of the bargain? Just suppose he attacked? Voilà. A war on two fronts."

"Britain isn't strong enough to attack," von Claus objected.

"She might be if we gave her time to rest. And what if the United States entered the war?"

From the kitchen came appetizing odors. Von Claus stood up and said loudly, "Come on, let's eat and soak up some of that liquid cordite." As Canaris stood up he again lowered his voice to a whisper, "You know what I think, Wilhelm? I think it might be a good idea if Stalin was warned that the Führer intended to attack. That way there would probably be no war at all and millions of Germans might not have to die."

"That possibility," said Canaris equally softly, "had not escaped me." He put his finger to his lips in a gesture that was only slightly theatrical.

The first of the two sources, on whom Canaris had decided to gauge the strength of the reports about Churchill's new policy, was like a sleek, well-fed cat.

His hair, gray at the temples, was sleek; his physique, aided by Savile Row suits, was sleek; when paid compliments, he purred.

He was one of the Abwehr's most trusted agents in Lisbon and unique because he never asked for money. Certainly, being a banker, he had more than enough, but it was the sad experience of the accountants on

Tirpitzufer that the richer the agent was, the more he charged. Apparently all that the banker required was recognition when Germany won the war.

Canaris met him by appointment at a ball given by a Brazilian coffee millionaire in one of the red-roofed mansions lying behind the casino at the coastal resort of Estoril, fifteen miles from Lisbon. The occasion struck Canaris as a bewildering anachronism. While most of Europe was blacked out, the mansion glittered. The guests, who arrived in splendid limousines, danced beneath chandeliers jeweled with light; the champagne frothed brilliantly; the gardens, designed for assignations, were strung with colored lights.

And the guests themselves were an astonishing mix in view of international tensions. Especially on the dance floor. In white ties and tails, in gowns from Paris, London, and New York, the partnering confounded politics. Americans, Spaniards, Portuguese, Germans, French, South Americans, Japanese—only the British seemed absent; they shunned the Germans whenever possible.

There was King Carol of Romania; Camille Chautemps, one-time premier of France; the elegant duke of Alba, former Spanish ambassador to Britain; Joseph Bech, the Grand Old Man of Luxembourg.

There was Otto Bauer, head of the Gestapo in Lisbon.

Ignoring him, Canaris, immaculate but uncomfortable in his evening dress, skirted the dancers spinning to a Viennese waltz, took a glass of champagne from a red-jacketed waiter, and made his way onto the terrace.

The banker, looking sleeker than ever, smiled at him, and together they strolled through the scented gardens until they were outside the glow of the colored lights. Beyond, they could see the moonlit waters of the Atlantic lapping the small Tamariz beach. (Palaces and casino apart, Estoril was more modest than Canaris had supposed.)

"A beautiful night," the banker purred.

"But a little cold."

"Cold? But, my dear Admiral, the air is like mulled wine."

"I would be cold in hell," Canaris told him. "What do you have for me?"

"An intriguing morsel." The banker's German was almost perfect. "No, more than a morsel, an entrée that I'm sure you and the Führer will devour hungrily."

Canaris sipped his champagne; in the darkness it seemed to lose its taste. Well, out with it, man, he thought and said, "How very intriguing," wishing that just sometimes spies could be straightforward, and reflecting how different this exchange was from the interrogation of Spearman.

The banker chuckled richly. "It's more than intriguing, Admiral, it's downright sensational."

"Am I right in assuming that it has something to do with British policy toward Germany?" hoping that von Claus had got it right; at the same time hoping he would deflate the banker into speeding up his revelations.

"Quite correct," undeflated. "I told von Claus roughly what it was all about. But I didn't tell him my source; that's what's so sensational."

Canaris stifled a sigh. "You mean your information is second-hand?"

"Of course, isn't all information second-hand unless the informant is the originator of his intelligence?"

Canaris smiled. Perhaps I should have brought a length of rubber hose, he thought.

"But my information is documented. And what a document!"

The banker moved closer to Canaris, his cologne overpowering the perfumes of the garden.

Canaris backed away.

The banker said, "I think you will agree, when you have read it, that my place in the postwar financial world should be assured."

"You have this document with you?"

"Of course. A letter. With a fascinating signature."

Canaris's patience was fast running out. "Then if you would be so good . . ."

The banker said, "Here you are, Admiral. Read it when you get back into the light. You will not be disappointed."

He handed Canaris an envelope, gave a little bow, and disappeared, purring, in the direction of the mansion.

Canaris moved swiftly into the light and, after glancing around, ripped open the envelope.

The letter consisted of only two paragraphs. They confirmed what he had expected from the banker. But he had to admit that the signature was a knockout.

Windsor.

As he picked his way through the gardens, he assessed the credibility of the letter. A handwriting expert would soon be able to confirm whether the signature was that of the duke who had so recently been Edward VIII.

But why should he write to a Lisbon banker?

Why not?

He had recently been staying in Estoril at the home of another banker, Ricardo Espirito Santo e Silva, known to the British as the Holy Ghost, while his wartime future was debated in Whitehall.

The duke's German sympathies were famous, but they in no way detracted from his patriotism. The duke merely thought that Britain and Germany should never have gone to war.

Hitler had been so impressed by the duke's point of view that he had ordered the foreign minister, the empty-headed Joachim von Ribbentrop, to try to persuade the duke to stay in a European country within the sphere of German influence, the idea being that one day he could return to the throne—along with his Nazi sympathies.

Of course von Ribbentrop, the one-time champagne salesman, had botched what had been a harebrained scheme in the first place. He had offered to put fifty million Swiss francs into a deposit account for the duke; then asserted that, if all else failed, *coercion* could be used.

In other words: kidnap him.

He had put Walter Schellenberg in charge of things. Walter, one of Heydrich's lieutenants in the Reich Central Security Office, the RSHA, which incorporated nearly every police department in Germany—with the exception of the Abwehr—was able enough, a charmer too. But he was well aware that von Ribbentrop was an ass and his plot fatuous.

He never really tried to implement it beyond getting word to the restless duke that British agents were gunning for him. And in the event, the duke had sailed from Lisbon on August 2 on his way to the Bahamas to become governor, which was just about the most ineffectual job the British could find for their ex-king.

So at least the circumstances for contact between the banker and the duke were established. And following the approaches from Schellenberg's henchmen, the duke would have known that the banker was his best clandestine shortcut to Berlin.

Canaris reached the terrace framed with bougainvillea and jasmine, slipped the envelope into the inside pocket of his jacket, and weaved his way through the guests.

Bauer, heavily built with cropped hair, intercepted him. "Do you always collect your mail in the garden?" He tapped the lapel of Canaris's jacket.

"Sometimes I read it in the garden," Canaris replied. "Especially when it's confidential. Especially when it comes from Berlin."

He watched Bauer field that one. Hitler, Himmler, Heydrich? All the Hs. The Bauers of the various SS security departments were always unsure how to treat Canaris; they sensed that Heydrich was poised to unseat him and gobble up the Abwehr, and yet Canaris seemed to ride out all such rumors with magnificent disdain. What's more, he was a confidant of Hitler, who used him as an emissary as well as a spymaster.

If they even suspected the truth, Canaris thought, how short a time I'd have left. He smiled at Bauer.

"Was the letter from your wife, Admiral?"

"No," Canaris said still smiling, "not my wife."

"You were lucky to get an invitation to the ball at such short notice."

"My dear Bauer," Canaris said, discarding his smile, "I was dining with our host when you were attending your first interrogation." He was pleased when the Brazilian millionaire clapped him on the shoulder and said, "Ah, Admiral Canaris, how are you these days?" studiously ignoring Bauer.

Together they strolled away, leaving Bauer staring after them. "A thug, I'm afraid," the Brazilian said, "but I have to think of the future, and I want to export my coffee to both the Germans and the Portuguese."

In the embassy car taking him back to Lisbon, Canaris reconsidered the letter.

If you thought about it, what better go-between for Churchill and Hitler? The duke had been friendly with both. In fact Churchill had backed him before the abdication. Churchill and Hitler in agreement! The mind boggled.

Canaris glanced out of the window of the Mercedes-Benz 170. Lights everywhere. Coming to Portugal was like walking out of a dark cave.

He touched the clipped tufts of his eyebrows. According to Abwehr intelligence in Lisbon, the duke had recently been in touch with Churchill, who, although he was conducting a war, had found time to reply. So the rapport was still there.

Canaris was inclined at this early stage in his deliberations to believe that the letter was genuine.

But would the suggestion it contained work? There was no reason, Canaris decided, spreading a traveling rug across his knees, why it shouldn't. Hitler had never wanted to go to war with Britain and, judging by his half-hearted invasion preparations, had no real wish to occupy it.

If he was given an alternative, he would grab it. And that's what Churchill, via the duke, was offering him. With a proviso. Russia.

Canaris switched on a reading light above his head and took the envelope from his pocket again. It bore no postmark and must have been handed to the banker by one of the duke's friends when the duke was well away from the complications it would cause. That, too, was in character.

He reread the brief typewritten text several times.

It has come to my knowledge through impeccable sources—Churchill of course—*that my country is willing to consider any course of action that will bring an end to the suffering that is, as I write, being endured by millions of innocent people; a tragedy that could in my opinion have been averted in 1939 by the use of the pen instead of the sword.* But not in Churchill's opinion!

It is common knowledge that the Führer is anxious to reach a peaceful settlement with Great Britain. . . .

Referring, Canaris assumed, to Hitler's speech to the Reichstag on July 19, when he had said, "In this hour, I feel it to be my duty before my own conscience to appeal once more to reason and common sense in Great Britain as much as elsewhere." Churchill had ignored the appeal, and Hitler had been grieved and enraged.

. . . and that feeling is now shared in the very highest echelons of Westminster, where it is believed that Great Britain could honorably cease hostilities with Germany if she abandoned her plans to invade our islands and turned her attentions to the menace which both countries have long considered to be the ultimate foe.

In his room in the German minister's residence on the Rua do Pau da Bandeira, linked to the legation by a secret underground tunnel, Canaris took off his evening clothes with relief, washed, brushed his teeth, slipped between cool sheets. Hands behind his head, he lay in the moonlight and waited for suspicions to present themselves, as they always did when he wanted to sleep.

Surely the whole setup was too facile. Could it be that the duke was playing a card in a masterly game of deception? That he was contributing far more to the British cause than he could have done in any other capacity? If so, history would gravely misjudge his postabdication record. He would be dismissed as dilettante instead of savior.

Wearily, Canaris climbed from the bed and went to the bathroom where he took a dose of Phanodorm. He should have taken it half an hour earlier, but even now when he was old enough to know better, he still hoped for the miracle: a night of natural sleep.

Soon the drug began to dispel the suspicions. But on the borders of sleep he glimpsed a terrifying vision: a mass grave filled with gray-haired corpses with clipped eyebrows.

When he finally slept, he dreamed that he was king of England.

Canaris met the second source the following morning at a rendezvous as macabre as the palace at Estoril had been sumptuous.

Why couldn't spies be content with the mundane? he wondered, sitting in the back of the Mercedes-Benz taking him to the Church of St. Vincent Beyond the Wall, outside Lisbon.

According to the cultured and knowledgeable Baron Oswald Hoyningen-Huene, German minister in Lisbon, the old church was decorative enough from the outside, the walls of its cloisters covered with glazed tiles depicting the Fables of La Fontaine; it was inside that the atmosphere became sinister because the crypt housed the mummified corpses of a dynasty of Portuguese kings, the House of Bragança.

As the black limousine glided to a halt outside the church, Canaris glanced at his watch. It was 11:55 A.M.; at least the informant had picked a civilized time, midday. The driver opened the door and Canaris stepped out, still wearing his leather overcoat despite the gathering heat. His bodyguard, a young man with a slight limp who had been wounded in Norway, climbed out from the front seat and stood at a respectful distance.

Overhead a hawk floated on the heat. Yellow butterflies flitted among blazes of poppies, and the air droned with insect noise.

Canaris hoped that the informant, as valuable in his way as the banker, would pull up outside; then he would suggest a stroll in the great outdoors. Almost anything was preferable to conversing in the company of corpses, however venerable.

He consulted his watch. One minute to go. He sighed. The informant was inside already. He turned on his heel and headed for the cadavers, followed by his bodyguard.

The crypt, lit by flickering candles, smelled of burning tallow, embalming fluid, spices, and prolonged death. The kings gazed at Canaris from black, glass-topped caskets scattered across the floor in historical disarray. A dynasty of Bragaças contemptuously reshuffled by a new republic.

Beyond the flame of a thick white candle, Canaris detected a movement. His hand reached for the automatic he carried in the pocket of his coat as a backup to the bodyguard.

A moth brushed against his face; he shivered but not with the cold this time. He thought he could hear breathing. As he stepped over a king, a man's voice said, "Perhaps you would be good enough to tell your man Friday to go away; there's enough death here already." He stepped out of the shadows. "I haven't got a gun, honest."

Canaris told the bodyguard, who was hovering at the door, to wait outside.

He let go of the gun in his pocket and said, "Was this really necessary?"

"It's one of the few places where we won't be seen. A superstitious lot, the Portuguese."

"Why," Canaris said, speaking in English, "must spies be so melodramatic?"

"Because when we discover our profession isn't, we have to create our own melodrama. I'm sorry I couldn't lay on a ball in Estoril for you. Do you have the money?" he asked abruptly.

"If you have the information."

"Nothing in writing. Just what I've been told."

"I seem to have heard that before," Canaris said. "May I suggest that you come a little closer. I don't like addressing you across half a dozen corpses."

Canaris had met Cross only once before, but again he was struck by the man's blend of sophistication and brutality. He wore a double-breasted gray suit, and his tan was a shock in this funereal place.

Canaris said, "Well?"

Cross told Canaris what he had implied to von Claus—that in the British embassy in the Rua São Domingos a Lapa he had heard reports that Churchill was ready to make a deal with Germany.

"Provided we divert our attentions away from the English Channel to the Soviet Union?"

"Yes," Cross said, tone surprised, "how did you know?"

"You aren't the only agent with his ear to the ground in Lisbon."

"The banker?"

It was Canaris's turn to be surprised. "Just other sources," he said. "Let's stick to the rules, Mr. Cross."

Cross brushed the dust from the glass on one of the caskets. Dom Carlos, one of the more recent Bragdanças, stared inquiringly at him, medals still pinned to his faded uniform.

"Rules? The Braganças stuck to the rules, and look where it got them."

"Nearly three hundred glorious years," Canaris said. "After Duke John of Braganca threw the Spanish out. In 1640, wasn't it?"

"Look where the rules got Carlos the First. Assassinated. In 1908, I think."

Canaris said, "I'm honored that I have been selected to convey this information to the Führer."

"I wonder," Cross said, "how *he* will shuffle off his mortal coil. Let's see if we can find Carlos." He moved from one casket to another, brushing the years from the glass lids. "Why do you think you've been honored, Admiral?"

"Because someone is aware that the Führer will listen to me."

"And will he?" inspecting a royal face that had been partly eaten away by rats. "No, that's not him," Cross said, moving on.

"Of course."

"But you don't believe what you've heard?"

"I don't believe, I don't disbelieve. Do you believe what you've heard in this instance, Mr. Cross?"

"He looks as if he died from undernourishment," Cross said, pointing at an emaciated monarch. "Yes, I do. The source was informed. . . . That's what sources are, aren't they?"

Canaris looked longingly at the daylight at the top of the steps. Cross had in the past proved just as reliable as the banker.

Canaris said, "Do you regard yourself as a traitor, Mr. Cross?"

"On the contrary, a patriot. However, I don't believe we should be at war with Germany. The real enemy is Russia."

"And you think Germany should do Churchill's dirty work for him?"

"It's more complex than that," Cross said, straightening up from a casket. "Britain isn't in a fit state to fight anyone and Hitler has always sworn that he would see off the Bolsheviks. What's more important is that Churchill can't be caught cooperating with the Germans, so there's no way Britain can fight on your side. It has to be done like this because this is the only way."

Canaris began to move toward the shaft of daylight; the sour, squalid, ancient smell of the place was making him sick.

Cross said, "I got the impression that speed was of the essence. The quicker Hitler attacks Russia, the better for everyone. According to my *informed sources*. That makes sense, doesn't it? If you want to break the pact with Stalin do it without prior warning and before he's reorganized the Red Army."

"Hitler hadn't intended to attack quite so precipitously."

"That was because he gave up hope that the British would seek peace."

Canaris took a small, anticatarrhal inhalant from his pocket, breathed some vapor into his lungs, and said between breaths, "I haven't decided what I'm going to tell the Führer."

Cross said, "Tell him what *you* believe."

"It would be better if I had some documented proof of Churchill's intentions," looking keenly at Cross to see if he reacted, if he knew about the duke of Windsor's letter, but Cross merely replied, "The point is that Hitler will believe you."

No, my friend, Canaris thought; the point is, do I want to tell him? Theoretically, he supposed, the answer was a resounding *yes*; a swift and comprehensive victory over Russia would leave the Third Reich triumphantly astride Europe and the western reaches of the Soviet Union. But do I want Hitler to lead us to that sort of victory? Do I want to give him a free hand to massacre all the Jews and other "subhumans" that he and Himmler decide have no place in the New Order?

The solution that he and Fritz von Claus had touched upon presented itself: advise Hitler to attack and at the same time warn Stalin. No war, no German casualties, no genocide.

"Of course there are other considerations," Cross was saying.

"Such as?"

Cross, stooped over a king, glanced up at Canaris. "I am in British Intelligence—as well as yours," smiling, "and it's thought you don't always see eye-to-eye with Hitler."

"Really? I'm afraid that observation doesn't say much for British Intelligence."

"What about the bomb in the Bürgerbräukeller in Munich on November 8 last year?"

Canaris said, "What about it?" He replaced the inhaler in his pocket and brought out his silver pillbox; he swallowed a mauve tablet.

Cross said, "Intriguing, wasn't it?"

"Not particularly. A botched assassination attempt by British Intelligence agents and a German carpenter. Or if you prefer the other version: a touch of uncharacteristic brilliance by the Gestapo to make the German people believe Hitler is immortal. As you know, the Führer cut short his speech and left by train for Berlin. Shortly after he left, the bomb went off."

"There are those in MI6," Cross said, walking toward the stairs, "who believe both versions are bullshit, that the assassination attempt was genuine enough. That it was carried out with the connivance of German Intelligence—not any of the SS groups,"—Cross raised an eyebrow at Canaris—"and when it failed, strenuous efforts were made by *someone* to confuse the whole issue."

"So?"

"We were discussing your allegiances. Führer or country. That sort of thing. I merely wondered if you had any theories about the assassination attempt."

"I've just told you what I know."

"Mmmmm. Did the Führer have any theories?"

"He was ecstatic, and gave the credit, as I recall, to divine intervention."

"Perhaps he would like to hear our theories."

And now I'm being blackmailed. The crypt became Canaris's own grave.

Cross went on, "More than theories, really. As you say, British Intelligence was involved. Two of our men were arrested, in fact."

Canaris shrugged. "You want me to convey some information to the Führer?"

"Really, Herr Admiral," Cross said, "it's not the sort of information you'd want to pass on, is it?"

Hardly, thought Canaris with a sigh. He'd often wondered if the British would ever try to use their knowledge of Abwehr complicity in the bomb plot as a lever. He had rather hoped they wouldn't because they knew there would be other plots. They really were quite desperate to convince Hitler that they were prepared to make a deal.

Thankfully, Canaris reached the foot of the steps. Choosing his words with extreme care, he said, "If we brought the Soviet Union to its knees with one preemptive strike, Hitler's position would be unassailable."

"I don't think anyone's position is ever really unassailable," Cross answered. "What's certain is that you can bring greater glory to the

Fatherland. And no one has ever doubted your patriotism, Herr Admiral. No one."

A tiny glow of pride lit Canaris's soul.

Cross said, "Well I must be on my way. I'll go first, if you don't mind."

"If you wish."

"So could you please tell your man Friday to get away from the top of the steps."

Canaris called out, and they heard the shuffle of feet.

Cross stretched out his hand and momentarily Canaris thought, "Mein Gott, we're going to shake hands, how very British," before realizing that Cross wanted his money and thinking, "That's very British, too."

Pocketing the escudo notes, Cross grinned, saying, "More grist for the casino," and ran up the steps two at a time.

Canaris gave him a couple of minutes. Then he heard a motorcycle start up; it must have been hidden. Riding a motorcycle in a suit? Ah well, Cross wasn't a conventional man.

Canaris walked up the steps into the sunlight and took a deep breath of fresh air.

6

September 18, 1940. On board Churchill's special train.

"So it worked."

Churchill, dressed in a bright blue, zip-up siren suit and black-and-gold Moroccan slippers, read with satisfaction the document Sinclair had brought him.

It was from General Hastings Ismay, Chief of Staff to Churchill in his capacity as minister of defense.

> ACCORDING TO INFORMATION RECEIVED HERE TODAY HITLER YESTERDAY GAVE ORDERS FOR THE INVASION FLEET FACING THE BRITISH ISLES TO BE DISPERSED. RECONNAISSANCE AIRCRAFT REPORTED TODAY THAT THIS PROCESS HAS ALREADY BEGUN.

The source of the first item of information, Churchill assumed, was ULTRA, the system based at Bletchley Park in Buckinghamshire by which Germany's top-secret ENIGMA messages were deciphered. It was ULTRA that had decoded Hitler's Directive 16, signed on July 16, 1940, announcing his invasion plans.

Churchill glanced at Sinclair. "My most secret source?"

Sinclair, wearing tweeds and brogues—did he ever wear anything else?—nodded. "But some of the ships are being left so that a force can be reassembled at short notice."

"Of course—if we renege on our promise. But I hope it will be too late by then." Churchill poured them both a whisky and soda and sat back in his seat. He liked trains, their clacking rhythms, their foraging, serpentine progress. He particularly enjoyed this train, equipped as it was with an office, bed, telephone, and on his insistence, bath. "Corporal Hitler has to keep his fingers on the screws to keep us in line. So don't expect any let-up in that cacophony," pointing with his cigar at the blacked-out windows and cocking an ear to the bark of the antiaircraft guns. "He dare not give us breathing space. And of course to an extent I'm responsible for it." He fell silent as melancholy touched his euphoria.

Sinclair said, "If you hadn't ordered the bombing of Berlin, then the Luftwaffe's attacks wouldn't have been switched from the airfields to our cities."

"And we would have lost the Battle of Britain," Churchill said. "Then the peace feelers we extended would have been genuine. It had to be done even at this appalling cost." They could hear more heavy thumps in the distance.

Churchill sat for a few moments brooding, while he pulled the zipper of his one-piece suit up and down. Then he said, "So we've won the first trick, and the next will be executed in Lisbon. Are you quite sure about the *identity* of this man Hoffman?"

"Quite," Sinclair said.

"And Cross, what do you think of him?"

"He's a great admirer of yours."

"Hardly a commendation for reliability."

"By definition," Sinclair said, with the faintest of smiles, "an agent, especially a double agent, must have certain flaws in his character."

"I suppose so. I knew him once, you know."

"I didn't know you'd even heard of him until recently."

"When he was a lad." Churchill didn't elaborate. "So it's all down to Cross and Hoffman?"

"And the girl."

"Yes," Churchill agreed, "and the girl."

The train pulled into a station. Churchill went to the door. Sergeant Thompson, Churchill's former bodyguard, recalled from his grocer's shop in Norwood, was already standing on the platform.

Churchill and Sinclair joined him. "Where are we?" Sinclair asked.

"Somewhere in England," Churchill told him. "To be more precise, somewhere in Kent."

"Why are we stopping?"

Thompson answered the question. "Mr. Churchill wants to make a telephone call to Chartwell, sir."

"Yes," Churchill said, "I must tell Clemmie I'll be home for dinner in half an hour."

7

Six days later, the girl to whom Churchill and Sinclair had referred flew over the strip of water in the Tagus reserved for Lisbon-bound flying boats.

Her name was Rachel Keyser. She was 23 years old, British and Jewish and aggressively proud of both. Of medium height, she had shingled hair so dark that it shone blue-black in the sunlight and an extravagant figure currently contained in a square-shouldered, narrow-waisted, lime green suit.

As she peered down at the molten waters of the estuary, she was frightened, and she was angry with herself for not being able to subdue the fear.

It was 11:25 A.M. and fifteen minutes earlier the captain of the Pan American Airways Clipper in which she had crossed the Atlantic had announced minor technical trouble.

The passengers had been aware of the trouble for the past five minutes. All they disputed was the term *minor*: one of the four propellers above them had feathered.

At least, thought Rachel, trying to divert her fear, the prospect of a crash landing had brought a small side benefit: it had dampened the ardor of the Venezuelan diplomat who had been trying to proposition her throughout the twenty-two-hour trip from the States.

Not that he wasn't reasonably attractive—or had been until he had suddenly subsided, white-faced and trembling, after the captain's announcement—but who wanted such attention when you were flying to meet your first love, or rather, lover?

The affair had been a revelation. She had met David Cross when they were both in Berlin. He had been a young diplomat at the British embassy, she the daughter of a first secretary there, who was engaged, outside office hours, in smuggling Jews out of Germany.

Cross had seduced her with ease, and she had found to her surprise that she responded pleasurably to aspects of his character that she had never encountered in anyone else, least of all in diplomatic circles. He was calculating, inventive, and a little cruel. She wasn't proud of her response to such qualities, but then again she wasn't ashamed.

During her stay in Germany, she had, through her father, witnessed terrible things happening to the Jews. She had seen them degraded and abused; she had seen families led away to God knows where; she had seen the bruised trust on the faces of children as they followed their parents.

And, after she had watched the tormentors laugh, she had sworn vengeance. Which was why, having qualified in Britain as a cryptanalyst, she was sent by the Foreign Office to Washington. Away from trouble.

Why then had they suddenly changed their minds and transferred her to Lisbon, where every day she would rub shoulders with Germans? And why the rush?

According to messages from Whitehall, she was needed to supplement the cipher department in Lisbon, which had become the European crossroads of coded communications.

But surely there were other talented operators not so savagely anti-Nazi and, therefore, not so much of a liability? Apparently not, according to Whitehall she was the best.

One other aspect of her new assignment bothered Rachel. She was delighted that she was going to be reunited with Cross, but it did seem rather a coincidence.

The Clipper lurched to one side. The diplomat closed his eyes. His hands were pressed together, his lips moving; and Rachel realized that he was praying.

She remembered reading about the Samoan Clipper that in 1938 had developed an oil leak over the Pacific; all that had been found of it was burned-out wreckage.

Rachel joined the diplomat in unspoken prayer.

Below them now were the relatively narrow reaches of the Tagus, which linked the Atlantic with the broader expanse of the estuary. To the left the faded red roofs, spires, and domes of Lisbon, tumbling down the hills to the waterside.

The Clipper righted itself, then dipped suddenly. The passengers in the spacious cabin sighed collectively. A woman fainted, a child began to cry.

The water was only a few hundred feet below them now. Rachel saw docks, plodding orange-colored ferries, fishing boats with Phoenician rig. The crying of the child reminded her of the Jewish children in Germany.

Another lurch. She noticed oil leaking from the engine cowling above her.

This surely wasn't how it ended. Not at my age.

She wished she had been kinder to her parents.

Masts of ships flashed past the window.

A noise like a tattoo on a tin drum.

The Clipper lifted, bounced, then touched the surface again, settled, and imperiously thrust aside the waters of the Tagus.

After the Clipper had been moored at Porto Ruivo, Rachel walked swiftly up the wooden gangplank to wait for her luggage. The diplomat made no attempt to follow her.

With her diplomatic passport, she sailed through immigration, porter in tow. Cross, waiting beside a green MG sports car, kissed her and said, "Welcome home."

"How brown you are."

She stroked his chest and belly.

"Estoril. In my business you have to go there. And I go on the beach."

My business? Well, now that she was a cryptanalyst she knew what that business was—she had always vaguely realized that he wasn't a conventional diplomat.

She kissed him and wished that he wasn't so controlled. He was obviously aroused—her hand crept toward his hip where the paler flesh began—and yet he didn't give. That was part of the cruelty: to try to bring her to such a pitch that she fell on him.

Well, it wasn't going to work, not this time.

He kissed her breasts, taking one generous brown nipple in his mouth, and opened her thighs with his hand, not that they needed much opening. And, of course, she was wet, much more of a giveaway than an erect penis.

His fingers began their measured persuasion.

But she didn't moan. She touched his glossy brown hair; it felt warm, as though the sun had been on it.

Gently, she took his penis in one hand and began to stroke it, up and down, as he had taught her long ago in an apartment with a view of the Tiergarten in Berlin.

Since then there had been three lovers. None of them had been as satisfactory as Cross, and two of them had been shocked at her practiced ways.

My trouble, she thought, trying to remain detached, was that my first lover was an expert. Now I have expertise instead of spontaneity, and there will never be any substitute until I find a man I truly love, and thank God, I don't love this man who is doing these wonderful things to me—control yourself you slut—even though I come alive with him.

He glanced up from her breasts, hair falling across his eyes, and smiled; and she thought, You bastard, as he lowered his head once more, hair brushing her belly, as he moved his face, his lips, his tongue to where she wanted them to be.

No!

What, she wondered absurdly, would her parents, now back in London, think? Would they be disgusted, or would they understand the passions they had passed on to her. Understand, perhaps, but not condone. Nor would they be condoned in many other Jewish quarters. Hypocrites! Soon, with the war, all that would change; morals were early casualties. "Let's make love, I might be killed tomorrow."

She felt the warmth of his tongue. The rationalization that had been her defense was dispersing. She was losing. Excitement and warmth spread through her. Such expertise. She found that she was moving her body rhythmically. This wasn't what . . . the damned moralists . . . taught you . . . to expect. You waited till marriage; then on the marital bed you gave yourself as a sort of reward to the panting male for doing the right thing by you. Coupling, copulation, intercourse . . . but this was . . . this was . . .

She used her mouth on him.

And he gave. She could feel it.

Did it have to be like this, victory or defeat?

"Oh God!"

But it was his voice.

And he was inside her and there was neither victor nor loser and it was
. . .

"Beautiful," she told him as they lay beneath a sheet on the bed in his apartment.

"We didn't waste any time," he said, lighting a cigarette.

She looked at her wristwatch on the bedside table. She had been in Lisbon for one hour.

That evening she explored Lisbon on foot. It fascinated her. It was a prewar shop window with glimpses of austerity between the showcases. She saw restaurants packed with diners gobbling down seafood; she saw refugees sharing a loaf of bread. She saw elegant women buying perfume from Paris; she saw women in black with autumn-leaf faces queuing up to buy rationed sugar.

The city seemed to be built on two main levels, so she took the street elevator built by Alexandre Eiffel "of Eiffel Tower fame" according to her printed guide—you could see his handiwork in the battleship-gray metal tower—to the upper level, the Bairro Alto.

There were only three other passengers in the wood-paneled cabin that smelled of disinfectant. A burly, middle-aged man with cropped, graying hair, who was smoking a black cigar, and a young woman with a hospital-pale face, holding the hand of a small boy wearing a peaked cap that was too big for him and knee-length trousers.

The man, who had bloodshot eyes and incongruously small ears pressed close to his scalp, drew deeply on the cigar and blew out a cloud of smoke. Deliberately, it seemed to Rachel, in the direction of the woman.

The woman began to cough, rasping coughs from deep in her chest. The boy moved closer to her and touched her dress with his hand.

As the elevator began to rise, the man exhaled another cloud of smoke in the direction of the woman. She put her hand to her breast as if in pain.

Rachel said, with studied politeness, "I think your cigar is upsetting this lady. I wonder if you could put it out."

The man smiled at her and said, in German-accented English, "Upsetting the Jewess and her brat? I'm doing Lisbon a service."

She stared at him. Surely he could see that she, too, was Jewish. Although some German men tended to forget their anti-Semitism if you were a young and reasonably attractive woman.

She said, "I'll ask you once again—"

"Please don't trouble yourself," the woman said in Yiddish and began to cough again. The boy peered at the man from under his peaked cap. Another jet of smoke.

It seemed to Rachel that she moved in slow motion. She snatched the half-smoked cigar from the man's lips, heard him yelp with pain, saw the blood on his lower lip, tossed the cigar on the floor of the elevator, crushed it with the heel of one of her shoes, ground the mess into shreds with the sole, stepped back, breast heaving.

The woman shrank into the corner of the elevator. The man touched his lips, then raised his hand as though to strike Rachel. It was then that the boy stepped between them; and then Rachel found to her further astonishment that she had a long nail file in her hand and was ready to use it as a knife.

The man reached for the boy, and Rachel said, "Don't."

He hesitated. The elevator stopped with a jerk, and the man dropped his hand to his side. "Jewish bitch," he snarled at her.

The door opened. The woman, still coughing, grabbed the boy's hand and pulled him outside.

The man said to Rachel, "Your name please, Jew."

"We're not in Germany now."

He grabbed at her handbag, but she dodged and walked briskly from the elevator.

She could hear him shouting, "Don't worry, Jew, I shall find out who you are."

Ahead of her, halfway across an iron bridge, the woman was pulling the boy along. Suddenly he broke free, turned around and grinned, and she called out to him, "Thank you for helping me." With one finger he tapped the side of his nose and she loved him. Still grinning, he rejoined his mother.

"Good to see such spirit," she said as the German strode past her.

On the bridge high above the Chiado, Lisbon's select shopping district, the elation left her. She paused and gazed down at the pigmy figures and felt dizzy.

On her very first day in Portugal, she had allowed her hatred of the

Nazis to erupt. How could she continue to live a normal life in a city teeming with Germans—and Jewish refugees? A few more such incidents, and she would be requested to leave, persona non grata.

She could only hope to coexist if she believed that she was in some way contributing to the ultimate downfall of the Reich. Then and only then would she be able to suffer their presence.

She went on across the bridge to the Largo do Carmo, found a taxi, and told the driver to take her to a restaurant in the Alfama.

There, one hour later, the purpose she sought was given to her.

"But why is this man Hoffman so special?"

Cross poured red Dão wine into their glasses. "I can't tell you yet."

"You want me to sleep with a man, but you can't tell me why?"

"That's the size of it," Cross said.

"You think I'm a whore?"

"I think you'll do anything for your people."

She was silent while the waiter served *lagosta à moda de Peniche,* layers of baked lobster cooked with onions, herbs, and spices soaked in port. Cross was selective about food even when he was asking his mistress to seduce another man.

He tasted the food. "Mmmmm. It's good." He sipped some wine. "Anyway I always thought *sleep with* was a misnomer. Surely people mean the opposite?"

"You," she said, "have got to be the most insensitive man in the world."

He had put the proposition to her almost as soon as they were seated in the restaurant; a neat, clean little place with whitewashed walls and green tablecloths. It had once been a furniture factory.

She had arrived in a yellow summer dress with amber beads at her neck, believing that, after all, she might be a little in love with Cross! He had destroyed that illusion with a few incisive sentences.

"You must be wondering why you've suddenly been brought back to Europe," he had said.

When she had asked him why in his apartment, he had told her the reason was her prowess with ciphers. She got the impression that since then he had taken advice from London. He held her hand; at least he did that!

She waited tensely.

"I remember your telling me," he said, "how you wanted to pay back the Germans for what they were doing to the Jews. Well, now you have your chance."

"What do I have to do?"

"Ultimately a lot. At the moment . . ." With a shrug he abandoned the pretense of caring and told her that all she had to do was seduce a man.

She bit into some lobster. He was right, it was good. She was surprised that she wasn't angrier. Of course she hadn't been the slightest bit in love with Cross; that had been a fleeting fancy—Lisbon and lovemaking. But she was intrigued, excited even. Rachel Keyser, perhaps you *are* a whore.

She sipped some wine—that was good, too—and said, "Let's start again. Who is this Hoffman?"

"He works for the Red Cross."

"Nationality?"

"He pretends to be Czech. In fact he's Russian; but don't let on you know. Perhaps I shouldn't have told you."

Oh yes you should, she thought, appraising him impersonally. Sleekly handsome features, gray eyes . . . Did the pigment of an eye really indicate character? If so, I should be as soft as a meringue, born for motherhood and unquestioning devotion. What a hope! She took in the white shirt, striped tie, and brass-buttoned blazer; all very British and decent—and totally misleading. *You intended to tell me, to feed me a few morsels of intrigue to jolly me along.* How well he knows me, she thought.

"What does he do in the Red Cross?"

"Helps the refugees."

"Age?"

"A little younger than you."

"Why did he leave Russia?"

"The same reason as any refugee. To escape oppression."

"He should have stayed and fought it."

He grinned at her. "Not everyone is as belligerent as you."

"Is he a pacifist?"

"Yes, he believes he's doing more good here than he could taking on the Red Army. As a matter of fact he's going to do much more good; more than he could ever dream of."

Another morsel.

"Do you know what this is all about?" she asked.

"I don't know the whole picture, but I know more than you."

"You will have to tell me why this man of peace is so important."

"Blessed are the peacemakers," Cross said, pouring more wine for both of them.

"Answer the question, David."

Four men came in and sat at a table on the opposite side of the restaurant under some chairs hanging from the ceiling, relics of the factory days. They were young and blond. "Germans," Cross told her.

"I hope one of the chairs falls on them," she said.

"And they," Cross said, pointing at a young man and a pretty girl who had just entered the restaurant, "are French."

"It's grotesque," she said. "Victors and vanquished sitting down to eat in the same restaurant."

"They're doing it in France."

"But not like this. Not as if they're all tourists who have bypassed the war."

"And he," said Cross, nodding toward a tall man who looked like a cowboy wearing a suit for the first time, "is an American. A Texan named Kenyon." He waved at him. "They're all fighting in their own way," he added.

"Spies?"

He nodded.

"You?"

"What about dessert?" he asked. "My mother always insisted that it should be called pudding." He consulted the menu. "The *sonhos* are very good. *Sonhos,* meaning dreams. In fact, they're fritters dished up with syrup."

Rachel was watching him. Finally she said, "Is that all I have to do, sleep . . . get him into bed?"

"For the moment, yes."

"I'm going to find it difficult making love to a pacifist," she said.

"Why should you? Opposite poles are supposed to attract."

"Repel in my case." She waited while Cross ordered the dessert and coffee. "Why me?"

"You speak a little Russian, don't you?"

She nodded.

"Well, that's one reason."

The waiter brought the "dreams," the fritters. On the other side of the restaurant, the Germans were speaking to each other in low voices. The Frenchman was kissing the pretty girl's hand. The American was drinking a martini and reading *The New York Times.*

"So," Rachel said biting into a dream, "I can assemble some of the evidence. A woman is needed to seduce a Russian. Qualifications? Obviously she must be reasonably desirable. She must be violently opposed to the Third Reich. She mustn't be inhibited by morals. . . ."

Cross said nothing.

"But it seems to me that there is a missing factor. One you've neglected to mention. Codes come into this, don't they, David. A Nazi-hating, code-breaking slut is what your people are after, isn't that it?"

Cross said, "Here comes the coffee. All the way from Brazil."

"Why codes, David?"

"I told you, I haven't got the whole picture yet."

"Messages to and from the Soviet Union?" She spooned brown sugar into the coffee. "It has to be. Through this man Hoffman."

Cross said, "You're making sense."

"What's his name?"

"Hoffman's? Josef."

"His real name."

"I'm afraid I can't tell you that."

"And I know why. Because you think that, in certain circumstances, I might use it. Don't worry, David, I won't be that abandoned, not with the sort of man Hoffman seems to be."

"I'm delighted to hear it," Cross said. "Brandy? The Portuguese brew's not bad. And don't get it wrong, the man's not a coward. Stretcher-bearers don't get VCs, but they deserve them—they don't even carry guns. And for that matter what about young men swanning around Lisbon in the diplomatic service when they should be in the army?"

Rachel said, "No, I won't have a brandy, and yes, but you are in the army. A secret army."

"Let's not be melodramatic," Cross said. He ordered a brandy for himself. "Can I take it you're willing to cooperate?"

"On condition that you tell me what the hell this is all about after I've got Hoffman into bed."

"If I know."

"You know," she said.

"I have conditions too," he said.

"I don't think you're in a position—"

"You've got to stop your private war."

She looked at him questioningly.

"Stop molesting Germans in the street. And no," holding up one hand, "it doesn't matter how I heard. You'll find out soon enough that the tom-toms beat all the time in Lisbon."

"He was a pig," she said.

"No one is going to deny it."

"You know him?"

"Of course I know him," Cross said. "He's the head of the Gestapo in Lisbon."

8

Cross drove Josef Hoffman/Viktor Golovin to the casino at Estoril in his open MG.

A visit to some of the fleshpots, he had told Viktor, was essential when you were helping refugees. At the top of the agenda was the casino, second the nearby Palácio hotel. In both you could meet the wealthy fugitives of war—and shame a few of them into digging their hands into their pockets on behalf of their less fortunate countrymen.

Viktor accepted Cross's invitation because he took most of his advice. This was Cross's world, and he was grateful for a guide. He was also grateful to Cross for putting him in touch with some of the peacemakers in Lisbon who were trying to persuade the Germans and British to lay down their arms. He thought their cause forlorn but worth trying.

My world, Viktor thought, as the evening air streamed past him, no longer exists. That world was a stuffy librarian's home, a university, a girl, and a future. It had all dissolved in a volley of gunfire in an abandoned theater.

What was left was escape. Escape but not escapism. He had been handed a cause: to help the victims of tyranny. What better place in which to offer his services than the Red Cross in Switzerland?

With his savings he had bought counterfeit documents from a forger who, thanks to Stalin, was doing brisk business in a cellar in the Arbat. He had crossed the Ukraine on a students' excursion, slipped across the border into Czechoslovakia, and found himself surrounded by the henchmen of another tyrant: Hitler's SS.

He had reached Geneva without too much trouble—the Nazis' bid to redesign Europe made a fugitive's lot that much easier—and, after training, had been sent to Lisbon.

At first he thought himself fulfilled in his work. Until a specter that haunts all emigrant Soviet citizens presented itself.

Mother Russia.

No matter how feverishly he worked the specter kept reappearing. As he fed and housed and dispatched the bewildered refugees, Josef Hoffman remembered that he was Viktor Golovin and grieved for his people.

And a question repeated itself in his mind: Humanity or country?

Cross's voice reached him. He was pointing along the coast, hair flapping across his forehead.

"I can't hear you."

"The Jaws of Hell," Cross shouted. "Good name, isn't it? There's an abyss there. The sea comes under a rock and booms like thunder during a storm. And here are the jaws of heaven," he said as they swung into Estoril.

Cross stopped the car beside the little railway station separating the beach from the road and the gardens. He pointed out the landmarks. The miniature castle on the promenade—"pretty but phony"—the ornate gardens leading up to the casino, the Palácio hotel—"which is where we'll go first," he said, gunning the MG into a tire-screeching U-turn.

In the crowded bar, Cross ordered two whiskeys. It was a decorous place furnished in autumnal colors, with a floor made of black and white marble squares, and a black marble bar.

Cross nodded at the barman juggling the bottles and glasses with great dexterity. "Joaquim Jerónimo, the most tight-lipped man on the Lisbon coast. He's heard more secrets than you've had hot dinners."

"You would know, I suppose," Viktor said. He accepted that Cross was in Intelligence and the only question was how deeply? Viktor suspected that Cross's involvement was very deep.

A man and an elegantly gowned woman vacated their bar stools. Cross took them and the two men sat down. He said, "You've been looking a bit broody lately, Josef, anything the matter?"

"Wouldn't you look broody if an assassin tried to kill you and you knew someone else might try and finish off the job?"

Viktor still hadn't rationalized the attempt on his life. How could the NKVD have discovered that he was in Lisbon? And in any case, was he so important that he merited a bullet in the back and the possibility of a scandal?

A pianist began to play gentle ripples of music in the background.

"So," Cross said, "how do you think the unholy alliance is holding up?"

"Which one? There are so many these days."

"Russia and Germany, of course," and to the woman who was standing behind them, looking around uncertainly: "Unaccompanied?"

"I've been stood up," the woman said.

"By a man with a white stick," Cross said. "Let me get you a drink. And let me introduce Josef Hoffman. Josef, Rachel Keyser."

Viktor looked into eyes so brown that they were almost black. At raven hair full of light. At olive skin and parted lips. At compassion and strength and vitality and perception.

And the night seemed to chime.

Viktor was suddenly conscious of the shabbiness of his gray, off-the-rack suit beside Cross's navy blue, tailored lightweight; of the unruliness of his fair hair beside Cross's barbered locks. At least he had the edge on height, but, standing on the terrace overlooking the moonlit lawns, he felt clumsy.

"What brings you to Lisbon, Mr. Hoffman?"

He told her. In his own ears, it sounded dull.

Cross said, "Josef is a Czech and a man of peace."

Rachel Keyser sipped her sherry and said, "The trouble in this world is that the men with the guns take advantage of the men with the flags."

He decided she was about twenty-four. Certainly older than he. Jewish . . . British. What was she doing here? He asked her. She told him she worked at the British embassy in the communications department. How long had she been here? Two days, she said, and he frowned because he had sensed a familiarity with Cross that was more than two days old. This was early, too, for her to be arriving unaccompanied at the Palácio. And who but a madman would stand up a girl like Rachel Keyser?

Cross said, "Look here, if you really have been abandoned, why don't you join us at the casino? If you've got any money to lose, that is."

She shivered as a breeze blew in from the ocean and hugged her stole to her shoulders; the breeze pressed her green gown against her body. "Yes," she said, "I think I'd like that. Are you a gambling man, Mr. Hoffman?"

"I haven't the slightest idea, Miss Keyser, I've never had any money to gamble with."

"In that case you aren't or you would have lost the clothes you stand up in by now."

No great loss, he thought and said, "And you?"

"I like the occasional flutter," she said.

Inside the casino, Cross slipped Viktor two thousand escudos. "Just to start you off," he said. "Pay me back when you've won."

Viktor tried to give him back the money, but Cross pushed his hand away.

The main hall of the casino had a sunken floor, showcases in which stuffed birds nested, divans, and walls covered with beaten silver and gold. Most of the patrons wore evening dress, the men's shirtfronts gleaming in the light of the chandeliers, the women's diamond necklaces and tiaras glittering. Viktor felt shabbier by the moment. Perhaps the security guards would mistake him for a pickpocket and throw him out.

Rachel Keyser gave Cross some money, and he bought some chips for her. She sat down at one of the eight tables and began to play roulette. Cross and Viktor stood behind her.

Viktor became aware that she was employing some sort of system. "A martingale," Cross whispered. "A shortcut to the debtors' prison."

But she was winning, playing only the even chances and doubling up when she lost.

Cross said, "If she hits a losing streak and finds herself having to double up on the twelfth throw, she's bust because that would take her above the house limit."

A uniformed attendant came past bearing a small blackboard bearing the name CROSS.

"Excuse me," Cross said.

She continued to win; not a lot, but more money than Viktor had possessed since he came to Lisbon.

The bored croupier droned his instructions in French and Portuguese. "Rien ne va plus . . . Nada mais."

Rachel Keyser turned and smiled at Viktor. "Why don't you make a bet?"

"Later perhaps." How could he explain to her how incongruous he felt, how he detested these people who would throw away a peasant's earnings for a year on the turn of the wheel and barely notice the loss. Was she rich, this devastating Jewish girl? The stole, and the green silk gown . . . and yet she wore them with care, as though they were special. Like I wear my suit because it's the only one I've got. And you don't get rich working in an embassy, but perhaps she had private means. He looked at her hands: well-cared-for but not pampered.

A German sat next to her. Did she flinch, or was it his imagination? *Miss Keyser, I want to know a lot more about you.*

"I'm sorry," Cross said, "I've got to leave. Urgent business. The ambassador . . ." As Rachel stood up, he placed one hand on her bare shoulder. "No, you stay here, we can't sabotage a winning streak. Josef will see you home." He pressed a wad of notes into Viktor's hand. "Won't you?"

Viktor hesitated; there was nothing he would like better. "Of course," he said, "but . . ."

But Cross was gone.

And then Rachel Keyser began to lose.

Her chips dwindled; those of the German sitting beside her mounted. Rachel's shoulders slumped.

She turned around. Viktor got a fleeting impression that losing such a quantity of money meant quite a lot to her, scared her. "What shall I do?" she asked.

"I don't understand roulette."

"I've doubled up eight times. I stand to lose a fortune. By my standards, that is."

"I told you I wasn't a gambler."

"Once more?"

"If you wish." After all it wasn't his money; but he hoped she would win.

She lost.

"Thank God for that," she said, leaving the table.

"How much did you lose?"

"A few thousand escudos. I'm not sure how much that is."

"In British money? One escudo is about a penny." He fingered the money in his pocket.

"I think I'd like to go home," she said.

"Good. This isn't my sort of place. Would you like dinner first?"

She shook her head. "I want an early night."

Because of the gasoline shortage, the black Citröen taxi summoned by the doorman was fueled on wood gas, towing a stove on a small black trailer. Its progress was slow; Viktor was glad. In the glow of the dashboard, he noticed a small, paper Union Jack. "If we'd been Germans, he'd have stuck a swastika there," he said.

"How long have you been here, Josef?"

"Several months. It's a beautiful city."

"Isn't it a bit of a backwater?"

"If you've got nothing worthwhile to do."

"And you have," she said quickly.

"It's very satisfying work."

"A curious way to put it. You aren't seeking self-satisfaction, surely?"

Rocks ahead, he thought. "I'm happy to be helping people in need of help. And by God they need it."

"I see," she said, but he felt she didn't.

"You've seen the refugees?"

"Only sitting around the cafés."

"Look," he said, "these people aren't criminals on the run. They had to get out of their countries. If they hadn't, they would have been rounded up, sent to camps, massacred. They're women and children and old people—"

"Not all of them," she interrupted.

He no longer cared about impressing her. "You're beginning to sound like a Nazi."

The cabdriver glanced over his shoulder and forced the taxi to go another mile an hour faster.

"I don't believe in weakness. Kid gloves never won any ideals, and if Britain had been strong, she wouldn't be at war now."

"These refugees are children of a war they never sought."

Unaccountably she softened. "I'm sorry." She told him about Berlin. "I always thought that if the rest of Europe had been strong, if the Jews themselves had been strong, the persecution would never have happened."

"And now you believe in vengeance?"

"Don't you, Josef? After all, the Nazis invaded your country."

"I don't know what I believe in," he said.

She let that one ride.

The taxi pulled up outside the Avenida Palace next to the railway station, between the Rossio, the main square, and the Praça do Restauradores. Viktor had been there a couple of times; it was old and elegant, hung with chandeliers and floored with marble, and reminded him of Vienna: Miss Keyser must receive a good allowance; the Avenida cost two hundred escudos a day, although he had put refugees in the salon for nothing.

"Only till they find me an apartment," she said, reading his thoughts. She handed him half the fare, but he told her to keep it; let Cross pay. The hotel doorman hovered outside. Rachel Keyser stepped out. "Well, Josef, it's been—"

"Stimulating." Should he offer to buy her a coffee in the hotel? See her to her room? Into it . . . Fat chance, you gauche peasant. "Goodnight," he said, waving as the taxi took him away.

The drivers of two cars, one a Volkswagen 60, the other a Chevrolet Standard, watched the parting of Rachel Keyser and Josef Hoffman with indecision. Should they follow Hoffman or wait to see if the girl reemerged? Both made different decisions. The Volkswagen followed Hoffman to his lodgings; the Chevrolet stayed outside the hotel. Both drivers had been aware of each other since they followed the taxi from the casino; both rather whimsically wished they could cooperate and ease the strain of surveillance; and both accepted the fact that there was no chance of this happening. One worked for the NKVD and the other for the Gestapo. In any event, they both stayed at their posts for two hours before deciding that their quarries had retired to their respective beds alone.

The knock on Rachel's door came fifteen minutes after she had left Hoffman, and she knew it was Cross.

"So, what happened?" he asked, closing the door behind him.

"You can see what happened. Nothing."

"You can't have tried very hard."

He sat down on a frail chair. The whole room had an air of genteel fragility about it—dressing table with matchstick legs, thin gilded mirrors, antique bed. From a picture frame on the wall, the Portuguese leader Antonio Salazar gazed down with approval.

She sat on the edge of the bed and said, "What did you expect? He's a gentleman, something you wouldn't understand."

"I wasn't aware that you appreciated gentlemen." Cross lit a cigarette. "When are you meeting him again?"

"He didn't make a date."

Cross said angrily, "Christ Almighty! You're brought halfway around the world to make one simple conquest and you act like some Victorian

111

maiden flirting with the vicar's son. Did you flutter your eyelids behind your fan?

"Sometimes," Rachel said, "I think you're a complete fool. Well, I can tell you this: *he* isn't. If I'd made a pass on the first night, he would have smelled a rat."

"What a romantic phrase. Jesus wept! Some seductress! Didn't it occur to you that you were supposed to manipulate the situation so that *he* made the pass? Believed that he was an irresistible, middle-European lover?"

"As a matter of fact," Rachel said, returning Antonio Salazar's steady gaze, "we had a row."

"Great. On her first date Mata Hari has a quarrel. Wonderful."

"An interesting row. The reverse of the norm. You know, overmasculine male showing coy female what a wow of a he-man he is."

"You mean he's a pansy?"

"I mean he's the pacifist and I'm the belligerent. Different."

"You seem remarkably casual about it all. You're supposed to be taking part in an operation that will change the course of the war."

"It's going to be an interesting relationship," Rachel said, kicking off her shoes and lying on the bed.

"You said he didn't make another date."

"But we'll be seeing each other again; I knew that when I first set eyes on him."

Cross stared at her speculatively. "Really? I didn't know I was quite such a matchmaker." He stood up, crossed the room and kissed her, loosening his tie at the same time. "But until your next meeting with him . . ."

"In Washington," she said, "I learned a lot of new phrases." She smiled up at him. "Go screw yourself, David."

When the door closed behind him she thought, "Not bad for a demure Victorian maiden."

9

Viktor telephoned her two days later.

With studied nonchalance, he asked if she would like to take a trip up the Tagus to a small town where on Sunday, the first Sunday in October, they would be running the bulls. "You'll see a bit more of the country," he said. "You know, Lisbon isn't Portugal."

She said she would love it.

With a surge of pleasure, he hung up the receiver in the musty bar opposite his lodgings near the Largo do Carmo. Then he went into the small square and sat on a worn marble bench opposite the headquarters of the Guarda Nacional Republicana to consider his good fortune.

Pigeons pecked at his feet; a guard in a green-and-white sentry box, wearing shiny black boots and a peaked green cap, scowled at him because no one had a right to look so happy.

It was quite extraordinary, Viktor thought. Normally he would never have been in a position to approach such a woman. He didn't visit five-star hotels, and she certainly didn't frequent bars where you spat your olive pips on the floor and drank wine for one escudo a glass.

Extraordinary. . . . Then the doubts returned, and the guard relented, because the smile faded from the face of the tall, fair-haired young man sitting opposite him.

It was more than extraordinary; it was miraculous and Viktor didn't believe in miracles. Had Cross arranged the whole thing? But why? Viktor frowned; a vestige of a smile crossed the guard's granite features.

The doubts took a different direction. How could he entertain such a woman on the money he earned with the Red Cross? What an escort he would be with his dreadful clothes, as shabby as a penniless refugee's.

And if all that wasn't enough, he was younger than she. It wasn't the years that mattered—two or three of them at the most—it was the experience. Rachel Keyser, he sensed, was a very experienced lady.

In many ways, he thought, he was older. He had witnessed death and betrayal, and he had become a fugitive. But as far as women were concerned, he was a novice. Well almost. There was Anna Petrovna and the plump little waitress in Geneva and Candida Pereira. It was only when he thought about Rachel Keyser that he felt gauche.

He looked so miserable that the guard almost forgot to salute an officer leaving the building in a black staff car and only just made it with a flourish of his sword.

The movement jerked Viktor Golovin out of his melancholy. It was no good brooding. He made his way through the pigeons, past a newspaper kiosk, where a German was remonstrating with the owner for displaying too many British newspapers, and up the hill to his lodgings.

He had one room and use of a bathroom down the corridor. The room was clean and whitewashed with a view of assorted rooftops; it contained a bed, a wardrobe, a tin chest covered with old hotel labels, and a wicker rocking chair.

His landlady was a tiny, toothless old woman permanently in mourning. In addition to paying her rent, Viktor brought her chocolate bars from the Red Cross, which she munched with gums as hard as bone. For the rent he also got breakfast—Brazilian coffee and bread hot from the bakery, buttered on Saturdays and Sundays.

Viktor shut the door behind him, unlocked the tin chest, and surveyed his possessions: a Bible that he had bought in Prague to cleanse himself of Bolshevism but never opened, a Leica camera with a broken lens, a fountain pen, some letters from the waitress in Geneva, a hunting knife, two fancy Swiss shirts two sizes too small for him, a blank photograph album—nothing Russian, in case the room was searched by the PIDE, the Portuguese secret police, who were very thorough, having been trained, so it was said, by the Gestapo.

The most he could expect from that lot at the flea market on the Camp de Santa Clara in the Alfama was a couple of hundred escudos.

Despondently he picked up the Bible. It was locked with a chain and a tiny padlock and key. He turned the key and the vellum pages opened at the Book of Jeremiah. Two hundred-dollar bills fell out.

Viktor felt them, rubbed them together, held them up to the light. Who, he wondered, was his benefactor? (He had bought the Bible in a street market.) A missionary from the New World who had decided to reward a convert? He's converted me, Viktor thought, stuffing the two bills in his trouser pocket and heading for a money changer in the Rossio.

He emerged, pocket bulging with escudos, and made his way to the cathedral. God wouldn't want it *all* back; God was beneficent, not grasping. Viktor placed the equivalent of fifty dollars in the poor box; then another fifty, because if he couldn't make a girl happy on one hundred U.S. dollars, he might as well give up trying.

They took a boat from the Terreiro do Paço. Sunshine lit the sweeping terraces, King José I on his bronze horse, and the crowded waters of the Tagus. The air was chilled, a few white clouds sailing in from the Atlantic, but by lunchtime it would be warm enough.

The boat, more rust-bucket than yacht, probably wasn't what Rachel had expected. It had one cramped cabin, a patched green tarpaulin over the deck, and a suspicious amount of water in the stern. It was skippered by a fisherman named Carlos, who was doing Viktor a favor because he had translated some documents for him—British share certificates that Viktor presumed were stolen.

Surveying the decrepit craft and glancing at Rachel, dazzling in white, Viktor decided that this was his most idiotic venture yet.

This opinion was confirmed as the vessel, the *Santa Clara,* weaved its way erratically between the big ships moored in the river. The cabin was too dirty for Rachel's pristine dress, so they sat under the tarpaulin roof. It was more than chilly in midriver; it was biting cold. From time to time spray spattered them.

"We can go back if you like," he said, as a wave hit the bow, splashing water onto his new flannel trousers and brown, herringbone jacket.

"I wouldn't dream of it. But what an idiot I was to wear a dress like this."

What would Cross do in a situation like this? Answer: Cross would never have gotten himself into such a predicament. But if he had . . . Viktor took off his jacket and draped it around her shoulders.

"Thank you," she said, "but you needn't—"

"I insist," he said.

Carlos, middle-aged, unshaven, and morose, steered the *Santa Clara* past a Panamanian cargo ship. Ahead lay clear water. The sun came out from behind a cloud. Things began to look up.

They reached the town at 1 P.M. It was an uninspiring place on the Ribatejo plain, but during *feiras* it was injected with vitality; the bulls ran, boats sailed on the Tagus, sardines were gobbled in great quantities.

They went to an open-air restaurant, sat beneath a fig tree that was losing its leaves, and drank white port.

Skinny cats patrolled the dust at their feet in the hope of sardines; dead fig leaves rustled in the breeze; half-naked children stared at them. From under the branches of the tree, they looked across at green meadows where black fighting bulls were bred.

"I'm glad I came," she said, filling Viktor with great joy. She raised her glass. "Nasdarovya!" He was almost caught. Was she trying to trap him?

"Why Russian?"

"Toasts should always be in Russian. They have fire. We should now hurl our glasses against the wall."

"You speak several languages?"

"English—badly," laughing. "Russian, German, Hebrew, and Yiddish. You?"

Carefully he said, "Slavic, as you know. Czech, but not so well. Portuguese, Polish, German, English, and Russian."

"How did you come to learn Russian?"

"I studied languages in Prague. Anyone who has a way with languages should learn Russian. It's one of the languages of the future."

"Not German?"

"They're not going to win the war," Viktor said.

"They're having a good crack at it."

"You forget the Americans," Viktor said. "And the Russians."

"But they're not in the war."

"They will be, it's inevitable."

"You're very . . . assertive for a pacifist," she said, sipping her port and holding the glass up to the sunlight.

"There's no reason why pacifists shouldn't be strong. That's a misconception. Cross has put me in touch with a lot of people seeking peace. They're not weak. Tough as old boots, some of them."

"But it's a contradiction in terms, surely?"

"No," he said, happy to see the waiter approaching with their meal, "no contradiction. You have to be strong to be peaceful. Anyone can fight; it's not difficult."

"A bellicose pacifist," she said, "that's different," and, "What's this?"

as the waiter, wearing a grease-spattered black jacket and a floppy bow tie, laid a plate in front of them.

"*Dobrada,*" he told her, grateful for the interruption.

"What's that?"

"Tripe," he told her. "Cooked with beans."

"Ugh."

"Try it."

She did and for five minutes they stopped arguing.

Afterward, figs and goat cheese and coffee and *medronho,* a brandy made from arbutus.

She looked as at home here, he thought, among the dust and the cats and the grubby children, as she would in the best restaurant in Lisbon.

Reading his thoughts, she said, "I don't really like casinos."

"Not when you're losing."

"Or at any other time. Shall we stop talking about pacifism and war?"

He liked that, too—she was the one who had raised the subjects each time.

"Let's go and see the bulls running. Do you like bullfighting?"

"I'm sure you think I do. In fact I've never been to a bullfight."

"They're different here," he told her as he paid the bill, which was practically nothing. "They don't kill the bulls, for one thing—not till next day, that is. The bull's horns are covered with leather, and the eight bullfighters have to master the bull. One of them tries to seize the bull by the horns."

"Shouldn't we all?" she asked.

While they were eating, Carlos, the boatman, was telephoning Lisbon. Two calls, two payments; the trip would more than pay for itself.

First, he telephoned the German embassy on the Rua do Pau da Bandeira and asked to be put through to a man named von Claus who worked in the Chancellery.

The conversation was brief. He told von Claus that Hoffman and the Jewish woman were spending their day as planned.

"Will you bring them back?"

"Sim."

"Call me when they get back."

"Sim."

The second call was to a Russian named Novikov who, like most

Russians in Lisbon, posed as a Balkan refugee; a wealthy one staying at the Aviz hotel. The conversation was identical.

Both calls were monitored by Britain's MI6 and relayed to Cross.

Sitting at a desk staring over the garden at the rear of the British embassy, Cross thought, "You'd better hook him bloody quick, Rachel my girl, or it will be too late."

The streets were barricaded with ranchlike wooden fences with escape exits, and although the bulls were past their prime, someone invariably got hurt.

Viktor and Rachel took up a position on the safe side of the fence, near an exit. Crowds packed around them, swaggered in the street, and leaned from balconies dripping with geraniums. The air smelled of wine and dust.

Beside them stood a thin man in a white shirt and black trousers; his fat wife, who was smiling from beneath a shawl; and their son, who was about six years old, with short black hair as bright as needles, and a smile given to him by his mother.

The man handed Viktor a bottle. "Drink," he said. "It will give you courage to face the bulls."

Viktor tasted the liquor: raw brandy. He tilted the bottle and felt it burn his throat and drop into his stomach like molten lead. "Thanks," he said in Portuguese, "but I'm not going out there. Are you?"

"In the past I have always gone. But this year, no. I promised my wife." His wife went on smiling. "Instead I get drunk."

Viktor turned to Rachel. "Do you think I should go?"

"Of course not. You can't call the Red Cross if you get hurt, you are the Red Cross."

"Your skin is very fair, senhor," the man said. "And your hair. You're not from Portugal?"

"From central Europe."

"And the senhora? I think she must be Portuguese, she is so beautiful."

Rachel smiled graciously at him. "I'm afraid not. I come from Palestine."

"Why did you say that?" Viktor asked in English.

"I don't know; it just came out."

As the bulls came down the street, goaded from behind with sticks, the little boy broke free from his mother.

The smile vanished. "Alfredo," she shouted to her husband. "Do something."

118

But her husband didn't understand what had happened and stood with the bottle to his lips, remembering the good years when he had run before the horns.

In front of the bulls came the heroes: youths and young men and older men, fired by liquor. They challenged the bulls, they fell before them, they darted into the escape hatches, they vaulted the fences.

It was Viktor who saw the boy first. The boy had wandered through the exit and was gazing at the bulls bearing down on him. Then he shouted for his mother and began to run toward her but on the other side of the fence.

His father dropped his bottle, tried to climb the fence, but lost his grip and slipped back.

The boy fell directly in front of them. The bulls were twenty yards away. Their tormentors, occupied with their own courage, didn't see the boy.

Viktor pushed back against the crowd to give himself room. The boy's mother was screaming. He cleared the fence with one leap, then fell.

Lunging at the boy was an old black bull, eyes angry, horns dipped for the kill. Viktor scrambled up, grabbed the boy, and as the other bulls stampeded past, threw him over the fence. He was vaguely aware of hands clutching the child, but the aged bull, deprived of its target, had rounded on him.

It was a powerful old warrior. Viktor dodged the horns once and tried to run for the fence, but the bull cut him off. He saw a blur of faces, Rachel's among them. Grabbing at the scything horns, he held on, tossed from side to side, while a man caught the bull's tail and pulled, and others shoved at its heaving flanks.

Then he began to twist the horns to topple the old bull on its side. As he twisted, and the others pushed, it began to lean. Viktor's arms arched. The skin had been rubbed from the palms of his hands, but he was winning.

But did he want to win? Why humiliate the old bull who had been thrust into the streets to chase the crowds and had done what was expected of him?

He let go.

The bull paused, righted itself. He and Viktor gazed at each other. Then the bull wrenched himself free from the others and was gone.

The spectators began to applaud.

Viktor dodged through the exit and pushed his way toward Rachel. She was holding the boy's hand. Viktor touched the boy's head. "You'll be a bullfighter yet," he said and was sure it was the wrong thing to say. To Rachel he said, "Come on, let's get out of here."

She took his arm and said, "Not bad for a man who hates violence."

"I had to take the bull by the horns," he said.

With bulls and crowds behind them, they walked through the center of the town with its pillory, where miscreants had once been suspended in a cage; across scrubland, where lean cats and scruffy chickens lived in peace; to a green and silver glade among the olive trees.

As they walked, she told him about herself. She had been born and brought up in the wealthy pastures of Hampstead, but she had sometimes felt her heart had been in the East End, on the other side of London. Her mother had owned a dress shop in Oxford Street, her father had worked at the Foreign Office. Before she was into her teens, she had become aware of anti-Semitism. Or had she sought it out? he wondered. It wasn't until her father was sent to the British embassy in Berlin—"One of the few Jews in the diplomatic service"—as an adviser on the Jewish situation in Germany and she witnessed the persecution of her people that she understood what hatred was.

Neither her father nor the embassy staff could manage to convey the gravity of the situation to Whitehall. Nor, for that matter, could the envoys of other European countries get the message to their capital cities. "No one really wanted to know," Rachel said.

After training in communications, she had been sent to Washington. "As far away from trouble as possible."

Viktor was puzzled. "And you were content? It's hard to believe that someone as red-blooded as you could sit there while Europe went up in flames."

"I had no choice."

"No choice?"

"If you want to fight, you have to gain experience. I thought if I just had patience, someday I'd be of use to my people. And I will be."

"Here in Lisbon?"

"Perhaps. If not, then later in Palestine. I'm a Zionist. I want the Jews to have a homeland."

"And you'll fight to see that they get one?"

"Yes."

He nodded. He felt as if he was coming to know her rather quickly. "Do you work with Cross?"

"He's a specialist."

Viktor grimaced. "You mean a spy."

"Isn't everyone in Lisbon?"

"I'm not."

"Every diplomat then."

"You?"

"We keep our eyes and ears open in communications."

"Are you doing so now?"

"This is developing into an interrogation," she said.

A flock of sheep wandered past, nudging each other along, shepherd and dog behind them. When they had gone, it was very quiet. They lay down beside each other under the silvery leaves, and then he leaned over and kissed her.

There had never been a kiss like it. It was in the mind, it was in the body, and it was on the threshold of emotions for which there were no names, only understanding.

Carlos the boatman interrupted the kiss.

He said from the edge of the glade, "We have to go, Senhor Hoffman, the tides . . ."

She looked up at Viktor and her eyes were lazy and sharing, flecked with gold; and she smiled at him. There will be other times, the smile said.

Viktor stood up. "How did you find us?"

"It's a small town, senhor. You were watched; the foreigner with the balls, who fought the bull."

"What did he say?" Rachel asked, but Viktor didn't translate. Nor did he believe the boatman's explanation; he had followed them. Ever since leaving Russia he had possessed this new awareness. "We have to go," he told Rachel.

And they sailed back on the *Santa Clara*. It was no longer a rust-bucket, and it floated on the golden waters of the Sea of Straw.

Two days later, Cross sent a message by King's Messenger to the head of Special Intelligence in London, Robert Sinclair.

Decoded, it read:

OPERATION RED CROSS PROCEEDING AS WELL AS
CAN BE EXPECTED. SUBJECT DRAWN CLOSER INTO

NET BUT WITH MINOR COMPLICATIONS, SOME AL-
READY ANTICIPATED. BOTH SUBJECT AND CONTACT
ARE UNDER SURVEILLANCE BY AGENTS OF ABWEHR
AND NKVD.

Contact was a bloody pedestrian word for a girl like Rachel Keyser,
Sinclair thought.

ABWEHR SURVEILLANCE PROBABLY ROUTINE INI-
TIALLY TO CHECK OUT NEW RECRUIT TO EMBASSY
BUT INTEREST MAINTAINED BY CONTACT'S ASSOCIA-
TION WITH SUBJECT IN RED CROSS. WE HAVE SUR-
VEILLANCE IN HAND BUT SUGGEST TIME APPROACH-
ING TO MAKE REVELATION BEFORE OTHER PARTIES
INTERFERE.
RECOMMEND MAKE NECESSARY DOCUMENTS
AVAILABLE SOONEST SO THAT WE CAN INSTIGATE
NEXT VITAL PHASE.
COMPLICATION NOT ANTICIPATED IS GROWING
AFFECTION BETWEEN SUBJECT AND CONTACT. THIS
UNEXPECTED DEVELOPMENT COULD HAVE UNPRE-
DICTABLE RESULTS.

Thoughtfully, Sinclair raked the glowing coals from the fire in his
office to preserve them for tomorrow and, as the sirens wailed their
warnings in the distance, left his office to walk to No. 10 Downing Street
to report the latest developments to Winston Churchill.

10

Before applying his mind to the conquest of Russia, Adolf Hitler decided to inspect his birdhouses.

He left the chief of the Luftwaffe, Hermann Göring, and the head of military intelligence, Wilhelm Canaris, in the house. He took with him Eva Braun and his German shepherd dog, Blondi.

It was a crisp October day, leaves of the deciduous trees turning red and gold, conifers thrusting dark green spears among them. In the distance stood the crumpled white peaks of the Untersberg Mountains.

This was the part of Germany that Hitler loved best. Obersalzberg in the Bavarian Alps, above the village of Berchtesgaden, close to the Austrian border.

It was here he had sought refuge when he was released from prison after attempting to seize power in November, 1923. It was here that he had finished writing *Mein Kampf,* "My Struggle," his credo, which he had begun in jail.

It was here that he had bought a modest house and converted it into his luxurious alpine retreat, the Berghof; and it was here that he had at last found direction to become the savior of the Fatherland.

He came here to rest and recuperate, to breathe the clean mountain air, and to walk on the wooded slopes. He had built feeding centers for birds and game and had forbidden hunting within the boundaries.

Hitler, dressed in a gray jacket and black trousers, followed Blondi into a wood. Pine needles crunched softly beneath his feet, and the dog's barks were lost in the trees.

Eva took his arm. She was gossiping about some of the members of their inner circle, and he only half-listened to what she said. They walked deeper into the wood until they came to a couple of birdhouses. All the food had been taken, and Hitler replenished each with bread, shelled nuts, and seed.

Suddenly Eva saw a movement in the grass and, reaching down, picked up a bird. Cupped in her hand, fluttering weakly, it looked like a robin; but the red on its breast was blood and it was a sparrow.

Hitler took the bird from her and gently felt its fragile body with the tips of his fingers. From one wing he took a pellet of shot, then another. "I can't understand shooting little birds," he said.

"But no one would dare to shoot anything here."

"It flew here after being shot elsewhere." And he knew where. Göring's own lodge was above the Berghof, and nothing delighted the fat Reichsmarschall more than shooting anything that moved.

"Can we save it?"

"I doubt it," Hitler said. "They don't have much resistance. This was a tough little devil. Usually they die of shock."

As he spoke, the sparrow in his hand died. He placed it in the branches of a tree, out of Blondi's reach, and turned back toward the Berghof with Eva. It was time to discuss the most important campaign he would ever undertake.

Hitler talked first to Canaris because it did Göring good to be left waiting.

Canaris, looking as wary as ever, was standing in the main reception room, with its sunken floor and marble stairs designed by Hitler, beside a log fire, lit specially for him.

A manservant poured coffee and left them. Hitler gestured to Canaris to sit down and said, "I summoned you to give me the latest news on Churchill's intentions."

Hitler had first announced his decision to invade Russia on July 29, just over two months ago. The announcement had been made to his personal chief of staff, General Alfred Jodl and, two days later, to Göring and Admiral Eric Raeder, commander in chief of the navy. The proposed date for the attack: May 1941.

All three had taken the notice of intent seriously but not the date. It was impossible—and even Hitler admitted this—to predict any date until Britain had been brought to heel. If that hadn't been accomplished by the end of the year, then no move against the Soviet Union could be accurately forecast.

Since then, Canaris had brought the pleasing news that Churchill was willing to make a secret peace if Germany turned her forces against the Communist menace in the East. It was a reasonable offer that sounded more reasonable because Churchill's detestation of communism was well known.

It was the answer to Hitler's dreams, and he had withdrawn his Sea Lion invasion fleet, sorely battered in any case by the RAF, and revised his strategy.

Canaris said, "There isn't a great deal more, mein Führer." He picked up a black briefcase and took out two sheets of teletype. "But this is further confirmation."

It was a cable from Churchill to Roosevelt that referred to "the dispersal of the German invasion fleet and the annihilation of the mutual enemy,"—Russia, of course. Coming on top of the letter from the duke of Windsor, it seemed decisive.

"Where did you get this from?"

"From Lisbon, where we have an Abwehr agent established in the communications department of the British embassy. Cross is his name."

Hitler began to pace up and down the room, hands behind his back. "I remember him from our last conversation. How did he get access to a cable sent by Churchill from London?"

"He's just returned from London. As a double agent he has access to many secrets there."

"It distresses me, if you'll excuse my saying so, Admiral, to put my faith in spies. Are you sure we can trust him?"

"He's one of the best we've got."

Hitler walked over to the window and stared at the mountains. Above the Berghof, approached by tunnel and an elevator 124 meters high, was the Kehlsteinhaus, the Eagle's Nest, the odd building perched on the spur of the Kehlstein Mountain and built at extravagant cost by Martin Bormann. Hitler didn't much care for it. What interested him more was the Untersberg Mountain, where Emperor Frederick I was said to be buried. He had been known as Barbarossa, Red Beard, and according to the legend, someday he would live again and would save Germany.

Hitler turned from the window and said to Canaris. "I'm going to call it Barbarossa."

Canaris looked puzzled.

"The conquest of Russia." Briskly, he said, "Keep me informed of any developments."

"Of course, mein Fuhrer."

"That will be all, Admiral. Please send the Reichsmarschall in to me."

Hitler watched Göring waddle in, click his heels, and give the Nazi salute.

The man was always loyal, but Hitler wondered how long his self-indulgence and inefficiency could be tolerated. It would have been different if he had fulfilled his promise to shoot the RAF out of the skies. But he had conspicuously failed.

Hitler told Göring to keep up the Luftwaffe's night attacks on British cities. Churchill, he said, must be constantly reminded of Germany's power. He told the Reichsmarschall no more than this, and their discussion lasted barely ten minutes. As Göring marched to the door, Hitler called out after him. "Just one more thing, Hermann."

Göring stopped.

"Stop shooting sparrows."

Göring carried out Hitler's orders zealously, continuing the bombardment of Britain's cities *and* adding a new dimension—fire. On October 15, in addition to 390 tons of explosive, his planes dropped 70,000 incendiary bombs on London.

But instead of causing moral collapse, the Blitz had the opposite effect. In London, and later in most of Britain's major cities, the people were more united than ever before. "We can take it," they said and did so every terrible night.

Whenever Churchill was assailed by doubts about the fate he had decreed for Russia and Germany, he did two things: he studied the anti-British propaganda pouring out from the Kremlin and the treachery of Communist agents trying to undermine Britain's war effort, then he visited one of the battlefields of Britain.

One day the battlefield was Peckham. A landmine had fallen, devastating acres of terraces of little houses that in South London shoulder each other toward the Thames.

On his way by car with the chancellor of the exchequer, Kingsley Wood, he peered out of the limousine at what London was taking. At the spaces in the terraces—like gaps left by cleanly pulled teeth; at the boarded windows and holed roofs and tiny, debris-spattered gardens, complete with stirrup pumps for extinguishing flames.

The car skirted a crater in the road; it had been roped off, and tin-hatted air-raid wardens, gas-mask cases swinging from their shoulders, were chasing gaping children who ran away to regroup.

At a street-corner tobacconist's shop, its bomb-blasted windows shored up with cardboard, people were queuing up for cigarettes, as they queued up for almost everything else: their four ounces of butter, their twelve ounces of sugar, their one shilling and ten pence' worth of meat. Guiltily, Churchill regarded the glowing tip of his cigar; he was about to squash it in the ashtray when he thought, "No, it's a symbol. And so am I, that is the main thing I have to offer these people."

A young woman in trousers and sweater recognized him and pointed. Smiling, he raised two fingers in his V-for-Victory sign, and she returned the salute.

The car stopped on the edge of the devastation. The crater in the center of the smoking rubble that had been thirty or so homes was fifty yards wide. On the stump of a wall, a poster fluttered, DIG FOR VICTORY. Above floated a silver barrage balloon.

Rescue workers were digging for the dead and the injured. Staircases and patchworks of homely wallpaper hung on swaying walls. The air smelled of bonfires and whitewash.

Within minutes of his arrival, crowds gathered around him. They cheered him and touched him, and it was when he thought, It's as though I have brought them great riches, that he had to dab the tears from his eyes with a handkerchief.

A fire officer told him, "Jerry must be pretty proud of these mines. They float down on parachutes and so the blast does maximum damage."

Churchill nodded grimly, and a group of children began to sing:

> Just whistle while you work
> Mussolini is a twerp,
> Hitler's barmy,
> So's his army
> Rub 'em in the dirt.

As he was driven away, a stout woman shouted, "Let the Jerries have it back, eh, Winnie?"

Oh yes, he thought, I'll let them have it back all right—and the Russians, too.

Churchill set aside an hour with Sinclair to discuss the latest developments in Lisbon.

There was no cabinet meeting that evening. At 9 P.M. he was dining with the secretary of state for war, Anthony Eden, who had shared his antiappeasement views in the late thirties—but he hadn't told Eden about Lisbon. Between 7:00 and 7:45, he had an audience with the king—like himself a symbol, and a noble one at that—who lately had taken to practicing at a shooting range on the grounds of Buckingham Palace, in case he had to go down fighting. So he received Sinclair at eight. It was a cold, clear October night, and the sky was swept by the beams of searchlights, which seemed to polish the cold stars. The air-raid warnings sounded just as Sinclair arrived.

Sinclair, who looked more like a dour Scottish laird every time he saw him, hesitated in the hall. "Aren't we going to the Annexe?"—the government block at Storey's Gate, overlooking St. James's Park, where an underground, bombproof War Room had been built.

Churchill shook his head. "I can't stand the place. In any case, the apartments there aren't finished yet and life here's much more exciting."

A few nights earlier, Churchill had rescued his kitchen staff from probable death. Bombs had been falling around No. 10 when, over dinner, he had suddenly remembered the huge plate-glass window in the kitchen. He told the butler to put the meal on a hot plate and dispatched the staff to the shelter. A few minutes later, the kitchen was wrecked by a bomb, the window blown into lethal shards of glass. Mrs. Landemare, the cook, had expressed annoyance at the mess.

Churchill took Sinclair by the arm. "I'm surprised the whole place didn't come down. It's two hundred and fifty years old and was thrown up by a jerry-builder named Downing. Jerry finishing off Jerry's work, eh?" He laughed. "Come on, my dear chap, and have a grog before we get down to work."

Churchill took Sinclair to his study. The mahogany furniture was covered with white dust shaken from the ceiling by a bomb; the curtains were drawn across blackout frames and steel shutters. The antiaircraft guns were barking outside; from time to time the building trembled.

"We've got some of the rooms shored up with wooden props," Churchill said, pouring them both a whisky.

"I think you should take more care of yourself," Sinclair said, sipping his whisky. "You owe it to the people."

"So everyone keeps telling me. But that's not the Churchill they want. He leaned back in a red upholstered chair. "Now tell me the state of the parties in Lisbon."

Viktor stroked the lovely contours of her body, and everywhere, it seemed, there was an answer to his touch. A movement, a pulse, a stirring. And when she touched him, he felt his body respond with an intensity he hadn't experienced before.

Not that there was anything hurried about their caresses. On the contrary, they were tentative, exploratory, the approaches to preordained fulfillment.

Nor was there any attempt by either of them to dominate. He had feared that, in lovemaking, Rachel's character would demand assertion; had feared that out of perversity he would try to take control. Instead they reached for each other, looked into each other's eyes, and became one.

There was no shame, no expertise, just awareness. The natural culmination of a kiss two weeks earlier beneath an olive tree.

"I love you," he said, as he became aware of rain tapping on the window of her room in the Avenida Palace.

"And I love you," she said.

But why was there sadness in her voice?

Sinclair said that, yes, he was ready to make the next move. Everything would be put into tomorrow's diplomatic bag and flown to Lisbon.

A bomb fell close by. No. 10 shook and a piece of plaster fell on the carpet between Churchill and Sinclair.

"There is one complication," Churchill said, touching the piece of plaster with the toe of his shoe. He was wearing a light gray pinstripe and a blue, polka-dot bow tie.

Sinclair, who thought there was more than one, looked at him inquiringly.

"Timing," Churchill said. "You've accomplished Phase One. It's October now, and Hitler will attack Russia as soon as he can. But we don't want him to do it too soon. Next June would be ideal; May could be disastrous because it might give him time to reach Moscow before the Russian winter sets in. If Moscow fell then, who knows, the Russians might even admit defeat. At the very least there would be a lull in the fighting, which is exactly what we don't want."

"According to our intelligence. Not ULTRA," Sinclair said and paused because Churchill was notoriously skeptical about other clandestine sources of information and had devised his own method of sifting reports. But Churchill didn't interrupt, and he continued, "According to these sources we may have an unexpected ally: Mussolini. Apparently he's mad as hell about Hitler's occupation of Romania and wants to put on a show of his own."

"A Grecian adventure?" Churchill nodded thoughtfully. An antiaircraft gun opened up in St. James's Park, and they heard shrapnel falling on the roof. "See if you can't make your agents in Rome encourage him to take on the Greeks. He'll botch it so thoroughly that Hitler will have to delay the Russian invasion for a few weeks to help him."

"We're already pursuing that line of persuasion," Sinclair said and thought he sounded rather prim. "Through Switzerland; and Lisbon, of course." He had been poised to make the point Churchill had just made.

"The Battle of the Conjurors," Churchill murmured.

"Sir?"

"An apt phrase to describe espionage. But that's the battle that's going to win the war; if we win it. Without my most secret source, we'd be under the Nazi jackboot today. If we hadn't known in advance where Göring's planes were going to strike, they'd have overwhelmed us." He cocked an ear as the gun in the park barked again and glass tinkled outside.

"The Battle of the Conjurors." Sinclair repeated the phrase and asked, "When you come to write the history of this war, will you write about this particular battle?"

"Out of the question," Churchill said briskly. "The people must believe it was sheer guts that won the day. As, in a sense, it will be. Of course, the truth always comes out and so it will in this case. First ULTRA and then what you and I've concocted. But no rush. Someday people will understand better what we found it necessary to do and will see it in a different perspective. If it were public knowledge now, many people would be shocked."

Sinclair nodded.

"Tell me now, what about Phase Two? How do we fool Stalin? Is Hoffman ready?"

"Hoffman is the spearhead, but we don't want to rely completely on one man. We can't be certain yet that he'll cooperate."

"Then you have other methods of confusing Stalin?"

"Yes," Sinclair said, lighting his pipe. "British Intelligence has been feeding trusted Soviet agents with false information to damage their credibility. In particular Richard Sorge, the Kremlin's master spy in Tokyo. He's been fed so many incorrect facts that if he warns them about Germany's intentions, Stalin won't believe a word he says."

Sinclair puffed away at his pipe for a few seconds and then went on. "We're also using a young man named Kim Philby, but in a different way. He works for British Intelligence, but he's been turned, by the Russians. A double agent, in other words."

"And you intend to make him a triple one?"

"Precisely. He's very well thought of in Moscow, and we're giving him access to all sorts of classified material in Lisbon. It's a very neat set-up."

Churchill smiled. "That all sounds very nice, Colonel, and as I've mentioned before, one of our best ploys will be the warnings we send to Stalin to the effect that Hitler *does* intend to attack. That man never believes anything we say, and personally, I'm not sure I blame him. He only thinks we're trying to create dissension between Hitler and himself. I've advised Roosevelt to send warnings as well."

The all clear sounded outside.

Churchill stood up and said, "Now let's see those documents of yours." He poured more whisky for both of them. "There is absolutely no doubt, is there?"

Sinclair took a sheaf of papers and a tape-recorder spool from his briefcase. "That Josef Hoffman is Stalin's son? Absolutely none."

PART THREE

11

Viktor perused the documents, watched anxiously by Rachel Keyser.

CERTIFIED COPY OF BIRTH OF INFANT. (Fee one ruble.)
DATE OF BIRTH: 1919.

No month, he thought.

PLACE: PETROGRAD. SEX: BOY. NAME OF FATHER:
JOSIF VISSARIONOVICH DZHUGASHVILI.

At least they had gone to the trouble to get Stalin's real name right.
(Student rebels at Moscow University never failed to recall that Stalin,
born in Gori, Georgia, was the son of a drunken cobbler named
Dzhugashvili.)

OCCUPATION OF FATHER: COMMISSAR OF NATION-
ALITIES.

They'd got that right, too.

Viktor glanced at Rachel. They were sitting in the bedroom of a palace
at Sintra, fifteen miles from Lisbon, where staff from the British embassy
were allowed to spend weekends. "Why?" he asked her.

"Finish reading them," she said and looked away.

MOTHER'S NAME: NADIA LATYNINA.

Who was she supposed to be?

OCCUPATION OF MOTHER: STUDENT.

But Stalin had then been married to his second wife, Nadezhda Sergeyevna Alliluyeva, the vivacious revolutionary who, according to gossip, had been driven to suicide thirteen years later by Stalin's boorish behavior toward her. So the British were alleging that he was the bastard son of Stalin, born the same year that Stalin had married his second wife. He had certainly gotten around!

There had, of course, been rumors about Stalin's affairs. In particular with Rosa Kaganovitch, a doctor and sister of a leading Bolshevik. But Nadia Latynina? Never heard of her. And there had never been rumors of illegitimate children.

Stalin's only children were Jacob (Yasha), by his first wife, Ekaterina Svanidze—she had died in 1907—and Vassily, and one daughter, Svetlana, born in 1925, on whom Stalin doted.

By all accounts Jacob was a neurotic who had once tried to commit suicide and was now a bureaucrat and a Red Army reservist. Vassily, a boozer and a rebel, was now a pilot in the Red air force; Svetlana was an attractive, red-haired student.

All three of them would have been astonished to learn that they had a brother born out of wedlock!

This was a forgery, and the fact that it was written in faded ink, the color of dried blood, only made it more pathetic.

Viktor picked up the next document.

It was another birth certificate recording his birth as Viktor Nicolayovitch Golovin.

FATHER: LIBRARIAN. Etcetera.

"There's a lot more yet," Rachel said. She picked up a *queijadas,* the sweet cheese pastries made in Sintra, but replaced it without tasting it. She lit a cigarette; Hoffman hadn't seen her smoke before.

The third document was a letter written in 1919 by Josef Stalin and addressed to Felix Edmundovich Dzerzhinsky, who in 1917 had been appointed head of the Cheka, the Bolsheviks' first secret police force.

Stalin had signed himself Commissar of Nationalities, and the letter was an appeal couched in relatively humble terms because, even though you were one of Lenin's lieutenants, you didn't antagonize a secret police chief, certainly not one as ruthless as Dzerzhinsky.

The letter implored Dzerzhinsky to use all his powers to obtain and destroy all documents *relating to the birth we discussed* and concluded with a request to Dzerzhinsky to destroy the letter itself after he had read it. Stalin (or the perpetrator of the forgery) should have known better; a secret police chief destroys nothing.

Next, another faded letter from Stalin, this time addressed to Nicolay Semonovich Golovin, his father. *My heartfelt thanks for your action in this matter. May I assure you that I shall follow the boy's progress with the deepest possible interest.*

This was followed by a note apparently written recently and signed by someone named Sinclair.

It said, *It would appear that Cheka agents called on Golovin and confiscated any subsequent correspondence from Stalin. The following transcripts of telephone conversations were probably recorded by elementary wiretaps instigated by successors to the Cheka embodied in the NKVD.*

The alleged transcripts were typed, badly, on sheets of yellowing paper, headed simply CASE 1385. The conversations, dated in the twenties and early thirties, all had a similar theme.

Viktor looked at one dated October 21, 1930, when Stalin was firmly in power after Lenin's death in 1925 and his bitter rival, Leon Trotsky, had been exiled.

Stalin: How is the boy?

Golovin: He's fine. He had a wonderful time on the Black Sea. We are very grateful to you.

Stalin: And how does he like his new school?

Golovin: Early days yet, but I'm sure he will settle down. Like his father, he adapts well and is capable of great concentration.

Grovel, Viktor thought.

Then he remembered, "I did go to the Black Sea in 1930. To Tuapse." He recalled sunlight on green water and an argument with his father about an ice cream. "And I did go to a new school that autumn: State School 42 in Moscow." He remembered the fears on the first day there: an unsmiling teacher who wore pince-nez; a bully with a birthmark on his cheek.

Stalin: You must make sure that he works at home, too.

Golovin: Of course, comrade Stalin.

Stalin: You must also make sure that his political education is not neglected. Politics is everything.

Golovin: We are already attending to that.

With scant success, Viktor thought.

Stalin: I will be in touch again in one month.

Golovin: Very well.

Stalin: Look after him well, Comrade Golovin. He means a lot to me.

Then June 1936.

Stalin: I understand that he is assured of a place at Moscow University.

Golovin: That is correct. He has done very well.

Stalin: But not as well as I had hoped in the political field.

Golovin: He is a very sensitive boy.

Stalin: And isn't that compatible with political aptitude?

Golovin: I didn't mean that exactly.

Stalin: Never mind, there is still time.

And how they had tried, Viktor remembered.

Stalin (after a pause): He is looking very well. A little pale perhaps...

How could Stalin have known? But, of course, those frequent walks in the Kremlin from Red Square past the Cadet Institute Pavilion, past a gloomy two-story house: Stalin's home. Had Stalin been watching him?

Golovin: He has very fair coloring.

Stalin: So did his mother. . . . Are the funds sufficient, Comrade Golovin?

Golovin: Quite adequate.

Stalin: Very well, guard him well. I will be in touch."

There were several more transcripts. Viktor didn't bother to read them. He leafed through the rest of the documents. The message was clear; there was little point in reading many more forgeries. He picked out two at random. One purported to be a memorandum from Stalin to Lavrenti Pavlovich Beria, the sinister head of the NKVD, whose two predecessors had been executed in Lubyanka. It was dated just before Viktor had fled from the Soviet Union.

For reasons that need not concern you, I want full surveillance mounted on a student at Moscow University named Viktor Golovin. His movements must be completely unrestricted. This order must be carried out without question and with maximum application wherever the subject chooses to go.

The evidence was becoming increasingly implausible. The NKVD had tried to kill him in Lisbon!

Viktor scanned the second document. Again from Stalin to Beria.

An attempt was made to liquidate Josef Hoffman in Lisbon two weeks ago. According to foreign intelligence sources this was an NKVD operation. Those responsible must be dealt with summarily in the normal manner.

"I don't understand," he said aloud.

She crossed the room toward him, but he ignored her and picked up another paper. It was a denial by Beria that anyone in the NKVD had been involved in the assassination attempt. Nevertheless three Lisbon officers, who could not satisfactorily explain their whereabouts on that day, had been dealt with "in the normal manner."

"But they did try to kill me," he said. "Why?"

"There is a lot to explain," she said. "I didn't understand any of it when I first met you. Only that you were Russian, not Czech."

She stood in front of him, her eyes pleading.

Through the window of the pink-and-gold room, he could see lawns and a garden laid out with box hedges and, beyond the palace grounds, farmland stretching away to the sea. It had been raining, and in the gardens a bird was singing, its notes like the last drops of rain.

"But it was arranged, wasn't it? You and me?"

She looked away from him and went across the room, walking on the deep pink carpet. "First listen to this. Then we can talk." She made some adjustments to a tape recorder, pressed a button, and the spool began to turn.

It was his father's voice right enough; pedantic and pompous but bereft of its didactic quality. "I don't know where he is. He came back from a journey into the country, and he was changed."

Guns firing, bodies falling in slow motion.

Another voice. (Stalin's? It certainly had a thick Georgian accent.) "Had he been with the girl?"

"Anna Petrovna? I don't know. I warned him about her."

"Nikolay Vasilyev?"

"Perhaps. I warned him about all such dangerous influences." A stammer of apprehension in that sonorous voice. "Then he just disappeared."

"Don't worry, Comrade Golovin, we know where he is."

"Will he . . . will he be coming back?"

"Perhaps. But not to you, Comrade Golovin. You have played your part. But your days as foster father are over."

Was that a woman sobbing in the background? His mother?

Stalin, if it was he, said, "I am very grateful to you and I have arranged for a suitable reward to be paid to you." And, unbelievably—if it was he—there was a catch in his voice.

"Thank you."

"Yes, thank you," a woman's voice. His mother's. No doubt about it. Click.

The tape continued to whir but the voices had been severed as though the throats of their owners had been cut.

Viktor thought, "They weren't such bad parents," and realized even that was inadequate for the love his foster mother had given him.

Rachel switched the OFF button and looked at him. "Do you believe it now?"

"That was my father's voice, yes."

"And everything you've just read?"

Believe that his true father was a tyrant and a mass murderer?

"No I do not believe it!" he shouted.

But he did.

Sintra isn't like any other part of Portugal. It is dark green and verdant, a little decayed, a little decadent. It is built on high ground, nestling amid soft hills, and contains a clutch of palaces, including the former summer residence of the Portuguese kings, an odd building with two conical chimneys like oasthouses.

Lord Byron had much admired Sintra, and it reminded Viktor of a small town in the foothills of the Swiss Alps, which had borrowed a little from Ruritania. It was a classic setting for intrigue. Could this have been, Viktor wondered, the unconscious reason why they had brought him here, for what he already regarded as "the Revelation?"

It had stopped raining, but the foliage was still dripping as he and Rachel, both wearing raincoats, walked down a narrow road lined with mossy walls.

Viktor's brain ached with questions, but every time he tried to put one into words, it slipped away. They passed a waterfall, green and white and cold, and he thought again, "I am the son of one of the most evil men in history," and then the first question came quite easily, "Who was my mother? Who was this girl Nadia Latynina?"

The stranger walking beside him said, "I wish we knew." *We!* "The birth certificate said she was a student, that's all that's known. But," glancing at Viktor, "she was obviously very fair, slim, tall, sensitive."

"Weren't there any other records? You seem to have been very thorough."

"They couldn't find any." *They* now. "She seems to have vanished."

"So all I have left is a Georgian gangster. If he destroyed her—and make no mistake, he did—you would think he would have destroyed *all* the evidence."

"He probably tried, but in those early days, he must have underestimated the secret police. Even later it couldn't have occurred to him that he was under observation. Or perhaps it did, but he had to risk everything to keep in touch with Nicolay Golovin. You see," she said, "he is very proud of you. He had antagonized his other two sons, Jacob and Vassily; he loved his daughter, Svetlana, still does, but she's a girl. You were the only son he hadn't polluted, and he wanted to keep it that way."

"You haven't mentioned that he didn't want any scandal," Hoffman said.

"That as well," she said.

They turned up a lane past a crouching, red-roofed house. The blue sky was hung with clouds, and the woods on either side of them smelled of summer. To one side, on a crag, they could see the Moors' Castle.

"How did your people find all this out?" he said.

"British Intelligence has a double agent in the NKVD. He copied the duplicated documents. They've known about you for a long time, Josef."

"They didn't exactly jump on me when I escaped from Russia."

"They must have wanted you to establish yourself."

"Before introducing the femme fatale. Yes, I can see that. Get the poor fool waving his Red Cross flag in Geneva or Stockholm or Lisbon, somewhere useful, before making a play. . . . But," he asked her, "for what purpose?"

"First," she said, "let's get everything else cleared up."

"Cleared up—that makes it sound very simple."

Rachel looked at him almost timidly and began to speak. She had told him the truth, she insisted. As far as she had known *then,* she had been sent to Portugal because of her expertise in communications—cryptanalysis, if you preferred it. Almost immediately, however, Cross had recruited her into Intelligence with the specific task of cultivating him. Yes, she and Cross had been lovers, but they weren't anymore. He could believe or disbelieve that, it was up to him.

Why should he believe anything she said? he asked, and she said she couldn't think of any reason.

She hadn't been told why she had to "cultivate" him. She only knew that the two of them were to play some vital part in defeating Nazism.

But she could see he wasn't listening. Suddenly he turned toward her and said, "So you knew from that first meeting in the casino that I was Russian. That's very funny. Did you have a good laugh about it with Cross when the two of you were getting laid that night?"

"Please." She stretched out a hand, but he evaded it.

A few drops of rain fell from a dark cloud hovering over them.

He said, "All we ever talked were lies."

"No, not always. Not—"

"Always," he said firmly. "I'm surprised you didn't invite me up to your room the first night. Oh no, how stupid of me. Cross was there, wasn't he?"

"He came there. Nothing happened. It doesn't matter, does it; not if you don't believe me."

"He must be quite a lover. Aggressive, sadistic even. Your type. It must have been hell having to screw a pacifist."

The slap was hard and unexpected, and it made him stumble. And then Viktor utterly surprised himself; he slapped her back, hard. She came at him, and he grabbed her wrists and held her off. She was panting, and her dark eyes were full of a meaning he was not certain he could make out; but she was tough. He let her go, and she said simply, "Let's get back, there's going to be a storm."

She was right about the storm. The dark cloud had swollen and fat raindrops were spattering on the cobbled surface of the lane. They walked quickly on, side by side, almost as if nothing had happened.

"Why did the NKVD try to kill me?" he asked.

"They didn't," she said crisply.

He stopped, and then had to hurry a few paces to catch up with her. "But they did."

Her black hair was pasted close to her scalp by the water, her lipstick was smeared, and there was a red mark on her cheek where he had hit her. He thought she was beautiful.

"No one was trying to shoot you," she said.

"But the man with the gun . . ."

"He wasn't Russian."

"What was he, then?"

She stopped and turned, hands on her hips, rainwater streaming down her face.

"He was British," she said.

Lying in a hot bath in the palace, a glass of whisky beside him, Viktor considered her explanation. He was a little drunk, and her reasons had become blurred, as though the steam from the bath had gotten at them.

It had all been a set-up to establish a relationship between Cross and himself; to make him grateful to the British for saving his life; a stepping stone to Rachel.

The set-up had been elaborate because Cross was a perfectionist in such matters. But Viktor had never been in much danger; the gun had been loaded with blanks.

A hefty tackle. *Assassin* sprawling. Whisked away in a car to Cross's flat. Man-to-man rapport established. Russian peasant only too happy to accept guidance from sophisticated savior.

You stupid prick, Viktor thought. He drank some whisky. How could he have ever believed that a woman like Rachel Keyser would fall in love with him?

You deserved all you got and more, he decided, climbing out of the bath. He stood in front of the mirror swaying slightly.

He peered into it.

Josef Stalin peered back.

It wasn't until next morning that anything made any real sense. He awoke at 7:30 A.M. with a sense of sleepy serenity. Then he felt the first stab of pain in his skull, and it awakened the previous day's revelations. They were like an old black-and-white movie, erratic and silent. Then gradually they gained color, sound, and continuity.

He turned his aching head to one side and saw Rachel lying beside him. She had pushed the blankets down to her waist and he could see that she was wearing a filmy black nightgown.

They had come to Sintra as lovers. But she must have realized that was over. Or was the arrogance of such women so indestructible that they believed their sexuality could overcome all obstacles?

Another pulse of pain in his skull. He hadn't drunk that much whiskey, but he wasn't accustomed to spirits in any quantity.

Hands behind his head, he stared out of the window at the gray sky, drained of rain, and let the movie run free. He saw his parents. How complacent they had been. With good reason!

He swung himself out of the bed, put on his dressing gown, and stood at the window. The fields below the hills were covered in mist; the sun was rising amid pink petals of cloud; a donkey was delivering olive oil to the palace kitchens.

"We've got a lot to talk about," Rachel said. She was sitting up in bed, blanket clutched to her breasts.

"Have we?"

"But not here," her voice businesslike. "The reason we came to Sintra was to avoid surveillance, but they may have picked us up by now."

"They?"

"Germans, Russians. The Germans are curious about us. As for the Russians—Cross thinks they've stepped up surveillance because of the German interest. A vicious circle. . . ."

A knock at the door. A maid in a black-and-white uniform brought in a tray. Orange juice, coffee, hot rolls, butter, and a selection of jams. They ate in silence.

He spoke to her while she was splashing in the bathroom; it was easier that way. "I want to get back to Lisbon," he said. "As soon as possible."

"I'll drive you," she called out. "But we'll stop on the way. I have to explain what it's all about. There was no point last night. Too much whiskey."

She sounded, he thought, like a superefficient secretary who has just slept with the boss.

She drove the little, stiff-backed black Austin the British embassy had loaned her, at a brisk pace. The town hadn't yet awakened and stray dogs stared at them, affronted by the noise.

The gray Citröen van picked them up on the outskirts of the town.

"They took their time but they made it in the end," she said.

"Russians?"

"Germans. They use Citröen vans a lot." The Austin accelerated around a bend in the road.

Viktor glanced behind. The van was still with them.

"He has a problem," she said. "He's supposed to be inconspicuous. But what can he do when we're rattling along at . . . ," glancing at the speedometer, "sixty-five miles an hour? Either he shows his hand or he loses us."

She swung the wheel, and the Austin swerved around a donkey laden with canisters of kerosene. A peasant shouted after them, jumping back as the Citröen van swept past him.

The still-wet road descended the hills in bends past gardens of spent

144

flowers. Part of the mist had been smoke from the fields below, and they could smell it inside the car. She pushed the accelerator flat onto the floor so that there was no speed left in the engine. The Citröen disappeared and reappeared in the mist and smoke.

She took a turn beside a field of gnarled vines, braked, and went into a long skid. She fought it. The Austin righted itself and accelerated down a straight stretch of road.

"Let's hope he's not so lucky," she said.

But he was.

There were patches of clear visibility now, the fields on either side golden. They raced past a plantation of cork trees, through a hamlet with chickens pecking at the sides of the road.

Ahead lay a hollow filled with mist. They dipped sharply into it. It was like driving through gray wool.

Tires screeching, they took a sharp corner, splashing through a stream that had overflowed in the storm. To the right, a cart laden with slabs of marble and pulled by two horses was just emerging from a yard. The Austin swerved around it and plunged out of the mist.

Fifty yards down the road Rachel pulled into a lane and waited.

The sound of the Citröen's engine reached them from the hollow.

"Now," she said.

The noise of the impact was savage. They heard metal ripping, glass smashing, and thuds as what they supposed were the slabs of marble hit the road.

They climbed out of the Austin and walked back. The Citröen was lying on its side, oil and water streaming from its engine; marble littered the road; the horses were still in their shafts and one of them seemed injured; the man in charge had run out of the yard and was trying to calm them. The driver of the Citröen sat on the roadside, hands covering his face, blood oozing from between his fingers.

Rachel Keyser and Viktor went back to the Austin.

At the next village, Rachel telephoned the police and told them about the accident.

Ten minutes later she turned suddenly into a dusty track. She stopped the Austin beneath the sails of a windmill. "Now listen to what I've got to say."

As she began talking, he became aware of a whistling that he couldn't place.

He forgot it as her words struck home.

She wanted him to return to Russia.

"Why, for God's sake?"

"For Russia's sake."

She explained. British Intelligence believed the Germans were secretly preparing to attack Russia. But Stalin, isolated from reality in the Kremlin, trusting no one's judgment but his own, would never believe the British warnings. He had struck his pact with Hitler. Although he knew that one day it would be broken, he didn't think that time was imminent. Any word to the contrary—from the British of all people—would be interpreted as mischief-making.

Stalin was well aware that most clandestine information, and disinformation, filtered through Lisbon. Hard put to distinguish one from the other, he would rely more and more on his instincts unless he found a source he could trust.

"Me?"

She nodded.

"You're crazy."

"Think about it," she said. "Stalin believes he is surrounded by betrayal. With the exception of Svetlana, even his own children have let him down. But throughout all this period of treachery, imagined or otherwise, he has isolated and protected one person. You. Kept away from you so that he didn't antagonize you as he did the other two boys."

Viktor stepped out of the car and sat on a hummock of yellowing grass beneath the sails of the windmill. The whistling seemed louder. He glanced up and noticed clay jugs attached to the ropes of the sails; as they turned they whistled.

He said, "You don't understand why I left Russia." And, when he had told her, he added, "You see why I can't return."

She was quiet and then said, "I know you care for the Russian people, and everything you've said makes me more certain of that."

Viktor looked away at a distant cloud and said nothing. Of course, she knew it, and she was right.

"You can help save them from a holocaust," she added.

"They have one already."

"Not compared with what the Nazis would inflict on them. The Jews to start with . . ."

"Are they all you care about?"

"No," she said. "Humanity."

She plucked a blade of grass and began to chew it. A breeze teased her hair. He could smell the smoke from the fields and dry earth after rain. He wondered how much of what she was telling him was the truth. They said power corrupted, so did intrigue.

The way she had deceived him had honed new instincts in him. He said, "You don't seem to include Germans in humanity."

"I know," she said. "That's something I have to work on. But if you were a Jew and you had seen what I have seen . . ."

"I saw much worse," he said softly.

An aircraft took off from the Sintra airport for Lisbon. A German JU 52 with crosses on its fuselage. Rachel stared at it speculatively, one hand shading her eyes.

She said, "Odd, isn't it, how differently we reacted to what we saw? I wanted revenge, you wanted escape."

"I wanted escape," he said, "so that I could work for peace. Were there so many opportunities for revenge in Washington?"

"I went there to be trained, and you damn well know it," she said.

"And there you would have stayed if it hadn't been for me."

"Don't worry, I would have got away all right despite you." She was silent, breathing quickly, trying to control herself. "The point," she said, "is that we can both do something for humanity. We've been thrown together, we're collaborators—if, that is, you agree to help. . . ."

He lay back and stared into the blue sky. The windmill's sails continued to whistle as she talked.

"I know that you're a pacifist. I can understand that." Forcing herself, he thought. "But what I'm asking you to do doesn't undermine any of your . . . principles. The reverse, in fact. You will be giving your country an opportunity to defend itself—"

"I don't understand Britain's sudden concern for Russia."

"I'm not going to insult your intelligence," she replied. "Britain is concerned about Britain. If Germany wins a runaway victory against the Soviet Union, then she will turn on the British. That's what they care about. But what you must care about is saving your own country."

She was leaning over him, brown eyes staring into his. As she moved closer, he turned his head away. You have betrayed me once, he thought, you could do it again.

She didn't drive straight back to Lisbon. Instead she drove through the little town of Mafra, which Viktor knew because he had put refugees

147

in the monastery there. It was a solid-looking place, built by King João V. According to legend, the king vowed he would build a monastery if God granted him a child, and God obliged with a daughter.

"An impressive-looking building," Rachel said to break their long silence.

"It was designed by a German," Viktor said. "Where the hell are we going?"

"To a mansion."

"I want to get to Lisbon."

"First the mansion."

"Do you mind telling me why?"

"Because," she said.

"I could jump out of the car."

"You could," she agreed pushing her foot down on the accelerator.

He estimated that they were five miles outside Lisbon when she swung the Austin off the road into a long, winding drive burrowing through thick undergrowth.

When he saw the mansion, gray and massive with collonnaded wings, he said, "How did the owner get this pile? Cork or port? Or wolfram, perhaps?" Fortunes were being made selling it to the British and Germans for alloying steel.

"Olive oil," she said.

She pulled up outside portals surmounted by baroque angels. They were welcomed by an elderly, fragile-looking man wearing a blue blazer with a pink-and-gray silk scarf at his neck. Behind him stood Cross, looking healthier than ever beside the old man.

"Good morning, Mr. Hoffman," the old man said in almost perfect English. No one introduced him.

Viktor nodded, ignoring Cross. They walked into a cool marble hall. It reminded him of the foyer of a museum.

"You were very punctual," the old man said.

"Was I? I didn't know." Viktor looked at Rachel.

The old man led them up a broad, curving staircase. At the top was a long landing guarded by suits of armor. Sunlight, colored by a stained-glass window, quivered on the parquet flooring.

They went into a library, its walls lined with books that had an unread look about them. Windows with small, leaded panes looked across lawns as smooth as moss and a dark, deep-looking lake.

A log fire was burning in a grate. In front of it a chair; beyond the chair a pair of slippered feet.

The old man approached the chair. Cross and Rachel Keyser stood behind Viktor.

The old man cleared his throat. It was when the occupant of the chair stood up that Viktor first began to suspect he might be traveling to Moscow. Because who could resist the oratory of Winston Churchill?

12

The following day, Viktor made contact with German Intelligence.

A necessary precaution, Cross said, if Stalin was to be persuaded that he had access to Nazi secrets. At the same time, the Germans would have to be convinced that he was worth recruiting.

"Oh, what a tangled web we weave," Cross said, handing him an envelope. "That's Churchill's itinerary for Lisbon. He's gone now, but it will show how valuable you could be to the Abwehr. Suppose they had known beforehand . . . God forbid!"

Viktor was startled by even this degree of vehemence. It wasn't Cross's style.

Cross caught the look and said, "He's the greatest man to ever walk the earth."

They were walking along the waterfront at Belém, near Cross's apartment. It was a gray day.

"We just barely won the last war," Cross said. "Then the yellow streak in politics—Baldwin, Chamberlain, all that lot—dissipated what we'd won. But Churchill will save us again."

It seemed to Viktor that Cross talked about Churchill the way some Germans talked about Hitler, and he wondered why.

"My father was in the navy," Cross said abruptly. "He knew Winston quite well. Churchill came to our house one day in the late twenties. I had always assumed I would follow in my father's footsteps, and so I would have done if I hadn't gone down with tuberculosis. My father didn't take kindly to it; he seemed to think I'd fallen ill on purpose to disgrace the family. Churchill was quite different. He saw to it that I was examined by a top naval specialist and I was finally cured. Not even Churchill could get me into the navy with a history of tuberculosis, but he got me this job, and he made sure I could play my part."

Viktor realized, at that moment, that Cross was as dangerous as a fanatical, young SS officer consumed by admiration for the Führer.

Half an hour later, Viktor walked down a steep, narrow street, the Rua Joaquim Casimiro, named after a nineteenth-century composer/ organist. The paint on the walls of the tall terrace houses was flaking; the balconies looked as though they had been stuck there with glue. Halfway down he came across two Judas trees, shiny round leaves just falling. Around Easter the branches, still bare of foliage, would be covered with mauve-pink blossoms; blushing with shame, according to legend, because Judas, the apostle who betrayed Christ, had hanged himself on such a tree.

At the bottom of the street which formed a T-junction with a busy road he entered a small café-bar. It was just below the surface of the road, and the rattle of trams was part of the acoustics, like the squawking of a parrot in the corner.

It was midday. A few men in blue work overalls sat at the long bar drinking beer or coffee and brandy. Viktor ordered a Bagaceira, fire-water distilled from the residue of grapes in a cask that has contained whisky, and sat, as instructed, beside a mirror bearing the words VINHOS DE PORTO. As arranged, he carried with him a copy of yesterday's *Diario de Lisboa* opened at the sports page and was smoking a Portuguese Suave cigarette.

Earlier that morning he had telephoned the German Legation and, on Cross's instructions, asked to speak to Fritz von Claus. "If I made the call, he'd smell a rat," Cross had said, from which Viktor had inferred that Cross acted in a dual capacity. An indiscretion? Viktor, with his new awareness, didn't think so; Cross merely wanted to emphasize how frank he was being. Viktor had told von Claus that he had valuable contacts with the British embassy and the Red Cross.

Cross had said that there would be no difficulty in recognizing von Claus. He was short and dark, with a deformed back that was almost a hunch. He was also one of the Abwehr's aces, devoted to Canaris. But, like the admiral, his loyalties to the Third Reich had been sorely strained by the activities, condoned by Hitler, of Himmler and Heydrich and their henchmen.

Viktor waited. Cross had predicted that von Claus would be late. "He'll give you the once-over first. A cautious man, Fritz."

He sipped his drink and coughed and thought about Churchill. He had been softer and pinker than he had expected, but there was no denying his persuasive powers. His words were like hammer blows on a golden gong.

"For the sake of mankind, Mr. Hoffman, I beg you to help us to help the one parent you should never deny." A pause. "Mother Russia, Mr. Hoffman. To accomplish this you must make contact with your other parent . . . Comrade Stalin. He trusts no one except, we believe, you, Mr. Hoffman. If you establish yourself in Lisbon as his link with reality, you will be able to appraise him of Hitler's true intentions. The Führer may abandon the whole shooting match, or he may mount another Blitzkreig; but whatever he decides to do, you will be able to advise Stalin and you will be believed."

"You are fond of sports?"

Viktor glanced up. The man standing beside the table was on the short side, and his back was deformed.

"As a spectator," as arranged.

"Do you mind if I join you?" Von Claus spoke in clipped English.

Viktor gestured to the empty seat opposite him. "A drink?"

Von Claus pointed at Viktor's glass. "Anything but that. It makes schnapps seem like mother's milk. A brandy, I think." He sat down.

While ordering the drink at the long bar, Viktor glanced at the little man sitting at the table. His thin black hair looked as though it had been painted on his scalp; his face bore the erosions of suffering; he was as dapper as a fraudulent nobleman.

When he placed the brandy on the table, von Claus said, "Danke schoen," and the parrot swore in Portuguese.

"A good cover, that bird," von Claus said, touching the brandy with his lips, "you can blame any indiscretion on him. Do you have any indiscretions to make, Herr Hoffman?"

"I thought I'd join what seems to be a growing profession in Lisbon."

"Espionage? Yes, it's very popular. But as in everything else, you only succeed if you have anything worth selling. Do you have anything worth selling?"

Viktor said, "I have access to information."

"Ah, access," as though he had heard that one many times before. "Proof is also a good, saleable commodity."

Viktor took the envelope from his pocket. "Here's the proof. I obtained it since speaking to you this morning. Where's the payment?"

"You're hardly in a position to bargain."

"For dynamite? I think I am. How about ten thousand escudos?"

"You seem very sure of yourself."

"But at this moment you are not. For all you know, this could be details of a new U-boat deterrent."

"And is it?"

"No."

Von Claus said, "Five thousand and hand over that envelope, please. You can't expect any more. Only buyers at de Beers buy unseen." He handed over his copy of *Diario*. "You will find the money in an envelope inside. It's what I had intended to give you."

Viktor shrugged. If nothing else it was the easiest five thousand he had ever earned. A few days ago, he would have spent it on Rachel Keyser; now he would spend it on Viktor Golovin.

Von Claus took the typewritten memorandum from the envelope, while Viktor watched him closely. The hollow features had obviously been trained not to show emotion, but the training failed. The skin on his domed forehead moved, his thin lips compressed.

Von Claus took a decent mouthful of his brandy this time, and then he said, "Am I expected to believe this?"

"You can check it out."

"Now that it's over—if it ever took place? Yes, I suppose I can. But tell me, Herr Hoffman, why do you imagine I would be interested in out-of-date information."

"One, because you were. It was a shock to you. You *should* have known about it. Think of the opportunities, if you had been prepared for a visit by Winston Churchill. Two, because it proves that I do have access to top-secret information. And three, it's quite possible that Churchill will return to Lisbon." He was proud of that one; it was his own brainchild.

"And I thought . . ." Von Claus took a small gold box from his waistcoat pocket and took a pinch of snuff.

I know what you thought. You thought you had all such eventualities covered—by Cross.

Von Claus returned the snuffbox to his pocket. "If you can obtain such good information, why didn't you tell me about Churchill before?"

"Because I didn't know before. But if I had, I wouldn't have parted with it for five thousand escudos. One hundred thousand, perhaps."

"May I ask who your informant at the embassy is?"

"I may be a novice, but I do know that's an improper question."

"Improper?" Von Claus smiled thinly. "That's the first time I've heard that word used in connection with espionage. However, I take your point."

According to Cross, von Claus would assume that the contact was Rachel Keyser. According to Cross, the NKVD would be observing his meeting with von Claus. A tangled web . . .

"First," von Claus said, "I shall check out this information," tapping the memorandum with one frail finger. "If it turns out to be true, then you can take it that we shall accept your services. In future, when you make contact, use the name Best. All subsequent meetings will be here unless you hear to the contrary. If I can't make it, a man named Schneider will meet you. He's easy to recognize; he's got a dueling scar across one cheek."

"Payment?"

"According to value."

"Then," Hoffman said, "you or Schneider had better bring more than five thousand escudos with you next time."

"I should certainly like to know if Churchill intends to return to Lisbon," von Claus said. "But in advance next time."

With an abrupt movement he finished his brandy; he stood up slowly and painfully. "I sincerely hope we meet again, Mr. Best."

As he walked out of the café, the parrot squawked a Portuguese obscenity that made the workmen at the bar smile.

The German Legation on the Rua do Pau da Bandeira was a pink palace. A cobbled drive led up to its doorway; immediately inside was a big echoing hallway; to the right of this a glittering ballroom, which had been likened to the inside of a cube of sugar, where Baron Oswald Hoyningen-Huene, the aged and cultured German minister in Lisbon, threw lavish balls attended by diplomatic representatives of most countries in Lisbon except the British.

In the garden at the rear stood a rubber tree said to have been planted by Vasco da Gama. Underneath the building was a secret passage leading to the minister's residence close by.

A ball was in progress while Otto Bauer, the Lisbon head of the Gestapo, studied a report on von Claus's latest foray for the Abwehr. Himmler's instructions had been blessedly simple: "Accumulate as much evidence as possible to discredit Canaris's organization in the eyes of the Führer."

From the ballroom below came the strains of "The Blue Danube." Bauer didn't dance; he wasn't built for it, and in any case, he preferred distractions of a more intimate nature. In the Chiado he had chanced upon a doorway whore who, for a price, submitted to all sorts of indignities. But he did like Viennese music, and lips pursed, he whistled along with the waltz as he read the agent's report stolen from Abwehr files and copied before being returned.

So von Claus had gone once again to the café at the bottom of the Rua Joaquim Casimiro. Why didn't the man vary his movements? That was the trouble with the old aristocrats, they were too rigid in their outlook. They even confined their instruments of interrogation to rubber truncheons, whereas the Gestapo . . . Bauer, who had once been complimented by Himmler on his ingenuity in this field, took the spittle-soaked butt of his black cigar from his lips and crushed it in the ashtray on his desk.

"Wine, Women, and Song" reached him from the ballroom. He began to whistle, then stopped, attention riveted by a sentence in the report. *In the café subject spent 23 minutes in the company of Josef Hoffman, a Czech Red Cross employee, who, you will recall, has also been under Abwehr surveillance.*

Of course he recalled it. He had learned about it from other documents stolen from Abwehr files. He had considered mounting his own surveillance operation. But what was the point when the Abwehr was doing all the donkey work, and he could read its reports?

His deputy had been surprised by the intensity of his interest in the case; after all it was only routine. But his deputy hadn't been humiliated by a Jewish bitch in a Lisbon elevator. A Jewish bitch who was currently being screwed by this Hoffman.

Now von Claus had entered the picture.

Bauer leaned his bulky body back in his swivel chair and pulled at the lobe of one of his small ears, all his predatory instincts aroused.

Von Claus paying money to a Czech—the agent had seen the usual newspaper change hands—who was consorting with a Jewess. Take it a step further and von Claus was accepting the word of the Jewess because she was obviously Hoffman's source of information.

156

Himmler would like that. Bauer lit another black cigar and inhaled with satisfaction.

But how much better if he could prove that von Claus was being taken for a ride by Fraulein Keyser. It wouldn't be too difficult to portray such naiveté as treachery. Perhaps it was treachery—like Canaris, von Claus wasn't renowned for his pro-Nazi sympathies. Nor for that matter was the minister in Lisbon, which was why Bauer had to maintain a façade of protocol; although in the end, fear of the Gestapo usually prevailed.

Bauer regarded the glowing tip of his cigar. Now that von Claus is personally involved, he thought, I shall have to act. No more of this second-hand surveillance via Abwehr files.

Find out what the hell Hoffman is up to. And perhaps *persuade* the Keyser bitch to come clean. The prospect of such persuasion caused Bauer to become physically aroused.

Downstairs, old Vienna had been abandoned. The orchestra was playing a modern quickstep.

At 7 A.M. the following morning, a man named Müller began to keep watch on the terrace house where Viktor lived. He was a thin, wiry man, prematurely gray, in his late thirties. He was fit except for a persistent cough caused by excessive smoking. Without the cough he would have been a top-class burglar instead of a mere housebreaker employed by the Gestapo to carry out robberies where little risk was involved.

He was insignificant enough as it was, but he went to great pains to make himself even less noticeable. This morning he wore grubby overalls and spectacles, fitted with plain glass, and strolled up and down the street as though looking for an address—he had learned long ago that the observer who remains stationary, as they do in the movies, is the most likely to attract attention.

As he paused outside a shop window filled with cheap jewelry, he remembered the green years in Hamburg when he had aspired to becoming Germany's most renowned cat burglar. What had gone wrong? He coughed; that was what had gone wrong.

The Gestapo had approached him while he was serving his third jail sentence. Cigarettes had been rationed in the prison, and he scarcely coughed at all when the two agents had visited him in his cell. If he had, they would probably have found someone else. As it was, they didn't give him much choice: steal for Himmler or spend the rest of your life in jail, enforcing the threat with a list of burglaries, supplied by the Kripo,

157

which he had carried out. They had then sent him to Lisbon where there was great scope for his talents.

He moved down the street. It was a brisk, sunny morning, and the air smelled of coffee and freshly baked bread. He lit a cigarette, flipping the match into the gutter. In the Largo do Carmo, the owner of the newspaper kiosk was hanging out his wares, *Berliner Morgenpost* to the fore, no doubt, with a good supply of British newspapers bringing up the rear.

Two expensively suited Germans strode past. Wolfram buyers probably. They looked as though they owned the place; perhaps one day they would.

The door of No. 18, where Viktor Golovin lived, opened. Viktor emerged, scarcely paying any attention to the golden day. When he reached the square, a small Fiat that had been parked down the street took off after him. Müller had been told to expect this. Then a Renault took off behind the Fiat. He hadn't been told to expect that, still it was none of his business.

He glanced at his watch. 7:45. Hoffman's landlady went to the market every weekday at 8:30. He relaxed and lit his third cigarette of the morning. Luckily for him she left the house at 8:15.

He gave her three minutes, time enough for her to discover it if she had left her shopping list behind. Then he walked briskly to the rear of the terrace, which he had cased at dawn. The back door was hidden from the rest of the terrace by a high wall. He walked down a short path and tried the door. It was locked, naturally, but the lock was a rudimentary affair. He selected a key from the bunch in the pocket of his overalls and slipped it into the keyhole. He turned the key gently but firmly and the door opened.

The kitchen was the woman. Scrupulously clean, old, and smelling of garlic. The whitewashed hall was cold and dark; like the Spaniards, the Portuguese hid from the sun. The stairs creaked as he climbed them; they always did. There were three doors on the landing. One was closed; that would be the landlady's—women always closed their bedroom doors. He peered into the room next to it. It was piled high with suitcases, books, and papers. The woman's life was in there.

Coughing, he turned and entered Josef Hoffman's room.

Viktor, on his way to the Avenida Palace to learn about codes—from Rachel Keyser of all people—had begun to walk down the steep hill leading from the Largo do Carmo when he realized that he had left his recently earned five thousand escudos in his room. In the Bible.

158

He hesitated. He was late already. So what? Codes could wait, so could she. A woman passed him wearing a familiar perfume. Rachel's perfume. He saw her lying naked on the bed; a knife turned inside him.

He turned and began to retrace his footsteps toward his lodgings.

The trouble was that Müller wasn't *exactly* sure what he was looking for. "Evidence," Bauer had said. But not evidence of what. "Forged documents," he had elaborated. "Ciphers, anything suggesting foreign connections, anything that would incriminate a man—and you would know about that, Müller. Anything Jewish," Bauer had added, pulling at his ear.

Müller went straight to the tin chest under Hoffman's bed. It was locked. A good omen. It took him thirty seconds to pick the lock. The contents smelled musty, not a good sign unless you were looking for a family heirloom. Still, there were plenty of those around in Lisbon these days, the refugees' passports to escape. Perhaps Hoffman had brought some diamonds from Prague. Müller brightened; he had been given permission to steal anything within reason to make his thefts seem like run-of-the-mill burglaries.

But first, *evidence.*

With meticulous care he began to examine Viktor's life, his soul.

The documents were at the bottom of the chest in a blue cardboard folder. Most of them were in a foreign language, Czech or Slovak he presumed. There, too, were his Red Cross papers, passport, and a photograph of a beautiful girl, Jewish by the look of her. Müller laid all these things on the bed and, with a miniature Leica, photographed them.

The last paper contained handwritten notes, which appeared to refer to some sort of journey. Surely if they were incriminating, Hoffman would have destroyed them. But with amateurs you never knew. Frowning, Müller photographed them.

Viktor slid his key into the lock in the front door. The door opened with a faint sigh. He closed it behind him and walked across the hallway toward the staircase.

Foot on the first step, he stopped. Someone had coughed. Was it out on the street? He froze. Another cough. From upstairs, no doubt about it.

Surely no one would bother to rob his landlady. Or him for that matter. Unless the Germans or the Russians had decided to extend surveillance to intrusion.

Stealthily, he climbed the staircase, pausing as a step halfway up creaked. Another cough. From my room!

He took the last stairs in two strides.

The gray-haired man in overalls was just closing the lid of the tin chest. Even by opening it, he had desecrated it.

The man looked startled but not scared. His eyes took in Viktor, focused on the open door behind him.

"No," Viktor said. He kicked the door shut. "Who are you? What do you want?"

"Nothing here," the man said calmly in bad German-accented English. "You haven't got anything. It was the cough, I suppose?"

Viktor walked toward him, fists clenched. They were separated by the bed. "I don't have much, but it's mine. What have you stolen?"

"Not a thing. Search me if you like," one hand instinctively searching for his cigarettes.

"I'm not that stupid."

"Have you got a match?"

"I'm not that stupid either." Viktor edged around the bed. "Why have you got a camera?"

"If you really want to know," the man said, "it's to cripple cunts like you with," as he swung the small camera on its strap at Viktor's head.

The camera hit Viktor just below the eye. Metal struck bone, and pain leaped through his head. The eye closed at once.

But he was on the intruder. They fought quietly and intensely. Viktor was younger and stronger, but his opponent was a street fighter: lithe, deceptively strong and dirty. Viktor hit him on the side of the jaw with his fist, and the man fell against a wall mirror, splintering it. When he got up he was holding a shard of glass like a dagger in his gloved hand. Viktor backed away. The intruder waved the glass knife at him. "Get out of the way, prick." Viktor backed farther away, then swiftly, he bent and tipped the bed toward the man. The dagger fell to the floor, breaking into a hundred smaller daggers. The man was breathing hard; youth over age, Viktor thought. "The camera," Viktor said, "give it to me."

"Come and get it," the man said. With one foot he pushed the bed toward Viktor. Viktor rounded the bed, closed in. "It's almost over," he thought—as the man leaped through the open window.

Viktor leaped forward. He expected to see the man spread-eagled on the sidewalk. All he saw through his one good eye was a woman lying on the cobbles, water spilling from the cask she had been carrying and, already well on his way toward the Largo do Carmo, the fleeing figure of the intruder.

Bauer gazed thoughtfully at the photographs of Hoffman's documents. In particular, at the handwritten notes. A few place names together with times.

So Hoffman was going places. But where? The trouble with the notes was that they were written in different languages. Portuguese, English, and Czech or Slovak. Madrid, Geneva . . . it looked like Red Cross business. Disappointing. He frowned at the last place name; it was almost illegible.

He sent for one of the translators on the legation's eight-hundred-strong staff.

The translator looked at the word. "Moskva," he said crisply. And when Bauer looked puzzled, "Moscow."

"Is it written in Czech or Slovak?"

"It's written in Russian," the translator said.

Cross reacted vigorously to the news that Viktor had been burglarized. "We'll have to move even quicker than we thought," he said standing at the window of his living room. "If the Germans know you're going to Russia, they'll want to know why. And they won't be choosy how they find out."

"But I'm working for the Abwehr."

"But not for the Gestapo," Cross said briskly. He sat down in the chair in which he had sat the first night Viktor had met him and opened his briefcase. "Here are some more documents for you. They should get you to Moscow. After all you do work for the International Red Cross."

"When am I going?" Viktor asked.

"Tonight," Cross said.

In his office on Prinz Albrechtstrasse in Berlin, Heinrich Himmler, head of the Waffen SS and all Nazi security organizations except the Abwehr, considered Bauer's cabled report.

He had issued orders that anything that could be construed as Abwehr disloyalty to the Führer should be referred immediately to him. Bauer's decoded cable, sent from Lisbon the previous night, had been on his desk at 8:30 that morning.

A Slav coupling with a Jewess—that was disgusting enough. What sort of child would two such subhumans produce? pondered the Reichs-führer, who was small and unprepossessing and wore steel-rimmed spectacles to correct his nearsightedness.

Disgusting, yes, but there were times when he had to control his loathing of such vermin in the interest of logical calculation. Such a time was now.

Bauer's report was only a strand in the evidence Himmler was accumulating against Canaris and his Abwehr, the so-called intelligence service of the generals, many of whom were disloyal to the Führer. But slowly and with infinite patience he was weaving a web with each strand.

So what do we have here?

A Czech working for the Red Cross in contact with a Jewess employed at the British embassy in Lisbon. A Czech who then offered his services to the Abwehr. So, indirectly, the Abwehr was using a Jewess. What more could you expect from a hunchback like von Claus?

But what was far more interesting was the journey on which Hoffman was embarking immediately after making contact with von Claus. Moscow. Why would a Czech Red Cross worker, in touch with both British and German Intelligence, suddenly decide to travel to Russia? Not on Red Cross business, according to Bauer, who had checked.

Why?

Himmler took off his spectacles, rubbed the bridge of his nose where the frame had left a red mark, and stared myopically at an oil painting of Hitler hanging on the wall.

It was almost as if this Hoffman had made his play with the Abwehr to prove something. To prove that he had access to German secrets. To prove it to the Russians. . . .

Himmler snapped his fingers.

Suppose Hoffman *did* have such access. Suppose von Claus was a traitor. Suppose he had told Hoffman about the Führer's plans to invade the Soviet Union.

Himmler replaced his spectacles, picked up a telephone, and told the operator to put him through to Communications. The cable he dictated to be encoded and sent to Bauer top priority, top secret, was brief: STOP HOFFMAN AND INTERROGATE.

What would I do, Bauer deliberated, if I were organizing Hoffman's journey to Moscow?

First, knowing that the notes for the trip had been copied, I would change the times. In particular, the departure flight. I would dispatch him sooner, Bauer thought. Much sooner. In fact, I would put him on an aircraft tonight.

Bauer consulted a timetable. There was a Tráñco Aéro Español flight to Madrid at 2135 hours.

That's the flight I'd put him on, Bauer decided.

He picked up the telephone and told his deputy to change the mode of surveillance on Hoffman. The battered old Mercedes-Benz with the souped-up engine instead of the small Fiat, because by now Hoffman had probably identified his shadow.

If Hoffman didn't try to catch the flight at 2135 hours, no harm was done. If he did, they would take him on the stretch of road bordered by thick woods five miles from Sintra airport.

"Why you?"

Viktor stared in astonishment at Rachel Keyser sitting at the wheel of a gray Morris 8.

"Only Cross and I are involved. He seemed to think I was the better driver."

Viktor glanced up and down the darkened street outside his lodgings. There was no sign of the black Citröen; a taxi was parked down the street and beyond it a battered Mercedes-Benz.

Rachel drove out of the maze of small streets and accelerated up the broad, well-lit reaches of the Avenida da Liberdade.

She said, "We'll have to work on the codes when you get back."

"Very businesslike," he said.

"One other thing. You'll have to produce a convincing story when Stalin asks you how you found out you were his son. And why you suddenly decided to return."

"I've thought about it," Viktor told her as the Morris rounded the Parque Eduardo VII. "It isn't difficult. I'll tell him I always suspected he was my father. That I overheard a conversation between my parents and that seemed to tie up with the privileges we enjoyed . . . But I was too scared to do anything about it. After all, if Stalin didn't want it out in the open, who was I to interfere?"

"But what will you say clinched it?" Rachel asked.

"Nothing clinched it. When I reach the Kremlin, I still won't be sure."

163

"Then why will you say you've returned? And, come to that, why did you leave in the first place?"

"That's the easiest part," Viktor said, "if you understand the Russian mentality. I left because I was disgusted by the atrocities being committed. I returned because I heard rumors that the Germans were planning to invade. Country over conscience. Very Russian. And I felt I had to warn him whether he was my father or not."

Rachel swung the wheel. The Morris passed the flaring oil lamps of a shanty settlement and bored into the darkness of the countryside. In the driving mirror she saw the flash of headlights behind her. She drove faster.

"We had something more elaborate cooked up for you," she said.

"Leave it to me," Viktor said brusquely. "I know what I'm doing."

"You think I don't understand how you feel, don't you?"

Viktor didn't reply. Their whole relationship had been a lie from the start; he wondered if it still was. He wanted to reach out and touch her, to feel her warmth. But to hell with it. Not now or ever. Even a peasant—the grandson of a Georgian cobbler!—had his pride.

The headlights swooped past. Taillights glowed for a moment or so before disappearing around a bend in the road.

The night was starless; the forest on either side of the road part of the night.

The light flashing in the middle of the road came as a shock.

Rachel braked sharply. The Morris stopped to one side of the road within a few feet of the light.

Rachel wound down the window and said to the man holding the flashlight, "What's wrong?" When she saw the pistol, she tried to drive away, but by that time, he had yanked the driving keys out of the lock. "Get out," he said in German-accented English, leveling the gun at her head. And to Viktor, "You too, but don't try anything, otherwise she gets it." He switched off the headlights.

Rachel climbed out of the car.

"Hands behind your head. That's right. Be good and you don't get hurt. And you," waving the pistol at Viktor. "And forget any two-against-one stuff because there are two guns trained on you over there." In the darkness, Viktor could just see the outline of the battered Mercedes-Benz.

The flashlight, he decided, was his target. One kick and they'd all be in darkness. The old Viktor would have reasoned, "But Rachel might get hurt." The new one thought, "Rachel might get hurt but that's a risk I've got to take."

He took one step toward the man holding the light.

The man said, "Now both of you get in the back of the Mercedes."

Viktor was about to kick when the first shot rang out. He thought for a split second that he *had,* because the flashlight exploded in the man's hand. Then there was only darkness.

"Get down!" he shouted to Rachel.

They waited for another shot. Nothing.

The Germans were shouting at each other.

A body hit Viktor, hands searching for his throat. Viktor brought up his knee sharply. Felt it sink into a crotch. The man screamed out in agony.

Viktor kneed him again in the same place. The man vomited.

In the Mercedes another light flared, weaker than the flashlight but dangerous enough. Its beam sliced through the darkness and found Rachel's face. Viktor flung himself between her and the ray of light.

Another shot.

The light disappeared as though it had been switched off and the bullet ricocheted off the bodywork.

Viktor rolled toward the grass shoulder, taking Rachel with him.

Across the road a bullet must have hit one of the Mercedes's rear wheels; the tire sighed and the silhouette of the car sank to one side.

Viktor thought, "It must be the Abwehr—or the NKVD perhaps." He whispered, "Let's get into the forest."

But suddenly they were illuminated as though by a spotlight. Viktor, Rachel, and the three Germans. For a moment they were frozen like insects under an uplifted stone.

Viktor looked behind him. Someone had switched on the Morris's headlights.

Crouching, he ran for the trees—as the gun fired again.

The man who had attacked Viktor reared up and fell back, blood pumping from his chest, bright red in the glare of the headlights.

Another shot hit one of the occupants of the Mercedes. The door swung open and he fell onto the ground.

But the third occupant had reached the car and was firing back. His first bullet doused one of the Morris's headlamps.

They heard running footsteps. A shuffling behind the Mercedes. Another shot. The sound of blows. A snap as though a bone had broken. A final scream.

"Come on," Cross said, breathing heavily, "get in the MG, we haven't much time."

Ahead they could see the lights of the airport.

The night rushed at Viktor, and Rachel squeezed into the passenger seat of the MG beside Cross. Cross had to shout to make himself heard.

"Bauer's smart. I knew he'd try to stop you leaving; I also thought he would guess you'd make a dash for it tonight. So I followed you."

"What about the bodies?" Rachel pointed behind her.

"Armed robbery . . . the Germans won't make a fuss. Three armed Gestapo thugs in nice, neutral Portugal? It's the last sort of publicity they want. As for the Morris—it hit the Mercedes, and you, Rachel, hitched a lift to the airport."

Rachel was conscious of Viktor's body pressed against her. She wanted to kiss him fiercely.

The MG slowed down and Cross said, "Here we are, the runway to freedom. Don't ask questions, just follow me."

The small departure and arrival lounge bore the legends Aero Portuguese, Tránco Aéro Español, Deutsche Lufthansa, British Airways, and Ala Littoria. Outside in the floodlights, they could see a German three-engined Junkers 52 and a British De Havilland Flamingo standing beside it.

Refugees swarming around them bargaining, cajoling, threatening for seats on the British Airways aircraft and planes from any other friendly countries that might have landed. The British, Germans, and Italians flew mostly by night to avoid confrontations in the air. They all wanted to use Lisbon, and none of them wanted to spoil the unwritten agreement that they didn't molest each other.

Cross said to Viktor, "Get out your Red Cross papers."

"The Red Cross don't even know I'm leaving," Viktor said.

"They do; Bauer told them. But that doesn't matter. Just show your papers."

A plump refugee with two diamond rings on his fingers saw the papers and thrust a wad of escudos at Viktor. Viktor thrust him aside.

Cross led the way through emigration with his diplomatic passport; Rachel followed with hers; Viktor brought up the rear with his Czech passport and documents from Geneva.

"This way," Cross said, pushing through the throng of passengers waiting in a bare-walled room on the other side of the desks. Outside a group of passengers was striding across the tarmac toward a Berlin-bound Junkers.

Cross led Rachel and Viktor to a door at the side of the room; he took a key from his pocket and opened it. "The Gestapo will presume you're on the Tráñco Aéro Español flight," he said, handing the key and a wad of escudo bills to an airport policeman on the other side of the door. "Let's surprise the bastards."

From behind the squat airport buildings they heard shouting and the squeal of tires. "Cops," Cross said. "Looking for armed gangsters. We'd better get the hell out of here."

He began to run toward a DC-3 standing in the penumbra of the floodlights. It bore the colors of a Portuguese charter company. As they approached, one engine fired, then the other. The slipstream hit them, pressing their clothes against their bodies.

"It's all fixed with control," Cross shouted. "There shouldn't be any hitch; I paid them enough. And we'll be okay with our diplomatic passports."

At the foot of the boarding steps, Viktor hesitated.

Rachel stared at him. A wave, a smile, a hint of understanding. . . . Anything, please.

Cross said, "For Christ's sake move, here come the police."

Viktor turned and ran up the stairs.

The door closed behind him, Cross pulled the steps away, and almost immediately the DC-3 began to taxi forward.

Rachel thought she saw his face at one of the windows, but she couldn't be sure.

The aircraft reached the end of the runway, accelerated, and climbed into the night.

Rachel waved. "Good luck," she called out.

Cross looked at her quizzically. "You make it sound as if you're both aiming for the same goal," he said. "You haven't forgotten that we're betraying him, have you? That when he's ready to warn Stalin that Hitler's going to attack, we're going to make damn sure the opposite message is sent in his name?"

"No," she said through her tears, "I haven't forgotten."

PART FOUR

13

In the dining room of his modest home in the Kremlin, Josef Stalin watched, absorbed, while a man named Zalutsky tasted his food and wine.

One of these days, Stalin thought, the plump, blotchy-faced Ukrainian would fall down dead on the floor. An appropriate fate for a suspected Trotskyite who was alive today only because it intrigued him to force a traitor to intercept poison.

What thoughts were going through his mind just now, as with trembling hand he raised a glass of red Georgian wine to his lips?

Stalin watched the glass all the way to Zalutsky's mouth. A sip, no more. Did he intend to keep it in his mouth and, with his back turned, spit it back into the glass? "Drain it," Stalin commanded.

While Zalutsky finished off the wine and turned his attention to the roast suckling pig, Stalin began to doodle on a coarse-grained sheet of notepaper. He drew a sharp-fanged wolf; the animal joined a pack of wolves that he had already created.

If Zalutsky fell to the floor one day, clawing at his throat, whom would he hold responsible? Regrettably there would be many candidates. Just as he had done in the past, he would liquidate them all. It was the most effective way of dealing with intrigue.

The pencil broke on the fangs of another wolf, and he said to Zalutsky, "Try a little more of that pig." In a perverse way, it would give him satisfaction if the Ukrainian did collapse.

Throughout his career, daggers had been raised behind his back. By Czarist *agents provocateurs* in prison camps, by Mensheviks in the

Revolution, by White Russian agents in the civil war, by Trotsky and other careerists after Lenin's death in 1924. But he had blunted, he had broken, he had averted all their knives.

"The Revolution is incapable either of regretting or burying its dead"—Josef Stalin, 1917. And just as true today.

"Now the potatoes," he said to Zalutsky, darkening the wolf's face with the broken lead of the pencil.

Whom had he trusted during his life? The heads didn't take long to count. His mother, who had wanted him to be a village priest—but had been proud of him when he became what he was; his first wife, Ekaterina, he supposed, who had died in 1907; certainly not his second wife, Nadya, the dark-eyed quicksilver revolutionary who had turned on him before her death in 1932; a handful of stalwarts such as Molotov.

As for his legitimate children—Jacob was an introverted washout and Vassily, although a pilot, was a drunken braggart. Svetlana, his red-haired, teenage daughter, was his darling, but she was a girl, which left:
Viktor.

Only that morning he had received news about the son of the girl he had loved more than twenty years ago. (She hadn't betrayed him—she had died in childbirth.)

He went to the window and stared at the Kremlin. Despite its bloody history, from primitive fort, to palace, to shrine of communism, it was a glorious place. Particularly on such a day as this, with its gold cupolas riding high in the bright sky, the first snow of the winter scattered on its lawns.

But in a way its glories made him uneasy. They weren't intended for a cobbler's son, nor for a Bolshevik, which was why he had kept his home as unprepossessing as possible.

He thought Viktor would have liked such a home. And the view of the Kremlin's baubles, of course.

He remembered the vow he had made to the boy's mother.

He turned around. Zalutsky had poured him a glass of wine. He picked it up and threw the contents in the Ukrainian's face. "Now get out!" he shouted.

Perhaps Zalutsky was poisoning the food after he had tasted it. Stalin swept the food off the table. Perhaps after all Zalutsky would have to be executed.

That vow.

Who would have believed that he, who, of necessity, used promises and pacts as utensils, would have honored it?

172

But honor it he had.

"Don't let him be tainted," she had said. "Keep him apart from it all. Do you promise, Josef?"

"I promise," he had replied, and she had smiled and died, nineteen years of age, in a bed in Leningrad.

Not that his motives for keeping his word had been purely selfless. He wanted one son who would grow up straight and tall, one boy whom he could trust from afar.

Even when Viktor had fled to Switzerland and then to Portugal he hadn't been too alarmed. Like his mother, whom he resembled in so many ways, he was headstrong. At university he must have been exposed to subversive elements. He had wanted to make up his own mind about values.

One day he would return. Perhaps even now; according to the NKVD report he received that morning, Viktor had left Lisbon for Madrid.

Stalin stuffed a pipe with his favorite tobacco from Jusuri, in Georgia, and lit it. Trailing a cloud of blue smoke, he sat at his desk in the book-lined room. On the desk were photographs of Svetlana and his mother, Keke, the only woman he had ever revered, apart from Viktor's mother.

Then he turned his attention to another promise, one of the more common variety, one that neither signatory had the slightest intention of keeping.

The problem was, Just when did Hitler intend to break the treaty of friendship signed in September last year?

Not for a long time, in Stalin's opinion. Hitler was quite mad, but not mad enough to expose his armies on two fronts.

To assess the intentions of the world's leaders, Stalin invariably applied his own standards. For instance, he understood perfectly well why Britain and France had allowed Germany, a beaten force in 1918, to rearm: they wanted the armaments to be turned against the Soviet Union.

That was why he was skeptical about warnings that Germany was considering attacking the Soviet Union. The warnings all came from interested parties, in particular Britain through their new ambassador in Moscow, Sir Stafford Cripps. They wanted to turn him against Hitler and make him go to war.

Well, Churchill wouldn't succeed with that ploy: it was too obvious.

And yet Hitler *had* moved his troops into Romania and Finland, thereby breaking promises.

And Richard Sorge, Russia's spymaster in Tokyo, *had* warned that Hitler was planning an invasion.

But lately Sorge's information had been suspect.

Stalin sat at his desk and slowly puffed his pipe. There was no one on this earth whom he could trust.

14

With Red Cross credentials it was relatively easy to travel across Europe.

From Madrid, Viktor took an Ala Littoria flight to Rome, which refueled in Sardinia. From Rome, he flew northeast to Vienna; from there he took a train through Czechoslovakia into Poland. Then he would cross the River Bug, going from the German-occupied sector near Warsaw into the Russian-occupied sector. With the forged documents he possessed identifying him as an NKVD officer, he wouldn't have any difficulty in reaching Moscow.

Viktor would probably have reached his destination with ease if a diligent Gestapo officer, acting on instructions from Berlin, hadn't spotted him changing trains on the Czech-Polish border.

The train was halted in a suburb of Warsaw, which was still lying in ruins after the German blitzkreig the previous year. The passengers in Viktor's compartment—a teenage German soldier, an old woman in black carrying a stinking cheese, a pretty girl in her twenties who had been crying a lot recently, and a sweating, middle-aged man—glanced nervously at each other.

The sliding doors were pulled open. In the corridor stood two men in civilian clothes. One looked plump and jolly, the other, wearing a black leather coat, had dissipated features and pouched eyes.

The man in the leather coat went directly to Viktor. "Your papers, please," he said in German.

"I represent the International Red Cross—"

"Papers," holding out his hand.

Viktor unzipped his canvas bag. His Red Cross documents and passport lay on top of his clothes and toilet bag; forged Russian papers were sewn into the lining of his overcoat. "Hardly subtle," Cross had said, "but where else?"

The man in the leather coat scanned them with minimal interest, thrust them into his coat pocket, and said, "You will come with us."

"But—"

The man leaned forward and grasped Viktor's arm. "Come."

The other passengers looked away. Viktor sensed their relief that it was he, not they; he couldn't blame them.

Shrugging, he picked up his bag and followed the two men along the corridor and onto the platform of a small, bombed-out railway station. "I want to know who you are and what authority you have to detain me," he said, as the train moved away.

The second man laughed hugely. "Authority? God in heaven, Kurt, they'll be asking to see our birth certificates next." It was then, to his surprise, that Viktor realized that this plump, jolly man, not his companion, the archetypal Gestapo sadist in a black leather coat, was in charge; he looked more like a dairy farmer than a secret policeman. "Now come along with us, like a good fellow, and stop asking questions, because that's our job," the jolly man said.

A gray Packard stood incongruously outside what was left of the station. It looked like a gangster's car. "It belonged to a Jewish businessman," the jolly man explained. "My name, by the way, is Lieber, and this is Adler, and that's really all you need to know about us." He smiled conspiratorially.

Adler got behind the wheel; Lieber sat beside Viktor in the back. Adler drove away from Warsaw into the countryside, which was powdered with snow. Viktor considered trying to escape, but it was hopeless—he would be gunned down as he fell onto the road. He would just have to bluff it out or escape later.

They took him to a village hall. The village itself seemed deserted, except for a couple of dogs and an old man in a black cloth cap standing beside a burned-out cottage.

The hall smelled of antiseptic and, faintly, excreta. There was a platform at one end facing rows of wooden chairs. Posters depicting German soldiers being welcomed by grateful Poles hung from the walls.

Two trestle tables, flanked by electrical units of some kind, stood between the platform and the chairs. Leather thongs hung from the tables, and there were stains on the floor that might have been blood.

Lieber led the way backstage. In the wings stood a few rudimentary stage props. What looked as if it might have been a Canadian Mountie's uniform lay in a dusty heap, above it a cardboard cutout of a snow-capped mountain.

"Rose Marie, if I'm not mistaken," Lieber remarked. "'Dead or alive, then we're out to get you dead or alive,' or something like that." He began to hum softly to himself. He pulled a rope and the moth-eaten red curtains closed, isolating them from the rest of the hall. "That's better," he said. "Now we can get down to business. What are you doing in Poland, Herr Hoffman?"

"I'm on Red Cross business, as you'll shortly find out."

"Not according to the Red Cross," Lieber said pleasantly. "Try again. We called Geneva. They called Portugal. You should have been at work in Lisbon today, Herr Hoffman."

From the other side of the curtain Viktor heard the tramping of feet, a rubbery sound as though the people entering the hall were barefoot.

He said, "It was a secret mission. Negotiating the transfer of Poles caught in the Russian sector."

"It's a funny thing," Lieber said cheerfully, "but in the propaganda films made by our enemies, the senior Gestapo officer is always depicted ordering his subordinate to soften up a prisoner. Not here," hitting Hoffman on the side of the face with the back of his hand, so that he fell against the cardboard mountain. "Not by any manner of means," kicking Hoffman just below the ribs, making him retch. "Not that Adler wouldn't like to flex his muscles, of course, and so he will, shortly, if you don't cooperate. Adler is much more refined than me. He is a talented specialist." He leaned closer and said, "What are you doing in Poland, Herr Hoffman?"

"I told you. Check with Geneva again."

"What made you join the Red Cross, Hoffman?"

"To help mankind."

"It's *you* that needs help now. Are you a pacifist?"

Viktor stood up. "When I meet people like you, yes."

"Heroics," Lieber said, "bring out the worst in Adler." He chuckled and consulted a notebook. "Five days ago you met an Abwehr agent named von Claus in Lisbon and gave him certain information."

From the other side of the curtain Hoffman heard a volley of commands. "What's happening out there?" he asked.

"You later made contact with the British agent Rachel Keyser, whom you already knew."

More commands in Polish.

"Then your room was burgled."

The sound of leather hitting flesh.

"Almost immediately you were driven to Sintra airport."

The blows stopped. They were followed by screams, two sets of them.

Viktor moved toward the curtains, but Adler kicked his feet from under him. Adler lit a cigarette.

Viktor said, "The Red Cross will hear about this."

More screams.

"You were in a great hurry to leave Portugal, were you not, Herr Hoffman?"

Silence. Adler peeped through the curtains like an actor checking the mood of an audience.

"You took off on a chartered DC-3 instead of the scheduled flight mentioned in your notes. In fact your whole itinerary was changed—"

The screams began again.

Viktor, still on the floor, tensed himself to leap at Lieber, but Lieber said, "I wouldn't if I were you—Adler's got a gun pointed at the back of your head."

Viktor turned. He had.

"And Poland wasn't your final destination, was it, Herr Hoffman?"

The screams stopped again. The silence that ensued was more chilling because it was a dead silence.

"You were going to Russia. Where are your Russian documents?"

"I haven't got any Russian documents."

"The documents authorizing you to negotiate the return of Poles to the German sector then."

"There aren't any. Geneva cabled the Russians in their sector."

"Search him, Adler. Linings first."

Adler found the NKVD papers within a minute.

Lieber was enormously amused. "Secret policeman meets secret policeman, eh? Now surely, Herr Hoffman, the game is up, as they say. Why were you going to the Soviet Union?"

"You'll have to ask the Abwehr," Viktor said.

"I'm asking you," Lieber said. He pulled the rope and the curtains parted a little. "Odd, isn't it, standing on the stage and watching the show in the stalls."

At the far end of the hall a group of naked men were being held at gunpoint by two SS Rottenführers armed with machine pistols.

Two other prisoners were strapped, naked, on the trestle tables. Beside each stood a man in plainclothes holding twin, rubber-handled electrodes. The men looked questioningly at Lieber, who nodded.

The electrodes were placed on the prisoners' genitals.

"A bit like electrocardiograms, aren't they?" Lieber remarked.

The operator nearest the platform flicked a switch. The naked body on the table bucked against the leather straps. His scream filled the hall.

Lieber nodded to the second operator. This time the prisoner bucked so violently that a strap broke and his back arched unnaturally. The operator cut the current and examined the broken strap with astonishment.

"They, too, refused to answer questions," Lieber said. "But I'm afraid these operators are amateurs, unlike Adler." He came a step closer to Viktor, put a hand on his arm, and said with a smile, "Why were you going to Russia, Herr Hoffman?"

"I told you."

Lieber sighed. "Very well, one last show before Adler gets to work. Come backstage again, Herr Hoffman." Adler prodded the pistol into Viktor's back.

Lieber pointed through a window. "These men, too, have been led by their ignorance into a difficult situation."

Viktor saw a dozen poorly dressed Poles lined up against a brick wall. They had their hands behind their heads. The German firing squad stood twenty feet in front of them.

So here he was, in a theater once again. He closed his eyes. He heard the shots outside the village hall. Then Lieber was shouting, the jollity quite gone from his voice.

Viktor opened his eyes. Through the window he saw the bodies lying on the ground, but they were the bodies of the firing squad. And all was confusion. Shots, shouts, running figures . . .

Adler was staring through the window. Viktor chopped at his forearm with his fist; the pistol clattered onto the floorboards. He snatched it up as Lieber went for his own gun. Viktor shot him in the chest and turned the gun on Adler.

"Turn around," he snapped. As Adler did so, he hit him on the side of the head with the butt of the pistol. He heard bone crack. Adler slumped to the floor beside Lieber.

Viktor felt full of a wild exhilaration. He ran to the curtains and, peering through an opening, saw the two guards, SS emblems on their steel helmets, waving their machine pistols at the group of naked men. The guards looked confused and dangerous.

One of the prisoners on the tables was turning his head from side to side. The one who had broken the strap was lying still.

From the group came a shout in Polish: "They've come to free us. Let's get these bastards."

The guards tensed themselves to shoot. Viktor took out the sentry on the right first, resting Adler's pistol on his left forearm. Despite the wildness inside him he was quite methodical. He lined up the sights on the guard's cheek and squeezed the trigger.

No neat hole. The man's face seemed to fall apart.

The second guard spun around, firing at the curtain. The bullets cut a line of holes above Viktor's head as he hurled himself to one side, falling beside the Mountie's red uniform.

The shooting stopped suddenly, and the noise that followed was sickening. Viktor looked through the curtains. The prisoners had swarmed over the second guard while he was shooting at the stage.

Viktor jumped off the stage and released the man strapped to the first table. The prisoner on the second table was dead.

At the end of the hall most of the guard's clothes had been ripped off, and naked feet were thudding into his face, belly, and crotch. His eyes, between slits in swollen flesh, were still alive.

"Stop it!" Viktor shouted. "Don't be like them."

One of the avengers looked up. "Was it you who shot the other bastard?"

He nodded.

"Nice shooting. Why don't you come and help finish this shit off." There was no point. Someone was beating the man on the head with a chair leg, and Viktor doubted that the eyes, which he could not see anymore, were still alive.

The door burst open and half a dozen men brandishing handguns stepped in. They wore winter clothes and boots. They were unshaven, and their faces, polished by the cold, had a starved look about them.

One of them fired a bullet through the roof. "Get your clothes!" he shouted to the naked men. "We haven't got much time—German reinforcements are on their way. Get dressed and follow us. And who might you be?" he asked Viktor as the Poles left the guard's twitching body.

Viktor told him he was from the Red Cross.

"With a gun?"

"He saved us," said a bearded man emerging from an anteroom carrying a bundle of clothes.

While the naked men dressed, the Pole who had fired the shot through the roof went to the door and peered up and down the street. He was powerfully built and completely bald. Viktor gathered that his name was Kepa.

He joined him. "What happens now?"

Kepa lit a cigarette. "What always happens. We split and go underground. We don't win battles, but we kill Germans and that makes it all worthwhile. I suppose you wouldn't understand that, Mr. Red Cross."

"My name is Josef Hoffman," Viktor said, "and I've just killed two men."

"Only two? You don't graduate here until you kill twenty."

"Can I come with you?"

"All right," Kepa said, taking a deep drag on the cigarette. "You're a temporary paid-up member. Stay with me and leave your ideals behind, we can do without them."

The blue had gone from the sky, and it was beginning to snow. The survivors were dressed now. Viktor collected his bag and his forged documents lying on the floor beside the body of Lieber. Adler was sitting up, hand to his shattered cheek, but his eyes were not focusing. Perhaps he deserves to die, Viktor thought, but I won't kill him.

He went out of the building. The partisans were fanning out, keeping close to the cottages. The clock on the church had stopped at 2:50.

"That's when the Krauts came," Kepa said, pointing. "That's when they killed my wife and little boy."

Just as they reached the end of the main street a machine gun opened up.

The burst was long and effective. Partisans and survivors from the hall leaped and fell as the bullets cut through them. Viktor and Kepa took cover behind the wall of a kitchen yard. A black cat, back arched, spat at them; behind them the curtains of the kitchen moved as though someone was peering through them.

The shooting stopped, then started up again, bullets hammering the wall.

Kepa, massaging his shining scalp, said, "There's only one way—get behind them. Have you ever used a grenade, Mr. Red Cross?"

"I'd never used a gun before."

"But you used it well. Survival is a great leveler. Would you have guessed that I was a schoolmaster?" He handed over a grenade; Viktor felt its cubed surface. "It's an old one," Kepa said. "A British Mills bomb, part of the Polish army's defenses! It might explode and it might not. We've only got two and I've got the other. We'll take them from different sides."

Kepa showed him how to take the pin out of the grenade. "Count to three and throw it, like this," making a lobbing movement from behind his back. "Make it four if you feel like it but not less than two; that way they throw them back at you. If they turn the gun on you, prepare to meet your maker—if he wants to see you anymore—that's an MG 42 they've got over there and it can fire twelve hundred rounds a minute."

As he spoke the gun shattered a window in the cottage behind them. Close by, a man screamed. The cat sat down and watched them warily.

Snow was falling faster. "Our cover," Kepa said. "You go that way," pointing to an orchard of bare-branched fruit trees ahead. "I'll go this way," ducking around the end of the wall.

The firing stopped again. Through a gap in the stone wall Viktor saw Kepa make a crouching run across the street. He heard shouts in German. The gun coughed into life; plumes of dust followed Kepa as he leaped over a leaning wooden fence and disappeared.

The gunner stopped firing and Viktor took off into the orchard, dodging between the squat trees, veiled by the falling snow, holding the grenade tightly in one hand, hoping that Kepa would reach the machine-gun position first.

From the village he heard sporadic shooting as the partisans fired small arms at the machine gunners.

He stopped at the end of the orchard and peered through the snow toward the village. The street on the other side of the wall had become a rutted track, frozen and gray, climbing toward a small hill. At the point where it linked up with the cobbled road through the village Viktor could just make out the machine gun. It was manned by three soldiers wearing camouflaged battle dress and steel helmets. The gunner was lying down, peering through the sights; one of the other soldiers was looking through a pair of field glasses; the third was opening an ammunition box.

Viktor had run farther than he thought, the wall around the orchard hiding him from the gunners. Now he had to retrace his footsteps, creep up behind the wall and . . . Where are you, Kepa, where are you?

Crouching, he reached the wall, but it was in a bad state of repair, with ragged gaps every ten feet or so. He moved forward carefully, still hoping that Kepa would get there first; Viktor Golovin, peacemaker, with a lethal egg in his hand. Wasn't it self-deception to take your time so that another man could kill them? Wasn't it better to kill these three men quickly before they murdered more partisans cowering in the street? But perhaps the three German soldiers had lived in a village such as this, and surely they had letters from parents and lovers in their pockets . . .

A breeze sprang up and blew the falling snow into his face. He wiped it from his eyes and tripped over a flint that had fallen from the wall. The grenade slipped from his grasp and dropped through a gap in the wall onto the track.

He heard one of the soldiers call out. He waited for the sound of running feet. For a shot. Nothing. He raised his head. The grenade was lying in the middle of the lane.

Where are you, Kepa?

Viktor crawled through the gap in the wall. The soldiers were quite near now. And they were shooting again, so perhaps they wouldn't notice him retrieving the grenade. He picked it up and crawled back behind the wall.

But one of the soldiers had noticed something. The shooting stopped. One of them was pointing.

He saw Kepa about fifty yards on the other side of the machine gun. He was kneeling behind a stone well. If I can see him so can the soldiers, Viktor thought, as the gunner shouted and swung the barrel of the gun around.

Viktor saw Kepa take the pin from the grenade and hold it behind him, heard his voice when they had been together. "Make it four if you feel like it but not less than two . . ."

The gun fired, a belt of cartridges rising from the ammunition box like a rearing snake, as Kepa threw the grenade; but a bullet must have hit him at the last moment because the grenade dropped halfway between him and the soldiers.

Kepa fell to one side; the gunners pressed themselves to the ground. The snow-muffled silence thickened.

Cautiously, the soldiers raised their heads. "It might explode and it might not," he had said. The soldiers began to laugh, and Viktor could see Kepa lying on the ground beside the well.

Leisurely, the gunner took aim. Viktor drew the pin from his grenade, realizing that the distance was a little too far, stretched his arm behind him, and counted, "One, two, three."

He threw the grenade, watched it fly high into the falling snow and disappear from view. Then he waited. And waited.

The explosion was sharper than he had imagined it would be. He stood up. Debris rained around him. Stones, parts of the gun, and parts of the soldiers. When he looked toward where he had thrown the grenade, he saw that their corpses were quite still.

He walked toward the devastation.

I did this, he thought. There was revulsion now, but there hadn't been as he threw the grenade. Not at all. Only the same wildness that he had experienced as he shot Lieber, clubbed Adler. Survival, that was it. But was that all? He picked up a steel helmet with a jagged hole in it. Around the hole were fragments of bone and hair. Survival, yes, but it was accompanied by celebration, so who am I to judge others? Perhaps that was how it had been with the Germans; it had all begun with survival, then the celebration had taken over.

"Well done, Mr. Red Cross."

Kepa was limping across the grass toward him. "I played dead, but they were going to fill me full of bullets anyway. Thorough, the Germans." He looked around at the shattered men and the twisted barrel of the machine gun. "But not as thorough as you, my pacifist friend. You saved my life. It seems to be a habit of yours."

Viktor didn't reply. This close to his handiwork he was nauseated and appalled.

"Are you badly hurt?" he asked Kepa.

"A flesh wound in the thigh." He bent down. "But let's get rid of this." He picked up the grenade he had thrown and hurled it away.

It exploded in midair.

They sat in a coal cellar in a house fifteen miles from the village.

"At least the Poles will always have coal," Kepa said.

He sat with his back to the wall, his wounded leg sticking out in front of him like a spare part. They had been driven to the house in a farm truck, covered with sugar beets, their escape made easier by the falling

184

snow, as the Germans began to raze the village. The woman of the house, whose husband had been killed by the Nazis, had bathed and dressed Kepa's wound.

"What about the others?" Viktor asked.

"They each knew where to go. A lot of them were already dead."

"Is it really worth it, this resistance? You lose so many men. Now the Germans are punishing the innocent."

"We were all innocent, and we are all punished," Kepa said, feeling his wound through the bandage. "What we have left is honor. We show the Krauts we still have balls. I saw horsemen in the Pomorze Army charge Guderian's tanks and send them scuttling. Not for long, mind, but they fought, and we have to make sure they didn't fight for nothing."

The woman came into the cellar and put a bowl of stew on the charcoal fire she had lit. "No smoke," she had explained when Viktor had pointed at the gleaming piles of coal.

The smell of the stew reached them immediately. Viktor realized that he was famished.

"Potato skins," she said. "Very good for you. Beets, carrots . . . a little meat, only don't ask where it came from."

She was dressed in black, passive-faced and huge-breasted, with a red scarf tied around her hair. Her face was touched with coal dust. Kepa and Viktor were covered with it.

Viktor held out an earthenware bowl, into which the woman ladled stew. It was thin, but it tasted good and strong.

"Pepper vodka," she explained, watching Kepa wolf down his. She looked at him fondly, but there was nothing maternal about the look, and Viktor wondered if once, long ago, there had been something between them, although they had both been decently married. If so, there was still a little of it left.

"What about women and children?" he persisted. "They'll be hurt because of what happened today. Perhaps taken away, perhaps lose their husbands, fathers . . . Is it worth it?"

"If you could ask them," Kepa said, sipping noisily from a spoon, "they would tell you yes. As they've told people like you throughout the history of Poland."

Viktor dropped it; but he wasn't convinced that Kepa was right. History was full of heroes who had led people to their deaths. It was the historians who had helped to make pacifism a crime.

And who are you, Viktor Golovin, to talk about pacifism? You rejoiced in the killings.

Kepa said, "Why don't you ask her what she thinks?" pointing at the woman.

"I only know," she said, "that war changes everyone."

"It unlocks feelings," Kepa said. "You forget I was a schoolmaster. I suppose I taught history for so long that when the time came I knew what to do."

"There was never any question about you," the woman said, "when the time came."

"Nor you," Kepa said fondly. He turned toward Viktor and stared at him appraisingly. Then he said, "So what is to become of you, Mr. Red Cross?"

"I want to cross the demarcation line," Hoffman said.

"Why, for God's sake?"

"I can't tell you."

"Then you can't expect much help, can you?"

"I saved those men from being killed and tortured. You owe me something."

"Is it for the good of Poland that you want to cross?"

"I shall be helping to defeat the Germans. Is that good enough for you?"

Kepa considered this. "And defeating the Russians?" He looked shrewdly at Viktor.

Cautiously, Viktor asked what he meant.

"They are worse than the Germans. As you'll see if you manage to cross over. There are many Poles who consider themselves lucky to be this side of the line."

"How can anything be worse than what I've seen today?"

"At least the Germans ask questions first. The Russians don't bother with such niceties."

"I don't believe it."

"Why should you disbelieve it, Mr. Red Cross? Do you have some affinity with the Soviets?"

The woman said suddenly, "Where do you come from in Czechoslovakia?"

"Bratislava," Viktor said promptly. *Russians worse than Germans?*

"The city?"

"Outside the city."

"I know the area well," she said. "Where?"

"A village called Cicov."

"That's a fair way from Bratislava."

"On the Danube," he said.

"I know, I've been there."

"And the geese still walk on the sidewalks," he said, managing a smile and hoping that the guidebook had been accurate.

It seemed to satisfy her. "Does it hurt very much?" she said to Kepa. Blood was seeping from beneath the bandage.

"It will be all right," and to Viktor, "So you don't believe it? I can tell you this, the Poles on the other side of the Bug have a greater need for your Red Cross than we do. You say you will be helping to defeat the Germans? Nothing wrong with that. I can think of only one better outcome—to smash the Nazis and the Russians both."

Viktor said, "You've been listening to German propaganda."

Kepa spat into the coal. "I listen to no one but my conscience." He paused. "But why should the Germans spread anti-Soviet propaganda. They have a pact, don't they? They're friends, allies, brothers-in-arms."

But, of course, he didn't mean it. "You know as well as I do," Viktor said, "that Fascists and Bolsheviks can never share a cause. It's an arrangement, that's all. Hitler probably hates the Russians more than the English."

"He never hated the English," Kepa the historian said. "But we're getting away from the point. You don't believe what I tell you about the Russians? Then you must go and see for yourself. At least I will have made a convert."

When the woman began to protest, Kepa said, "You should have seen what he did today."

But they were Germans, Viktor thought. The enemy. What if they had been Russians?

"I can get you to the river," Kepa told him. "And I know people on this side of the river who will help you. You have papers?"

"Yes."

"The Krauts didn't seem to think much of your papers. But the Russians will, eh?"

"It's a chance I have to take," Viktor said, evading the question. "How do I get to the river?"

"By night," Kepa said and told him how it could be done.

The German staff car was hidden beneath a pile of rusting vehicles in a scrap yard.

As dusk fell, the day after the battle in the village, Viktor went there with two other partisans. Together they manhandled the car away from the wrecks.

The moon was shining and Viktor could see that she was beautiful. A Maybach tourer with a long, low-slung hood and a leather top. Through the windshield was a hole surrounded by radials of splintered glass.

"A wonderful shot," one of the partisans remarked. "Right between the eyes." From the trunk he took a gray-green uniform. "The driver's," he said. "He was a general's chauffeur, but he hadn't got the general with him, more's the pity." Appraising Viktor, he said, "It should fit you. And we've cleaned the blood off."

Pulling on the jacket, he thought, "You're a Russian posing as a Czech posing as a German who will shortly be posing as a NKVD officer. Not bad."

"Yes," the partisan said, "it fits—well, almost." Like a tailor trying to disguise bad cutting, he gave the jacket a tug. Then he handed Viktor some papers. "Your name is Otto Stieff and you're a private soldier in the Wehrmacht. Read these papers and memorize as much of them as you can. Head east and you can't go wrong. Good luck," and he was gone.

Viktor Golovin read the papers in the moonlight, then switched on the engine. It throbbed powerfully. What the partisans didn't know was that driving was the least of his accomplishments. Students didn't drive the few cars there were in Moscow, and in Lisbon there had never been any reason to practice.

He found reverse and backed the car erratically out of the yard. Then he headed east toward the River Bug, the demarcation line between German and Soviet Poland, a hundred miles away. And it wasn't until he had reached Siedlce, halfway there, that he was stopped.

The roadblock was primitive but effective; a truck parked sideways across the road, and three sentries guarding the space to its right. The license plate of the Maybach had been changed, according to Kepa, but if the Germans had a description of the stolen car, he was finished. If Otto Stieff's name had been circulated as missing, he was finished twice over.

The officer in charge of the roadblock approached the car deferentially, but his attitude changed when he realized there was no one important in the back.

He shone a flashlight in Viktor's face. "Papers." He was a middle-aged second lieutenant with petulant features. A roadblock, Viktor decided, was the highest command he would ever have.

He scanned the papers, then said, "Get out and let's have a look at you."

Viktor climbed out of the car. "So your name's Stieff. Where are you from, Stieff?"

"Dresden," Viktor said.

"I have a rank."

"Dresden, Lieutenant."

"What are you doing driving through the night by yourself, Stieff?"

"Going to pick up the general, *Lieutenant*."

He couldn't help the sarcastic emphasis. Stupid.

"So you're only accustomed to showing respect to generals?"

"No, Lieutenant." Controlled this time.

"That's a strange accent you have," the officer said. "I haven't heard anything like it before."

Viktor, who had imagined his accent was pure Berlin, said, "My mother was Polish, Lieutenant. I was brought up on the Polish border—the old Polish border, that is."

"And you drive a general?" The officer seemed amazed that a mongrel should be permitted to drive a high-ranking German officer.

"My accent doesn't affect my driving, Lieutenant." Stupid again. What had come over him?

The officer turned to a corporal standing beside him. "Search the car."

Viktor said, "I don't think the general would like that, Lieutenant." His papers were under the rubber lining in the boot; he felt his heart thudding.

"I'm quite sure he would endorse any security measures we thought fit to take."

Viktor sighed. "With respect, you don't know the general." If they found the papers he might just be able to shoot all three of them with the pistol concealed inside his jacket. "I have to pick him up in—" he glanced at his wristwatch, "in one hour exactly. In two and a half hours he has to be back in Warsaw. It's a very tight schedule."

"This will only take ten minutes or so."

Viktor shrugged. "Very well, Lieutenant. I'll tell General Wolff to explain to Heydrich that you thought the search was necessary."

The officer's head jerked up. "Who?"

Viktor said, "I understand that Reichsführer Himmler has dispatched Heydrich to Warsaw to meet General Wolff."

The officer thrust the papers at him. "Get on your way, man, and don't forget to show respect to officers."

189

Viktor stepped back and gave the Nazi salute. "Heil Hitler." He climbed into the Maybach and drove away, laughing. God help the next driver stopped at the block.

The potholed road led into a belt of forest. He was about forty miles from the river. Ahead lay God knows what. He thought instead about what he had left behind. Kepa and the woman in the cellar. He hoped they found some happiness before the inevitable overtook them.

Twenty minutes later, he saw a gleam of silver in the distance. The River Bug. On this bank, Germans keeping watch for unauthorized departures. On the other bank, Russians watching for unauthorized arrivals. He drove faster and just as badly.

Hunched in the old gray coat he had worn during the civil war, Stalin read and reread the latest report from the NKVD headquarters in Dzerzhinsky Square.

First hope, then despair, and finally anger, overcame him.

They had checked out Viktor from Lisbon, lost him briefly, picked him up at Madrid. From Madrid he had flown to Rome, then on to Vienna.

It was when he read that Viktor had boarded a train traveling east that Stalin had truly begun to believe that his son was coming home.

When he had got that far in the report he had pulled the coat closer to him and murmured, "Keep him apart from it all . . ." the words that Viktor's mother had used all those years ago.

He read on.

The NKVD had lost him on the outskirts of Warsaw. "German officers believed to be Gestapo took him away in a car. Regrettably we were unable to follow."

Regrettably! Crass, cowardly, treacherous bastards. He would have them recalled to Moscow and beaten to death in Lubyanka.

He poured himself a glass of vodka, tossed the spirit down his throat, and hurled the glass against the wall. Then he smashed his knuckles down on the desk, three times until the blood flowed.

15

Bauer picked up Rachel Keyser outside the Avenida Palace.

It was 7 P.M., an hour of expectancy in Lisbon. The cafés were awakening, crowds hurrying along the black-and-white sidewalks, trysts being kept or broken.

Rachel approached the hotel from the Praça dos Restauradores. Opposite the obelisk commemorating the end of Spanish rule in 1640, she bought an evening newspaper. The headline read, HITLER MEETS FRANCO. The story speculated on whether the Spanish leader, consolidating his position after his victory in the civil war, would make a deal with the Führer and let German troops attack Gibraltar from Spain.

Another story on the same page expressed the views of Portugal's aesthetic bachelor dictator, Dr. Antonio d'Oliveira Salazar. According to the article, Salazar was confident that Spain, like Portugal, would continue to observe strict neutrality. Portugal and Spain could not afford to be anything but cautious, for if the Germans wished they could conquer them as easily as they had conquered Poland.

Poland. Where was Josef now? Cross was confident that he would reach Moscow without a hitch. He was Red Cross all the way to the demarcation line—not even the Germans liked to upset them—and he was Red Cross even when he passed into Soviet-held territory. Once there, his position was even stronger: he was Red Cross *and* NKVD.

Bauer said, "I wonder if you could spare a moment, Fraulein Keyser."

He was smoking one of his black cigars. He smelled of cologne, and his cropped, gray hair glistened.

Rachel said, "Go to hell," and tried to walk past him, but he gripped her arm. "We have made contact with Josef Hoffman."

"Who?" She had stopped, and she wished she could disguise her fear.

Looking her in the eye, Bauer smiled. Then led her into the hotel bar, brought her unprotesting to a table, ordered a beer and schnapps for himself and a glass of white wine for her. She could see he was enjoying himself.

He took off his black topcoat and undid the jacket of his gray, double-breasted suit, displaying his big drum belly beneath a striped shirt. While the waiter poured the schnapps, he licked his lips. He drank it in a gulp and told the waiter to pour another. Then he drank some beer, licking the froth from his upper lip with the tip of his tongue.

At last he spoke. "A very enterprising young man, Josef Hoffman. Or should I say he has enterprising masters?"

"Where is he?" Rachel asked, abandoning pretense.

"Somewhere in Europe. That's how war stories are datelined, aren't they?" He drank some more beer. "Do you mind my speaking in German?"

"Why should I?" What did he mean, *made contact?* She bit the inside of her lip and tasted blood.

"Ah, of course not, you spent a long time in Berlin, didn't you? An enjoyable period of your life, Fraulein Keyser?"

"An interesting time."

"Ah, you must have had reservations about our handling of the Jewish problem."

"Your problem," she said.

"Last time we met," he said, "I got the distinct impression that you felt strongly about Jews. Being one yourself, that is. I seem to remember you didn't much like my cigars either." He lit another one and blew the smoke into her face.

"You haven't brought me here to discuss the Nazis' anti-Semitic policies."

"True, true. I'll come to the point, Fraulein. Josef Hoffman is currently in the custody of the Gestapo, but you can save him."

Despair lurched inside her. "I don't believe you."

Bauer took two sheets of paper from the inside pocket of his jacket. One was a cable, the other was the decoded version of it. He handed it to her.

JOSEF HOFFMAN DESCRIBING HIMSELF AS RED

She knew what that meant and she thought, "I have done this to him," but all she said was, "That's against international law."

Bauer examined the wet tip of his cigar. "In my opinion the Red Cross is as useless as the League of Nations was. However I agree that if he had been pursuing genuine Red Cross business we would not have detained him. As it happens, he wasn't. Neither Lisbon nor Geneva has any record of his mission; in fact they are both quite disturbed by his departure. I don't think," Bauer said, leaning across the table, "that your friends at the British embassy are quite as clever as they think they are. They made the mistake of underestimating German Intelligence." *Me,* he implied. His voice took on a grating quality. "They thought it was sufficient to murder three Germans and to change Hoffman's timetable, and he would reach Moscow just like that." Bauer's bloodshot eyes stared at her intently. "Why Moscow, Fraulein Keyser?"

"All right," she said, sipping her wine, "I do know Hoffman. In fact I'm fond of him—"

Bauer interrupted impatiently, "We know perfectly well that you've been sleeping with him."

"—but Moscow? I haven't the faintest idea what you're talking about."

"On the contrary, you drove him to the airport. Who killed my men, Fraulein Keyser?"

"I read that they were ambushed and robbed."

"Was it Cross? I believe he works for . . . certain sections of German Intelligence."

"*If* he works for German Intelligence he would hardly kill three of your men, would he?"

Bauer let that one go. He ordered more beer and schnapps from the waiter. Pulling at the lobe of one ear, he said, "You understand the implications of interrogation by the Gestapo?"

She closed her eyes for a moment.

"I sent a cable to Warsaw instructing our agents there to postpone interrogation until I conducted certain consultations in Lisbon. There is, in fact, only one consultation, and this is it."

The waiter gave him another beer and refilled his schnapps glass. "That one's on the house, Herr Bauer," he said.

"At least he knows who's going to win the war," Bauer remarked.

Despite everything, Rachel managed a small lie. "He doesn't charge the English for any drinks."

Bauer ignored it. "First they will soften him up a little," he said. "You know, the rubber hose treatment. Then if he doesn't talk—"

"Everyone knows about your methods." If he didn't stop she would pick up his glass of beer, smash it on the table, and grind the jagged glass in his face. But then Hoffman would surely die.

"—they will use more refined methods. We have an expert there named Adler. He's in a class all his own."

"You disgust me."

"Fingernails first. One by one with a pair of pliers. There's something about the wrench of a nail from a finger that makes people talk."

Please God don't let it be so.

"Then electric shocks if he's really stubborn."

What have I done to you?

"On his genitals. You would know about those, Fraulein."

"I'm going," she said. "I don't have to listen to filth from a fat pig like you."

"You don't want to save him?"

She took a gulp of wine.

"Adler's very good with the electrical side of things. He knows just how much current to give without killing the subject. It's said to be the worst pain known to man."

When I met you, Josef, you dreamed of peace and I derided your dreams.

"If you cooperate," Bauer said, "you can save him all that pain."

"But I can't help you," hearing him scream.

"Why was he going to Moscow?"

"I understood he was going to Geneva . . ."

"The fingernails one by one . . ."

". . . on Red Cross business . . ."

". . . until the tips of his fingers are pulp . . ."

". . . and then coming back to Lisbon . . ."

". . . electrodes on the testicles . . ."

". . . said nothing about Russia . . ."

". . . the body arches . . . the backbone has been known to break in the hands of amateurs . . ."

"I don't know anything!"

194

Bauer said softly, "What a pity. Then Hoffman will die. Slowly."

"He wasn't going to Moscow," she said.

"Really?" Bauer regarded her cynically, the look of a man who has heard many lies squeezed out by intolerable pressures. "Where was he going? The moon?"

"He was leaving the train at Warsaw."

"Going on vacation?"

"On Abwehr business," she said and noticed a slight compression of his lips. At least it was some reaction.

"What sort of Abwehr business?" Bauer asked harshly.

Encouraged, she said, "I don't know. I just heard he was being sent on a mission for them." And, innocently, "But surely you must know if he's acting on behalf of German Intelligence."

"Can you find out?"

"If," she said trying to control her eagerness, "you guarantee that no harm will come to Hoffman."

"I can guarantee that he won't be interrogated for a while. But don't tell Cross that I asked you to find out."

For the first time since they sat down Bauer seemed to have lost direction. *Abwehr business*. The two words had kindled an interest in him that appeared to be at least as strong as any patriotic considerations.

By instinct she had bought Hoffman respite. For how long?

Bauer said, "The elevator where we first met. I'll meet you at the top, on the bridge, at eight tomorrow evening. Please be there—with full details of this *Abwehr business*.

He paid the bill and left.

Bauer learned two hours later that Hoffman had escaped from the Gestapo. Not only had he escaped, but apparently he had killed one of his captors and maimed Adler, the specialist, for life.

Bauer stood up, ground his cigar viciously into an ashtray, and paced the room. He would have to go to the house near the Botanical Gardens and beat his whore black and blue. That always calmed him. How the Jewish bitch, Keyser, would laugh when she heard this!

He paused. But how long would it be before she did? It was not easy for men on the run to address communications across the whole length of occupied Europe. Bauer stopped near the window and smiled. He would keep his appointment with Rachel Keyser, and because of her great fear, she would tell him things.

As for the whore, he would beat her anyway but perhaps not quite so hard.

He lit another cigar and strolled out of his office, past the guards, and down the broad staircase of the legation.

"Abwehr business? Ingenious." Cross and Rachel sat beside each other in a pew at the rear of St. Rock Church, where they had arranged to meet in an emergency. "Now we'll have to think of something to substantiate your ingenuity."

A priest walked down the aisle. Rachel stared at the paintings on the wooden ceiling depicting the Apocalypse.

"We could cause a lot of soul searching in the Kraut secret services," Cross said. "But whatever we do it will only be temporary as far as Hoffman is concerned." He knelt, cupping his hands in front of him, as the priest, smiling gently, walked past. "Despite what Bauer promised you, they'll still interrogate him, and only by a miracle could he come up with the same explanation as ours."

Kneeling beside him, she thought, "So I've failed."

"But, as you say, you may have bought him time. They may wait to see what you come up with and then try it out on him. Abwehr business . . ."

She was no longer listening. She was praying in this Christian place of worship for Hoffman's life, praying to the Deity who surely listened whether you were in church, mosque, or synagogue.

"If we could persuade Bauer," he was saying into his cupped hands, "that Hoffman"—his name brought her back from prayer—"had gone to Warsaw at the instigation of the Abwehr to report on the atrocities there. After all, he does work for the Red Cross. Perhaps if we could convince him," Cross said, conspirator's imagination taking hold of him, "that von Claus had provided Hoffman with details of the places to investigate. Mass graves and suchlike. We know that Canaris abhors Himmler's treatment of the Jews. As for Moscow—well, that would be a good escape route for a Red Cross official who wanted to avoid contact with the Gestapo."

"But it won't save Josef, will it?"

"As I said, it might buy him time. Time to escape. Time to be rescued by partisans. Who knows . . ." Cross glanced at her curiously. "Tell me something. If telling Bauer the truth meant saving Hoffman but losing the war, what would you do?"

She didn't reply, but she knew what she would do and it terrified her. She closed her eyes and began to pray.

As instructed, Viktor left the Maybach in a barn at the end of a lane five miles from the river and began to walk across the fields, searching in the moonlight for the landmarks Kepa had mentioned.

It was 1:30 A.M. The scattering of snow had thawed and the ground underfoot was muddy. A few minutes later he was knee-deep in marshes. Kepa hadn't said anything about marshes. A duck took off with a flapping run and flew low overhead, squawking. Somewhere here, there should be a ruined farmhouse. He stopped and stared around, but all he could see was water and dark tufts of marsh grass.

Kepa wouldn't have sent him across a bog. Unless Kepa didn't want him to reach the Russians. Hoffman took a step forward, but there was only water beneath his foot.

He stepped back—and fell back into more water. Clumsily, he swam to a hillock of muddy grass. He had left the jacket of the uniform in the car, and he began to shiver.

He retreated again, reaching firmer ground. An aircraft droned overhead. A small animal broke from some reeds to his left, rushed into the marshes, and swam away, making an arrow on the moonlit water.

He gestured hopelessly to the starlit sky and changed direction. A couple of minutes later he found the farmhouse. It was more of a ruin than Kepa had led him to expect, almost swallowed up by the bog.

A path just riding above the water led to the east. Viktor stepped onto it, aware that he presented a perfect target, clear-cut and slow-moving. As he walked, a stiff breeze flattened his wet shirt against his chest; he couldn't stop shivering.

It was another quarter hour before the shot came, and by that time he had reached firmer ground. He threw himself into a ditch and waited, pistol in hand. At first there was nothing except the hooting of an owl; then, faintly, he heard footsteps and muted voices. He gripped the pistol tightly.

When the voices were almost upon him he realized they were speaking Polish, not German. "Where did she go?"

"I don't know. Perhaps you missed her."

"If we stay here much longer the Germans won't miss us."

A cloud passed over the moon. A thin flashlight beam came from the direction of the voices. It ran along the ditch, stopping at Hoffman. He leveled his pistol and said, "I've got you covered. Put out the light."

The light snapped out, and one of the voices said, "Now who the hell might you be?"

"Not a duck, for sure," said another voice.

And a third from behind him, "Now you'd better drop that gun, because *I* have got *you* covered."

In a cottage on the edge of the blacked-out village, the three duck shooters regarded Viktor curiously. They had examined the papers that he had taped to his chest in a waterproof pouch and read the letter from Kepa.

One of them said, "Does Kepa still wear his hair long like Jesus Christ?" and Viktor, cold, exhausted, and sick of being tested, snapped, "He's as bald as a coot and you know it."

A gaunt young woman entered the room and asked, "Well, where's breakfast?"

A man named Emil, unshaven and with an aggressive tilt to his face, said, "We didn't get a duck, we got this instead."

The men did their duck hunting by night. By day, they would be the quarry. They could only risk one, or at the most two, shots before the German patrols came to investigate.

"We can't eat him," the woman said. There was no humor in her voice.

"He does look a bit tough." Emil agreed. One of the men sniggered, but when the woman looked at him he pretended he was clearing his throat.

"So what's our baby going to live on?" the woman asked.

Emil pointed at her breasts. "Milk."

"To get milk you have to feed *me*." Her hands went to her breasts. "There's nothing there anymore."

Viktor felt hostility gathering around him. One more shot and they might have had food.

Emil fingered the black stubble on his chin. "You were lucky," he said after a while. "This is the house Kepa meant you to come to."

The woman said, "He's not staying here."

Emil said, "You keep out of it."

"It's my house as well as yours."

They stared at each other with something approaching hatred. Viktor looked away. On a crowded shelf on the wall stood a photograph of Emil and his wife on their wedding day. They looked posed and awkward and proud of each other. *I only know that war changes everyone.*

She pointed at Viktor's trousers. "German," she said, but he had explained that to the men, and they explained it to her. She didn't look convinced.

Suddenly she was gone, door slamming behind her, making a china ballerina on the shelf dance.

Emil took off his padded, hunter's jacket. "Put this on, you'll freeze to death."

Outside, perhaps, but not in this room, which, with the red-hot stove in one corner, was like an ornate furnace. So they meant him to go.

Somewhere in the house, the baby began to cry. Above the wail Viktor heard crisp footsteps on the street outside.

"A German patrol," one of the men said.

They waited. The footsteps got nearer.

A door banged in the house, quieting the baby for a moment. Floor-boards creaked.

The footsteps were directly outside.

The sound of a bolt being drawn.

Emil flung open the door of the living room and grabbed his wife as she turned the key in the lock of the street door.

He flung her onto the floor and she stayed there, at the foot of the stairs, whimpering.

The footsteps seemed to hesitate. Then continued, faded, died.

The woman looked up at her husband. "They would have given us food if we had turned him in."

"Bitch!"

"No, she isn't," Viktor said.

The baby began to cry again.

Emil said, "Come, you have to go now," and standing in the bare kitchen, added, "The baby is sick." He opened the back door.

Clouds had covered the moon and stars. There were three hours till dawn.

"The rowboat's that way," Emil said, pointing into the darkness, "just as Kepa said it would be. It's about half a mile. You'll have to pull strongly because the currents are strong." He handed Viktor back his pistol. "I don't know why you want to get there, but Kepa says you're okay."

It took Viktor half an hour to reach the river. Again, he had to pick his way through marshes. He found the boat hidden in some rushes; the rushes whispered to him in the darkness.

The water was as black as the night. There were no lights on the opposite bank. Rivers such as this were supposed to have been Poland's defenses against invasion. To the north lay Brest-Litovsk, where in the last war the Russians had made their peace with Germany. Dipping the oars gently into the water, Viktor began to row for the far bank. He was between two juggernauts, two tyrannies. Between two tyrants certainly, but he refused to believe the Russian people were like the Germans: their failing was their national persecution complex. That was why they had allowed Stalin to carry out his purges.

And if Stalin's megalomania is so obsessive that he believes no one, not even those who seek to warn him about Germany's hostile intentions, then I must tell him for the sake of Russia. Just then, the beam of a searchlight hit the rowboat, blinding him.

The chain-smoking, plainclothes NKVD officer sitting at the table in the dugout on the eastern bank of the Bug said, "You contradict yourself."

Fatigue overwhelmed Viktor. His bones ached, his head was heavy, lolling. "Contradict?"

"You say you are a NKVD officer. Then you must know that no NKVD officer would be taken in by this shit." The officer threw the forged documents at Viktor. "That's the contradiction."

"Check me out," Viktor said. His voice seemed to belong to someone else. "Check me out and you'll be in the shit, my friend, up to here," lifting one heavy hand to his chin.

The officer lit another yellow, cardboard-tipped cigarette, and staring at him, said, "You're too young for your rank." But his tone wasn't as confident as his words. That was the snag in being trained in suspicion: you suspected your own reasoning.

"Check," Viktor said. Sleep was a warm fog and its tendrils were reaching for him.

A field telephone rang beside the officer. He took a deep breath of cigarette smoke and picked up the receiver.

The effect of the voice on the other end of the line was electrifying. The officer stubbed out his cigarette and looked as though he might leap to attention and salute.

Viktor watched in amazement.

When the officer replaced the receiver he was trembling.

"I must apologize, comrade. You are to have an escort—to Moscow."

16

8 P.M.

Bauer was waiting on the caged-in platform at the top of Eiffel's gray elevator tower when she arrived.

He was staring down through the wire mesh at the rooftops of the elegant shops in the Chiado; behind him in the darkness she could see the lights of ships on the Tagus.

A wooden barrier had been placed across the platform; beyond it the cage was being repaired and a gap yawned into space.

One push, she thought, and his heavy body would crash through the planks of the barricade. She imagined his fat carcass turning slowly as it plummeted toward the rooftops.

"Don't worry, Fraulein," he said as she joined him, "I'm far too heavy for you to push. Too many creamcakes, too many schnapps. But it's a beautiful night, isn't it? Cold—but then a man of my size doesn't take too kindly to the heat."

She stood beside him and stared at the lights of the cars and trams— shining beads pulled slowly along on strands of gossamer. A breeze coming in from the river made her shiver, and she pulled her Persian lamb coat more tightly around her body.

"Well, Fraulein Keyser," he said, "what have you to report?"

"What about Hoffman?"

"He is alive and well."

"Where is he?"

Detained in a village twenty miles outside Warsaw. Now," he said, "what about this Abwehr business?"

She told him what Cross had told her to say. That von Claus had provided Hoffman with details of Nazi atrocities in Warsaw; that Hoffman had gone there to expose them. "A personal crusade rather than a Red Cross mission," she added.

"You wouldn't be trying to set one German intelligence organization against another, would you, Fraulein?"

"I'm trying to save Hoffman."

"And failing miserably," he said matter-of-factly. "Since you mentioned the Abwehr I've checked every move they've made in the past month. They enrolled Hoffman, true. Since then there hasn't been any contact."

"If the Abwehr suspect you have access to their files, they wouldn't record it," she said. But she felt the hopelessness of it all. The Gestapo still held Josef and they would check her story with him, and it was too much to hope that he would chance on the same explanation.

She tried a last ploy. "There is something else."

"Really?" He turned to face her; she could smell his cologne.

"Bring Hoffman back to Lisbon and I'll tell you."

"Why should I do that? If you want to save him you'll tell me anyway. What is this morsel?"

"No morsel, Herr Bauer. It is something beyond your comprehension. If you were responsible for relaying it to Berlin you would join Himmler, Göring, and Goebbels at Hitler's side."

She saw the greedy interest in his face.

"If you bring Hoffman here," she said desperately, "we will make a deal. His life for the greatest secret of this war. You would know how to arrange such an exchange so that there were no tricks."

The elevator stopped beside them. The doors opened; a handful of passengers walked across the bridge spanning the Chiado to the Largo do Carmo.

When they had gone Bauer said, "I have another suggestion to make. As we hold Hoffman, it makes far more sense. You tell me what this secret is and I will authorize his release. Refuse to tell me and I will authorize a slow and lingering death for him."

She would have to tell him.

"Come, Fraulein. Otherwise I shall assume you are bluffing. What is this priceless piece of information that will place me on the rostrum with the leaders of the Third Reich?"

Of course she would have to tell him. You didn't consign a man to the sort of suffering contrived by the Gestapo for *any* cause. Not even victory over the Nazis . . . From the streets of Berlin the bewildered faces of the children stared at her.

"Tell me—now—or Hoffman dies."

The children had gone to God knows where, but Josef was still alive. I have betrayed him once, she thought, and it must never happen again. I have no right.

"Tell me."

She knew she had to tell him.

She spat in his face and walked briskly across the bridge.

On the bed in the Avenida Palace where they had made love, she stared at the colors of the spectrum shivering in the chandelier and thought, "At least he will never know that I sent him to his death."

If he did, would he understand?

Would I understand, in his position? Of course, but it was so easy to make such affirmations when you were free from pain, from terrible, terrible pain.

Were they torturing him now? He who had wanted none of this. He who had been seduced into a war of which he had wanted no part. By me.

And when I could have saved him, all I did was spit.

The bedside phone rang.

It was Cross. Using the chess terminology they had agreed upon, he said, "The pawn is passed."

Hoffman in Russia? Cross had got the terminology wrong.

Cross's voice came to her from a long way off. "Can you hear me . . . hear me?" Words echoing. "Passed . . . Do you understand?"

Passed the border, of course she understood, as a great joy suffused her, as the colors in the chandelier merged into blood-red, as the telephone receiver swung from the bedside table.

When she had regained consciousness, she thought, "I will have to tell him," wondering if any man would ever understand that a woman who professed to love him could have knowingly dispatched him to a terrible death.

Viktor sat in the back seat of a black Volga staff car beside a young Red Army lieutenant.

The lieutenant obviously had no idea why Viktor was getting such preferential treatment.

The car was heading toward Pruzhany. Beyond lay the northern reaches of the Pripet Marshes.

Viktor, dressed in a coarse gray suit and black sweater provided by the NKVD, tried to make conversation.

"Have you been in Poland long?"

The lieutenant was hardly more than a boy and had cropped hair as thick as fur. He examined the shiny peak of the cap he was holding in his lap and thought for a few seconds about what answer he should make. Finally he said, "From the beginning."

"I sometimes wonder if we needed to occupy so much of Poland."

The lieutenant stared at the red star gleaming above the peak of the cap. By now he was probably convinced that Viktor was an *agent provocateur*.

"It was necessary," he said. And after a pause, "We had to create a buffer zone to keep the Germans away from our border."

The car was approaching a village of wooden houses. A group of peasants standing at the side of the muddy road stared at them sullenly.

"I thought," the lieutenant said, "that you might like to stop here for coffee."

Viktor looked at his wristwatch. It was 11:30 A.M. "All right," he said. Never before had he commanded such respect.

The driver pulled up in the village square in front of an ornate wooden church. At the other end of the square stood a platoon of Soviet troops wearing forage caps, tightly belted tunics, and mud-spattered jackboots. There were no Poles about, although once or twice Viktor thought he saw a curtain flutter.

The lieutenant led him into a hut that served as an inn. It contained a wooden bar and a handful of tables and chairs and smelled of sour liquor. A middle-aged man stood behind the bar, a pot of coffee steaming in front of him.

The lieutenant conferred with the barman while Viktor found a table. The young Russian officer spoke in a curt, contemptuous voice to the civilian and then, taking something from him, tilted his head back. Vodka, of course.

The lieutenant brought Viktor a mug of coffee. He returned to the bar. His head tilted again, and when he came back he was more relaxed.

They sipped their coffee, appraising each other through the steam.

"We've a long journey ahead of us," the lieutenant said at last. "Seven hundred miles as the crow flies, longer by road." He lit a cigarette. "At any rate, we'll be out of this stinking country soon."

"Are the Poles so bad?"

"They're treacherous bastards," the lieutenant replied. "They booby-trapped a patrol car in the next village this morning. Three of our soldiers were killed."

"And Poles?"

"Ten for every Russian. We'll shoot thirty of them and make them dig their graves first," the lieutenant said, putting no particular emphasis on the words.

Viktor put his mug on the table. The bleakness that he felt must have shown, because the lieutenant said, "Something a little stronger, comrade?"

Viktor nodded. When the lieutenant placed the carafe on the table, he poured the first shot straight down his throat. He took the second more slowly, feeling it burn his tongue. "Surely," he said, "all Poles can't be bastards. After all they produced Chopin, Conrad, Paderewski, Madame Curie . . ."

Wariness descended on the lieutenant again.

"After all," Viktor went on, "it must be hard to have your country occupied by two foreign armies."

The lieutenant stared at him suspiciously. "The Jews are the worst," he said.

Rachel Keyser appeared before him. Standing on the runway at Sintra as he took his seat in the DC-3.

The lieutenant frowned. "Are you all right, comrade?"

"Yes," Viktor said, "I'm all right."

The lieutenant shrugged. Perhaps this man he was guarding *was* a Jew. "By lunchtime," he said, "we shall be back in the Soviet Union. A little more firewater?" He poured them both vodka. "Nasdarovya!" Together they tossed back the liquid explosive.

With the telephone receiver held to one ear, Stalin pored over a map of Eastern Europe.

"So where is he now?" he said into the receiver.

"Close to the border," said the voice of Lavrenti Beria, head of the NKVD.

When his son had escaped from the Soviet Union, Stalin had confided in Beria, his sadistic fellow Georgian; but he had discovered that Beria already knew about Viktor Golovin.

It hadn't really surprised Stalin. Years ago he had personally destroyed all the relevant documents, but of course photographic copies had been made. He had also taken the precaution of liquidating anyone with any possible access to the deception. But in Moscow's vicious political climate you couldn't completely suppress such knowledge; it lingered in secret hiding places, in film negatives, in scheming minds.

There was only one way to control such knowledge, and that was through fear. Beria, formerly chief of the secret police in Georgia, was the man to look after that. The trouble then was that Beria had to be controlled. But my record of disposing of NKVD chiefs should take care of that, Stalin thought, running a finger down the border between Poland and Russia.

"How long will it take him to reach Moscow?"

"Two days," Beria said.

Stalin was overcome with joy; he had never experienced emotion quite like it before. His son was coming home, a son who might have suffered pangs of idealism, which was not entirely a bad thing, but who could not, apparently, resist the call of Mother Russia. "Keep him apart from it all," the boy's mother had said. Now that he had reached such enlightened maturity the truth could be revealed.

Stalin smiled and said into the telephone, "You've done well, Lavrenti."

Which he had. There had been that terrible period when NKVD operatives in Warsaw had reported that Viktor had been taken prisoner by the Gestapo. But he had escaped. My son, Stalin thought proudly. And all observation posts on the Russian side of the demarcation line in Poland, in particular the River Bug, had been re-alerted to watch for a man answering his description. He had apparently assumed the identity of an NKVD officer, which had made it easier for Beria to lay on transport to Moscow.

"Thank you," Beria said.

"And what about your men in Warsaw who allowed the Gestapo to take him?"

"Liquidated," Beria said.

"And the officer who began to interrogate him in the observation post on the Bug?"

"Liquidated," Beria said.

"And the escorting officer?"

"He *will be* liquidated," Beria said.

"Good," Stalin said, "we can't be too careful." He pulled at his thick mustache. "You wouldn't lie to me about any of this, would you, Lavrenti?"

"I would swear to everything I've told you on my mother's grave."

"Good," said Stalin, beaming. "Because if you're lying, you'd better start thinking about your own grave."

By the following day they were close to Smolensk, 250 miles west of Moscow.

The sun was shining thinly, and the lieutenant suggested that they eat out in the open. They bought bread and cheese and beer and stopped in a wood.

With a bottle of beer in his hand, Viktor sauntered through the woods. A few, stubborn last leaves clung to the branches of the trees, wasted brambles tugged at his ankles, a squirrel made a looping run for its winter home.

Twigs cracked behind him. He looked around: the lieutenant was following. "We'd better make a move," said the lieutenant, who didn't look as though he wanted to move at all.

"Another ten minutes," Viktor said.

They walked on together until they reached a belt of pine trees.

The noise filtered through to Viktor gradually. At first he couldn't place it. Then it came to him: shovels on earth and stone.

He quickened his pace. On the edge of a clearing a sentry appeared, rifle pointing at them. The lieutenant spoke to him. The sentry lowered his rifle, impressed—not many men who came this way had escorts to Moscow.

The lieutenant said to the sentry, "What's going on, anyway?"

The sentry answered him, but Viktor didn't catch his words. He walked into the clearing. And stopped, stunned.

In front of him, teams of workmen were shoveling soil into a deep depression that had been recently excavated. Piled high in the crater, in parade-ground order, were thousands of corpses. The bodies were clothed in the uniforms of Polish army officers. Each had been shot in the back of the neck. So regimented were they that, at a word of command, Viktor expected them to leap to attention.

He noticed some of the Red Army guards grinning and pointing at the uniformed corpses.

Viktor turned to the lieutenant and said, "What is this?"

"The sentry said that they're Polish officers who refused to accept the authority of the Red Army." He shrugged. "After all, what does one do with four thousand Polish officers?"

"You mean we shot them all?"

The lieutenant looked at him curiously. "They're only Poles," he said, "and some of them Jews at that."

Turning, Hoffman went back through the woods toward the car.

He didn't speak until they were on the outskirts of Moscow. Then all he said was, "What was the name of that place?"

"The village near there is called Katyn," the lieutenant said.

17

There is a short period of autumn in Moscow that is not a good time for neurotics.

Cold freezes the city at night, snow falls. In the morning, sunshine brings a thaw and the melted frost and snow condense into fog. Sometimes this lingers all day, sometimes it is washed away by rain. At dusk the cycle begins again. This continues until one raw morning when there is no thaw, when the air crisps your nostrils, and you know that winter has finally arrived with its white baggage for a six-month stay.

During this transient time neuroses, fed by the indecision of the weather, sprout in sickly growth. The morning sunshine brings hope; the afternoon mists, depression; the night, despair.

Standing at the window of his study, watching clouds droop and settle over the towers and domes of the Kremlin, Stalin felt the morning's optimism seep away. Where was Viktor? He should have reached Moscow by now.

The fog thickened and assumed monstrous shapes that dissolved when you stared at them. Pain throbbed in his left hand, the legacy of an ulcer, itself the manifestation of blood poisoning that had nearly killed him during his undernourished childhood.

Puffing at his pipe, he paced up and down. He stopped in front of his desk and stared at three framed pictures: Keke, his mother; Svetlana; and Lenin, engrossed in a copy of *Pravda*. But they would never be joined on his desk by Viktor. Seeing a new picture there, his enemies would sense scandal and pick up its trail.

Also on the desk were reports from various sources that Hitler was contemplating an invasion of the Soviet Union.

211

Seeking distraction, Stalin scanned the documents. Two of them were from Soviet agents who had recently been discredited for transmitting information that had been proved to be false. Others emanated from British sources who patently wanted to cause a rift between Germany and Russia. One report differed from the others: it was from an up-and-coming young British agent whose activities had been brought to his attention by Beria. His name was Philby, he had good contacts in Lisbon, capital of espionage, and he was quite positive that Hitler had no intention of attacking "in the foreseeable future."

Stalin was under no illusions about Hitler's strategy. One day he intended to invade, but not until he had brought the whole of Europe outside the Soviet Union to heel, in particular Britain, which he was currently demolishing with bombs. Stalin planned to wait until Germany was fully extended, and perhaps a little bruised, and then launch his own attack. Already he had established his launching pads by taking a slice of Poland, part of Finland, and the Baltic States. He envisaged attacking the Wehrmacht some time in 1942, after the Red Army had been completely refurbished.

Meanwhile, through his foreign minister, Vyacheslav Molotov, he continued to conduct meaningless negotiations with Hitler. Talks, for instance, about a four-power pact—Russia, Germany, Italy, and Japan—which he would torpedo with impossible conditions.

But was it just possible that Hitler was going to launch a premature attack? Surely not—he wasn't prepared for the Russian winter, and it would defeat him just as it had defeated Napoleon. But supposing he reached Moscow next year *before* winter set in?

Frowning, Stalin tossed the papers back on the desk. If only he had one source of information that he could really trust. What a hope when he was besieged by conspirators, and surrounded by liars.

He turned back to the window. He could just see the silhouettes of his guards through the mist; he wished winter would set in, hard and implacable.

Condensation had formed on the window. With one finger he traced the head of a wolf; a drop of water slid from one fang to the bottom of the pane of glass. Then the outline dissolved, turning the beast into a ghoul.

Stalin poured himself a glass of red Georgian wine.

Where was Viktor?

He peered into the swirling mist. It parted for a moment, and in the courtyard below he thought he saw—No, it was an illusion. He closed his eyes and opened them again and there, accompanied by Beria and two men in plainclothes, was his son looking up at the window.

Stalin's glass of wine crashed to the floor. He's come home, he thought.

They sat on either side of the table, a private feast laid out between them.

The first thing that had struck Viktor about his father was how much smaller he was than he appeared to be in pictures. The second thing was the benevolent and yet wary expression of his yellow eyes.

Stalin was dressed in a gray jacket buttoned up to the neck and in black trousers. He had some sort of infirmity in one arm, and when this troubled him he pulled at his shaggy mustache with his fingers. He ate greedily and drank copiously.

Now that they sat appraising each other, Viktor wondered what he looked like to Stalin. They had finished with the first round of small talk, and Viktor had already answered the inevitable questions.

Stalin's son? Yes, he had known for years. He had overheard a conversation between his foster parents, and this clandestine knowledge had been confirmed by the privileges he enjoyed. Why had he done nothing about it? Well, if the ruler of Russia wanted the existence of an illegitimate son kept secret then the son would be ill advised to confront him with it.

Viktor had answered his father's questions firmly but with trepidation. By all accounts, it was not difficult to provoke a murderous rage.

Why had he left Russia?

He told the truth. He was aware that no other story could be more convincing, and Stalin probably knew anyway. He mentioned the grief he had felt at the thought that his father authorized the mass execution he was witnessing.

Even at this no storm had burst. Instead the dictator of all Russia had pleaded with him to put aside the natural sensitivity of youth and realize that the armed forces were undermined with traitors who had to be exterminated for the sake of Russia.

It was at this point that Viktor had understood that he, not Stalin, was in control.

"So how does it feel to find you're the grandson of a cobbler and a washerwoman?"

"I have no thoughts about that. You might well ask me how it feels to be the son of the leader of the Soviet Union."

Viktor sipped at a glass of vodka. He could feel his father's eyes on him. That isn't the way to drink it, they said. He tipped back the glass and poured the fiery liquid down his throat.

"So why did you return?" Stalin said abruptly.

"I couldn't stay away when my country was threatened."

"Threatened by whom?"

"By Germany."

Stalin considered this. Then he said, "I've heard the rumors. Of course Hitler will try to stab me in the back some day. But not yet."

"The rumors are pretty strong in Lisbon," Viktor said.

"Do you believe them?"

"I think it would be a mistake to ignore them."

Stalin pulled at his mustache. Head tilted, he stared at Viktor. It was a long time, Viktor assumed, since anyone had openly questioned his judgment.

He picked up a slice of suckling pig with his fingers. "I haven't ignored them," he said, bad, Georgian-accented Russian worsening, "I have been considering them. I think they're basically propaganda inspired by the British. After all, the British must be bitterly aware that they were responsible for my signing the pact with Germany."

Viktor looked at him questioningly.

"I sought an alliance between Britain, France, and the Soviet Union, but Chamberlain wouldn't agree to it. Although I must admit," he said, face full of cunning, "that at the same time I did ask Merekalov, our ambassador in Berlin, to sound out that idiot Ribbentrop about the possibility of a pact with Germany." He popped the slice of pig into his mouth.

Viktor got the impression that Stalin was enjoying confiding in his son. "So what's your strategy now?" he asked.

Stalin said, "Britain and France, and, of course, the United States would like to see Russia and Germany exhaust each other. That's why they are spreading these rumors. Well, I want to see Britain and Germany exhaust each other—with help from the United States. Then I will bring the Germans to heel. That's something that must be done. Years ago Hitler was referring to the Ukraine and Siberia as part of Germany. Siberia!"

"Suppose," Viktor said slowly, "that Hitler has anticipated your long-term plans and acts first?"

Stalin's eating and drinking slowed down. He rolled a piece of black bread into a pellet. He looked uncertain for the first time.

"He wouldn't be that stupid."

"If he thought you weren't prepared he might be. Especially if he attacked in April or May, giving himself time to reach Moscow before our winter set in."

Stalin threw up one arm in a gesture of futility. "You'll never know how many times I've sat here and thought about that. If I had only one single source of information that I could trust, everything would be different. Nevertheless, I'm glad you warned me."

It was then that Viktor began to guide the conversation toward what he had in mind.

Coffee and cognac. The smell of burning tallow from two white candles on the table and Jusuri tobacco smoldering in Stalin's pipe. Snow hovering outside the windows.

All these things made talk come more easily.

"In Lisbon," said Hoffman, who felt replete and just a little drunk, "I have access to a lot of information."

"Good information?"

"The best."

"Red Cross?"

"To an extent."

"And British?"

"That as well."

"And German, of course."

Hoffman realized that Stalin knew his movements. Cross had been right in making sure that he made contact with the Abwehr.

"Information comes from all sides in Lisbon," Hoffman said. "You have to be discerning. You have to know which are genuine sources."

"And you know?"

Hoffman nodded.

"Why did you make these contacts?" Stalin said, splashing cognac into his black coffee.

"I wasn't sure at first," Viktor said. "Gradually, I began to realize that the intelligence I was gathering was vital to Russia. To you."

Stalin leaned back meditatively in his chair. The tobacco in his pipe glowed brightly, throwing red light on his cheeks, while outside the snow fell thicker.

"I always hoped," he said, "that one day you and I might be partners somehow. You see, you have to trust someone." He sounded, Hoffman thought, like an old man turning to God. "When you're a leader it's difficult. Everyone has his own cause to promote. Politicians, bureaucrats, soldiers . . ."

Then, in barely comprehensible Russian, he said, "I've always wanted to have one adviser I could trust. And suddenly you're here."

Viktor hesitated, hardly knowing what to answer. Then he said, "That's why I came back to Moscow."

Stalin was silent for a moment, then he thrust his hand across the table, and as Viktor took it, said, "You're my intelligence source, you tell me what's going to happen."

Despite everything he had seen, Viktor was deeply moved.

Winter settled that night. In the morning, Viktor walked the streets in the center of the city. Snow was falling heavily; snowplows were out and the air rasped with the sound of *babushkas'* shovels on the sidewalks. As he strode along beside the Moskva, the snow stopped falling for a moment, and across the black wound of the river he glimpsed the Babylonian towers of the Kremlin. Toward it all threads of Soviet intrigue led.

He brushed snow from his eyes and thought, "And I am the son of the architect of all that intrigue." What would they say if they knew, the Muscovites around him, burrowing, heads down, through the vanguard of winter as though looking for nests in which to hibernate?

Before going to bed the previous night, he and Stalin had discussed his identity. Obviously, if he was to keep his Red Cross front he had to remain Josef Hoffman. (Cross would have to handle the Gestapo.) One day perhaps . . . Stalin had gazed fondly at him through the tobacco smoke billowing in the halos of candlelight.

Of Viktor's mother he had said very little. Only that she had been a student in Leningrad, that she had been beautiful. But he had told him about the oath he had sworn to her as she lay dying after childbirth. "Now that you have come to me of your own free will I don't feel bound by it any longer," he had said.

As the snow began to fall again, a blizzard of it, Viktor recrossed a bridge over the river. When he reached the gate leading to the Kremlin from Red Square, his coat and new sealskin hat, with its spaniel-like earflaps, were pasted white.

Stalin was waiting for him in his study. His handshake was firm, his eye steady. On his desk was a tray bearing caviar and smoked salmon, bottles of Stolichnaya vodka and Narzan mineral water. Stalin was already drinking. Viktor wasn't sure that he could face any more liquor; but he supposed it would please his father to see that, like him, his stomach was lined with asbestos.

As snow poured past the window, they toasted trust.

Stalin beamed.

Then they discussed practical ways of communicating when Viktor got back to Lisbon.

Which was when the Judas Code was born.

18

Seventy feet below Piccadilly, Churchill slept fitfully.

The cause of his interrupted slumber was twofold.

In the first place, he didn't like this dungeon, built before the war by the Railway Executive Committee in anticipation of bombing. But Mr. Josiah Wedgwood, M.P., had made such a noise in Parliament about his vulnerability during the Blitz that he had been forced to burrow beneath the West End until the shelter at the Annexe overlooking St. James's Park by Storey's Gate was made stronger. Lying there feeling London's foundations shudder, he was acutely aware of the plight of the populace, who were taking cover in Anderson shelters, in the new Morrison shelters (metal tables enclosed with steel mesh), and in underground railway stations. "London Can Take It," ran the slogan. Soon, Churchill feared, all the other big cities would have to take it as well.

The second cause of his fitful sleep was the dearth of good news.

This, he brooded as he awoke at 3:10 A.M., was only equaled by the surfeit of bad news.

He swung himself out of bed and prowled around his wretched subterranean quarters. On a chest of drawers beside the iron bed were his family photographs. His children, Diana, Randolph, Sarah, and Mary. And, of course, his wife, Clementine. It was at times like this that he needed Clemmie.

Only she understood these moments of loneliness and, yes, despair. She was the only one allowed to. If the public heard about them, they too would despair. His chief importance was not to be a visionary or a strategist but to be the lion's roar for the people of Britain. He was an old predator led out from the back of the cage to snarl defiance through the bars.

Glass of water in hand, Churchill rested his plump frame on the end of the bed. The truth was that he could not share his greatest fears with anyone. Not even Clemmie. Because they concerned the looming possibility of a defeat for which only he could be held responsible.

Quite simply, if Mussolini couldn't be persuaded to create a diversion, and Hitler launched his invasion of Russia as early as May next year, he might be capable of reaching Moscow before winter clamped down. Then, with the Red Army in frozen, bloodstained tatters outside its capital and Stalin seeking peace, the Führer would turn to England for that tacitly promised pact. If it wasn't forthcoming he would take Britain with one swipe of his panzers.

And by encouraging him I would be responsible for this last body blow to these islands of ours. The end of beleaguered valor, the end of our insular heritage, the end of reason.

How could he explain any of that, even to Clemmie? Even if the Grand Deception still succeeded, he would be responsible for a holocaust. One day, perhaps, he could explain to her that he had tried to avert suffering on an even greater scale; that he had plotted to prevent two bloodthirsty warlords carving up great tracts of the world as they had carved up Poland.

Churchill lay back on the uncomfortable bed; he thought he could hear the all-clear above ground. Normally he would either have been up there watching the show from a rooftop or in a deep sleep.

Not tonight.

There was one person in whom he could confide. Sinclair, who had seemed too soft for his job until bereavement had made him pitiless in that deceptive, Anglo-Saxon way that so often baffled foreigners. With Sinclair he could discuss every aspect of the Grand Deception—except his own fear. Sinclair wouldn't want to know about fear: Sinclair wanted revenge. In that respect Sinclair was the man in the street: he wanted the roar not the whimper.

With a sigh not far removed from a whimper, Churchill pulled the sheet and blanket up to his chin. He closed his eyes. He slept. He dreamed about Knickebein, code word for the Luftwaffe's system of beam navigation. (The British were now bending the radio beams, causing the German bombers to drop their loads off-target.) He dreamed about his negotiations with Roosevelt—fifty aging American destroyers in exchange for leases on British bases in the Atlantic; he dreamed about the Italian army advancing toward Egypt; he dreamed about the defense of Malta. When he awoke again he discovered that all these momentous considerations had occupied eight minutes of his life.

His head ached. He considered his intake of liquor the previous evening. No more than usual. Which wasn't to say it wasn't considerable.

He took a pinch of snuff to blow the headache away.

He slept again and this time he dreamed that German storm troopers were besieging the gates of the Kremlin.

When he next awoke, there, on his breakfast tray, was good news.

What was good news for Churchill was uncommonly bad news for Hitler.

He first heard about the intention of his Italian ally, Benito Mussolini, Il Duce, to attack Greece, in Berlin on October 24.

He had no doubt about Mussolini's motive: jealousy at the victories of the German war machine. When he had heard about the movements of Wehrmacht troops in Rumania he had obviously decided it was time Italy stole a little glory.

But Greece! There was only one argument for having the big-mouthed blacksmith's son as an ally and that was keeping the British occupied in the Mediterranean. A military campaign against the tough Greeks could be a disaster that would embroil Germany.

Hitler swore softly as he stared at the snow-covered countryside from the window of his special train. He was on his way to Florence to dissuade his ally from taking on the Greeks. That was one of the troubles with leading a crusade: you encouraged second-rate comrades-in-arms to try and emulate you.

Two hours from Florence he learned that his trip to Florence was abortive, that at dawn that day Italian troops had invaded Greece from Albania, which they had occupied in 1939.

When he alighted at the platform at Florence the cock-a-hoop Il Duce greeted him with the words, "Führer, we are on the march."

Hitler managed to remain cordial, despite the fact that Mussolini had embarked on an adventure that could have consequences far graver than he anticipated. If his troops failed to take Greece swiftly, if the Balkans were set alight by his actions, if the Germans had to go to the Italians' aid, Barbarossa might have to be postponed.

PART FIVE

19

The door looked innocuous enough. It was painted cream and was located on the fourth floor of the Avenida Palace hotel in Lisbon. It might have been the door to a linen cupboard or, perhaps, a staff room.

It was neither. It was an exit to the railway station next door and was used by, among others, Antonio Salazar, when he wanted to leave the hotel secretly. That way, sightseers, journalists, or more sinister observers could be left waiting on the sidewalk for hours before they realized that he was long gone.

What helped to make it so deceptive was its altitude. Who would have thought that you could walk off a fourth-floor landing straight into a railway station? But, of course, if the station was built on a hill—and what part of Lisbon wasn't?—then it was quite rational.

The existence of the door was made known to Hoffman by Cross while they were sitting near the statue of Peter Pan overlooking the mossy waters of the Serpentine in London's Kensington Gardens. Even in wartime there were a few nannies wheeling their charges around, but most of those abroad in the park were in uniform. The November day was raw, the silver barrage balloons that had been part of the summer skies suddenly seemed incongruous, like rain-filled clouds that had failed to burst.

"First," Cross had said as they sat on the park bench, "we must get the Gestapo off your back. That shouldn't be too difficult."

"And you," Viktor said brusquely, "can change your attitude. You're aware of what's happened to me since you last saw me?"

Cross nodded.

"Then I'm entitled to a more intelligent approach. I'm not your pawn anymore, Cross, I'm your king. Without me, nothing. Right?"

Cross glanced at him quizzically. "Whatever you say. You've done bloody well."

After the initial meetings with Stalin, Viktor had spent ten days in Moscow building solidly on the foundation of trust. Then he had sailed for London on a cargo ship from Archangel, which, flying the neutral flag of the Soviet Union, was safe from attack by the British or Germans.

Viktor said, "It won't be difficult to get the Gestapo off my back? Come off it, Cross—to use an expression of yours—it will be bloody difficult. My skin, not yours."

Cross, wearing a trench coat, shoes made of soft, black leather— Portuguese probably—and a tan as incongruous as the barrage balloons, looked surprised. "By God you've changed," he said.

"You should know, you changed me."

"War—"

"—changes everyone."

Cross shrugged. "Whatever you say. *You* may have changed, nothing else has. The object of the exercise is still to make sure that Stalin believes Hitler is going to invade Russia before he launches his attack. You're his confidant now, and we've got to make sure that you stay good and alive. So we've got to fix the Gestapo. You made their acquaintance, I gather, in Poland?"

"Oh yes."

A Wren, black-haired and impudent in her sailor's cap, navy blue uniform, and black stockings strolled past on the arm of an Australian soldier. Cross smiled at her. She ignored him—he was a civilian.

"One of the prices I have to pay," Cross said. "However, I can get hold of silk stockings, so I'm still in with a chance." He lit a Three Castles cigarette. "The point is that we have to get the Abwehr on our side."

"We've already got them. Von Claus . . ."

"We have to get them on our side to the extent that, in your case, they wield more power than the Gestapo. Thank Christ, despite Himmler and Heydrich, Canaris still has Hitler's ear."

A rowboat skimmed past them. The oars were wielded by a muscular young man in an Air Force blue shirt. Opposite him, looking cold but valiantly aware of the play of his muscles, was a blonde nurse. Viktor envied them. At least the war had liberated love. He thought of Rachel

Keyser. What a presumptuous liaison that had been. The clouds began to seep rain.

Viktor turned up the collar of his black topcoat. "What you're saying," he suggested, "is that we should give the Abwehr a coup so that Hitler calls off Himmler's thugs."

"You're learning," Cross remarked.

"Simple. We just tell them about some attack planned by the British. A few hundred lives lost. So what? My credibility has been restored."

Three Spitfires streaked low across the leaking sky.

"You know something?" Cross said. "Cynicism doesn't suit you. Leave that to me." He flicked his cigarette end across the path. "In fact we *have* come up with something, in our cynical way."

"We? Who's we? You and Churchill?"

"Leave any shabby maneuvers to me. Anything Churchill does is for the sake of Britain."

"So it can't be shabby? For Christ's sake, Cross, don't start trying to sell me Saint Winston. The man's a politician and a warrior. He may well win the war, but don't tell me he's not capable of pulling a shabby trick."

"I think we're talking about the greatest Englishman who's ever lived."

Skirting this idolatry, Hoffman asked what secret he was going to convey to the Abwehr.

"The existence of a new installation on the south coast—near Littlehampton—equipped with beam-bending devices. You know, the Krauts think they're bombing Croydon Airport when in fact they're blowing up a few unfortunate cows in a field. They know we've got this equipment," Cross said, "but they don't know where we've got it."

"And I'm going to tell them, just like that?"

"You," Cross said, "are going to tell them where there's a base made of plywood equipped with precisely fuck-all."

Viktor digested this, then said, "But won't their agents over here blow the deception?"

"Almost all of their agents here have been turned. They'll tell their masters what we want them to tell them. The Luftwaffe will smash the plywood base to smithereens and your rating with the Abwehr will go up a couple of notches."

"But if we go on bending the beams," Viktor said, "they'll smell a rat. Guess that they've bombed a dummy."

"As it happens," Cross said, "they're about to produce a beam that we can't bend; not for the time being anyway. So it will all be academic. We hope the Abwehr will believe that we're not bending them because, thanks to you, they destroyed our equipment. Canaris will think you're the answer to a spymaster's prayers, call on Himmler, and tell him to call off his gangsters. I would like," Cross said, "to be present when Bauer gets his instructions."

An air-raid warden walked past. His arm was in a sling, and he was still wearing a steel helmet. He stared at Cross and Viktor with unseeing eyes.

The rain thickened, the rowboats headed for the boathouse.

"But it's more than a question of merely saving your skin," Cross said, taking his last cigarette from a silver case and lighting it with a Dunhill lighter.

"I know—I'm important. I've got to save Russia from the Nazi hordes."

Cross appraised him. "Don't you want to?" He blew gray smoke into the rain. "Did anything happen over there that you haven't told me about?"

"Don't worry, nothing's changed."

"I hope not," Cross said quietly. A raindrop hissed on his cigarette, extinguishing it. He tried to relight it without success. "Shit," he said and tossed it away. "What I meant was," he said, "that it's not merely a question of preserving you to warn Stalin. You will be a double-bladed weapon."

"The Germans?"

"Yes," Cross agreed, "the Germans. You'll be a veritable fount of misinformation." Viktor sensed that he had meant much more than that, had been close, or as close as he was ever likely to get, to an indiscretion. Viktor couldn't imagine what it was. "And that leaves the Red Cross," Cross said, diverting the conversation. "What are we going to do about them? You abandoned your post and since then they've had some disquieting questions asked about you. The last thing they want is their impartiality questioned."

Viktor said, "You'll think of something."

Fifty yards away a soldier pushed a WAAF against a tree and began to kiss her passionately. They didn't appear to mind the rain.

"Your parents in Czechoslovakia," Cross said. "You heard they were in trouble with the Germans. That they had been interrogated, that your father was injured, that he was dying."

228

None of this surprised Viktor; nothing surprised him anymore.

"You flew to Prague using Red Cross documents. You're very sorry about that," Cross said prodding a finger at Viktor. "When you got there you found that they'd been taken to a camp in Poland. They're Jewish, of course."

"If you say so."

"You traced them. Helped them to escape. But, apart from traveling on Red Cross papers to begin with, you at no time involved the Red Cross. You are truly penitent, and thank God, your boss in Lisbon is an understanding man. A Jew, I believe."

"You mean I'll be forgiven?"

"You'll get a bollocking, but, yes, you'll be forgiven."

"Someone must have a very persuasive tongue if all that's going to be accomplished."

"Jan Masaryk," Cross said, "is a pretty accomplished Czech diplomat even though he's in exile in London."

Still unsurprised, Viktor asked, "So when do I go back to Lisbon?"

"Tomorrow night," Cross said. "The following day you have a rendezvous with von Claus—in the railway station. But you don't go directly to the station."

Which was when Cross told Viktor about the secret door in the Avenida Palace.

20

The Gestapo reestablished contact with Viktor in the Praço dos Restauradores.

The agent, a thin-faced Austrian who also worked for the German news agency DNB (standing, according to the British, for Do Not Believe), took up the trail with extreme caution, being uncomfortably aware that several Gestapo operatives had already died after being assigned to Josef Hoffman. The agent spotted Viktor walking past the Palácio Foz and followed him until he entered the Avenida Palace. The agent parked his Citröen across the street. It was 1:18 P.M. Perhaps Viktor was lunching at the hotel. Or visiting the Jewess. Whatever he was doing, the Austrian expected him to emerge within a couple of hours.

After three hours he became worried, after four, frantic. He left the Citröen and approached the hall porter, a Swiss named Riem. Yes, Riem remembered a man answering Hoffman's description entering the hotel; if he wasn't mistaken he had left half an hour later.

Impossible. The Austrian ran up the stairs to the first floor, where a handsome, crinkly haired young Portuguese ran the switchboard. There had been a call for Hoffman about three and a half hours ago, which he had taken at reception. After that . . . The Portuguese shrugged. Was there another exit from the hotel? Another shrug. That was the business of the management. The Jewess's room number? Jewess? What Jewess? Desperately the Austrian tried to remember the girl's name. Kaufman? Koestler? An author named Koestler, Arthur Koestler, sometimes visited the hotel, the switchboard operator remarked. Keyser, that was it. Her room number? He wasn't permitted to divulge numbers, but he could try the room. He plugged in a lead. Together they waited. Finally he said, "There's no reply from Miss Keyser's room" and looked pleased about it, damn him.

The Austrian searched the big, chandelier-hung dining room and the salon and the courtyard, lined with potted plants, and the bar, where he had a large brandy. The barman, Domingos, hadn't seen anyone resembling Hoffman. The Austrian consulted his pocket watch. He had been out of contact with Hoffman for nearly five hours. By now another of Bauer's men might have picked him up.

He telephoned the legation from a callbox outside the hotel.

Bauer was brusque, cutting short the Austrian's timetable of surveillance. "What you're trying to tell me is you've lost him?"

"He might still be in the hotel."

"Only if he's taken up residence." Bauer's voice was a stiletto. "You realize that Reichsführer Himmler is personally interested in this case?"

The Austrian said he did.

"You can imagine his reaction."

He could.

"If you haven't found him within an hour I shall have to report your failure to Prinz Albrechtstrasse. You appreciate . . ."

He did.

"There's a plane to Berlin tonight."

"I haven't the slightest doubt—"

"Find him!"

The stiletto plunged deep into the Austrian's brain, twisting.

In fact, Viktor had spent less than five minutes in the hotel. The porter had been mistaken about his leaving by the main entrance. There had been a phone call—from the Red Cross—which he had taken just before leaving.

From reception he had taken the stairs to the fourth floor and, using the key that Cross had given him, gone through the cream door, emerging in the railway station.

The station wasn't large—only ten platforms—but it was busy enough. One train was just departing, billowing steam that collected under the glass roof, and one had just arrived. The footsteps of the arrivals were sharp on the marble floor, those of friends and relatives who had just said good-bye softer and slower. Through the entrance to the station Viktor could see sand-colored buildings and a couple of palm trees.

Von Claus said, "Restless places, stations, aren't they? Sad and exciting." He took Viktor's arm. "Let's sit over there," pointing at a seat beside a silver-painted pillar.

"So," he said, "I gather you're a lucky young man still to be alive." He was wearing a gray fedora and a black coat cut to minimize the hump on his back. He looked extremely dapper.

Viktor said, "You know what I think? I think I should have gone to the Gestapo in the first place. Your people don't seem to have any control over them."

"We are an intelligence service," von Claus said, "not a bunch of bully boys. Which doesn't mean to say we can't be tough. You should have told me you were going to Russia. You were a gift horse to the Gestapo— Czech consorting with a Jewess, pulling the wool over the eyes of the Abwehr, and suddenly rushing off to consort with the Bolsheviks." He paused. "Why did you go to Russia, Herr Hoffman?"

Viktor had discussed the answer to this question with Cross. As it stood, the Gestapo had one explanation, the Red Cross another. Cross had decided to let them both stand. To give the Abwehr the same story Viktor had given to the Gestapo (assuming that Adler had lived to repeat it): He had been heading for Russian-occupied Poland to negotiate the transfer of Poles trapped there. And to persuade the Red Cross in Lisbon, already sympathetic to Josef Hoffman and his fictitious Jewish parents in Poland, to corroborate the story. Viktor told it to von Claus.

Von Claus wet his lips as though tasting the story. "But why were you so special, Herr Hoffman? Why did the Red Cross send you halfway across Europe to negotiate the transfer of a few Poles?"

"Not a few. Thousands. And there aren't many employees of the Red Cross who speak German, Polish, Russian."

"And were the Poles in the Russian sector really so anxious to return to the Germans?"

"Yes."

"That's very complimentary to the Germans."

"Not really," Viktor said, remembering the place named Katyn, "they were the lesser of two evils."

A family of refugees ran past them toward a train that was about to depart. They had probably abandoned hope of leaving Lisbon and were going to settle in the country. They ran as if they were pursued; perhaps they were.

Von Claus said, "But why Moscow, Herr Hoffman?"

A precaution. The Red Cross thought I would probably have to go there to complete the negotiations. A necessary precaution, as it happened."

"And these poor Poles, have they been repatriated?"

"We've done everything we can. It's up to the Russians now. They have promised . . ."

Von Claus grunted his view of Soviet promises. "I should have thought," he said in his precise voice, "that there were far more worthy causes. However I accept your story—for the time being. What do the Russians think of Germany?"

"They're not happy with the German incursions into Finland and Rumania, if that's what you mean."

"I think Molotov made that perfectly clear in Berlin," von Claus said. He smiled. "With a little help from Churchill, who laid on an air raid, so that Ribbentrop and Molotov had to take to the shelter during their discussions. When Ribbentrop assured Molotov that Britain was finished, Molotov said, 'If that is so, why are we in this shelter and whose are those bombs which fall?'" Von Claus shrugged. "So the story goes. What I really meant was, do they think the pact will hold?"

"Between Germany and Russia? They think it will hold, yes. Not forever. For another couple of years, perhaps."

"Your sources are good?"

"Modest, but reliable." If you only knew, Viktor thought.

Von Claus seemed to accept what he had said; it probably concurred with his own intelligence from Moscow. "And what about England?" he asked. "You really do get around, don't you?"

"I have good information from England, but it will cost you."

"Allow me to evaluate it," von Claus said.

"Five hundred American dollars. In dollars—they buy more."

"Nothing you can tell me is worth five hundred American dollars."

"If I told you how the Luftwaffe can stop dropping bombs on fields instead of cities?"

Von Claus looked at him quizzically. "I presume you're referring to the British method of bending radio beams to divert bombers from their targets?"

"If I told you where it was being done, would that be worth five hundred dollars?"

Von Claus tried to straighten his body. His back seemed to be paining him. "It might," he said eventually. "But I'd have to have proof before paying out."

"Two-fifty now, two-fifty when I've proved it."

"Mercenary, aren't we?" He tapped his pockets with thin fingers. "I haven't got two hundred and fifty American dollars with me."

"In one hour's time," Viktor said. "I'll wait here."

Von Claus considered the proposition. "Very well, but if the information is false I'll hand you over to Bauer."

When he had gone, Viktor strolled around the station. He enjoyed the atmosphere, even if it did smell slightly of fish. He bought himself a coffee and a copy of *Diario de Lisboa.* Birmingham had been bombed, so the beam-benders hadn't been of much use that night.

Von Claus returned one hour later with the money inside a copy of *Signal.* Viktor told him where the plywood installation was on the south coast of England.

Von Claus made a note and said, "I suppose this isn't an elaborate ploy to save your skin from Himmler's assassins?" He thought about his own words. "But why then should your skin be so important to the British?" He frowned.

"The question," Viktor reassured him, "doesn't arise, because there isn't any ploy."

"But it does seem odd that a Red Cross official should be privy to such secrets as this."

"You forget that people trust the Red Cross with their secrets. They're not even aware that they're letting them out."

"I suppose so." Von Claus didn't seem wholly convinced. "'Careless talk costs lives.' I believe they have posters to that effect in Britain."

"But people don't take too much notice."

Von Claus stood up. "Just out of interest," he said, "What are you going to do with all that money?"

"Count it," Viktor said.

The hour was almost up. Two more minutes before he was due to telephone Bauer. Hoffman almost certainly wasn't in the hotel, and he wasn't in his lodgings, because the landlady hadn't been lying—the thin-faced Austrian was adept at picking up the ring of truth.

Fearfully he made his way to the callbox in the Largo do Carmo. He had no doubt what fate awaited him in Berlin. The question was whether to make a break for it before he reached Sintra airport.

One more minute.

No sign of Hoffman.

He dialed the legation number.

Bauer said, "Where is he?"

The thin-faced Austrian said, "He's just rounded the corner of the Largo do Carmo and is heading toward his lodgings." And so joyful was he that he essayed a little joke: "And do you know something? He's really on our side—he's carrying a copy of *Signal*."

On November 22, 1940, the day the Greeks inflicted a shattering defeat on the Italians at Koritsa, a German reconnaissance aircraft was spotted high over the south coast of Britain. Two days later, three Ju 88 bombers, escorted by Messerschmitt 109 fighters, dropped fifteen thousand pounds of bombs on and around a camouflaged installation two miles inland from the seaside resort of Littlehampton. The installation was destroyed, and for weeks afterward householders in the area were able to supplement their allocations of coal with pieces of shattered plywood.

In the new year, transmitting information gathered by Britain's ULTRA cryptanalysts, Viktor was able to convince Stalin that, through contacts in Lisbon, he had penetrated the inner sanctums of the Reich Chancellery. Using the Judas Code, he anticipated, among other things, the dispatch of Luftwaffe aircraft to Italy and the appointment of a new German army commander in North Africa. The commander's name was Erwin Rommel.

21

"But why *Judas* Code?" Rachel Keyser asked.

About time, Viktor thought. It was now February, and he had been waiting for three months for her to start probing for details of his method of communicating with Stalin.

"Why not?"

He tapped out Victory V—three dots and a dash—on the transmitter on which, under Rachel's supervision, he was practicing Morse code in her apartment, overlooking the Parque Eduardo VII. Rain sweeping across the deserted park and spattering against the window added its own tattoo to the Morse.

"I don't know. It's just that it sounds so biblical."

"Judas . . . treachery. We're in a treacherous business, you and I."

"That's not the whole reason, is it?"

So she could impale the small untruths he uttered. Even though there was no longer any physical love between them, there was still understanding. What if she perceived the greater untruths that he might have to perpetrate?

She got up from the window seat and wandered around the small apartment. It was old, and despite the new paint, a little musty. She hadn't tried to rejuvenate it, but she had installed green plants, a couple of mottled mirrors, and a chaise lounge with moss-colored scatter cushions.

"Would you like some tea?"

He shook his head, varying his touch with the transmitter, as she had taught him, so that he couldn't be identified by experts. "Your touch can be as distinctive as a pianist's," she had told him.

Why had she left it so long to sound him out? He was still being used—he had no illusions about that—and he would have thought she would have made it her business to discover how he spoke to Stalin, in case anything went wrong.

Once, of course, she would have found out in bed. But that was before Sintra.

She went into the kitchen and, beneath a ceiling hung with dried herbs, made tea. Her voice issued through the serving hatch: "You say we're engaged in treachery; I don't agree. If we're betraying anyone, it's the enemy."

And ourselves?

He abandoned the transmitter and sat on the cushion she had vacated. Day after day, Viktor had been confined to this room with her, learning his new craft, what they euphemistically called communications. And they had barely touched hands. It was ridiculous, naïve, unnatural; it was also a strength.

Supposing she wasn't still deceiving him?

"So why Judas?" she asked again. Cup and saucer rattled; he smelled tea above the aroma of the herbs. "There's no secret about it, is there?"

Oh yes, there was a secret. Such a secret! And only two people knew it: Stalin and himself. It was the twist, the ultimate safeguard.

When he didn't reply she said, more loudly (perhaps Cross had been getting at her), "I mean, we're supposed to be in this together. And I have taught you everything you know."

True. He could encode and decode with the best of them. He could use a one-time pad—transmit or receive a code that was virtually unbreakable. Relatively simple when you knew how. You just used a page from a pad containing a sequence of, say, five-digit numbers representing the letters of the alphabet and added a previously arranged number of the alphabet—27, perhaps, for *A,* descending to plain 2 for *Z.* As the original numbers had no pattern the result was well-nigh indecipherable to a code-breaker. After each message had been sent and received, you destroyed that leaf of the pad and there on the next page was another virgin sequence of random figures available only to you and the recipient of the message. She had even told him about the Voynich Manuscript, an apparently coded volume 204 pages long that, since its discovery in Italy in 1912 by an American, William Voynich, had defied analysis.

Yes, she had taught him a lot. Love and deception included.

As for his method of communication with the Kremlin, well, she wouldn't be all that impressed. It was one of the oldest known methods of sending coded information. All you needed was the key. But until you had that key it could give you migraine.

The key was a book. They had agreed on that in the Kremlin, he and Stalin. The Bible was the first book that Viktor had thought of—it had been his benefactor once before!—but he had rejected it because it would probably occur immediately to a cryptanalyst and because he didn't think his father would appreciate it.

They had agreed upon *War and Peace*. It was singularly appropriate. And from a specialist at the NKVD's Moscow Centre he had learned how to tally numbers with letters and to vary references, to confuse hostile cipher experts if the key was discovered.

If it was discovered. It was quite probable that it already had been, all 1315 pages of it—hidden with the transmitter he used to contact Moscow in the room he had rented in the Alfama. Without a doubt he was under surveillance. Perhaps, even as she made the tea, Rachel knew about *War and Peace*.

But when the time came, he could change the key. And she didn't know the ultimate secret of the Judas Code.

Cup and saucer in hand, Rachel came back into the room, dressed in a navy suit, black hair longer than when they had first met, a couple of spiderweb creases at the corners of her eyes that hadn't been there in those days.

She sat opposite him, sipping her tea. "The Bible?"

"Judas? No. It's a personal thing. Stalin doesn't even know I've called it that."

"It's not your code name?"

He shook his head. His code name was Dove. But why make Cross's job easier? Then again, why should Cross and Rachel want to deceive him? But they had done so once before.

"I wouldn't mind betting," she said, nibbling a chocolate biscuit, "that because you're a man of peace you've chosen a code name like Dove."

"*Was* a man of peace," he said. "You can call me Judas. You and Cross. And Churchill."

"You didn't tell me everything that happened in Poland, did you?"

"I told Cross. That was enough, wasn't it?"

A clock on the mantelpiece chimed. The day felt like a Sunday, but it was Wednesday.

She said sadly, "We should have told you everything right from the beginning. Cross will pick his own pockets one of these days. Double-Cross—very funny, very true."

But does he still make love to you? He hadn't displayed any symptoms of jealousy. He wouldn't, would he, if he was a satisfied lover?

"You were so different," she said, "when you came back."

"I hadn't killed anyone before I went away."

"Not just tougher," she said. "More . . . insular."

"Secretive?"

"Self-contained. And older," she added.

"Then I've just got to adapt, haven't I," he said.

"Just got to adapt," he tapped out, returning to the transmitter.

"All right," she said, voice brisk again, "now the second part of the lesson. Transmitting *and* receiving. I'm going over to the embassy. Wait here, I'll start transmitting in fifteen minutes."

From the window he watched her cross the street, five stories below.

"Are you receiving me?"

"Loud and clear," he tapped back.

"Anything to report?"

"I had a visitor this afternoon."

"Friend or bandit?"

"I wish I knew."

"Not bad. You could speed it up a bit."

He speeded it up. "I recognize your touch. Vary your touch—like you taught me to."

"Are you taking down the messages?"

"Of course. Object of exercise."

"Try this." Tap, tap, tap.

He looked at what he had written.

He replied, "Please repeat message."

A pause. "Is it so terrible?"

"Please repeat."

"I . . . love . . . you."

"Report back to base," he tapped out.

It was the fastest response he had ever transmitted.

So the cliché was true. First contact, after a long, long time, *was* like electricity.

No, she had said when she had returned, no preliminaries, and they

240

had taken off their clothes and lain on the bed in her small, blue-papered bedroom, and the electricity had darted between them, melded them; and she had pulled him down onto her, into her.

Then because he was still inside her, and for the moment at least, he was hers, and because she had begun to lose hope, and because he was so thin and proud, she had wanted to weep; but instead she had smiled at him and said, "There."

"I had forgotten," he said.

"I hadn't forgotten. I had begun to despair. But it will be all right now," she said, wanting him to say yes, because that was something, even if she knew it wasn't true because of what she had to do. But in war all that mattered was *now.*

"Yes," he said, "it will be all right now."

But the wariness was still there.

"I don't want it ever to happen again," she said. "That terrible thing that came between us."

"Don't worry," he said. He raised himself on one elbow, stroked her hair, her breasts. "Don't worry."

"I should have told you . . ."

"It wasn't your fault." He kissed her breasts. "But now . . . You wouldn't deceive me again, would you?"

"If I was going to deceive you I would still say no, so my answer can't bring you any satisfaction."

She noticed that it had stopped raining and the raindrops on the window were sparkling in pale sunshine.

"That's a very complicated answer," he said without surprise. "Just say no—if that's your answer."

"What I want to say is even more complicated. I want to say that you must trust me, whatever happens. I want to say that, because of this terrible bloody war, a person's actions may be misunderstood. I want to say that, no, I won't deceive you, but if circumstances change . . ."

"Then you will?"

"I won't." What else could she say? If she told him the truth she would lose him. What if she told him that she had refused to bargain for his life when he was in Poland?

He lay back on the blue-and-white coverlet, and when he spoke the wariness was still there.

"Aren't you going to ask me about the Judas Code again?"

"To hell with the Judas Code. Will you take me out to dinner?"

"You were very interested in it just now."

"Just its name, that's all. It sounds very . . . ominous. Or shall I take you to dinner?"

"I'll take you. The Germans are paying anyway. But shouldn't you know more details?"

She ran her hand down his body. It was thin but it was muscular, too. Muscles sheathing the sides of his ribs moved when he shifted his arms. She rested her hand in the blond, curly hair at his crotch.

"Why should I? You send the messages."

"Supposing something happened to me?"

We made a mistake there, she thought; at least Cross did. I should have got the details as soon as he got back; now his suspicion has germinated. If I'm not careful he will realize that we know about the room in the Alfama, about *War and Peace,* about the elementary method of encoding he was employing, about the transmitter. And he will know that even now I am deceiving him.

She kissed him and said, "You're right, of course."

"But only if something happens to me."

"I don't understand."

"I've left the details of the Judas Code in a sealed envelope with a lawyer named Eduardo Alves, who has an office on the Avenida da Liberdade. He has instructions to deliver it to you in the event of my death."

"You don't really trust me, do you?"

"I want to," he said.

He turned and kissed her eyes, mouth, breasts; the electricity was regenerated; she moved above him and sank onto him; and this time they were lost together for much, much longer.

And it wasn't until they were eating lobster and drinking white wine in a little restaurant in the Alfama that she again thought about his code. It was so basic. Could there be more to it than was apparent?

Why Judas?

Rachel Keyser had her second presentiment of danger later that night.

When she got back to her apartment Cross was there; the gramophone was playing, and he was looking for hidden microphones.

"It seems to be clean," he said after a while. "But just in case . . ." He turned up the volume of the gramophone. Bing Crosby singing "Pennies from Heaven."

"Do you have to come as late as this?" She sat in an armchair and crossed her legs; she was tired and all she wanted was to lie down and relive the evening.

"Why, are you expecting loverboy?" He pointed through the open bedroom door at the rumpled coverlet. "Is he insatiable?"

She realized for the first time that Cross was jealous. There could be nothing more perilous to a delicate espionage operation than a jealous partner.

She said, "It's what you wanted, isn't it?"

"It's obviously what *you* wanted." He had been drinking, but he wasn't drunk. "What made him succumb again after all these months?"

Love, she wanted to say, but "My natural charms" were the words that emerged. "What do you want?"

"Have you got a drink?"

"One," she said, "then out. The whisky's in the kitchen."

When he returned he had a glass of whisky in one hand and a photograph of a document in the other.

"Do you know what this is?" waving the photograph.

How could she possibly know?

"It's Directive 21, the brainchild of one Adolf Hitler, dated December 18, 1940. It's called Barbarossa and it's the blueprint for the invasion of Russia."

"When?" interest revived.

"May 15. But thanks to Mussolini, he will probably have to postpone it for a few weeks. Listen to this." He read from the foot of the photograph. "*The German armed forces must be prepared, even before the conclusion of the war against England, to crush Soviet Russia in a rapid campaign.* Dynamite, eh?"

"But not if it falls into Stalin's hands. It would finish everything we've been working for."

"Don't worry," Cross said, "I got this from an exclusive source. He assured me there aren't any other copies flying around and I believe him." He gulped his whisky, went into the kitchen, and refilled his glass, and she thought, Bastard! You know I'm not going to throw you out until you've told me what this is all about.

"So what we have to do," Cross said, chinking ice in his glass, "is make sure that loverboy feeds Stalin enough information about the German army's movements to maintain his credibility. The information must be good but it mustn't alarm Uncle Joe too much. The actual figures," he said, "are staggering."

"Stagger me," she said.

"Apparently Hitler intends to move three million, four hundred thousand men, six hundred thousand horses, and six hundred thousand vehicles up to a line stretching from the Baltic in the north to the Black Sea in the south."

"You've staggered me," she said.

"Yes, but what matters is the present deployment. As far as we know he's so far managed to move twenty-five divisions into position." Cross took a typewritten sheet of paper from his pocket. "This is what I want loverboy to transmit."

Rachel took the sheet of paper and read, *Understand considerable German troop movements in easterly direction. These easily explained by Nazi concern with Bulgaria, Rumania, Hungary, and Yugoslavia and her designs on Greece.*

Cross said, "That should allay Uncle Joe's fears for a while." He finished his whisky. "You don't really give a damn for loverboy, do you?"

His jealousy surprised her. It was the last emotion she had associated with him. She had known him for so long; it was he who had awakened her. Perhaps she had been so absorbed with that awakening and the subsequent pleasures that he had brought her that she had never noticed other characteristics.

She wished Hoffman had been the first, the only one. No, that was ridiculous, schoolgirl talk.

"Well, do you?"

"Yes," she said, quietly, "I do."

"You stupid bitch. If you let your emotions take over, you could jeopardize the whole thing."

"Don't worry," she said, "I won't do that, I promise."

"Is he good?"

"Good?"

"In bed."

"It's none of your business. Now for God's sake get out." She stood up. "You've had too much to drink."

"I should think he's very good. Since he met you, that is, because you must be a very good tutor. It's important to have a good tutor. You did."

He grabbed her jacket. Silver buttons flew across the room. Then her blouse. The silk ripped easily but, oddly, what she feared most was the thought of his kissing her.

He said thickly, "Come on, you bitch, don't pretend you don't like it rough," which was when she hit him with the back of her hand, hard across the face, amethyst ring on her finger drawing blood.

She backed toward the serving hatch and picked up a kitchen knife. "Touch me again," she said, "and you get this." She felt quite calm.

He touched his cheek. The sight of blood on his fingers seemed to surprise him. He took a handkerchief from his pocket to staunch it.

He managed a smile. "God help the Arabs if you ever get to Palestine," he said. He opened the door and walked into the corridor.

At the same time that Cross was leaving Rachel Keyser's apartment, his "exclusive source" was lying in bed elsewhere in the city torturing himself with doubt.

Had he done the right thing by handing over details of Barbarossa?

Although the window was closed, he could hear the plaintive notes of the *fado*; that didn't help. He shivered, and with his feet searched for the hot-water bottle, but it was almost cold. Switching on the bedside lamp, Admiral Canaris got out of bed and fetched another blanket from a cupboard. It wouldn't make much difference.

He put on his thick, gray dressing gown, sat on the edge of the bed, and from his briefcase took his own copy of Hitler's Directive 21. The British would almost certainly pass details on to Stalin. What if the Red Army made a preemptive strike and smashed its way through Eastern Europe?

Canaris ran his hand through his gray hair and studied the details of the Führer's precocious brainchild. He intended to marshal three great armies. The southern group would plunge across the Ukraine to Kiev; the northern would strike from East Prussia toward Leningrad. But the main attack would be launched by the central group toward Smolensk and Minsk with the object of cutting off vast portions of the Red Army.

In addition Hitler intended to send a detachment from Finland to take Murmansk, the all-season Arctic port.

Some German generals were against the whole concept. Notably Guderian, King of the Panzers. Others, such as von Brauchitsch, Paulus, and Halder, disagreed about strategy after the initial attack. Hitler wanted to mop up industrial and agricultural areas and the Baltic States before taking Moscow. The three generals wanted to seize the Soviet capital as soon as possible and deprive the Russians of their communications and administrative center.

Canaris had no doubt whose view would prevail. Although they were often appalled by his unconventional strategies and disgusted (like

Canaris) by the extreme nature of his anti-Semitism, the generals couldn't deny Hitler's flare or the frequent accuracy of his predatory instincts.

No, Hitler would brook no argument. He was convinced his armies would reach a line east of Moscow, stretching from Archangel in the north to the Caspian Sea in the south, by October 15. Five months in which to smash the resistance of the biggest country in the world.

Not if I have my way, Canaris thought, putting the directive back in his briefcase and climbing back under the blankets, because Barbarossa is the ultimate act of madness. A war fought on two fronts (if the British break their word) and a campaign that could freeze the Wehrmacht to death in the Russian winter.

He switched off the light.

Am I really a traitor? he wondered. All I want to do is save German lives, hundreds of thousands of them. But, armed with Directive 21, would Stalin strike first?

I wouldn't if I were he, Canaris comforted himself. Not with my army catastrophically purged, not with my obsolete guns and prehistoric aircraft. Not if my army couldn't even thrash the Finns convincingly. No, I would merely move my divisions up to the border to show the Führer that I was ready for him.

Not even Hitler would then risk a drawn-out engagement with the endless ranks of Soviet troops—Stalin had no shortage of available bodies. Another pact would be sealed, and the two warlords would start exchanging birthday greetings once again.

Of course that's what would happen. Savior, not traitor.

And what would happen if anyone discovered that he had handed over Directive 21 to a British agent? Canaris turned his head on the pillow. The fresh blanket had only made him colder.

22

The Grand Deception, Churchill thought, pressing a brick into its bed of cement, was reaching its climax.

By midsummer he would know if he had succeeded in tricking the two archenemies of democracy into a wasting war.

And success or failure would be determined this month, March.

"This is the vital month," he said to Brendan Bracken, who was watching him build a garden wall at Chartwell.

"In what respect, Winston?"

It was always refreshing to hear Bracken asking a question, because he was usually occupied spouting facts. But there was one subject about which he knew nothing: Judas and his mission. Nor did Churchill's deputy, Clement Attlee, nor did Eden, nor did Beaverbrook, nor did Clemmie.

He answered Bracken in general terms. "This is the month when Hitler will have to decide whether he's going to get Mussolini off the Grecian hook. If he does, he will have to postpone Barbarossa—and that could bring him face to face with the Russian winter." With his trowel Churchill removed a wad of cement squeezed from under the brick.

"And we both know the deciding factor in that context," said Bracken, getting into his stride. "Germany, or Austria if you prefer it, is separated from Greece by four countries—Hungary, Romania, Bulgaria, and Yugoslavia. The first three have all succumbed; Yugoslavia is still holding out. To march on Greece, Hitler needs Yugoslavia's cooperation."

Churchill handed Bracken the trowel. "Here, let's see if you know everything there is to know about bricklaying."

He stood back and watched his ginger-haired parliamentary private secretary, incongruously dressed in a charcoal gray suit and stiff white collar, pick up a brick.

He frowned. Something Bracken had said had alerted an instinct. He knew the feeling well: an idea was about to surface.

Bracken pushed the brick home and sliced off errant cement. He picked up another brick. By the time he got back to Westminster he would be the world's greatest authority on bricklaying.

Churchill wandered a few yards away and stared across the garden. It was bathed in delicate sunshine. Daffodils and narcissi trembled in a breeze that smelled of rain to come. For twenty years Chartwell had been his haven. Soon he would have to leave it and make do with Chequers, because it was going to be used as government offices. But he would return when the war was won.

When . . . Yugoslavia. What had Bracken said? *To march on Greece, Hitler needs Yugoslavia's cooperation.* Not a particularly profound observation. But what, Churchill speculated, if Yugoslavia were persuaded *not* to cooperate? What, his enthusiasm rising, if they were persuaded to resist?

Excitedly, he returned to Brendan Bracken, bricklayer. He pointed at the Irishman's handiwork. "Crooked," he said. "Terrible. Don't bother to apply for membership to the union, I won't give you a reference."

He took Bracken by the arm and led him toward the house. "Are you staying the night? Good," before Bracken could reply. "I've got to pay someone a visit. Clemmie will look after you while I'm gone."

"But you said—"

"That we'd have a long talk. So we shall, Brendan, so we shall. But something's come up."

"While I was laying those bricks?"

"Yes," Churchill said, "while you were laying them crookedly."

"Am I permitted to know whom you're going to see?"

"No," Churchill said, giving his arm a squeeze, "you're not. But I've been thinking, Brendan. You know so much about so many things. What if I were to make you Minister of Information?"

He winked at the astonished Irishman and summoned his driver to take him to the only man in whom he could confide his own plans for Barbarossa, Robert Sinclair.

It was dusk when he arrived at the house in Berkshire. Sinclair was just about to take his dog for a walk. Churchill asked if he could join them, and Sinclair said yes, why not. But as they strolled through the thick, overgrown woods, Churchill sensed he was an intruder; this was the time that Sinclair put aside to commune with his son, who had been dead for nine months. But Sinclair listened just the same, making brief and astute responses when they were needed.

Churchill approached the reason for his visit through an assessment of the war—felt his way to see if he had strayed along any false trails.

"One of our greatest victories," he said, "was last November."

"Roosevelt?"

"When he was reelected we were no longer alone. Roosevelt said the United States would be 'the arsenal of democracy.' A nice phrase—I wish I'd thought of it. And, by God, Sinclair, that's just what it has become. Lend-lease—America's intervened without intervention."

"Now we must hope that Hitler's Barbarossa will be a victory—for us." The dog scampered away, barking. "Which, I presume, is why you've come to see me."

"An off-shoot," Churchill said. "Yugoslavia."

"The back door to Greece."

"To Greece and Mussolini's beleaguered army. You know something, Sinclair, we're almost as lucky in the Führer's choice of allies as we are in our own. At least he seems to be behaving honorably to Il Duce."

"He doesn't have much choice," Sinclair remarked. "He can't allow Mussolini to lose his footing in Greece. It wouldn't do to let Britain have bases there, would it? Or Crete for that matter."

The dog brought the stick back and waited for it to be thrown again, tongue hanging from laughing jaws.

Churchill said, "You know what I'm getting at?"

"I think so."

"I wouldn't describe you as expansive, Sinclair."

Sinclair said, "With respect, it's fairly obvious. Yugoslavia is on the point of doing a deal with Hitler. When that happens the Wehrmacht will swoop on the Greeks and polish them off. Hitler will then be ready to finish his buildup for Barbarossa. We don't want that just yet."

Churchill swung at a clump of dead bracken with his stick. "What we want is at least a month's grace."

"So an anti-German coup in Belgrade would do the trick?"

"I had been thinking along those lines," Churchill said, as the dog returned with the stick.

"It's already in hand," Sinclair said. "I was going to be in touch this evening—for your final approval."

For once Churchill was speechless. Finally he said in an aggrieved tone, "Very well, you've got my approval."

"That's all right, then. Shall we return to the house?"

They walked back in silence, followed by the dog.

On March 25, Viktor was given a scoop to convey to Stalin. It was so good that he wasn't sure whether he could believe it.

Before taking it to the room in the Alfama to encode and transmit, he said to Rachel Keyser, "How the hell would the British get to know something like this?"

"Ours not to reason why," she told him.

"It had better be right," he said. "If it isn't we're endangering the whole project. One piece of false information and we lose credibility."

"It's right," she said.

The message he transmitted simply said, ANTI-NAZI COUP EXPECTED IN BELGRADE TOMORROW NIGHT MARCH TWENTY FIVE STROKE TWENTY SIX.

Hitler didn't hear about the coup until March 27. The news threw him into a fury.

Apparently a Yugoslav air force general, Bora Mirkovic, had overthrown the government in the name of the young heir to the throne, Peter II. Crowds were celebrating in the streets, and the German minister's car had been spat upon.

Immediately he called a council of war in the Chancellery. So passionate was his rage that he didn't wait for von Ribbentrop, or the commander in chief of the army, von Brauchitsch, or chief of the army general staff, Franz Halder, to arrive before launching into a diatribe.

Yugoslavia, he said, would have to be crushed with "unmerciful harshness." To Hermann Göring he said, "You must destroy Belgrade in attacks by waves."

Then he issued Directive 25, authorizing an immediate attack on Yugoslavia. The directive stated, "It is my intention to force my way into Yugoslavia . . . to annihilate the Yugoslav army."

He ordered his generals to draw up invasion plans that evening.

He went to bed in the early hours of the twenty-eighth, after cabling a letter to Mussolini in Rome setting out his intentions.

But it was a long time before he slept. Every time he closed his eyes he was awakened by his own words ringing out to his generals and ministers in the Chancellery:

"The beginning of the Barbarossa operation will have to be postponed up to four weeks."

For the first time since his armies had rolled across Europe he wondered if he had made a mistake.

Churchill's reaction to the Belgrade *coup d'état* was less dramatic than Hitler's. He ordered a bottle of slivovitz, the national drink of Yugoslavia, and sent it to Sinclair by special messenger.

While Hitler mustered his tanks to crush Yugoslavia and Greece, Viktor Golovin bought a bicycle.

It was by far the best way to shake off surveillance. Gestapo, Abwehr, NKVD, or MI6. If you were on a bicycle they couldn't follow you on foot, and when you dived into one of the narrow, hillside lanes of Lisbon they couldn't follow you by car. So they, too, had to take to bicycles, and there was no way you could conceal yourself hurtling through a precipitous maze on two wheels.

Viktor also enjoyed cycling. He could pedal at a leisurely pace through the city and admire its landmarks: the Belém Tower on the Tagus waterfront, the eleven-mile-long aqueduct of Aguas Livres, the palaces and parks—then suddenly launch himself down a lane as steep as a chute.

The bicycle was a Raleigh, austerity-built and painted entirely in black to prevent reflections in the blackout in Britain. Viktor guessed that a British seaman had traded it in the Alfama for a crate of local brandy or a girl. It had three gears, which helped him up the hills and whooshed him down them.

On April 1, April Fool's Day in Britain, the devil got into him.

Who was on duty? He accelerated along the Rua do Ouro, the Street of Gold, so named because of its jewelry shops, and glanced behind. A bicycle had also accelerated. Seated on it was the thin-faced Austrian. Gestapo. Viktor was glad. He enjoyed confounding Himmler's secret police force more than the others.

In his pocket he had details about German troop movements in the region of Yugoslavia. But there was no hurry to transmit them. The attack there wasn't due to be launched until April 6, according to British sources; and they, it seemed, were always right.

He stopped outside a cinema bearing an old legend, *animbiografo,* which was showing a German propaganda film, and went inside. The thin-faced Austrian, he felt, would be embarrassed by the experience, because although the Portuguese showed such movies to appease the Nazis, they treated them derisively. They didn't let him down. The film was about the French, Belgians, and Dutch welcoming blond Germans dedicated to wiping out corruption in their cities. There were a few saboteurs but they were all Jews. The Germans were catcalled by the audience, the saboteurs cheered.

Viktor departed by the rear exit. Behind him he heard a commotion, as the Austrian, who had just sat down, got up again to leave. Viktor mounted his bicycle, which he had chained to a lamppost, and headed for the Praça do Comércio.

There he wheeled his bicycle onto an orange ferry bound for the opposite bank of the Tagus. The Austrian just made it; he stood in the stern of the ferry while Viktor rode in the bow. There was a lot of activity among the ships lying at anchor. The previous afternoon, a German U-boat had surfaced a mile downriver and loosed off a couple of shots at a British cargo boat before submerging again. There had been an official protest, and the Portuguese navy was making a show of looking for the U-boat, which was probably halfway across the Atlantic by now.

The ferry butted its way between looming hulls and Phoenician-rigged fishing boats. Sunlight danced on the water.

When they reached the far bank, he waited. The Austrian hesitated; plainly it was ludicrous for just the two of them to stay on board. Head bowed, he wheeled his bike up the gangway; Viktor stayed behind. Just as the ferry was about to return, the Austrian hurled himself on board. He was sweating and he looked worried. If he hadn't been Gestapo, Viktor would have felt sorry for him.

Back on the city shoreline, Viktor mounted the bike and pedaled along the waterfront. He rounded a corner. Ahead stood a group of muscular women wearing head scarves and carrying wooden boxes filled with sardines that shone as bright as quicksilver. The Austrian, Viktor guessed, would accelerate, fearing he had lost him at the corner. Viktor drew his bike in close beside the wall of a building and waited. He had felt how slippery with fish scales the street was beneath the wheels of his bike, and as the Austrian turned the corner, he took off, fast, rounding the group of shouting women. The Austrian didn't round them—he plunged into them like a shark hitting a shoal of fish.

The shouting and swearing that ensued was an education.

Viktor cycled slowly toward the English Bar. It was an old-fashioned place with shelves of dusty bottles, ceiling fans, and hunting prints on the walls. As its name suggested, it was frequented by the British.

Next door stood the British Bar. It had a black marble bar and a similar atmosphere to the English Bar. Except that, contrary to its name, it was frequented by Germans.

Across the street stood the Bar Americano. That, too, was similar to the English Bar, except that it had a stag's head on the wall.

Viktor drank first in the English Bar, then moved swiftly to the British Bar, catching a glimpse of the Austrian staring into a tobacconist's, before crossing the street to the Bar Americano, where a fight was taking place.

The contestants were American sailors, and they were systematically wrecking the place. Viktor ducked into a corner and ordered a beer from a phlegmatic barman.

"Soon," the barman confided in English, "the stag's head will go."

"How do you know?"

"Because it always does. The Americanos seem to like swinging from stags' heads. I think they see too many films. You know, in the fights one of them is always swinging from a chandelier. Well, we haven't got a chandelier, we've got a stag's head."

As he spoke a sailor leaped for the stag's muzzle and the head came away from the wall.

"We don't screw it in too tight," the barman explained. "There is no point, is there?"

The sailor picked up the stag's head and charged two brawling comrades, drawing blood with the horns.

The barman said, "Always they do that. One day someone will die."

Viktor ordered another beer. He glanced at what remained of a clock on the wall. He had been in the bar ten minutes. Soon the Austrian would come in, fearing that he had left through a rear exit.

One minute later, the Austrian sidled through the door and was hit on the head with a bar stool by a sailor attacking the stag's head. He fell to the floor unconscious.

Viktor stepped jauntily over his body into the street. As he mounted his bike, a clock struck midday. In Britain it was time to stop all April Fool's tricks.

In Portugal too, he thought, grinning, as he pedaled away in the spring sunshine.

He left the bicycle padlocked to some railings in the center of the city. From there he took a yellow tram up the hill to the castle.

The metal thighs of the tramcar brushed against pedestrians, and the rails glistened behind it like thread spun by a spider. On either side balconies dripped with pink and red geraniums.

Viktor alighted three hundred yards from the castle walls.

He looked up and down. The city was lazy in the midday warmth; like a cat stretching out in the sun, except that its voice still had a vigor alien to sleep.

He couldn't see any pursuers.

It wasn't far from here, he remembered, that it had all begun; that a man had pretended to try and kill him; that he had been rescued by men whose last consideration had been rescue. Nothing was as it seemed and he shouldn't be deceived by a street that looked so innocuous.

He turned into an alley. Then he ran, twice doubling back on his tracks.

Finally he dodged into a patio, where blue-and-white *azulejos,* tiles, were for sale. The proprietor smiled lazily at him. Why should he worry if a crazy refugee chose to pay him good money, dollars, for a room he didn't occupy?

Viktor went through the patio into a second courtyard stacked high with tiles. In the center stood a dusty statue of a saint and, in one corner, a small Judas tree vivid with pinky mauve blossom.

He waited. There was no following movement. From his trouser pocket he took a key and inserted it into the lock of an old door studded with nails.

The door swung open. Viktor backed inside, still watching. Farcical, perhaps, but in the past few months he had learned.

He closed the door and switched on the light. A gecko took to the shadows.

He sat on the earthenware tiles of the floor, listening. Nothing. He levered four tiles from a corner of the room, watched by the gecko.

Carefully he removed *War and Peace* from the cavity, then the transmitter.

It took him half an hour to encode the message in Russian.

He consulted his watch. It was time. He plugged the lead into a primitive connection in the whitewashed wall.

254

He made contact immediately. "Dove here."

"Come in Dove. Receiving you loud and clear."

He began to transmit. OPERATION MARITA (the original German plan to take Greece) REVISED AS FOLLOWS... LUFTFLOTTE IV COMMANDED BY COLONEL-GENERAL ALEXANDER LÖHR TO RAZE BELGRADE . . . PANZERGRUPPE KLEIST TO MOUNT ASSAULT . . . 32 DIVISIONS OF WHICH TEN ARE ARMORED AND FOUR MOTORIZED . . .

So it went on.

As he transmitted he wondered if anyone had previously managed to follow him to this room in the Alfama. The British, for instance. If they had, it didn't really matter.

From Moscow: RECEIVED AND UNDERSTOOD. IS THAT IT.

That was almost it. Watched by the gecko, he sent the final five words: IN THIS INSTANCE DISREGARD JUDAS.

UNDERSTOOD. He could almost see the uncomprehending frown on the forehead of the receiver at the Moscow Center.

OVER AND OUT, Viktor sent, signing off, DOVE.

A week later, Viktor managed to find berths for a family of five Czechs on a Liberian cargo ship bound for New York. The Red Cross were surprised at his success, because the captain had been demanding a bribe on top of the fares, which they weren't prepared to pay. Viktor paid him with money saved from von Claus's payments. The deal gave him as much satisfaction as any he had concluded: Germans unwittingly paying for the escape of their victims.

With the balance of his savings he bought a tuxedo, and that night he took Rachel Keyser to Estoril. They traveled on the little train that skirted the coastline from Lisbon and arrived just as the sun was setting. But the air was warm and scented from flowers in the gardens sweeping up from the railway station to the casino.

They strolled under the palms to the Palácio. Beyond it stood the Hotel do Parque. "Favored by off-duty German spies," Rachel told him. "The British and Americans stay at the Palácio. It's all very insular— until they start spying, of course."

They had a drink in the bar at the Palácio. "Where we met," he said. "I felt very gauche."

"You certainly don't look it now," she said. "More like a Hollywood croupier, except that they're always dark." They sat at a table. The bar

255

hadn't filled up yet, and the pianist was playing and singing "Tea for Two."

Rachel said, "When it's all over, when we're living... wherever we are living . . . we'll have to return here."

Viktor sipped his scotch. Rachel looked glossily beautiful in shimmering green, her favorite color, with amber beads at her neck. He wanted her always at his side; without her he was incomplete. He wanted to tell her this, but he had acquired the instinct of caution and, if he were honest, suspicion.

"I wonder," he said, "how many couples are sitting together at this moment wondering where they'll be when it's all over."

"Palestine? Would you like to visit Palestine, Josef?"

"Would you like to visit Moscow?"

"With you, yes. If . . ."

She closed her eyes for a moment.

So many unfinished sentences, he thought.

An urbane-looking man wearing a white tuxedo entered the bar with a pretty blonde. Catching sight of Rachel, he smiled and bowed slightly. The couple sat at the next table; Viktor could hear him speaking English with a slight stammer.

As they walked through the gardens toward the casino, he asked Rachel who the man was.

"Kim Philby," she told him. "A useful contact," she added but didn't elaborate.

The casino hadn't filled up, and the only games being played were roulette, baccarat, and French Bank.

Viktor bought twenty dollars' worth of chips, which they lost in style. Before buying any more they watched the roulette.

Viktor stood behind Rachel, hands around her waist. He could feel her warmth, smell her perfume. She leaned against him.

"I never thought I'd be a gambler," he said.

"Twenty dollars, you call that gambling?"

"I wasn't thinking about roulette, I was thinking about us. We're gambling, aren't we?"

She didn't deny it. "If it wasn't for the war we wouldn't be."

"If it wasn't for the war we wouldn't have met."

"This gamble you're talking about—do you think you're going to win?"

"I think you know," he said. He felt her move fractionally away from him. "Don't you?"

256

"Why don't you buy some more chips?" she said.

He returned with ten dollars' worth. "Odds or evens?"

"Blow the lot. All ten dollars on one throw. Wow!"

"On us?" He didn't know why he was doing it. Perversity. Hope?

"If you wish."

"Red or black," he said. He kissed the back of her neck. "Red says you're not setting me up for anything I don't know about." He placed the chips on *rouge*.

The wheel spun. The ball bounced, danced. He could feel she was holding her breath. The wheel slowed. The ball dropped into a red pocket; then with a last exhausted jump made it into a black.

She fled and a man standing beside Hoffman exclaimed, "She must have lost a fortune!"

"More than that," Viktor said. She had disappeared, and he ran to the exit. A security guard in evening dress stopped him, asking him, in Portuguese, what the hurry was.

"A girl in green. Did you see her run out just now?"

"What if I did? If she wants to get away from you that's her business. May I suggest you go to the bar and calm down?"

She could have gone to the washroom or left the casino, Viktor thought. He decided she had left, and he ran down the front steps of the casino. The moon was riding high, and chauffeur-driven limousines were lining up to deposit their passengers.

Where would I go if I were she? Toward the sea. He set off across the gardens. To his left he thought he caught a glimpse of flying skirt, but he couldn't be sure.

The sea was a gleam of silver ahead of him.

Why the hell had he made the stupid gamble he wondered as he ran. In war you hold onto what you've got until it's taken away from you.

When he reached the road he ran straight in front of a Rolls-Royce. The driver swerved, hooted, shouted. Viktor ran on. When he reached the beach he stood listening; but all he could hear were the lick of small waves and the creak of rope on wood.

He began to walk, between the waves and a line of pink, candy-striped tents, toward the mock castle at the end of the deserted beach. He searched for footprints, but the sand had been scuffed during the day.

If he had lost her, it was his fault. The possibility scared him.

He found her in the last tent, sitting inside the open flap, staring across the Atlantic.

He sat beside her and put his arm around her. She felt cold.

"I'm sorry," he said.

She didn't answer.

"It was a stupid thing to do."

Still she didn't answer. A ship hooted and the moonlight was cold on the sea.

He kissed her cheek. "Let's keep whatever we have," he said. "While we can."

And at last she turned to him and rested her head on his shoulder.

Rachel Keyser had always shrunk from asking how the final deception would be accomplished. All she knew was that when Hitler was poised to attack Russia a message to the contrary would be transmitted to Stalin.

The time when that message would be sent was drawing close, and the day after her visit to Estoril she confronted Cross.

She met him at a sidewalk table outside the Nicola café on the Rossio. It was a fine day, sunlight dancing in the fountains in the square and opening the buds of the flower sellers' wares.

Cross threw a newspaper on the table. "On the ball again," he said. "Hitler attacked Yugoslavia on the sixth. Belgrade's being razed by the Luftwaffe, and the panzers are moving in for the kill. I don't give the Jugs much longer than a fortnight."

"So our operation can't be far off?"

Cross sat down and ordered a beer from a black-jacketed waiter. "Well, Hitler's got to beat the Greeks first. They'll be a tougher nut to crack: they've sharpened their teeth on the Italians. But they can't last all that long, not even with British help. Then maybe the Krauts will have a go at us on Crete. Then—"

"I've got to talk to you," Rachel said.

"Go ahead." He drank some beer.

"It's too risky here."

"Okay. When I've finished my beer we'll walk. I can guess what it's about," he added.

He paid the bill, and they walked around the Rossio and down the Rua Augusta toward the river, catching up with a funeral procession. The horse-drawn hearse looked like a coronation coach, decorated with gold-painted wooden garlands and surmounted with a crown. The sides of the coach were made of glass, and you could see the coffin inside. The coffin was also glass, and the corpse, a benign old man with a gray beard, rolled with the motion of the carriage.

"The information Hoffman gave Stalin about the coup in Yugoslavia," Rachel said. "Was that ULTRA?"

"That and the details about the German attack. Churchill's *most secret source*. Stalin must be very impressed with his son."

"So we'll know as soon as Hitler is about to attack Russia?"

"We virtually know now. Round about June twentieth. It depends on Greece, Crete, British resistance... But Hitler hasn't put a foot wrong so far. Let's hope Barbarossa is his first mistake. I think it will be. Churchill, with his limited resources, hasn't put a foot wrong either. Isn't it fantastic to think that he's relying on you and me?"

"And Hoffman."

The bearded old man rolled to one side; he seemed to be smiling at Rachel.

"Without him there would be nothing."

"Without him there would have been another plan. Winston is nothing if not ingenious."

"I don't happen to share your hero worship."

She walked faster, but the horses seemed determined to keep pace with her.

"So," Cross said, "what did you want to talk to me about? How we're going to stage-manage the finale?"

"Well, how?"

"You know the basics—that Stalin has got to be persuaded that Hitler doesn't intend to attack."

"The basics," Rachel said, "aren't enough. If I'm going to cooperate I've got to know how. I presume," and she had presumed all along without facing up to reality, "that you're not going to allow Hoffman to transmit the message."

"You presume correctly." Cross looked surprised. "How the hell could he? He imagines he's saving Mother Russia. He's hardly going to do that by failing to warn his old man that Hitler is about to attack."

"So how are you going to do it?"

"Leave that to me," Cross said.

The old man rolled to the other side; Rachel noticed that although his beard had been neatly trimmed the hair at the nape of his neck was unkempt. She thought he must have been a nice old man.

"I want to know," she told Cross, "and you're going to tell me, because if you don't I'll blow the whole thing."

"Really? What about those poor Jewish children in the streets of Berlin? Would you really abandon your cause because of one man?"

259

"I want to know," she said.

He was silent, weighing up her determination. "Very well," he said, "he will have to be . . . overcome."

"How?"

"It won't be difficult." Nothing, according to Cross, was difficult. "We'll receive the coded message from London at the embassy. Hoffman needn't even know that it's arrived, so he won't be on the alert."

"And?"

"We put him out for awhile. Drugs probably. We go to this room of his in the Alfama and send the message to Moscow on his behalf. HITLER HAS NO REPEAT NO INTENTION OF LAUNCHING ATTACK. Stalin will rejoice that his own son has confirmed his own views and relax. The Red Army won't be put on alert, and wham! Hitler will wade into the Soviet Union. But Hitler, thank God, doesn't have any real idea of the reserves of Soviet manpower. He'll be the victim of his own successes, and he'll march straight into the Russian winter."

Rachel considered this. She slowed her pace, but the horses slowed theirs, and the old gentleman was still beside her.

"If," she said after a while, "Hoffman doesn't know the message has arrived from London, why does he have to be overcome?"

"Because he might catch us transmitting the message in the Alfama. That's obvious, I should have thought."

She tried again. "Haven't you overlooked something? The message will have to be transmitted in Russian."

"Which is why," Cross said, smiling at her, "an interpreter from the Foreign Office who is fluent in Russian arrived in Lisbon by plane this morning. He will assist you because, of course, you will be transmitting the message."

Touch, that was it. Whoever was receiving the message in Moscow would recognize that it was not Hoffman transmitting. She told Cross.

"And so," he said, "you will be even more valuable than we ever dreamed. You've trained Hoffman—in more ways than one—and you know his touch. You can simulate it, his speed, everything."

The funeral procession turned down a side street. As it turned, the old man rolled toward her for the last time. But his lips had opened and the smile had been replaced by a look of horror.

Cross said, "Meanwhile, everything is proceeding according to plan. Every other agent that Stalin treats seriously has been fed misinformation to discredit him. This man Philby has been a godsend. Apparently they think very well of him in Dzerzhinsky Square. He's been fed two stories that we knew bloody well he'd communicate to Moscow. Both of them were bullshit. Even if he, or any of the others, gets wind of the date for Barbarossa, he'll be ignored."

They reached the Terreiro do Paco. It was from here, Rachel recalled, that she had set out by boat with Hoffman the day she discovered a pacifist can be brave.

A stiff breeze blew in from the river, flattening their clothes against them. She said suddenly, "How would you drug him?"

"Me? No, my dear. You would do that. After all, you're closer to him than I am."

She sensed that his answer wasn't spontaneous, that if she had been chosen to drug Hoffman she would have been prepared already for the task.

Suddenly she understood. How could she have been so stupid? It was quite simple. Cross intended to kill Hoffman.

23

Nine thousand miles away, in Tokyo, a man with scarred legs and a prematurely lined face was being bathed by a young girl whose name meant Camellia.

But for once her hands, now strong, now gentle, brought him no relief from the worry with which he lived these days.

There had always been worry—you could hardly be a spy without it—but recently the worry visiting Richard Sorge had become erosive.

Twice now, information he had passed to Moscow Centre had been incorrect. He couldn't understand it: he had the best contacts in Japan. And so he should: it had taken long enough to perfect his front.

Sorge, aged forty-five, son of a Russian mother and a German father, had lived in Berlin before joining the German army in the last war. His legs were savaged by shrapnel, and having witnessed the futile carnage of what he had regarded as capitalist wars, he had become a pacifist and a communist.

In 1925, he went to live in Russia, where he learned Russian, French, and English. He also added espionage to his qualifications. He visited Los Angeles, Stockholm, and London and spent three years in China spying for the Russians.

Then he returned to Germany to reestablish his patriotism. He met many of the top Nazis and in 1934 went to Tokyo as a journalist representing *Frankfurter Zeitung*.

Almost immediately he penetrated German diplomatic circles through an assistant military attaché named Eugen Ott. When Ott became German ambassador, he made Sorge his press attaché.

With this status Sorge promptly moved into Japanese diplomatic circles. Moscow was euphoric. Through fifteen years' application, they had established one man with access to their two potential enemies, Germany and Japan.

And Sorge didn't disappoint the Kremlin. He advised them about the pact among Germany, Italy, and Japan; he forecast Germany's attack on Poland on September 1, 1939.

Then things started to go wrong.

Information obtained from Ozaki Hozumi, a Japanese journalist with contacts among British espionage agents, had proved to be a disaster. Sorge had assured Moscow that the British had no intention of counter-attacking in the Western Desert. What had happened? Operation Compass was what had happened, and Wavell's tiny army had decimated the Italians.

The girl named Camellia massaged his neck and shoulder muscles with strong fingers. He closed his eyes. The oil she used smelled of lemons. "Is that good?" she asked him anxiously, because it was her duty to please him.

"That's fine." He patted one of her hands, smiling at her through the steam. But it wasn't fine at all; the worry had spread to his muscles, and they ached with it.

The fact that he had misled Moscow about Operation Compass wasn't in itself such a calamity. What was disastrous was that it began to throw doubt on his credibility. When he got the big one he wouldn't be so readily believed. And he was convinced that there was a big one in the pipeline.

Then Ott, of all people, had misled him. Ott, his mentor, his prime contact. Ott told him that reliable Japanese agents in Hong King had heard from "an unimpeachable source" that on April 9 Britain was going to seek peace with Hitler through a Swedish intermediary. What had happened on April 9? The RAF had bombed Berlin, that's what.

And made an idiot of Richard Sorge.

Which again wasn't catastrophic, but it was another sizable bite out of his plausibility.

He said to the girl, "Let's go over to the couch." From beside the bath he picked up the waterproof pouch containing a message to be passed on to a GRU (Soviet Military Intelligence) agent in Tokyo and slipped it under the pillow.

It wasn't a couch really, it was a massage table. Sorge lay on his stomach, while Camellia applied herself to his naked body.

What principally concerned the Kremlin was Japan's attitude toward Russia: whether they planned an attack. Sorge suspected that soon he would have news of a more imminent peril: Germany's intention to attack Russia.

The girl's hands dug into his buttocks, then began to work their way up his spine. At last he felt himself beginning to relax.

The message in the pouch wasn't that important strategically, but it was important to the reputation of Richard Sorge. One more fiasco, and he would be blown as far as the Kremlin was concerned. One more item of good, accurate intelligence, and his star would be in the ascendancy again.

Her hands were at the base of his neck. Strong and gentle, commanding, coaxing, reaching nerves through muscles. He closed his eyes.

"Am I pleasing you?" she asked.

"Mmm . . ."

Staring down at his body, the girl named Camellia smiled, but it wasn't a smile of professional pride; there was a touch of contempt about it.

There was, Sorge thought as he hovered on the brink of sleep, a common denominator to both items of inaccurate information that he had sent. The British. Hozumi's contact had been British, so, he had discovered, had Ott's "unimpeachable source."

And the item in the waterproof pouch? There couldn't be much doubt about this one. Again it came from Ott, but this time the source was Berlin. The Führer intended to invade Crete on or about May 20.

If he was proved to be right about that date . . . her hands were coaxing him into unconsciousness, blurring his judgment . . . if he was proved right, the next message he sent . . . he was awake and yet he was asleep . . . then the next message . . . the date of Barbarossa . . . the big one . . . would be believed.

When his breathing was shallow and regular, the girl reached beneath the pillow with one hand, maintaining the massage with the other. With slim, strong fingers she opened the pouch and removed the manila envelope. From the folds of her kimono she produced an identical envelope, substituted it, and replaced the pouch under the pillow.

Then she dug deeply into Sorge's shoulder muscles with the balls of her thumbs, so powerfully that he awoke with a gasp. One hand delved below the pillow. Satisfied, he turned on his back.

"All right," he said, "that's enough. You did well. I'll be back tomorrow," swinging himself off the massage table, draping a white towel around his belly. Outside the bathhouse he handed the envelope to the GRU courier bound for Moscow.

Half an hour later another patron claimed the attentions of Camellia. He said he was an American, but Camellia thought he was British.

He was direct to the point of rudeness, but there was a certain masterfulness about him that appealed.

"Well," he said, "did you do it?" Apparently he wasn't even going to bother with a bath or a massage, which was a pity.

"Of course. As I told you, he never leaves anything important with his clothes."

"You have the original?"

She took the envelope from her kimono and handed it to him. He ripped it open and read the contents. He seemed satisfied. He handed her a wad of yen. "Go and buy yourself a bathhouse," he said and was gone.

The following day a GRU cryptanalyst decoded the message brought by courier from Tokyo. UNDERSTAND HITLER HAS ABANDONED PLAN TO CAPTURE CRETE RICHARD SORGE.

The message was relayed to the NKVD and taken to Foreign Minister Vyacheslav Molotov and Stalin, who were conferring at the generalissimo's home in the Kremlin.

Stalin said, "This will make or break Sorge."

Molotov, as inscrutable as ever, said, "We shall see."

Stalin, cup of lemon tea in hand, went to the window and stared into the melting day. Not that it matters, he thought, I have my own source.

Eleven hundred miles northeast of Lisbon, in Lucerne, a slight, shabbily dressed man, with sad eyes behind spectacles that seemed too big for him, fought two battles. One with his black chess pieces, the other with his conscience.

His name was Rudolf Roessler. He was forty-four years old, although he looked older, and he was a German publisher who had come to live in Switzerland in 1934. He was also a spy.

His opponent at chess was a British businessman from Bern named Richard Cockburn, pronounced, he had told Roessler, *Coburn*, "like the port." Cockburn was a flashy-looking man with longish silver hair and a fierce mustache that he frequently stroked with thumb and forefinger.

Roessler didn't like him. What he was saying made sense, but Roessler knew a bully when he saw one, even if he was disguised in a Savile Row suit, and he had resisted such men all his life.

"Well?" Cockburn said, "will you do it?"

"It's your move," Roessler said. He wished he were playing white; bullies didn't like playing black.

Cockburn studied the board.

Roessler said, "If this is going to take a long time, do you mind if I make some coffee?" He lived on the stuff; it was his only indulgence.

"Make some by all means," said Cockburn, clearly grateful for the extra time. Like a bully, he had attacked too precipitously on the board and overextended himself.

Roessler went into the kitchen of the small apartment that he shared with his wife, Olga. It was in Wesemlin, a suburb of Lucerne some three miles from his publishing house, Vita Nova Verlag, at 36 Fluhmattstrasse.

It was from Fluhmattstrasse that Roessler poured out his hatred of one particular breed of bullies: the Nazis.

Like Richard Sorge, Roessler had fought in the trenches in the last war. Like Sorge he had emerged a pacifist and propounded his views through writing and lecturing. He was still a patriot but when, in 1933, the bullies came to power he knew that decent patriotism had, for the time being, been buried.

When he came to Switzerland, however, he brought with him more than just memories: he brought contacts with leaders of the German armed forces who secretly abhorred Hitler's racist policies. Among them Admiral Wilhelm Canaris.

Already he had given Bureau Ha, the Swiss intelligence organization in Lucerne, the correct dates for the German invasions of Poland, Belgium, Holland, and Denmark.

He had also made sure that the information reached the British, but they had ignored it. Which was why he had joined a Soviet spy ring headed by a jovial Hungarian named Alexander Rado. Roessler was code-named Lucy (Lucerne), and the agency was known as the Lucy Ring.

Now suddenly, impudently, the British wanted his help.

Roessler filled his cup from the percolator. As he picked it up he was overcome with a fit of coughing. An attack of asthma was something he could do without while pitting his wits against the Englishman.

He fought the attack, regained control of his breathing, and, cup and saucer in hand, returned to the dining room.

Cockburn looked up, a complacent smile on his face. So, Roessler thought, he thinks he's outmaneuvered me. He sat down and studied the board: he hadn't. Cockburn was so obvious. He reminded Roessler of a confidence trickster who preys on widows.

Obvious or not, the widows often succumbed. Will I succumb in the battle with my conscience?

The trouble was that Cockburn's arguments were logical.

"It's very simple," Cockburn said—he preferred to talk when Roessler was concentrating on the board—"just two phony items, that's all we need."

"But that will destroy my credibility."

"Not for long. When Moscow realizes that you've given them the right date for Barbarossa you'll be right back in favor again."

"I suppose you're right." Roessler moved a pawn. Cockburn underestimated pawns. "A pity your people didn't pay more attention to my earlier reports."

"We've realized our mistake. I've apologized on behalf of the British government. Now let's put the record straight. You've seen the evidence," gesturing at the documents on the dining table.

Roessler didn't warm to Cockburn's candor, but the documents seemed genuine enough. What shall I do? Roessler wondered, waiting for Cockburn to move his bishop.

He looked around the dining room. Cheap furniture, molting carpet, family portraits on the mantelpiece, and a couple of paintings of lush Bavarian scenery on the walls. Not much to show for a publisher who had once been a member of the Herrenklub in Berlin.

But I still have my ideals . . .

Cockburn moved his bishop.

. . . which are more precious than material posessions . . .

Cockburn sat back, pleased with his move and himself.

. . . although now they are under attack . . .

"Your move," Cockburn said.

. . . and have to be defended.

Roessler moved his knight and picked up the documents again.

What Cockburn was suggesting was incredibly devious. *Ironic how my ideals have always had to be maintained by double-dealing.* Cockburn was saying that if Stalin believed Hitler was going to attack he would shore up his defenses.

268

Obviously.

Then there would be no Russo-German war.

Right.

Which would leave Germany just as brutally strong as she was now.

Wrong. I don't want the Nazis strong, Roessler had thought.

He remembered the first intelligence he had transmitted from Switzerland. Details of a policy statement drawn up by Reinhard Heydrich, Himmler's deputy:

"The Third Reich will not rebuild Poland. As soon as the conquest has been completed, the aristocracy and the clergy must be exterminated. The people must be kept at a very low standard of living. They will thus provide cheap slaves. The Jews will be grouped into towns, where they will remain easily accessible. The final solution will take some time to be worked out and must be kept strictly secret."

The final solution. Roessler had no doubt what that phrase implied.

No, the Germans—"my people"—must not be left in a strong position.

It was at this point that Cockburn had made the point that neither should the Russians. And produced documents, collected by British Intelligence, showing that Russian atrocities in Poland were just as bad as those perpetrated by the Nazis.

"So what we have to do," Cockburn had said, "is to make sure that the Soviet Union is not prepared for a German attack. That way the Germans will be enticed into the wastes of Russia; that way two tyrannies will cripple each other."

"So where do I come in?" Roessler had asked.

"Simple. You will get advance warning of the date when Hitler intends to attack."

"So?"

"Your information has hitherto been so good that Stalin will believe you." Cockburn spoke good German, Berlin-accented; but so would any competent confidence trickster dealing with a German.

"So what do you want me to do?" Roessler had asked. "Send him the wrong date?"

"On the contrary. I—we—want you to dispatch two incorrect items of information. Then when Stalin gets the true date of Barbarossa from you he won't believe it."

Cockburn castled. Into trouble, in Roessler's opinion.

"So what have you decided?" Cockburn asked, pulling at the wings of his silver mustache.

"I haven't decided anything."

"You left Germany because of what they were doing to the Jews, the gypsies, the mentally deficient. Stalin will do the same, worse. You are in a position to prevent this."

"Me alone?"

"Not completely," Cockburn admitted.

An uncharacteristic display of honesty.

Roessler slid a bishop in behind his queen.

Cockburn saw the danger and covered his king's knight's pawn with a knight. *But that's not enough Mr. Cockburn—sorry,* Coburn.

Roessler sipped the last of his coffee and went to the kitchen to get some more. The doctors had said he should lay off the coffee. What would that leave him, for God's sake? He coughed. When the bout had spent itself he could hear his breathing whistling and singing in his lungs.

One thing was certain: he would get the date—and time—of Barbarossa before anyone else, with the possible exception of Richard Sorge in Tokyo. With his contacts, he couldn't fail to do so. He wondered if he would ever find his way into the history books, and, if he did, would the historians ever discover that among his contacts had been the head of the Abwehr?

Returning to the dining room, he swept a rook across the board. The sort of move that Cockburn would have enjoyed—if he'd had the wit to move with more caution in the first place.

Cockburn looked nonplussed. He abandoned his mustache and stroked his hair. He must have been hellishly handsome as a young man—still was, in a theatrical sort of way.

Roessler said to the frowning Cockburn, "What are these false items you want me to send?"

"Nothing devastating. Details of a commando raid that never takes place, British moves against Iraq. None of it matters as long as it's wrong, wrong, wrong."

Cockburn touched the queen, then withdrew his finger. He was now obliged to move the queen; instead he moved a pawn. Roessler could have made him move the queen, but he didn't bother. Why should he? Cockburn was doomed.

Roessler moved in for the kill with his knight. "Check." One move later, Cockburn resigned with bad grace. He should have quit three or four moves before.

So, one battle won. "All right," Roessler said, "I agree." The other battle lost. Or won? Who was to say?

Three hundred miles from Lucerne, in a luxurious apartment overlooking the Bois de Boulogne in Paris, two homosexuals were having an impassioned argument.

One, Pierre Roux, was in his early thirties, a physical fitness fanatic who had left the army after the 1940 debacle and returned to the Parisian underworld. He managed a nightclub near the Place Pigalle that featured a transvestite cabaret and was popular with certain elements of the German army of occupation.

The other, Jean Capron, one of the transvestite dancers, was as willowy as Roux was muscular. He was wearing a black silk dressing gown embroidered with gold dragons and a little makeup, although his mascara had been smudged with tears of rage.

Roux, in addition to running the club, worked for the French Resistance and kept a radio transmitter under the floorboards of the club—under the feet of the Germans who came to see his young (and not so young) men waggle their hips and raise their skirts.

Capron, in addition to being one of the stars of the show, acted as an informant for the Soviet spy ring known as the Red Orchestra, masterminded in Paris by a Pole named Leopold Trepper, who carried a forged Canadian passport bearing the name Adam Mikler.

The row had begun at midday when they tumbled out of bed. It had now consumed one hour of time, half a bottle of Ricard, and, in Capron's case, ten Gauloise cigarettes.

"I won't do it," Capron said. "I just won't and that's the end of it." He walked across the white carpet and examined his face in a gold-framed mirror, brushing ineffectually at the smudged mascara with one finger.

"You'll do what I say," said Roux, calmly. He felt his biceps under his sweatshirt, a habit of his. "Otherwise—"

"You mustn't threaten me. You know what the doctor said—"

"That you're neurotic? I didn't need a doctor to tell me that." Roux stared into his cloudy drink; he had drunk too much and would have to run in the Bois de Boulogne later to sweat it out. "So be a good girl." He yawned; the quarrel was becoming a bore.

"I won't," Capron repeated. "It's deceitful."

"Since when did that bother you?"

"I don't know why you're so terrible to me."

"Look," Roux decided to try one last appeal to reason. "All I'm asking you to do is to feed your Red Orchestra with a couple of false leads. The reason needn't concern you. I'm not sure that I understand it, but I trust my sources."

"On the radio?"

Yes, Roux agreed, on the radio. In fact, he had met a British agent dropped by parachute near Melun.

"But everything I've told them so far has been true."

"Of course. The information you get at the club is good. Germans are warned about not divulging secret material to girls, but no one's ever warned them about keeping their mouths shut in the presence of the queens of Paris."

"So what will happen if the Orchestra suddenly discovers that my information is unreliable."

"They'll slap your wrists," Roux said. He took one last sip of his Ricard. "It might hurt a bit, but you won't mind that, will you?"

Capron lit another Gauloise. "And what will you do," he asked, blowing a pout of smoke toward the ceiling, "if I refuse?"

"First of all, throw you out of the club."

"I can find a job somewhere else. I'm *very* popular, you know."

"And denounce you to the Krauts."

"Two can play at that sort of game."

"And maybe kill you."

Capron sat down. The hand holding the cigarette was shaking, sending the stem of smoke into lacy patterns. "You're joking, of course?"

"I was never more serious."

"But I thought you cared . . ."

"I don't give a fuck for anyone who doesn't do what I tell him."

"You're a brute."

"So?"

"I still won't do it." Capron managed to look frightened and coquettish at the same time.

With a sigh, Roux stood up. He rolled one fist in the palm of the other. "I had to discipline you once before, remember?"

"But that was before we lived together."

"I've been too lenient with you. Are you going to do what I've told you?"

"I can't betray people. I have my standards."

"Standards? Don't give me shit. What standards did an old Pigalle queen ever have?"

"Not so old," Capron said.

"Yes or no?"

"You don't scare me."

"We'll see," said Roux as he hit Capron around the side of the face with the flat of his hand, knocking him out of the chair. He picked him up by the lapels of the dressing gown and hit him again on the other side of the face. "We'll see," letting him fall again.

Capron stared up at him, breathing hard, blood trickling from the corner of his mouth. "Do what you like to me," he said, a note of excitement in his voice, "I don't care."

"Very well." Roux picked him up again. "This time I'm really going to hurt you. You know, with a razor . . ."

Capron began to sob. "I thought you cared . . ."

"You'll do it?"

"Yes, yes. What do I have to do? You're so cruel."

Roux threw him in the chair. All he had to do, he told him, was convey two items of information about German troop movements to the Red Orchestra. There was one proviso about them: they both had to be wrong.

"Do you agree?" he asked Capron.

"On one condition." Capron swallowed the rest of his glass of Ricard.

"Condition? You're in no position to lay down conditions, ma chère."

"That we stay together."

"But, of course. I wouldn't want it any other way." Roux pointed to the bedroom. "Come, let's seal the bargain."

How much longer, he wondered, would the British insist on his consorting with this tiresome creature? Really, war was hell.

24

Two factors persuaded Viktor Golovin that it was time to change the location of his code book and second radio transmitter. One was the inexorable buildup of the German army on the Baltic-Black Sea line dividing them from the Russians; two, the discovery that a Russian linguist had been imported into the British embassy.

The conclusion was obvious: one way or the other his mission was reaching its climax. Either he was going to send the ultimate message to Stalin his own way, or the British were going to meddle.

He found out about the Russian one fine morning at the beginning of May when he visited the British embassy on Red Cross business.

Summer heat was beginning to settle on the city, but a breeze coming in from the Atlantic caused the Union Jack to flutter defiantly above the low, rather shabby building on the Rua São Domingos a Lapa, a genteel but poor place compared with the German diplomatic HQ.

With Viktor were two refugees who had fled from the Russians rather than from the Germans, which made a change. They were Ukrainians. They claimed they were influential, and they wanted to see the British ambassador to pass on details of Ukrainian underground movements. Deputies had been suggested and rejected, only the ambassador would suffice.

The three of them were waiting in the entrance hall. With its cracked, black and pink floor tiles and worn carpet covering baronial stairs, it reminded Viktor of an exclusive men's club in London. Any moment now a bandy-legged octogenarian with a yellowing boiled shirt would lead them into the ambassadorial presence.

But His Excellency was obviously busy: he couldn't be anything else in wartime Lisbon. Thirty minutes passed. The Ukrainians began to talk angrily to each other in a heavy, regional dialect that Viktor had difficulty understanding. Not so the wispy-haired, bespectacled man who emerged from an office.

"What's the trouble?" he asked, using the same dialect.

One of the two sturdy, bleak-faced, neckless men told him, with an air of importance.

The stranger said, "You should be used to waiting if you come from the Soviet Union."

Viktor, who understood him better than he had the two Ukrainians, said in Muscovite Russian, "I didn't know there were any Russians in the British embassy."

The wispy-haired man looked at him with surprise. "I'm not, I'm what they call a Russian expert. In other words, I can speak Russian; not many people in Britain can do that, you know. And you?"

"Czech," Viktor said. "But I have a way with languages."

"Me too. People mistake it for brains." He smiled brightly.

"How long have you been at the embassy?"

"A couple of weeks, that's all. There doesn't seem to be very much for me to do. But I gather they've got an important job coming up."

I bet they have, Viktor thought and said, "Communications?"

"I liaise with them, yes . . ." He frowned. "Well, I must be on my way," and giving them another bright smile, walked hurriedly away as if pursued.

That evening, Viktor sent his last encoded message from the old room in the Alfama.

ONE HUNDRED FORTY FIVE GERMAN DIVISIONS MOVING TOWARD SOVIET CONTROLLED FRONTIER STOP AN ESTIMATED THREE MILLION SOLDIERS SUPPORTED BY PANZERS COMPRISING 2400 TANKS COMMA MOTORIZED INFANTRY ETCETERA STOP ALSO UNDERSTAND FINNISH AND ROMANIAN UNITS ASSEMBLING STOP LUFTWAFFE SUPPORT PLANES IN REGION OF 2000 ALSO BELIEVED TO BE STANDING BY THROUGHOUT EASTERN EUROPE STOP.

Before signing off, he again added a rider: DISREGARD JUDAS.

Then he waited for the acknowledgment.

After a couple of minutes, the receiver stuttered into life: RECEIVED STOP HERE IS ONE FOR YOU.

After the operator in the Centre had finished transmitting, it took Hoffman half an hour to decode it, using *War and Peace*.

The message, signed Hawk, Stalin's confidential code name, sought elaboration of previous messages that Hoffman had sent. Was it possible that the military buildup was a diversion from Hitler's true purpose; the invasion of Britain?

Three million men a diversion? Jesus Christ!

And did Viktor have a date for any supposed attack on Russia? Supposed! Was the man blind?

During his conversations in Moscow, Viktor had, to an extent, understood his father's reasoning. He didn't want to provoke Hitler in any way—a Soviet buildup would be just such a provocation—so that he could buy more time to rearm. And he didn't believe that Hitler was crazy enough to make the same mistake as Napoleon.

But that was before three-quarters of the Wehrmacht had started rumbling towards the border!

Viktor sent a formal acknowledgment. No, he hadn't any date, and yes, he would investigate Lisbon's assessments of Hitler's motives.

What, he wondered, would happen if and when he did get a date? *If,* because he suspected that Cross wouldn't pass it on to him. The wispy-haired linguist must have been brought out to translate a message into Russian, which could then be encoded by . . .

Rachel. Who else? He covered his face with his hands.

When, because he had every intention of getting the date from the British.

He packed up the transmitter, Tolstoy's bulky masterpiece, pads, and references. But this time he didn't replace them beneath the floor. Instead he removed six *azulejos* from a portrait of St. Anthony of Lisbon; the saint regarded him balefully through his one remaining eye.

Viktor passed the black suitcase containing the tools of his trade through the opening into the tunnel that lay beyond. Then he replaced the tiles.

Dusting himself down, he emerged into the patio and walked into the street. It was full of noise and people and heat that had built up during the day, but Viktor knew that he could pick out any shadow easily enough—he was experienced in such matters these days. He wasn't disappointed.

He strolled down the Beco do Mexias, past the inner patio where the housewives did the washing in a fountain; under balconies blooming with geraniums and dripping with laundry, through a ring of dancing children, past pigmy shops selling spices and nuts and fishing tackle, and into the black mouth of a bar.

He ordered a glass of port. The barman, as listless as an overfed dog, poured the ruby liquid, Portugal's blood, and returned to his stool, while his customers continued to argue heatedly about bullfighting and fishing and women.

Viktor, sitting beneath a photograph of Salazar, watched the doorway. Soon his pursuer would peer in with studied nonchalance.

Five minutes passed. He ordered another glass of port. As he began to sip it, a swarthy, middle-aged man, with a sad mustache and a burgeoning belly, peered in. Then he went on his way. Viktor sipped and waited. The swarthy man—Portuguese by the look of him—returned. Viktor assumed that, tonight, he was the only watchdog. Employed by whom?

Viktor finished his port, paid the barman, and strode into the cramped street. Then he lengthened his stride. Below, he could see lights glittering in the streets, pulled into watercolors on the river.

He made a series of quick turns. Wherever he went the lament of the *fado* followed him. So, at a distance, did the man with the sad mustache.

Viktor glanced at his watch. It was nearly midnight. He turned, passing his pursuer, and ran to the railway where he had chained his bicycle. He unlocked it and set off down the hill. The man with the mustache ran behind him.

At the bottom of the hill Viktor changed gear and pedaled furiously across the Baixa. He dismounted near the elevator and chained the bike to a lamppost. Then he joined the queue.

What would I do if I were the pursuer? he wondered. I would race the elevator, he decided, and wait at the point where the overhead bridge joined the Campo do Carmo.

The elevator rose slowly, occupants staring everywhere except at each other. When it reached the platform at the top, Viktor emerged, then doubled back round the observation platform, clambering over a wooden barrier marked DANGER in English, German, and Portuguese.

He waited.

The elevator descended with a sigh.

He could hear the traffic far below, an aircraft droning across the starlit sky, the farewell siren of a departing ship. Footsteps approaching across the bridge.

He shrank back. To his left was the reason for the danger sign: the metal fencing around the platform had only been partly repaired.

He pushed himself against the inner wall.

First a hand rounding the corner. Then a foot. A pause. Then the belly. Then the face with the drooping mustache. Like a Mexican bandit's in an American film, Viktor thought.

As he rounded the corner Viktor kicked his legs from under him and, as he fell forward, clubbed him over the back of the neck with the blade of his hand.

Grunting, the man tried to stand up, going for a knife at the same time. Viktor brought up his knee into his groin.

The man doubled up and vomited. The knife fell from his grasp, bounced on the platform, and fell into space, glinting like a silver fish.

"Who sent you?"

He could hear the elevator starting up again below.

"PIDE."

Portuguese secret service? Why should they be interested in me? He put his foot on the man's throat. "Who sent you?"

The man grabbed his foot and Viktor lost his balance. The man was on top of him. They rolled to one side. The metal fencing broke and swung open like a gate.

Viktor's head was over the brink of the platform. Far below he could see the lights of street lamps and traffic. A fist crashed into the side of his face.

He rolled away from the edge.

The platform shuddered as the elevator began its ascent.

A breeze suddenly sprang up; it caught the swinging flap of metal and slammed it shut. The flap hit the man on the side of the head. He loosened his grip.

Viktor broke loose. He grabbed the man by the neck as he tried to sit up. "Who sent you?"

The man stared at him.

Hoffman pushed him forward. The flap swung open again. The man's head was suspended over space. "Who?"

"The British." Even though he had half-expected the reply, it sickened him—the Russian at the embassy, Rachel knowing . . . He thrust the man's body farther over the edge of the platform hearing, without comprehending, his scream.

The two men who hauled them back were Americans. "Christ," one of them said, "what the hell was all that about?" He was elderly, shuddering from the exertion.

Viktor stood up and leaned against the wall. I was going to kill him, he thought. Who am I to pass judgment on men of violence?

He stumbled away. One of the Americans shouted, "Hey, you, stop!" but he broke into a run, through the crowds, across the bridge, into the Largo do Carmo, up the street, through the door of his lodging house, up the stairs, and onto his bed, where he lay as though dead.

Ten minutes later he got up. He went to the bathroom, stripped, and poured a jug of cold water over himself.

He dried himself, put on flannel trousers and shirt, and went out into the night again. He walked downhill to the Baixa, where he unlocked his bicycle. Swiftly he pedaled back to the Alfama, up through the still-crowded alleys to a basement beside the ramparts of the castle.

With an iron key he unlocked the heavy, studded door. It opened with a groan. He shut it behind him and lit a candle. At the rear of the basement was a flight of stone steps leading down to a cellar. A tunnel led from the cellar to the back of the tiled portrait of St. Anthony in the room where Hoffman had been transmitting. When he had discovered the existence of the tunnel he had promptly rented the basement.

He crawled along the tunnel. There, at the end, was the suitcase. He hauled it into the cellar and placed it in a cavity he had prepared beneath a flagstone.

He left the cellar by another flight of steps emerging in the grounds of the castle where Romans, Visigoths, and Moors had once ruled. Now, it was neutral, just as the world should be, Viktor thought as he breathed deeply of the cool night air.

He didn't return to the lodging house that night. Instead he went to Rachel Keyser's apartment, where he made love to her with an abandonment that frightened both of them.

When she finally slept, he thought, "What has happened to you, Viktor Golovin?" *War changes everyone* ... but what if there had been no war?

And what is true character? What is my relation to the character I thought I had?

How many murderers had been quiet, unprepossessing men until a slumbering passion was aroused?

In the morning, realism settled coldly upon him. After breakfast he went out and purchased a gun.

280

He bought it from a Polish refugee who had made it known he had one for sale. It was Russian—a TT 1930 modeled, according to the refugee, on a Colt M 1911, which meant nothing to Viktor. Obviously he had to learn how to use it.

He crossed the river by ferry and boarded a bus for the port of Setúbal. He alighted halfway there, and carrying gun and ammunition in a canvas bag, headed across fields of corn and wheat. When he reached a clump of eucalyptus he stopped and gazed around; the green countryside stretched to the horizon shimmering in the midday heat; there was no one to be seen.

He had brought with him a book about handguns borrowed from the British Library. Consulting it, he managed to load the gun, an automatic.

With a piece of chalk he drew a target on the trunk of a eucalyptus. He walked back ten yards and took aim; he was surprised how calm he felt. He fired; the bullet whined viciously off a boulder beside the tree.

He fired again; a chip of bark flew off the trunk a foot from the target. He held his breath, took aim again, and fired. A little nearer. He was enjoying it. When a bullet smacked into the outer circle, he grinned fiercely.

He sat down and took a bottle of cheap red wine from the canvas bag. He took a swig of it, wiping his mouth with the back of his hand. Then he reloaded the gun.

Slowly he raised it, keeping his arm stiff and straight. He lined up the sights with the target. He saw the face of the man on the platform of the elevator, he saw Cross, the two Gestapo officers in Poland . . .

The bullet dug a hole dead center of the target.

Viktor licked his lips. Fired again. Another bullseye. He drank some more wine. A celebration. A few more shots. No more bullseyes, but most of the shots were on target.

He laid down the smoking gun, with its grooved butt bearing the letters CCCP, and took bread, goat cheese, and olives from his bag and ate them, washed down with the rest of the wine.

Then he lay down beneath the whispering fronds of the wounded eucalyptus and slept.

He was awakened by a dog sniffing him. He sat up and saw a shepherd with a flock of sheep regarding him. The shepherd, toothless and shriveled, pointed at the trunk of the tree. "Why shoot a tree?" he asked.

"It won't hurt it," Viktor said, but he felt ashamed.

"It might kill it."

"No. Eucalyptus look beautiful, but they are also tough."

"It will do it no good."

Viktor picked up his bag. "I am sorry for what I have done to the tree."

"But why shoot it?"

Viktor left him and began to walk back toward the road. It was very hot and he felt drowsy with wine.

When he reached the road he thumbed down an old Citröen, driven by an oyster farmer from Setúbal. What, he wondered, would the farmer say if he knew his passenger carried a gun in his bag?

He would probably sigh, "Se Deus quizer," if God wills, which reflected the Portuguese philosophy: fatalistic and easygoing, with an appreciation of all things melancholy, which could erupt into spontaneous gaiety.

Viktor thought he would have liked to have been born Portuguese, but it seemed that, instead, his veins ran with Tartar blood.

The farmer dropped him in the center of Lisbon.

Viktor took his gun to his lodgings and locked it in the tin chest. Then he cycled to Rachel's apartment.

"What have you been doing?" she asked.

"Completing my education," he said.

PART SIX

25

Nervously, the pilot of the Messerschmitt 110 scanned the evening sky for British fighters. It wasn't merely his own skin that concerned him: he was frightened that his sacred mission might never be completed.

Below him lay the North Sea, as calm as sheet metal. Ahead the coastline of Scotland. He didn't doubt that his aircraft would be picked up by radar; but he didn't think the British would bother to launch a full-scale attack on a solitary aircraft.

He consulted the instrument panel. He had taken off from Augsburg at 1745 hours. Destination: Dungavel. As far as he could make out he was on course, on schedule. As anticipated, fuel was running out.

It was the fuel factor that should confuse the British. Why would a Messerschmitt 110 be flying over Scotland when it couldn't possibly have enough fuel to get it back to base?

Well, they would find out soon enough.

He was over Scotland now, the end of his 900-mile flight almost in sight. He began his descent.

The pilot, forty-six, with a face that was part saint, part fanatic, and part brute, checked in his flying suit to make sure that he had the photographs that would identify him. He was slipping them back when the fuel ran out.

He did what he had known he would have to do: he bailed out. When he hit the ground he felt a bone in his leg snap, but he managed to roll up his parachute and limp to a cottage.

The door was opened by a farm laborer. The pilot told him that his name was Horn, of which only the *H* was correct. His real name was Rudolf Hess, and he was Adolf Hitler's deputy.

Hess had worshiped Hitler for more than twenty years. As a young man he had taken part in the Munich *putsch* and been jailed with Hitler at Landsberg, where he had helped him to write *Mein Kampf*. He had become third in the line of succession to Hitler—Göring was second—in 1939.

But recently, as Hitler became more absorbed with military strategy than politics, he had been forced into the background by men of war. There was only one answer: to prove himself once more to his god, who had rebuilt Germany from the ashes of humiliation.

So far, one task had eluded Hitler: he had been unable to persuade the British, whom he admired, to seek peace. So Hess had decided he would do it to remind Hitler of his devotion and his genius. As it happened he had the contacts, in particular the duke of Hamilton, a friend of the son of his own political adviser, Karl Haushofer.

The duke was also Lord Steward—a confidant of the king and, no doubt, of Winston Churchill. So Hess determined to fly to the duke and tell him that Hitler merely sought friendship from the British—on the Führer's terms, of course.

He had been a little perturbed when Canaris had approached him just before he took off from Augsburg. If the wily admiral knew what he was up to, how many other members of the wolfpack surrounding Hitler knew? But Canaris had reassured him: "It is my job to know about such matters, but I haven't confided in anyone else."

In fact Canaris had merely elaborated on Hess's mission. Why not show Churchill how Hitler planned to crush the Soviet Union? Anyone could see from the plans that it would be a swift and devastating victory. Then Hitler would turn on Britain. Unless . . .

". . . Churchill agrees to make a deal," Canaris had said. "In other words, pressure him a little. With Russia in flames on one flank, the Führer can't fail to crush Britain on the other. Even Churchill must appreciate that."

And Canaris had given him the details of Barbarossa, complete with date: June 22.

Churchill was told about Hess's arrival while he was watching a Marx Brothers film. He told Eden to arrange for Hess to be interrogated.

It was the results of the interrogation that absorbed him as he stood in the ruins of the House of Commons, hit by a bomb the night Hess arrived. It had been a barbarous night, that Saturday. Two thousand fires had been started, and with the Thames at low tide and 150 water mains smashed by bombs, the fire fighters hadn't been able to cope. Three thousand people had been killed or injured, nearly every main railway terminus blocked, five docks and scores of factories hit.

In a way it made what he was perpetrating easier to contemplate. The wreckage around him proved that the Germans had no compunction about bombing civilian targets; nor would the Russians. Let them do to each other what they were both perfectly willing to do to the rest of the world.

But why did he have to keep reassuring himself?

Stick in hand, hunched in his topcoat, he glowered for the photographs.

One day, perhaps, people would understand that he had saved their children from monstrous oppression. Forty years—that was about the time it would take. Four decades had a middle-aged ring of responsibility about them. Perhaps young Hoffman, who would then be in his sixties, would tell the story. "I wouldn't mind if he did," he thought. "If he lives, I shall have to give him some authorization to do so."

Churchill picked his way through the rubble, past the spot where, some forty years earlier, he had made his maiden speech. How many of those listening that day had realized how nervous he was? But he had acted his way through the ordeal; acted his way through the rest of his public life; given a vast audience the act they wanted.

He reached the car and told the driver to take an indirect route back to No. 10. He wanted to think. The car moved away; he gave a V-sign to the crowds, then settled back in the cushions.

Ironic how closely Hess's idea corresponded with his clandestine proposal to Hitler to call off the invasion of Britain and attack Russia.

Some hope! Churchill grinned and lit a cigar.

They were close to Victoria Station. He glanced out of the window at the sand-bagged scene. *Black Vanities* was playing at the Victoria Palace Theatre, *The Philadelphia Story* at the New Victoria cinema. On the theater wall was a poster, LET US GO FORWARD TOGETHER, complete with a photograph of the star of *that* show: Winston Churchill.

The car turned into Downing Street. June 22—that was the date Hess had given for Barbarossa. That corresponded with other reports Sinclair had received. But the date would not be given to Lisbon until June 18; Stalin had to be kept on a tight rein—given as little time as possible in which to question his son's intelligence that Hitler did *not* intend to attack.

June 18-22. Four days in which the future of the world would be decided. He climbed out of the car and strode purposefully into No. 10.

June 17.

In his country residence at Kuntsevo, Stalin agonized over the evidence of Hitler's intentions.

He moved from one of the three main rooms—each furnished with a long table and a sofa—to the other, keeping in the shafts of dusty sunlight trembling on the floor. Despite the warmth, log fires burned— to keep the wolves of doubt at bay.

He still believed that Hitler was bluffing. That the army massing on the border was a feint to conceal his intent to invade Britain. That in any case Hitler would deliver an ultimatum before making a move against the Soviet Union.

That he, Stalin, would then be able to make a few concessions while he organized the Red Army. That Hitler would be insane to take on the Russian winter.

The trouble, Stalin brooded, was that no one agreed with him and the only informant he could trust, his son in Lisbon, had been out of touch for days. If Viktor didn't make contact tomorrow he would have to reinforce the border. And provoke Hitler into attacking?

Head aching, he sat down at a table and reviewed the warnings he had received.

The United States. Three months ago the American secretary of state, Cordell Hull, had handed over a copy of what was alleged to be a copy of Barbarossa to the Russian ambassador in Washington, Konstantin Oumansky. It was said to have been obtained by the U.S. commercial attaché in Berlin, Sam Woods.

Stalin had totally disregarded that one. It was in the interests of America, Britain's undeclared ally, to persuade Russia to take military steps that *would* provoke Hitler. Vicious mischief-making, pure and simple.

Britain. In April, Churchill had cabled a warning through his ambassador in Moscow, Stafford Cripps. What else would you expect from an anti-Bolshevik capitalist warmonger?

288

Richard Sorge. On May 19, this once-trusted spy had sent details of the German military buildup on the border. On June 1, he had outlined the tactics the Nazis would use. Two days ago, he had given June 22 as the date for the invasion.

But Sorge had got Operation Compass wrong and a lot more besides. His final coup had been a message that Hitler didn't intend to take Crete. On May 20, Hitler had attacked Crete!

So much for Richard Sorge.

The Lucy Ring. According to Marshal Golikov, head of military intelligence, the information provided by this agency had been the best in Europe. Until recently. Suddenly the intelligence supplied by a master agent named Rudolf Roessler had become suspect. A British commando raid that never took place, British policy in Iraq totally wrong . . .

The Red Orchestra. Another spy ring that was supposedly milking the Third Reich of its secrets. They, too, had botched up their last two messages.

Stalin sat up abruptly.

Why should I take any notice of any such sources?

He felt better. He lit his pipe and blew coils of smoke into a shaft of sunlight. From the wall Lenin smiled at him approvingly.

There was still the evidence seen through Red Army field glasses: a vast army *was* concealed in the pine forests, marshes, hills, stretching from the Baltic to the Black Sea.

But a bully has to flex his muscles.

No, Hitler won't attack. Stalin poured himself some vodka, drank it, and munched black bread and pickled gherkins.

Or will he?

The headache returned.

Speak to me, Judas. Speak to me, Viktor.

Three weeks after leaking details of Barbarossa to Hess, Canaris had visited Hitler at Obersalzberg.

Martin Bormann, who was taking over from Hess, had been there with Frau Bormann and Eva Braun and her mother and sister. Canaris could never understand Hitler's liaison with the dumb little shopgirl. Perhaps she was an accomplished performer in bed; but then again it was by no means sure that Hitler had sex with her—Canaris's intelligence stopped at the bedroom door.

More likely she was a good listener, as everyone close to the Führer had to be. Including the brutal, balding Bormann, who, when Canaris arrived at the Berghof, was stomping around the grounds pointing out to the Brauns his achievements in reconstructing the whole Obersalzberg area.

While Bormann continued to show off, Canaris took the opportunity to speak to Hitler in his study on the first floor. At Hitler's feet lay Blondi. From time to time Hitler stroked the dog and tickled it behind its ears.

Canaris, who assumed that Hess must by now have passed on details of Barbarossa to the British, told Hitler that he feared a British agent in Lisbon was poised to pass on details to the Kremlin. Why hadn't he been liquidated? Because, Canaris said, the Gestapo had botched surveillance and alerted the agent.

Hitler gave Blondi a final pat and straightened up. "So you consider this man to be a real danger to Barbarossa, Herr Admiral?"

Canaris said he did.

A rasp of anger edged Hitler's voice. Barbarossa forestalled by one British agent, by Gestapo bungling. He said, "Then you will stop him, Admiral. I hold you personally responsible."

"In that case," Canaris said, "perhaps you would be good enough, mein Führer, to give me written authority."

From a drawer in his desk, Hitler snatched a sheet of personally embossed notepaper and an envelope. He scrawled rapidly across the paper.

He folded the paper, thrust it into the envelope, and threw it across the polished surface of the desk to Canaris, who picked it up and put it in his pocket without reading it—that would have been a mistake.

Canaris stood up, clicked his heels, gave the Nazi salute. "Have no fear, there will be no leak from the British agent in Lisbon." He stood up, turned, and walked briskly away. Escaped.

So at least I've reported the Lisbon conspiracy. A point in my favor. If things go wrong and the true source of the Barbarossa leaks is suspected I can point out that I reported the matter to Hitler. Hardly the behavior of a traitor.

What's more, he had obtained Hitler's authority to eliminate the leak. A traitor didn't seek permission to destroy his own channels of communication. And, he congratulated himself, he had also managed to lay the blame for the negligence at the door of the Gestapo.

He ignored Bormann's friendly wave and climbed into the back of his

Maybach. As the car glided through the green valley he felt his pulse—fast. He told the driver to stop at an inn, where he swallowed a pink tablet with a glass of water.

When he got back to his office in the Tirpitz Ufer in Berlin, he sent a cable to von Claus in Lisbon. Josef Hoffman would have to be liquidated. And Cross, of course. And Rachel Keyser.

Von Claus was in command and he was enjoying it.

In his office, on the desk separating him from Bauer, lay the written authorization from Hitler. You would have thought it was primed to explode, the way Bauer was looking at it.

"So I am taking complete control of the Hoffman case," he told Bauer. "As from now, there will be no Gestapo interference whatsoever."

Bauer tugged furiously at one of his little ears. "Of course, if that is the Führer's wish."

"No more agents being hit on the head with bar stools," von Claus remarked. His back had been aching earlier this morning, but this exchange was so stimulating that the pain had disappeared.

"An unfortunate accident," Bauer said. "The agent concerned has been dealt with. He has been sent back to Berlin."

"So you'll be meeting him there?"

Bauer leaned forward over the desk; he was sweating profusely. "What do you mean by that?"

"The Führer was far from pleased by what's happened over here."

"But nothing has happened," Bauer said.

"Precisely. In fact so little has happened that I understand you may be recalled to Berlin to explain this dearth of activity. Himmler and Heydrich like action, I understand."

"But you've done even less!"

"On the contrary," von Claus said. "We picked up certain radio transmissions."

"What radio transmissions?"

"That needn't concern you." The conversation really was the best fillip he had enjoyed for years. Not that his cryptanalyst had been able to decode Hoffman's messages. But the British-Soviet connection—it had to be Barbarossa.

Bauer lit one of his filthy black cigars. "Is there to be a . . . liquidation?"

"That needn't concern you either."

"If it is, my men can—"

"No help," von Claus snapped.

"May I ask when?"

Von Claus shook his head happily. "By the way," he said, "I just spoke to Canaris on the telephone. He said Himmler was in a filthy temper. I can't think why, can you?"

By the expression on his face, Bauer could.

Von Claus stood up to indicate the interview was over. "I thought this might be of some use to you," he said. He handed Bauer a timetable listing airplane connections to Berlin.

26

Judging by the German military buildup, Barbarossa was imminent. So why hadn't any information reached him from London?

On Wednesday, June 18, Viktor decided to contact Moscow to see if Stalin had reacted to the deployment of Nazi troops.

He wheeled his bicycle from the hallway of his lodgings at 8 A.M. and set out across the city. It was going to be a lovely day. Mist from the Tagus lay in pools at the foot of Lisbon's hills, but soon the sun would burn it away.

The air smelled of coffee and hot bread. Newspaper vendors were shuffling their morning editions, flower sellers arranging bunches of carnations and bird of paradise blooms in green buckets. Weaving in and out of the trams and taxis, Viktor made his way to the Alfama and padlocked his bicycle to some railings.

He paused for a moment, then darted into the mist. A few phantoms loomed up, briefly gaining substance before vanishing again. He was satisfied that he had shaken off any pursuers. Thank God for the mist.

He made his way toward his new HQ, unlocked the heavy door, removed the transmitter from below the flagstones, and got through to Moscow.

The response came back as though the operator at the Centre had been poised waiting for him. It was brief and he decoded it while keeping contact.

SOURCES HERE ASSERT GERMANS PLANNING ATTACK JUNE TWENTY SECOND STOP PLEASE CONFIRM OR DENY URGENTEST REPEAT URGENTEST HAWK

Viktor sent back WILL DO DOVE and cut the connection.

He sat for a moment. If Moscow had a date—provided, of course, that it was the right one—why didn't London? Strange, because the British had incomparable sources of information.

Thoughtfully, he replaced the transmitter under the flagstone, locked up, and made his way back to his bicycle. The mist had cleared, and the Alfama was as busy as a street market once more.

As he pedaled around the Rossio he thought, "Perhaps the British *do* have a date." And then, "But what reason could they have for withholding it from me?"

Rachel's apartment was locked but he had a key. On the table was a note: "Gone to buy bread, back in fifteen minutes."

So she wasn't going to the embassy this morning.

Viktor stared through the window at the sunlit park.

When she came back he would ask her about June 22. But would she tell him the truth?

There had to be another way to find out and, of course, there was. He fetched the other transmitter from her bedroom. He knew her call sign, he knew her touch. What he didn't know was how long she had been away from the apartment.

He placed the transmitter on the dining-room table and made contact with the British embassy. The old Viktor Golovin would have asked naïvely, DO YOU HAVE A DATE FOR BARBAROSSA?

Not the devious replacement. Using her call sign, Raven, and her touch he asked:

CAN YOU CONFIRM BARBAROSSA DATE JUNE 22 NOT 21 RAVEN

A pause. Outside he thought he heard the elevator.

Come on, he entreated the silent machine.

The clang of the elevator door shutting. Footsteps.

The machine came to life.

The footsteps stopped.

Letter by letter he wrote down the message. C . . . O . . . N . . . F . . . I . . . R . . . M . . . E . . . D . . . There had never been a slower operator.

A key in the door.

T . . . W . . . E . . . N . . . T . . . Y . . . S . . . E . . . C . . . O . . . N . . . D . . .

The door opened and he said, "Hallo Rachel, I was just practicing," and Cross said, "In that case you won't mind showing me what you've written on the pad."

294

Viktor said, "It's none of your—" and looked into the barrel of an automatic.

Cross waved the barrel impatiently. "Hand it over."

"Come and get it," Viktor said, one hand on the pad.

"Don't be under any illusions, my dear Judas, I will have no compunction about killing you."

"And then who will send your message to Moscow?"

As he spoke, he knew. Rachel. How could he have been so stupid?

Cross said, "Pass it over very slowly, no sudden movements."

Viktor handed Cross the pad. What they didn't know was the new location of the second transmitter. But they didn't have to, did they? They could transmit from here; Rachel could do the job quite adequately. Call sign, touch, and, of course, they had details of the code from his first HQ.

Russian? No problem: they had the wispy-haired interpreter from the embassy.

If only Rachel . . . a controlled rage possessed him. He wasn't going to allow them to get away with it. They had to learn that he wasn't that gullible.

And he wasn't! He had one card left—the refinement of which they knew nothing, the Judas Code. But if the card wasn't played correctly it could destroy everything.

Cross said, "So you've got the date."

"Weren't you going to tell me?"

"Tell you, lover boy? Why should I? You'd warn Uncle Joe and then what would happen? He'd rush his troops up to the border. Stalemate. The two warlords left evenly balanced. Don't you understand? We want them to destroy each other."

"But I understood—"

"That we wanted to save the Bolsheviks? How can you have been so naïve? I was scared at one time that you'd catch on. But no, not you. You were too prick-happy. Rachel played her part very well, didn't she?"

Superbly well, Viktor thought. Surely Cross wouldn't risk shooting him here.

Cross prodded the automatic toward him. "Stand up and turn around, hands behind your head."

The scrape of the chair as he stood up synchronized with the key turning in the lock of the door.

From the doorway, Rachel, two loaves of bread under her arm, shouted, "No!"

Without taking his eyes off Viktor, Cross snapped, "Keep away," fingers tightening on the butt of the automatic.

"No!" she shouted again and threw herself at Cross. As he staggered back she grabbed his wrist, pushing it down. Cross thrust her aside as Viktor came at him. The gun went off as they grappled, the bullet smashing the window. Cross tore his wrist from Rachel's hand and clubbed her on the head with the gun.

As she fell, Cross broke free from Viktor and aimed the automatic at his chest. From the floor Rachel hooked a foot around one of his legs; as he staggered Viktor hurled the transmitter at him. It hit him on the side of the head and he collapsed.

Viktor knelt beside Rachel. Her face was terribly pale, but she said, "I'm all right . . . You must get away."

On the other side of the room Cross was trying to get to his feet.

As he slammed the door behind him Viktor heard Rachel call out, but he couldn't make out the words. He thought he heard the word "love," but he wasn't sure.

The elevator was on another floor.

It wasn't until he was running down the stairs that he remembered that his recent purchase, the Russian automatic, was stuck in the belt of his trousers.

The man chosen by von Claus to kill Hoffman—then Cross and Rachel Keyser—was an albino.

But, although his eyes had a pinkish tinge to them, his sight was perfect, the eyesight of a marksman.

Seated at the wheel of a BMW 326, he was taken by surprise at the speed of Hoffman's exit from the apartment block. He came out on a bicycle, would you believe, which he must have left in the hallway.

Shit! The albino had heard about this bike. Difficult to follow on foot, equally difficult by car in the narrow lanes of the old town. But here there shouldn't be any difficulty, especially if Hoffman decided to cycle down the Avenida da Liberdade with its broad lanes of traffic and island gardens. It was a mile long, and if he couldn't pick him off in that distance, he didn't deserve his job. From a shoulder holster he took a Luger pistol.

He let in the clutch and took off after the black bicycle.

The only drawbacks were the trams and the police on duty at the intersections. Hoffman didn't seem to pay much attention to either.

The BMW with the rakish hood and flaring fenders was capable of 80 MPH. As Hoffman rounded a tramcar picking up passengers, the albino put his foot down. But to his consternation Hoffman swerved to the left, ignoring a policeman's outstretched hand. Should he follow suit?

Swearing, the albino slowed down. The policeman waved him on, glaring at him as he lifted one foot off the clutch abruptly and rammed the other on the accelerator.

Through his pink eyes he saw Hoffman take a right. Soon he would be approaching the old quarter, the Alfama. If I don't get him before that I'll have to chase him on foot. Himmel Sakrament!

50 MPH . . . 55 . . . 60 . . .

Hoffman, bowed over the handlebars, was a hundred yards in front. 70 MPH . . . The albino leaned out the window and aimed the Luger.

Which was when he became aware that a green MG was about to overtake him.

That morning Stalin, back in his gloomy apartment in the Kremlin, received another warning about Hitler's intentions. It came from a Soviet spy in Switzerland named Alexander Foote, a British member of the Lucy Ring.

The punchline of the message read, "General attack on territories occupied by Russians dawn of Sunday 22 June 3:15 A.M."

So now they weren't just giving dates, they were giving times.

Stalin glanced at the wall clock. It was midday, the time he had intended, against his better judgment, to put the Red Army on full alert, even if such an action did provoke Hitler.

But since then he had received word from his son. Three words, to be precise. WILL DO DOVE. Viktor was checking out speculation about June 22.

Stalin decided to give him another hour.

Viktor speeding down a hill behind a yellow tramcar, glanced behind him.

He saw a gray sedan. A very blond man with a gun in his hand was leaning from the window. He was just about to be overtaken by Cross in his MG.

Viktor ducked. Nothing happened.

He glanced back again. The MG had drawn level with the gray car. It was lower than the sedan but, as Viktor watched, its windshield struck the arm of the blond man holding the gun.

Then Cross's MG was in between the sedan and his bicycle.

So now there were two assassins trying to kill him.

What chance did he stand on a bicycle? Unless he could plunge into an alleyway.

He noticed a narrow road to his left. He tried to turn and found that he couldn't. He wrenched the handlebars but nothing happened. He continued to speed straight ahead behind the tramcar, with the two pursuing cars behind him.

He tried to turn the other way. Nothing. He peered down and realized that the wheels of the bicycle were trapped in the tramlines.

He stood up and pedaled furiously, aware that he was presenting a better target. But he was gaining on the tram. Passengers stared at him curiously.

He glanced around again.

Cross was aiming his gun at him.

Viktor was ten yards from the tram. He swung one leg over the saddle so that he was balanced on one pedal.

He heard the crack of the gunshot as he jumped. The cycle continued, riderless, along the tramline.

And he was running faster than he had ever imagined he could, the impetus of hitting the ground bowling his legs along.

He reached the running board of the tram as another shot cracked out. He grabbed the rail. It felt as though his arm was being pulled from its socket. Hands reached him and pulled him in, and he shouted to the passengers, "Duck, for God's sake, duck!" as another shot rang out.

He peered over the window of the platform. The driver of the gray sedan was trying to push the MG off the road. Just ahead of the two cars, still speeding along the tramline, was his bicycle.

Cross fired again.

The bullet shattered the window above him, ricocheted above the heads of the crouching passengers, and hit the driver in the chest. As he slumped to one side the tramcar gathered momentum.

He saw the MG hit the bicycle and knock it flying. The sedan crunched over it.

The tramcar gathered speed.

298

Another bullet shattered a window. Viktor couldn't tell who had fired it. Passengers were screaming, the two cars, side-by-side, were gaining.

Viktor lay on the floor of the driverless tram and peered around the side. The driver of the sedan was aiming his gun, not at the tram, but at Cross. He must have missed, because the MG didn't waver.

The tramcar breasted a slight rise in the street and plunged down a steep hill, swaying wildly. Beside Viktor, a small boy was sucking a lollipop with evident enjoyment. His mother was screaming.

At the bottom of the hill, Viktor remembered, stood a street market specializing in second-hand goods: clothes, electrical goods, cracked china, books.

As the tramcar left the rails and charged the stalls, Viktor jumped. He hit his head on the ground and spun sideways. Stunned, he saw the tramcar toss aside a couple of stalls like a charging bull and smash into a wall.

Where were the gunmen?

He crawled behind an upturned bookstall, listening to the cries of the wounded. He peered around a heap of books and saw the sedan and the MG abandoned a hundred yards away. Of Cross and the other assassin there was no sign.

Gripping his automatic in one hand, Viktor wormed his way through the debris. When he reached the end of the stricken market he straightened up and ran.

Cross came at him from one side, the blond man from the other.

As he ran, he aimed the gun at Cross and pulled the trigger. The gun jerked but Cross kept running.

He reached a small, dusty square. He heard gunshots. People scattered until there were just the three of them.

He fired again at Cross, then at the blond man.

He saw Cross stop and take careful aim, gun balanced on his forearm. He dived into the dust beside a mangy dog as Cross fired. On the other side of the square the albino screamed, reared up and fell to the ground, blood pumping from his chest.

Rachel managed to reach the telephone, blood seeping from the wound on her temple. She called the British embassy and told them that she was injured.

Not that she really cared what happened to her. She had betrayed the one man she had ever loved, and provided he escaped, the plan had failed.

She saw him before the horns of a bull, she saw the passion on his face as he made love to her beneath the chandelier in her hotel bedroom, she saw the realization in his eyes that she had lied to him . . .

She sat down and wept.

Gun in hand, Viktor ran through the Alfama toward the ramparts of the castle. The crowds scattered before him. A policeman drew his gun, but Viktor dodged through a courtyard hung with laundry into another alley.

Behind him came Cross.

Viktor ran past bars, shops, stalls, churches. Bells chimed; the *fado* mourned lost ideals, trust.

He was staggering now, but so was Cross. He put on a last spurt, reached the door of his new HQ, slid the key in the lock, and fell into the cool darkness.

Behind him he could hear labored breathing.

He switched on the lights and ran down the stone steps into the cellar, then backed into the mouth of the tunnel, aiming the gun at the head of the steps.

Cross stood there swaying. "Josef," he shouted, "you've got to listen. You don't understand."

"Oh but I do," Viktor said, and shot him in the head.

From beneath the flagstone he took the transmitter. He was through to Moscow within a couple of minutes. With trembling fingers he sent his message:

CONFIRM GERMANS DO PLAN TO ATTACK ON TWENTY SECOND STOP REPEAT DO PLAN TO ATTACK . . . DO PLAN TO ATTACK.

EPILOGUE

"But I don't understand," I protested to Judas. "You warned Stalin that Hitler *was* going to attack, but he still didn't take any notice."

As the world knows, the Germans had attacked on June 22. Four months later, they had been poised to take Moscow. Then they had encountered the Soviet winter, the indomitable will of Mother Russia, and her inexhaustible supplies of manpower. Germans had continued to fight Russians for another three and a half years.

Josef Hoffman, or Viktor Golovin, or whatever he called himself these days, gave a small, conspiratorial smile. "But you don't understand the Judas Code." He had guarded the secret for more than forty years and was reluctant to part with it.

Three days had elapsed since we met in Madame Tussaud's. We were sitting on a bench, beneath the chestnut trees in the Broad Walk of Regent's Park. Hoffman was talking into a microphone plugged into a small tape recorder, as he had been for hour after riveting hour. I hadn't been home since that first meeting, staying instead in a small hotel in Baker Street.

The air smelled of the shower that had just spent itself and of spring blossoms; lovers strolled past arm in arm; children played on the grass.

I waited, but the slim, contented-looking man in his mid-sixties, fair hair only just beginning to turn gray, wasn't going to put me out of my agony. Not yet, anyway.

I approached from another direction—the story had made me devious. "So what happened in Lisbon after you sent the message?"

"Oh, I cleared out. I was tired of being used as a target." The sun was warming up; he unbuttoned his raincoat. Beneath it he wore a Harris tweed sports jacket and sharply creased gray flannels. "I assumed yet another identity. The one I use now." He didn't elaborate.

"There must have been an almighty hue and cry."

"There was. But in Lisbon in those days almost anything could be covered up. Some maniac had loosed off a gun at a tram—miraculously no one was killed in the crash—and he was caught in the Alfama after a chase. Cross recovered from the bullet wound"—a note of regret there?—"and came back to England. He's still very much alive."

"And Rachel Keyser?"

He didn't reply to that one. Instead he said, "But once I had sent the message, anything that happened in Lisbon was of trivial importance."

Very well. "So what about the other protagonists?"

Hoffman named them one by one, according each a terse obituary.

Stalin. Died at Kuntsevo on March 5, 1953, following a cerebral hemorrhage.

"Did you ever see him again?"

Hoffman seemed surprised. "Good God, no. He would have had me hung, drawn, and quartered." The surprise brought out a few middle-European accents in his almost perfect English.

"Did he ever realize what had happened?" I asked hopefully.

But Hoffman wasn't to be drawn.

Hitler. Committed suicide with Eva Braun in the Führenbunker beneath the ruins of Berlin on April 30, 1945.

Hoffman stared into the distance, into time. "The British were quite right, of course. The Germans were routed, and the Russians lost so many lives that they couldn't sweep through the rest of Europe as they would have done if they had been stronger."

There was something about his intonation that alerted me to an unintentional clue: he sounded as though he had known about the British conspiracy *before* it was carried out.

I asked him. His reply was the most unsatisfactory so far. "Not really." What was I supposed to make of that?

His voice became suddenly harsh. "The Russians lost twenty million lives, Mr. Lambert. Can you imagine what it's been like to live all these years with the knowledge that you were responsible for all those deaths?"

Certainly the magnitude of such guilt was beyond comprehension, if he *had* been responsible. But he had warned Stalin that Hitler *was* going to attack . . .

Canaris. Hanged, naked, on April 9, 1945, for alleged complicity in the abortive plot in July, 1944, to assassinate Hitler with a bomb.

Sinclair. Died of natural causes on May 18, 1960. After the war he had opened a home for underprivileged children.

And finally:

Churchill. Died on January 24, 1965, aged ninety, from a stroke, after lying in a coma for fourteen days.

"Did he suffer the same guilt as you?" I asked.

Hoffman shook his head firmly. "Churchill was convinced that he had acted for the good of humanity. And he had, hadn't he?" gesturing around the placid park. "You and I wouldn't be sitting here free to move and think and do as we please if it hadn't been for his Grand Deception. All he did was match against each other two massive armies intent upon aggrandizement. That's terrible enough to contemplate. Can you imagine what would have happened if they had combined? If Stalin had been prepared to repel a German attack? If, realizing this, Hitler had done a deal? Britain today could well have been a colony of Germany or Russia or both. In any case, I didn't say I suffered guilt. Responsibility is a different quality altogether."

He seemed to lose some of his purpose. He had, after all, been talking for something like twenty-four hours. I glanced at him. He was staring down the Broad Walk at a figure approaching about 100 yards away.

"Did Churchill authorize you to tell the full story?"

"Written authorization. I have it here." He took a yellowing envelope from his pocket and handed it to me. "I got it from the solicitors this morning. You can open it if you like."

Inside was a brief letter written on faded notepaper bearing the address 28 Hyde Park Gate, signed by Churchill, and dated August, 1945. It stated that he gave Josef Hoffman, "or Viktor Golovin, or whatever identity he chooses to adopt," permission to publish the full story relating to the German invasion of Russia not less than forty years after June 22, 1941.

Hoffman told me to keep the letter—"You may need it."

"Why 1945?" I asked, glancing at the date of the letter.

"Because he had just lost the election. He expected to, but just the same he felt a sense of betrayal. He felt that one day, when he was dead and passions were less likely to be aroused by such revelations, those who had voted against him should know that his achievements were far greater than they had ever dreamed they were."

"What kept you?" I asked. "It's 1983 now."

"I didn't really know if the truth should ever be told, even though Churchill wanted it to be. Then you inserted that advertisement in *The Times*. It was as though Churchill was nudging me. Reminding me that I was reneging on a promise."

I was debating how to ask him again about Rachel Keyser—how could I write the story without knowing what had happened to her?—when the figure that Hoffman had been gazing at stopped in front of us.

"Rachel," he said to the woman smiling down at him, "I want you to meet Derek Lambert. Mr. Lambert, my wife."

She was an elegant woman dressed in gray, with a healthy complexion and silver hair, who had grown gracefully into her sixties. As I stood up I peeled back the years, and there she lay wounded in her apartment in Lisbon, raven-haired and voluptuous, calling out to the man she thought she had lost. And the one word he had thought he heard, "love," was what it must have been.

Hoffman switched off the recorder, disconnected the microphone, and put them both in a black case. Then he, too, stood up. "Let's take a stroll," he said, and she tucked her arm in his.

"So Josef has told you everything?" she asked as we passed a young couple, absorbed with each other, with many years ahead of them.

"Not quite all."

"Ah, the Judas Code. I'm not at all sure that he will. He's had it locked away for a long time."

But he did.

When he had finished, he stopped walking. He handed me the case containing the tape recorder and shook my hand. "And that's the end. Tell it well."

"But there might be a few more queries. The young man in the zoo—your son?"

Rachel Keyser smiled a mother's smile. "He works for the United Nations."

"And Palestine," I said desperately. "Did you ever go there?"

"For awhile," her husband said. "Happy years. And now we really must go. If you have any more problems you will have to solve them yourself. You don't know our present name and you never will. We are now returning to obscurity."

"And happiness," said Rachel Keyser, kissing him on the cheek.

Another shower had blown up, and I was glad because I wasn't sure whether there were tears on my cheeks.

304

Together, they walked across the grass, past the children and the young people and the parents and the grandparents whom they had saved from oppression.

When I got back to my apartment I found Chambers, the man who had warned me not to pursue Judas, sitting in my armchair. He reminded me once again of a City businessman, with the reservation that City businessmen don't usually aim pistols at your head.

"Mr. Cross," I said, "you might as well put that thing away—there are two policemen waiting outside," I lied.

He considered this. "Cross . . . So you didn't heed my warning?"

"On the contrary, it inspired me."

"How very stupid of you. I don't believe there are two policemen outside, and now I have no alternative but to kill you."

"Whereas Hoffman's bullet only grazed your cheek."

His free hand went to the scar. "You've seen Hoffman?"

"He sends his regards. I presume you're protecting the good name of Winston Churchill?"

I sat down opposite him and stared into the barrel of the gun. It was larger than the Browning he had previously wielded—a Magnum, quite capable of blowing my head off.

"Why, yes. As Judas has no doubt told you, I think he was the greatest Englishman who ever lived."

"And you're determined to stop anyone telling the truth about his part in Barbarossa?"

"Correct, even if it means killing them. Why should the public be given a chance to misunderstand him, revile him?"

"I shall write it so that they don't."

"Except that you won't be writing the book," finger tightening on the trigger of the Magnum.

"Someone will. The tape on which Hoffman recorded the story is in a safe-deposit box." That at least was the truth—it was at Harrods.

That stopped him, but the madness didn't leave his face. "Give me the key."

"I haven't got it with me." Again the truth. I had put it in a registered letter and posted it to myself. While he considered this, I followed up with, "But I do have a letter."

"Letter?" he frowned. "Who from?"

"Winston Churchill," I said.

That sank home. "You're crazy!"

"Supposing I were to tell you that Churchill wanted the book written?"

"Then I would say you were certifiable."

"The letter's in the inside pocket of my jacket."

"That, if I may say so, is pretty corny. What have you got in there? A derringer?"

"Come and find out."

"No," he said, "I have a better idea. Stand up and take your jacket off and throw it on the floor in front of me. Not in my face, that way I blow your head off and put a hole through that nice jacket as well."

I stood up and, very slowly, removed the jacket of my blue suit. I threw it on the floor, and still keeping the gun leveled at my head, he withdrew the envelope from the inside pocket. I sat down.

He read the letter. I watched his eyes. He read it again. And again.

When he looked up, his face was washed of emotion. He looked tired and ashen-faced, as though he needed some sun on the beach at Estoril.

He said what I had expected him to say: "How do I know this isn't a forgery?"

"You don't. You'll just have to believe me until you get the signature checked out by a handwriting expert."

He considered this. He looked much older than he had a few minutes earlier.

Finally he said, "Very well, I'll take your word for it—for the time being," and put the gun back into the shoulder holster beneath his jacket.

I slumped back in my chair. Then I asked him, "Would you like a drink?" He didn't reply, but I poured him a large scotch and soda just the same, and an even larger one for myself.

When he had drunk the whisky he said, "You know, one thing has always puzzled me. If Hoffman warned Stalin that Hitler was going to attack, why didn't Stalin do anything about it?"

"The Judas Code, of course."

"I never fully understood what that was. I suppose Hoffman was smarter than I imagined," he admitted. "Did he tell you?"

It was too good to be true. "No," I said and grinned at him because now he would never know, and the question would haunt him to his grave.

The Judas Code, Hoffman had told me as he and his wife walked with me in Regent's Park, was really invented by a Mafia gangster named Frank Costello. Realizing that all his mail was scrutinized by the FBI, he used the very simplest of codes: he told all his confidants that they were to infer the *opposite* of what he wrote.

If he wrote that he would *not* be dining at a particular restaurant on Lexington Avenue in New York at 8 P.M., he meant that he would be there all right. The FBI never cracked this crudest of codes, possibly because it was too obvious.

Hoffman had heard about the ploy in Lisbon from an Austrian refugee who had once laundered Mafia money. He had suggested it to Stalin as their ultimate safeguard, to be applied only to Barbarossa. Stalin had been delighted with the idea.

For CONFIRM GERMANS *DO* PLAN TO ATTACK ON TWENTY-SECOND read CONFIRM GERMANS DO *NOT* PLAN, et cetera.

"One last question," I had said to Hoffman.

"Why, in my own way, did I go along with the British? Why? in other words, did I send the affirmative message?"

I nodded. It was the crux of the whole story.

"It's very simple: I went to Poland. I saw the horrors perpetrated by the Germans. Then I went to Katyn. It was then that I realized that my own people were capable of committing atrocities just as terrible as those perpetrated by the Germans."

"And you knew all along what Cross and Rachel—your wife—were planning to do?"

Hoffman said that he only suspected that he was going to be double-crossed; that he had always hoped Rachel would tell him the truth. But whatever they intended to do was irrelevant. "After Katyn, I had decided to mislead Stalin. As it happened, Churchill and I chanced on the same idea."

"A horrendous decision for a man of peace to make."

"But I wasn't a man of peace anymore. War changes everyone. I don't know whether or not you find your true character. But I do know this: you learn to understand yourself." He paused. "Perhaps, Mr. Lambert, you are too tactful to ask why I married the woman who had betrayed me?"

I had been leaving the question to last. "Why?"

Hoffman said, "Because I understood her. War had done that for me. I understood that, even though she loved me, what she had to do was more important. And, of course, we were both trying to achieve the same ends."

"I wonder what happened to those children in Berlin," his wife said. "It was their eyes. Every time I wanted to confide in Josef I saw them looking at me. Pleading."

"And do you know why I called it the Judas Code?" He answered his question himself. "Because it was the ultimate act of betrayal, that's why."

On the landing outside my apartment, Cross and I stood waiting for the ancient elevator to haul itself up from the ground floor.

As it made its laborious approach, Cross said, "You know something? I think you *do* know the secret of the Judas Code."

I smiled in a self-satisfied way.

"I said just now," Cross went on, "that I never *fully* understood it. But I have my theories. That Hoffman and Stalin agreed that the opposite of what Hoffman transmitted would be the truth. How does that grab you?"

I tried to maintain the smile as the elevator shuddered to a halt. Cross opened the doors and stepped in. "You've enjoyed your little triumph," he said. "Now it's my turn."

I could feel my smile fading.

"Just suppose," he said, "that the Judas Code has become a habit with Hoffman. That what he told you . . ."

"Was the opposite of the truth?"

"Not all of it, of course." Cross's hand strayed to his cheek again. "There are certain parts of his story that undoubtedly occurred. But how much of it, and which parts? That is what you'll have to decide . . . and your readers, too."

He pushed the ground-floor button and disappeared from sight.